WHO TO TRUST

CAROLYN RUFFLES

Who To Trust is an original work of fiction and any resemblance to actual persons, living or dead, is purely coincidental.

WHO TO TRUST
First Edition
March 2020

Copyright©2020 Carolyn Ruffles

For my boys: Mark, Rob, Harry & Max.
And for my wonderful dad, Colin.

PROLOGUE

1 am

Under cover of night, the doctor slipped through the door and into the hospital. The reception area stood eerily empty in the half-gloom. Drink and confectionary machines stood silent as sentries; shuttered shop facades were the only witnesses.

The doctor strode down the deserted hospital corridor, stethoscope bumping in rhythm against the crisp, white coat. Without warning, a whey-faced nurse appeared from around a corner. A brief stab of panic, a slight nod of acknowledgement, then the woman was gone. Nothing to fear. Another turn; another empty space. Not far to go now.

Maternity ward. A moment's hesitation before peering through the glass. A stroke of luck. The nurses' station was unmanned. A bolt of elation fired renewed hope. It was possible. The doctor straightened, shoulders back, a figure of authority, before using a key card to gain entry. No-one saw. The murmured hum of voices drifted from the bay at the far end of the ward. Perfect. It was fate; it was meant to be.

The doctor crept into the nearest bay, enveloped in darkness. Only one bed was in use, a grey mound silently sleeping. A wheeled crib stood beside it. The baby girl briefly opened her eyes wide, pools of blue innocence, as the doctor loomed over her. An intake of breath. Waiting ... The eyelids fluttered and closed. It had to be now. Slowly, gently, the doctor pushed the crib to the entrance of the bay and peered stealthily around the curtain. The coast was clear. Another deep breath. Now or never.

With a burst of feigned confidence, the doctor wheeled the sleeping infant out of the ward and along the corridor. The hardest bit was done. Swiftly along to a storeroom by the stairs at the rear of the hospital. Empty. A quick glance around. No-one there.

Abandoning the crib behind the door of the storeroom, the doctor cradled the baby, crooning softly. 'Nearly there, my lovely.'

Down the stairs, the click of shoes beating a guilty tattoo and out into the night ...

CHAPTER 1

Anna
May, 2019

Later, looking back, I could pinpoint it exactly – a moment of silent recognition, a stab of disquiet. It was then. When it all started.

Driving to Norwich along the A47 in my black Fiesta, the sky benign with Mediterranean blues, I was unaware of what lay ahead. I'd turned off the dual carriageway, following the signs for the city centre and waiting at the first set of traffic lights. Queen's 'Don't Stop Me Now' was playing on the radio and I was belting it out when the words caught in my throat. That's when it was – a glimpse of blue in my wing mirror. At the time, I didn't appreciate the significance. But that was when the fear started and my life changed for ever.

Then, it gave me pause and I adjusted my rear-view mirror for a better look. It was an electric blue Peugeot 206. I frowned, turning my head, craning my neck to see more. A beep from behind jolted me forward, foot twitching against the accelerator pedal. The road was busy and we crawled forward to the next set of lights. Another look in my mirror. Impossible to tell. The Peugeot was about six cars back and in the same lane. I was trying to see if it had a large dent on the nearside front bumper. As the lights changed again, I switched lanes and kept checking my wing mirror. After a few seconds, the Peugeot also pulled out; I could see the dent clearly. It was the same car. And it was following me. Again.

I'd first seen the car last Saturday, driving to Swaffham to visit my parents, noticing it only because they'd bought me one, the same colour and model, for my seventeenth birthday, nine years earlier. Since its sale, two years ago, when I bought my Fiesta, I'd looked out for my trusty, old car. On that occasion, I spotted the dent in the front bumper.

'Poor Percy!' I'd exclaimed, the name I'd christened it. 'Have you had a bit of a bump with your new owner?'

As I reached the drive to my parents' house, the Peugeot had continued onwards and I'd checked the number plate. It wasn't Percy. If only I could remember the number. Unfortunately, as soon as I realised it didn't start with AU, I'd dismissed it from my mind.

I noticed the Peugeot with the dented bumper behind me once again on route to the Queen Elizabeth Hospital in King's Lynn where I was taking Edith Swainsthorpe, a client of mine, for a knee x-ray.

'Obviously belongs to someone local,' I observed to Edith after telling her the Percy story.

Having spotted the same car twice more that week, always behind me, I began to wonder, with creeping unease, if it was something other than coincidence. I started to look out for it every time I took to the road. Then, today, as I turned off the A47 towards the city, there it was again.

Still I couldn't quite believe it. Why would anyone be tailing me? It must be a mistake. I clamped down on the first fluttering of panic and decided to use the next set of traffic lights as a test. They were red and I sat in the middle lane, heading for Norwich city centre, planning my move. When the lights turned green, I accelerated and indicated left, nipping in front of the white van beside me with an apologetic wave. My eyes flicked again to the rear-view mirror. The Peugeot had also manoeuvred across the lanes and now sat four cars behind me. I felt a surge of anger towards the unknown driver. Who was he? What did he think he was playing at? My fingers gripped the steering wheel as I pulled out to overtake a cyclist. The Peugeot remained, locked on to the rear of my Fiesta like a guided missile.

What could I do?

Anxiety stiffened my spine as I processed my options. Pull over; let him pass. My mind played out the scenario. The Peugeot might pull in behind, prompting a confrontation. The thought of that held little appeal. Maybe it would continue past me and lie waiting, further ahead – a nerve-tingling game of cat and mouse. I didn't like that idea either. Another option would be to do nothing, to continue on to Chapelfield's car park. Wait and see what happened. But car parks are dark, anonymous places where a person might easily disappear. The thought sent my pulse skittering. The remaining choice would be best. Somehow, I would lose him.

A rush of adrenalin, knuckles whitening. Images from film car chases flashed through my head – drivers shooting between cars, avoiding oncoming vehicles, tyres screeching, horns blaring. *Don't be silly, Anna.* I wasn't about to attempt anything like that. It would have to be something more subtle, slipping out of sight somehow before he realised. *Think, Anna!* The voice in my head sounded urgent, panicky. Despite the air-conditioning, droplets of sweat tickled my brow as I waited for my chance …

Without indicating, I swung my car left down a tree-lined avenue and then first left again, veering wildly around a parked car and earning an angry blast on the horn from the vehicle coming the other way. I swerved left again and raced to the end of the street preparing to turn right, back to the traffic lights. Cars streamed ahead of me, coming from both directions, forcing me to screech to a halt. Another glance in the mirror. The blue Peugeot was just turning into the street, wary now, maintaining a distance between us, perhaps wondering if he'd been spotted. A tiny gap allowed me to shoot forward and take my place in the steady flow of traffic. This time the lights were green.

'Come on, come on!' I exhorted the drivers ahead of me. They were moving so slowly; the lights would change at any moment. Sure enough, the amber light flashed and the car in front of me braked, ready to stop. Then, at the last moment, the driver changed his mind and continued forward, deciding to risk it. As I also sped past, the lights had already changed to red. I checked my mirror; no blue Peugeot.

I exhaled, not realising until then that I'd been holding my breath. Still, my eyes flipped between the rear-view and wing mirrors. At any moment, I expected to see him behind me. Every red traffic light set my heart racing; the wait for a green light felt interminable; the fear he would catch up consumed my thoughts. Another look. No blue Peugeot. I shook my shoulders, trying to relieve the tension. Surely now I was safe.

As my breathing steadied, I started to feel a bit stupid. I'd over-reacted. Nothing in my recent sightings of the blue Peugeot suggested that the driver wished me harm, I reasoned. If he'd wanted to attack, abduct or kill me, there had been opportunities.

My fear had been amplified by panic. That happened. I'd suffered from anxiety for as long as I could remember. It crept up on me, sometimes stealthily but often unexpectedly, sheer, gut-wrenching terror which left my insides squeezed dry and my muscles stiff with knots.

Still, the voice in my head argued, he was definitely following me. Perhaps I should inform the police. Almost immediately, I dismissed the notion. What could they do? No crime had been committed and I had no clue to the identity of the driver. I couldn't even tell them the registration number. No, I'd be wasting their time. After all, they'd been unable to do anything when Alice Drinkwater, another client, had been burgled while she lay asleep in bed.

'They just gave me a number – a crime number, I think they called it – and told me they'd let me know if they recovered any of the stolen property,' Alice wailed over a cup of tea, her many chins shaking with a combination of indignation and distress. 'As if I'm worried about *that*. It's the invasion of my *home* I'm worried about. I can't *bear* to think of someone creeping about, rifling through my things, while I'm tucked up in my bed. I haven't slept a wink since.'

Poor Alice. She had not been in the village very long and her husband of thirty-six years had recently left her for his PA. I did my best to reassure her, stayed with her while a locksmith changed the locks and put her in touch with the Neighbourhood Watch co-ordinator. Apart from that, there was little, it appeared, anyone could do.

I reached Chapelfield's car park and reversed into a parking space. The dim, artificial lighting, the rumble of car engines and echoey thumps and rattles did little to soothe my frayed nerves. My mind might insist I was over-reacting but my body still quaked with pent-up fear. As I walked away from my Fiesta, I glanced nervously over my shoulder. The incident had shaken me, no question about it. A flash of blue in my peripheral vision made my heart lurch and muscles tense in anticipation. He was still following me; I hadn't got away! I slipped through the glass doors and up the staircase leading to House of Fraser before I risked another look behind. No need to panic – it wasn't him after all, not even a Peugeot.

'Pull yourself together, Anna!'

An elderly woman walking towards me, laden with bags marked 'Sale' in big, red letters, gave me an odd look and I realised I'd uttered the words aloud.

'Are you alright, love?' she asked kindly. 'You look very pale.'

'I'm fine, thanks.' I hurried on.

Why would someone be following me? Was he watching for a regular pattern, planning his move, deciding when best to pounce? If so, he'd soon discover I didn't have a set routine. Most of my time was spent at home writing. I also did occasional, part-time work as a Girl Friday which meant I travelled when and wherever I was needed. These were usually one-off jobs; my writing schedule made me reluctant to commit to anything more regular. Today though, I wasn't working. I'd driven the twenty-five-mile trip into Norwich for a shopping day with Madison, a close friend from university. A glance at my watch showed I was running late and I quickened my step.

Madison was waiting by the entrance to the café, her stocky frame leaning against the wall in an attitude of resignation. She was dressed casually in jeans and peering at something on her phone. With her shaggy, auburn curls, soulful, brown eyes and bouncy exuberance, she always reminded me of a spaniel puppy and the sight of her brought a smile to my face.

'At last!' she exclaimed as she greeted me with a hug. 'I was wondering if you'd forgotten.'

'Sorry.' I clung to her a fraction too long. 'Let's get coffee. I'm buying.'

'Is everything OK?' Madison's eyes narrowed as she stepped back. 'You're trembling!'

'I'm fine.' I flashed another smile, meant to reassure.

Her lips tightened as she watched me fumbling for my purse. Clearly, she wasn't fooled but she waited until we were sitting at a corner table before interrogating me further.

'OK,' she said firmly as I clattered the tray onto the table. 'What's happened?'

'Nothing.'

She frowned, her raised eyebrows indicating disbelief.

'Honestly, it really *is* nothing. I've probably just over-reacted to something, that's all.' As usual, I was reluctant to discuss my fears. I'd had a lot of practice at hiding things. My issues were a weakness I preferred to keep secret.

'Anna, I'm sorry but I don't believe you. Tell me what's happened.'

I gave in. 'You're going to think I'm daft ... the whole thing seems surreal now. Maybe I was just imagining it.' I told her of my encounters with the blue Peugeot, concluding with today's drama.

'It *could* just be coincidence,' Madison said slowly. 'Have you told the police?'

'No. It was only today I actually felt like I was being followed. Do you think I should?'

'Maybe. It's difficult when you have no evidence ...' She paused. 'If you see that car parked anywhere near your house, you should definitely ring them ... and you need to get the number plate.'

'No kidding, Sherlock!'

'Sorry!' She gave me a rueful look. 'If someone *is* following you, do you have any thoughts who it may be? I was listening to a programme on the radio the other week and they were talking about stalkers. Apparently, the majority are known to the victims, often ex-partners. Have you been out with any weirdos recently – anyone you haven't told me about?' She looked at me thoughtfully. 'I know what you're like. Men always make a beeline for you and you never have the heart to tell them to get lost.'

That was true. I'd even invented an imaginary boyfriend to put them off. Not all took rejection well.

'You've been leading me on all night,' one lad had sneered just a few weeks ago, slamming his beer glass down on the bar and pushing past me as he shuffled off. 'Bitch!'

Disquiet at that latest incident came flooding back. What was his name? I couldn't remember. Dave? That didn't sound right but it was something like that. I was at a bar in Norwich with a group of friends from my spinning class. One of the girls, Fran, was celebrating her thirtieth birthday. The guy, whoever he was, had spent the evening telling me about his dad who had just been diagnosed with cancer. I'd tried to get away a few times but each time he'd forestalled me.

'Just hang out with me for a bit longer, babe,' he pleaded. 'I don't have anyone else to talk to and you're a good listener.'

When he insisted on buying me another drink, I resigned myself to being a sympathetic ear for a little while longer. However, when he snaked his arm around my waist, I pulled away. That's when I told him about Jeff, my boyfriend in the Marines whom I'd fabricated for just such occasions.

'Is he here tonight?' the guy asked belligerently. 'If not, what he doesn't know won't hurt him.' He reached for me again and I spun away, irritated.

'Sorry. Look, I'm here with friends,' I said firmly. 'I really must get back to them.' He stalked off with a few more choice epithets. Could he have followed me home that night and been doing so ever since? The thought chilled my bones. It was terrifying to think someone I'd met might wish me harm.

'What about that guy you went out with a while ago? You know, the gorgeous, dark one who was a bit off the rails. What was his name?' Madison's voice interrupted my thoughts.

'Ewan Jacobs.' I knew who she meant. He *was* good-looking and definitely wild. Our relationship was erratic, to say the least, and ended when I suspected he was taking drugs. He wasn't one of my better choices. Now, I put it down to my rebellious phase.

'Yeah, Ewan. I reckon he'd be the type to hold a grudge. He always acted like the world was against him. Had a bit of temper too … and you did finish with *him*, not the other way around.'

I filtered through the possibility. 'No,' I said, 'I can't see it. That was all done and dusted ages ago and I haven't seen him since we broke up. Anyway,' I smiled as something occurred to me, 'it definitely couldn't be him. You know what he was like. He wouldn't have been seen *dead* driving an old, blue Peugeot!'

'Good point. Well, I suppose it *could* be some random weirdo.'

'Cheers for that happy thought.'

'Sorry.' She pushed back her chair. 'Look, let's go and hit the sales. A bargain will help you forget your troubles.'

My heart wasn't really in it but I made an effort for Madison's sake and relaxed as the day wore on. Initially, I found myself scanning fellow shoppers for anyone who might be paying me undue attention but soon wearied of the task. I'd never make a detective, I thought, trudging back to my car, laden with purchases, at the end of the day. Madison insisted on accompanying me to the car park and together we scoured the ranks of cars on the same level of the multi-storey. To my relief, there was no blue Peugeot with a dented bumper.

'Right,' said Madison, giving me a farewell hug. 'If you see that car following you on the way home, I want you to turn around and come straight back to mine. Then we'll phone the police together.' She paused and gave me a stern look. 'And make sure you're extra vigilant at home too.'

'Yes Mum.' I tried for a confident smile but it fell a little short. In truth, my nerves had started jangling as the return journey loomed closer. I threw the bags onto the back seat of the car and slid behind the wheel. 'I'll phone when I get home.'

'Make sure you do.'

***

Madison watched as her friend folded her tall, curvy frame into the driver's seat and pushed her long, blonde hair behind her ears. With a final wave, Anna turned the key in the ignition and steered towards the exit.

'Safe journey home,' Madison called as the black Fiesta disappeared from view.

Balancing her many shopping bags on one arm, she reached for her phone from the capacious depths of her brown, leather handbag. As usual, prickles of guilt fluttered in her chest as she scrolled through her contacts.

'Sorry Anna,' she murmured while she waited for her call to be answered, 'but it's for your own good.'

CHAPTER 2

Jack
Tuesday 16th July, 1996

Had he known this would be the last day he'd see his daughter, Jack would have indulged her more. As it was, he was bored of standing thigh-deep in the pool, watching as she kicked her way over to him, blonde curls bobbing up and down inside her duck-shaped inflatable, her chubby face a picture of fierce determination. She was only three but at this rate she'd be swimming unaided in no time, maybe even by the end of the holiday. They had another week still to enjoy at the beach resort of Alla Mora on the east coast of southern Spain. There was definitely time.

'Daddy wants a rest from swimming now, Pumpkin,' he said as his daughter reached him. 'Time to get out.'

'Not yet,' she wailed in response. Defiantly, she turned, kicking in the opposite direction.

'Not so fast, young lady.' Within a few strides, he caught her and scooped her up into his arms. She giggled, allowing herself to be lifted out of the water and wrapped in a towel on a striped sun-lounger. 'We'll go back in the pool in just a little while,' he promised.

'OK.' She was an easy-going child. 'Daddy, can I go and play by the swings now?'

He nodded, happy at the thought of a respite. It was hard work keeping a small child entertained. Nice to have a few minutes to himself. He watched as she skipped to the small, enclosed children's area in her damp, spotty swimsuit and bare feet. The play park was conveniently sited adjacent to the pool on the edge of the beach. He waited until she was happily playing with a small group of children building sandcastles before he allowed himself the luxury of leaning back on his lounger, the sun warm on his face. This was the life. When Selina, his wife, had insisted on coming out here for a family holiday, he hadn't been keen. His childhood had always been about camping. 'Holidays in far-flung places are a waste of money,' his own father maintained. 'Plenty of nice places in this country.' He'd approached his first time abroad with some trepidation but now would wholeheartedly recommend it. He felt relaxed and content. The gentle lapping of waves soothed away all his worldly cares. Here, he could forget his troubles with work, his concern for his recently widowed mother, his money worries. He had found his oasis. Selina was right. Even though they really couldn't afford it, this break was a godsend.

'Excuse me but if you don't mind me saying so, that's a gorgeous, little girl you have there.' The American drawl, a woman's voice, was directed at him and he turned his head.

'Thank you,' he replied, his smile widening as his eyes took in the sight of the woman lying on the lounger to his left. He hadn't seen her around the pool before; he would have noticed. She was stunning – petite and perfectly proportioned, with smooth, golden skin and long, dark hair. He felt his groin tighten as she grinned back, full lips slightly parted to reveal even, white teeth, and snatched up his paperback to hide his embarrassment.

'Is it just you and her? Or is there a mom lurking somewhere?' Her voice flowed over him like warm honey.

'Yes ... no ... that is ...' he stuttered, 'my wife and son have gone off on a boat trip. They're hoping to see some dolphins.'

'Cool.' She picked up a tube of sun lotion and he returned to his book. It was difficult to concentrate on the words though; from the corner of his eye, he watched her smoothing the cream into her skin with languid strokes. When she leaned forward and worked her long, slender fingers beneath the turquoise fabric of her bikini top, he swallowed hard and averted his gaze. Carelessly, she dropped the tube and turned on her side to face him.

'I'm Suki, by the way.' She stretched her arm towards him and he took her hand briefly in his.

'Jack.' Electricity tingled where their fingers touched and he released her abruptly, as if he'd been stung. 'Good to meet you.'

'It sure is good to meet *you*,' she replied, deliberately letting her eyes trail his tall, well-muscled body.

Jack inhaled sharply, her bold, intense stare scorching his skin, a physical burn. *Get a grip*, he rebuked himself. He was a married man, for God's sake; he adored his family. This woman was toying with him, passing an idle afternoon with some harmless flirtation.

'Daddy, can we go back in the swimming pool now?' Maisie had bounded up to him, blue eyes pleading.

The interruption was a welcome distraction but he sighed, the long-suffering sound of a pestered parent. 'Maisie, we were only just in the pool. I said we'd go back in shortly – not yet.'

'Oh, please Daddy.' She tugged his arm with insistent fingers. 'Now. You promised.'

'Hi, Maisie.' Suki pulled off her sunglasses and smiled at the child. She had cool, grey eyes, slightly at odds with the seductive fullness of her lips. There was open appraisal, warmth but also calculation lurking in their depths.

'Hello.' Maisie turned politely to the stranger, acknowledging her presence before turning back to Jack. 'Please Daddy.' She increased the pressure on his arm.

'You sure do have pretty hair.'

Her eyes still wary, Maisie touched a hand to her blonde curls. 'Mummy says it needs a haircut,' she said solemnly.

'Well, to me it looks perfect.' Suki swung her slim legs off her lounger in one fluid movement. 'Hey, d'ya know what, I could use a dip in the water to cool off.' She held out a hand to Maisie. 'I'll take you in the pool if you like ... and if Daddy is OK with that?' Her eyebrows arched in question and Jack immediately felt flummoxed.

'No, no,' he protested, shifting himself into a sitting position. 'I'll take her. I don't want to put you to any trouble.'

'No trouble at all.' Her smile was dazzling. 'What d'ya say, Maisie?'

Maisie stood uncertainly, still clinging to her father's arm. 'Daddy?'

Jack gave in, helpless under the wattage of Suki's charm. With a reassuring grin, he patted his daughter's hand. 'This is Suki. Would you like her to take you in the water? I'll be right here, watching. Maybe I'll come and join you in a minute.'

'OK.' Obediently, Maisie slipped her small hand into Suki's perfectly manicured one and Jack watched as the woman led his daughter away.

CHAPTER 3

Anna

My head was pounding by the time I pulled up outside the three-bedroomed semi I shared with my friend Ellie in the sprawling Norfolk village of Lewton. No wonder. My shoulders, neck and jaw were rigid with tension after the drive back home. There'd been no blue Peugeot prowling in my wake but I couldn't relax. Even as I pulled into Hamilton Close, my eyes darted left and right, searching for anything untoward, anything suspicious. Was this what it felt like to be hunted – constantly on tenterhooks, jumping at shadows, imagining the worst?

I took a deep breath and shook my arms, attempting to loosen the bands of stress gripping my limbs. The pain throbbing at my temples was like a sledgehammer. What I needed was a long, luxurious soak in the bath and some paracetamol. I'd have liked nothing better than to stay in this evening but it was Thursday, the day I always drove ten miles to the market town of Swaffham for dinner with my parents. For a brief, tempting moment, I considered cancelling but knew I couldn't. It would be harder to face their disappointment and inevitable concern. I *never* missed a Thursday evening.

With one final scan of the neighbourhood, I reached for my shopping bags and stepped out of my Fiesta. The familiar sounds of neighbours cutting grass and children playing were a welcome return to normality. Ellie, my housemate, was not yet home from work and I remembered her saying she was going straight round to her boyfriend's house that evening. My stomach curdled at the thought of Dan. I had good reason to dislike him but my feelings were unknown to Ellie. I'd made a mistake in not telling her from the start and now it was awkward, a guilt-ridden secret between us.

Less than one hour later, I was heading for Swaffham, my body tense, hunched over the steering wheel. I was being ridiculous but I couldn't help it. Inside my car, I felt helpless and vulnerable, like a crane fly trapped against a window pane. Would he appear behind me? *Stop thinking about it. Forget him.* The stern rebukes didn't help. I was jumping at imagined shadows, allowing my fear to take root and flourish and helpless to stop it.

A rational explanation for the behaviour of the Peugeot driver would help but I'd struggled to come up with anything. Not anything positive at any rate. I didn't want to think of negative reasons.

Why would anyone want to follow me? It didn't make sense. I was ordinary. Yes, I'd had a book published but I wasn't a celebrity – not even well-known. Was that it, though? Was the stalker perhaps a fan? My parents were horrified when I published using my real name, rather than a pseudonym, and had warned of crackpot fanatics. I'd laughed at that. I couldn't imagine my work having that much of an effect on anyone. My parents ... perhaps that was it. Dad was a wealthy man. From an early age, I'd been warned of stranger danger and kidnapping. Was that what someone was planning? Unlikely. Dad was retired now, not the figure of renown he'd once been. The timing was wrong.

I glanced again at my rear-view mirror. A white transit van was following, so close I could see tattoos on the driver's arms. My right foot pressed down harder, increasing my speed. I didn't think the Peugeot was behind him but I couldn't be sure. On the outskirts of Swaffham, I turned left through the open, wrought-iron gates at the bottom of my parents' driveway. The van sped impatiently past, an empty road behind. A rush of relief. I composed my features into a fixed smile as I parked outside the large, imposing, red-bricked house. I wasn't going to mention the Peugeot to my parents. They would only worry and that wouldn't help the situation. Even though I was twenty-six years old, they still used any excuse to treat me like a child. It was best, I'd learnt, to keep problems to myself.

The front door burst open and my father, Geoff Blake, strode towards me, a tall, muscular figure dressed in a short-sleeved, checked shirt and brown trousers. 'Anna!' His voice was deep and rich, like melted chocolate. He clasped me to him, a fierce, possessive hug. 'Lovely to see you, darling. I hope you're hungry. Your mother's cooking up her usual storm in the kitchen.' He stepped back and held me at arms' length, his hooded, brown eyes searching my face. 'And how's my girl? Is everything alright? You look a bit peaky.'

The inquisition had started. 'Of course. I'm just a bit tired after a day in Norwich with Madison. She really did want to shop until I dropped. How are you and Mum?'

'We're fine. All the better for seeing you.'

He followed as I led the way into the spacious hallway where the grandfather clock was chiming a quarter past the hour. I was assailed by the smell of paint and wrinkled my nose. 'Are you having some work done?'

He rolled his eyes. 'You know what your mother's like. She thought the whole downstairs needed redecorating. It doesn't seem five minutes since it was last painted.'

'Well, I'm sure it won't take long!' I linked my arm with his as we walked through to the kitchen. 'Mmm, that smells *good.*'

'I'm surprised you can smell anything other than that awful paint!' Dad grumbled good-naturedly and I left his side to greet my mother, Mariella, a slight, immaculately-tailored woman with short, ash blonde hair and sharp, grey eyes. She worked part-time at the Norfolk and Norwich hospital as a highly-regarded paediatrician and had a reputation for cool, calm professionalism.

Turning a smooth cheek to receive my kiss, her lips curved briefly. 'Chicken cacciatori,' she said, her voice clipped and precise, no words wasted. 'Almost ready.'

'Lovely.' I returned to the warmth of my father and squeezed his arm. I'd always been a daddy's girl.

Mum glanced towards us, her lips thinning at the gesture. 'As it's such a nice evening, I thought we'd eat in the conservatory if that's acceptable.' It was an instruction rather than a question.

'Lovely,' I said again. The truth was if Mum had suggested we eat in the cellar, I'd have responded in the same way. It was best not to disagree.

'How's the latest masterpiece coming along?' Dad asked as we strolled through the French doors into the large conservatory overlooking the garden where the table was laid for three.

'Fine thanks. Almost halfway.' I ignored the dig. I knew that my parents were disappointed my books were decidedly 'chick-lit', not literary masterpieces. After graduating from my course reading English and Creative Writing at Lancaster University, I'd returned to the family home intending to write a work worthy of merit and make my parents proud. I had tried, I really had, but it had been a slog, leaving me frustrated and disappointed with my efforts. Their attempts to help made it worse. They enjoyed arguing ideas across the dinner table every evening, often giving conflicting advice. It had just added to the pressure and my anxiety levels increased. Something had to change. Surreptitiously, I began casting around for alternative accommodation.

One evening, two years ago, when I was trying to cheer up Ellie, another university pal who had just split up from her boyfriend of five years, a solution presented itself. 'I'm going to have to move out of my house,' Ellie had wailed, 'unless I can find someone who wants to share with me. I can't afford the rent on my own.'

'I could share with you,' I'd said instantly.

It had been the answer to my prayers but meant several difficult conversations with my parents. Stubbornly, I'd stood my ground and moved to Lewton, despite emotional appeals and then anger. I'd set my faltering, literary novel aside and began writing *Love on a Treadmill*, a romantic comedy about a hapless fitness instructor named Jemima. Much to my surprise, an agent, Helen Barton-Thomas, had liked it and agreed to take me on. My first book had been published, with a moderate degree of success, last year. The second, a sequel entitled *Dumb Belles*, was scheduled to appear in bookstores in the autumn and I was now working on the third instalment, *Baby Gym*. Despite my burgeoning success, I was aware my high-achieving parents were disappointed I hadn't produced anything they considered worthy of a place on their coffee table. At least, they'd come around to the fact I'd moved out and our relationship was, thankfully, back on an even keel. I worked hard to keep it that way.

Mum appeared, carrying a bowl of buttered noodles. 'Geoff, can you bring the chicken out while I start serving? I don't want the food to get cold.'

He rose obediently to his feet and she narrowed her eyes as she looked across at me. 'You're looking pale. Is everything alright?'

'Of course. I was just telling Dad. Anyone would be a bit tired after shopping with Madison!'

'There's nothing else the matter?'

I gave her my best, reassuring smile. 'Of course not. Everything's fine. You and Dad are such a pair of worryguts!'

She shrugged. 'When you're a parent yourself, you'll understand. Put it there, Geoff.' He'd reappeared with a red casserole dish. 'No, not there … on the mat!' There was the usual tension in the air, like a pinched nerve, throbbing and pulsating between us. I watched as Dad's lips tightened.

'And where's the wine? I asked you to open a bottle of chianti.' Mum's voice had taken on the grating quality of a vinyl record stuck on a turntable.

'I *have* opened it. I just forgot to bring it out here. Won't be a minute.' Dad smiled apologetically at me as he once more left the table.

'Honestly,' she tutted as she spooned noodles onto plates. 'He's so forgetful these days!'

'How are things at the hospital, Mum?' I asked in an attempt to divert the subject away from Dad's shortcomings.

She shook her head. 'Pretty bad. This latest round of cutbacks has left us hopelessly understaffed. The Government seem to be trying to run the National Health Service into the ground. I'm glad I'm only there for three days a week.'

'Why don't you retire then, like Dad?'

She snorted. 'Your father hasn't really retired. He's still going down to London once or twice a week. I've told him that he needs to leave all the poor staff alone to get on with it but you know what he's like. That bank is like his second child.'

He'd founded the hugely successful merchant bank, Sampson Blake, along with his erstwhile boss and mentor Phil Sampson, twenty years earlier. When Phil died suddenly from a heart attack, Dad became the sole spearhead of the company but the pressures had taken their toll on his own health. Four years ago, he'd suffered a heart attack himself and had been told he needed to change his lifestyle. Realisation of his own mortality had shocked him into announcing his retirement and moving from London to Norfolk. He'd become obsessed with fitness, biking, swimming and using the gym regularly, and enjoyed competitive games of golf with his new circle of friends. He didn't do anything by halves. But he couldn't quite let go of Sampson Blake's reins; I doubted he ever would.

'Well, it *is* hard for him.' As usual, I leapt to his defence. 'He's always been an all-or-nothing guy.'

'I know.' She looked up and frowned. 'Anna, for goodness sake, leave that ear alone. It's high time you outgrew that habit!' My hand snapped away from my left earlobe which I'd been compulsively twisting between thumb and forefinger.

Geoff arrived with the wine. 'Leave the girl alone, Mariella! She's a grown woman.' He shot me a sympathetic smile and winked. 'I've always found it quite endearing.'

'The chicken's delicious, Mum.' Once more, I changed the subject.

The evening passed, as it so often did, with Dad holding court, entertaining us with his stories. He was a witty raconteur and, for a few hours, I managed to forget my stalker. I chuckled as he described how one of his golfing buddies, Alan, had accidentally driven his golf buggy into a bunker. I did suspect his recounts were embellished – poor Alan could not possibly suffer as many mishaps as Dad claimed – but he told them with great comic timing and a real knack for observational humour. I'd often thought he could have had a career on the stage as a stand-up comedian.

Dusk was hooding the sky and I was suddenly eager to be home before dark. The thought of being followed at night filled me with terror. Something about the blackness, about the anonymity of car headlights, magnified the threat. Pleading tiredness, I helped carry the dishes and plates through to the kitchen and gave Mum a farewell hug. Dad walked me out to my car.

'You *would* tell me if something was wrong?' he asked.

'Of course.' My response was automatic. 'It's time you stopped worrying about me.'

'I'll never do that. Make sure you text me when you're safely back home.'

I gave him a wry smile. 'Yes, Dad. I always do. Love you.'

Raising my hand in farewell, I pulled away from the house and down the drive. When I reached the junction, I looked nervously for a car lying in wait but the road was quiet. Still, I was unable to relax and drove home faster than usual. When I was safely indoors, I sped around the house, checking all the windows were closed and doors were locked. I'd never worried about being alone at night before but now I definitely felt spooked – jumpy and alert to every sound.

Later, as I lay in bed, willing myself to sleep, my brain remained stubbornly busy. Madison had said almost all stalkers were known to their victim and possible candidates paraded themselves, like contestants in a game show. The presenter's voice boomed in my head. *Will the real culprit please reveal himself?*

My thoughts turned to my parents. I didn't like deceiving them. Perhaps I should have told them about the Peugeot after all, especially as they'd both expressed concern about me. It was strange how they always seemed to know when something was up.

Car lights spun across my curtains and an engine was switched off, somewhere close by. I tensed, listening, waiting. *Clunk.* A door slammed shut. Footsteps on tarmac. The rattle of keys. Another door closing. A neighbour's. *Relax!*

But I was too wired to relax and the identity of my stalker once more took centre stage. Over and over, my mind churned. It was hopeless. He could be anyone; after all, how do you know who you can trust? That disturbing question tossed and twisted in my brain like a kite in the wind until I succumbed, at last, to uneasy sleep.

CHAPTER 4

Anna

I was running, straining every muscle and sinew to gain extra speed but it was no use. He was gaining. I could hear him behind me, pounding ever closer. I could almost feel his breath warm on my neck, a whisper of intent. He would catch me. The chase was relentless. Lungs bursting with effort, I veered left and scrambled over a ditch. The wood was my only chance. Somewhere in its tangled darkness, I could find cover, somewhere to hide. I surged forward, heedless of branches and brambles tearing my skin, weaving through the densest part of the wood. Ducking my head and keeping low to the ground, I plunged on. Behind, I could hear him cursing. The tortuous route I'd chosen was slowing him down, giving me an advantage.

I knew now where I was heading. There was a massive oak tree I used to climb as a child. If only I could reach it without him seeing, I could shelter within its branches and watch him thunder past.

So close now; one final surge of adrenalin.

There it was. Panting, gasping for breath and praying for strength, I grasped the lowest branch and hauled myself up onto it. It was lower than I remembered; I would have to go higher, much higher, to be fully concealed. A knot in the trunk would provide a foothold up to the next branch, I remembered, but I needed to find it. My hands searched feverishly. I was running out of time. If he appeared now, I would be in full view and there would be no escape.

There it was! With a triumphant yelp, I swung my foot into position and pushed upwards, reaching for the branch above my head. Almost there; I could do it; one last push ... and then I felt my foot give way. The bark was wet and slippery and I slid down, grasping once more for the first branch as I fell. Almost sobbing with desperation, I righted myself and gritted my teeth for another attempt.

Then, to my horror, I felt fingers close around my ankle, ripping me cruelly from my perch. 'No!'

I shot upright, my heart thundering in my chest, staring in confusion at the tangled disarray of sheets around me. For a few, panic-ridden moments, I poised for flight before realising I was safe, in bed. My body was drenched in sweat and I took a shuddering breath to calm my nerves. *Just a dream.*

With a jolt, I remembered the stalker. Little wonder I was having night terrors. The clock on my bedside table was showing quarter to six. I might as well get up and start work. The thought of sleep had lost its appeal and immersion in the frothy, comedy world of my main character, Jemima, would calm my frazzled nerves.

By the time I'd showered, made coffee and eaten a breakfast of muesli and fruit, I felt better and, by ten o'clock, I had almost two thousand words under my belt. As I sat back and stretched, my mobile hummed.

'Hi, Dad.' I pressed the speaker phone button while I saved my work.

'Morning, darling. Just ringing to see how you were.' His warm, deep voice prompted a wave of affection.

'I'm fine. Working hard. What are you up to today?'

'Not much. Just popping down to the office but it'll be a flying visit. I'll be back home this evening. Now…' His voice took on a note of concern. 'You would tell me if anything was bothering you, wouldn't you? I did think you seemed tense last night.'

'Of course, but everything's fine.' My reply was automatic. 'You have a good day and don't give poor, old Hamish too much grief, will you.' Hamish McDonald had taken on the role of managing director when Dad had moved to Norfolk.

He chuckled. 'Don't worry. It's no more than he deserves. Alright darling, look after yourself and call me if you need me. Love you lots.'

'You too.'

I ended the call, uncomfortable now with my deceit. Lying to my parents, albeit white lies, to save them from worrying, had become an essential part of retaining my independence. Dad would quite happily run my life for me if I let him.

The phone rang again. This time it was my housemate, Ellie. 'Are you OK, Anna?'

What was it this morning with people ringing to check on me?

'Yeah, sure. Why do you ask?'

'I've spoken to Madison. She rang to see how you were after your scare yesterday and filled me in. You should have called me, Anna, and I'd have come home.' I detected a reproachful note.

'No need.' My voice remained determinedly cheery. 'I was fine and I really didn't want to spoil your evening. How's grumpy Graham this morning?' Graham Pearson was the dentist for whom Ellie worked as a receptionist, a dour, miserable man in his early sixties.

'Same old. Look, I'll be home this evening and, in the meantime, if you see any suspicious vehicles or people around the house, call the police. This stalker thing has made *me* feel spooked so I can't imagine how worried you must be.'

'Please don't change your plans for me, Ell.'

'No, I'm not. Dan is out with his mates tonight so, if you're not doing anything, we could walk round to the pub, or just have a girly night in with a bottle of wine.'

'Sounds good. See you later.'

At one o'clock, I made a sandwich and reviewed the morning's work. The third book was on track and I was confident I'd meet the publisher's deadline of July 30th for completion. I switched off the laptop to get ready for my second job. About nine months ago, I realised writing at home, day after day, was an isolating experience. I missed interaction with other people. That was why I decided to advertise my services as a 'Girl Friday.' Getting out and about and doing a succession of varied jobs provided a welcome change of scenery after hours cooped up inside. Best of all, it provided an opportunity to meet a cast of different characters who proved a rich source of inspiration for my writing.

This afternoon, I had a gardening job at The Old Rectory for a new client, Josh Fielding, who'd recently moved into the village. I was looking forward to it. I'd spent many happy hours as a child trailing round after a succession of gardeners employed by my parents, learning about all the plants and what they needed to flourish. My expertise had grown as I completed a number of gardening jobs in the local area and the word had got around. Although I advertised my services as a 'Girl Friday,' the majority of my recent jobs had been garden-related.

Less than an hour later, I stepped out into the sunshine. Immediately, I was assailed by the sensation someone was watching me. The skin at the base of my neck prickled with apprehension. I swallowed hard, forcing myself to look around. There was no-one there. An unfamiliar black Range Rover was parked by the side of the road but it was empty.

Cautiously, I approached my car. Blood roared in my ears as I imagined someone crouched behind the driver's seat, waiting to grab me. I peered inside; the space was empty. *Get a grip, Anna.* Feeling stupid, I opened up the garage, collected up my gardening equipment and loaded it into the boot of my Fiesta. Several nervous glances over my shoulder slowed the task. The air throbbed with the heaviness of my fear. Invisible eyes scorched my back as I slithered behind the steering wheel and started the engine.

The Old Rectory sat next to the church in the centre of Lewton. I spent the few minutes it took to complete the journey trying to still my mounting panic. *It's just your imagination. Think about the job ahead.* I forced myself to revisit the phone call I'd received a few days earlier. Josh Fielding had said he was doing up the house and the garden needed 'some work.' His voice had been deep with a sardonic edge and I had the impression he would not suffer fools lightly. I'd better be on my best behaviour.

By the time I pulled into the sweeping, gravel drive of The Old Rectory, my breathing had returned to normal. The sense of being watched had evaporated and I berated myself for my foolishness. I spotted Josh straight away, a tall, muscular figure dressed in faded jeans and a navy T-shirt. My breath instantly caught in my throat. *Oh, my days!* He was younger than he'd sounded on the phone, maybe early to mid-thirties, with short, tousled dark hair, a narrow face and amazing brown eyes. My heart did a funny sort of skip in my chest and I risked an involuntary glance at myself in the mirror. *Oh Lordy!* I was dabbing at a smudge of errant eyeliner as he approached.

'You're late!' he barked, eyeing me with disapproval. 'I've had to hang around waiting for you to turn up.'

I snatched a look at my watch. Damn, he was right.

'I'm really sorry,' I said, hoping my look of contrition would melt his frigid expression. 'I'm not usually late and it's not much more than five minutes and ...'

'Save it,' he snapped. 'Come on. I've got things to do.'

He headed round the side of the house with long strides and I scrambled to follow him, annoyed at starting off on the wrong foot and irritated by the way Josh Fielding was making me feel like a naughty schoolgirl.

The garden behind the house was large and rambling with mature borders filled with overgrown shrubs. It was just the sort of project I liked to get my teeth into and I renewed my charm offensive, affording Josh my best, confident, professional smile.

'What a fantastic garden! I can't wait to get started.'

'Just get it tidy and in some semblance of order,' he barked. 'I'm hoping to cut the grass later but I don't know anything about plants so I'm trusting that you do.' The look he gave me was so full of distrust I struggled not to laugh.

'I'll do my best,' I said solemnly.

'Right, I'll leave you to it. I've wasted enough time as it is.'

It was all I could do to restrain myself from saluting his retreating back. What a horrible man! His appeal washed away like water down a drainpipe. I couldn't bear arrogant men and Josh Fielding was just plain rude.

The next half hour was spent assessing the garden and deciding what to do first. It was a riot of colour: heavy, crimson peonies; rose bushes drooping with burgeoning buds; climbing clematis toppling over a trellis; elegant, blue irises; wild flowers like red campion; and cow parsley. All were being strangled by an impressive array of weeds and overshadowed by large shrubs such as choisya, japonica, ceanothus, weigela and others I didn't recognise. I inspected them carefully, jotting my observations in a notebook. They all looked in serious need of pruning but spring was not the time to be doing that. I would have to wait until they'd flowered. Instead, I decided to start by pulling up the largest weeds and cutting out any dead wood; then I could see what would be revealed beneath.

There was no sign of a wheelbarrow or any garden tools and I congratulated myself for bringing my own equipment – fork, spade, trowel, secateurs, loppers and a large bag for garden waste. There was a brown bin by the wall so at least I could dispose of the rubbish.

Itching now to begin, I returned to my car and collected the implements I'd need, along with my crusty, old gardening gloves. As I headed back, Josh stuck his head out of a rear door, glaring with fierce, brown eyes.

'What do you think you're playing at? It's taken you thirty minutes to get started. Are you sure you know what you're doing?'

I bit back an angry retort. 'Just making a plan,' I smiled, tapping my notebook. 'Don't worry. So far, I've had no complaints.'

'And you don't need all that.' He gestured towards my tools. 'There's gardening stuff in the shed.'

He disappeared back indoors, leaving me seething. 'Now he tells me! What a charmer!' I muttered as I set to work.

After three hours, the garden was definitely looking tidier although by no means finished. I dumped the day's final bag of garden waste into the bin and stretched my aching back. The one thing I *had* forgotten was a bottle of water and my throat was parched. Another black mark against Josh Fielding. I couldn't remember the last time I'd worked for someone at their house without being offered a drink. Still, I shouldn't expect it; my raging thirst was my own fault.

I'd already loaded my equipment into my car and was about to tell him I was leaving when I spotted a pile of weeds and dead wood I'd forgotten to clear. *Damn.* I didn't bother putting my hot, sweaty gloves back on. The stuff was dry and wouldn't take a minute to shift. I traipsed back across the lawn and scooped up the debris. It certainly wouldn't do to give him any further cause for complaint.

'Ouch!' With a yelp of pain, I dropped the rubbish and clutched my left hand. There must have been a piece of glass in amongst the pile for blood was seeping from a nasty gash across my palm.

'Oh bother!' I was going to have to run it under some water to clean it. With trepidation, I headed for the back door and gave it a sharp rap. No answer. Diffidently, I pushed it open and peered inside. The room, the kitchen, was a building site. Units had been removed from the walls and were stacked in a heap on the floor. The sink on the far wall looked usable and I headed towards it. Surely, he wouldn't mind me bathing my injured hand?

'What have you done *now*? Oh, for *goodness* sake!'

He appeared behind me, his tone filled with exasperation, as I washed rivulets of blood down the sink.

I resigned myself to another telling-off. 'I cut myself on a piece of glass but no real harm done. Have you got anything I can put on it to stop the bleeding, please? A plaster?'

He peered over my shoulder, oozing disapproval. 'I don't have a first aid kit handy. Here ... use this.' He handed me a clean tea towel. 'That looks quite deep. You should probably get it looked at ... and get a tetanus jab.'

I forced a bright, nonchalant smile as I wrapped up my hand. 'I'm sure it will be fine. Thanks for this.' I wasn't going to tell him I'd had a tetanus injection barely three months earlier when I'd tripped and cut my knee on a rusty piece of metal in someone else's garden. He'd think I was totally hopeless. Realistically, he probably already did.

'I'll be off then. I've made a really good start on the garden. Same time next week?' I wasn't holding my breath. No way he'd want me back. His loss.

He grimaced. 'Actually, if your hand is OK, I could use some more help tomorrow. I was hoping to cut the grass myself but ...' He shrugged. 'Well, the work's there if you want it.'

I was tempted to tell him what he could do with his grass but found myself nodding agreement.

'Right,' he said. 'Same time ... but don't be late! And get the hand looked at.'

What a moron! Still, at least I had another chance to rescue my reputation. Tomorrow he would see only efficiency and competence. And punctuality, of course ...

CHAPTER 5

Jack
Tuesday 16ᵗʰ July, 1996

He wasn't going to lie. It was a pretty riveting sight, one from which he found it hard to look away. The lithe figure of the dark-haired woman in a turquoise bikini, frolicking with his daughter in the pool, occasionally glancing his way, was the stuff of any hot-blooded man's dreams. They were both laughing. He could hear Suki's drawl, encouraging Maisie as she paddled furiously from one side to the other. Back and forth they went. Suki's patience seemed limitless and, after her initial wariness, Maisie was now confidently swimming into the woman's arms, squealing with triumph at each milestone accomplished.

'Did you see me, Daddy? Did you see me?'

He waved across at them both. 'That was amazing, Pumpkin. Your best yet.'

'Watch me Daddy!'

'I'm watching.'

The sun was blisteringly hot and he manoeuvred his lounger across to a parasol to take advantage of the shade. Remembering his wife's instructions, he wondered if Maisie should have another application of sunscreen. When she got out of the water, he decided. Let her enjoy her swimming lesson.

He licked his lips, his mouth dry as dust. There was a bar about two hundred metres away and he glanced at it longingly. A drink would have to wait. Looking once more towards the pool, he saw Suki and Maisie had joined in a ball game with a thin, dark-haired boy and a young woman in a yellow bikini. He watched as Suki swam smoothly to retrieve the ball when it was launched too far. She was laughing as she threw it back, her long, dark hair now completely wet and slicked back from her face. Her face was sharply angular, like the planes of a prism, yet softened by the perfection of her glowing skin and generous, smiling mouth. Jack sighed. He adored his wife. There was no way he would ever consider being unfaithful to her. But there was something utterly compelling about this woman, from her stunning looks to the way she interacted with his child. She seemed completely natural with

Maisie. Originally, he'd thought she was indulging in idle flirtation, that *he* was the one who had piqued her interest. Now watching her, he had to re-evaluate. She seemed totally focused on his daughter, enjoying their interaction as much as Maisie was.

He wondered about joining them in the pool but decided against it. Safer to keep his distance. He could still feel the heat from her fingers where they'd squeezed his hand. The sun fierce on his face, he lay back on his lounger, allowing himself to indulge in the fantasies about Suki crowding his mind ...

They were alone in the pool. She was wearing the same turquoise bikini as she pressed her body against his. Laughing, she undid her bikini top, revealing full, golden breasts ...

A pang of guilt interrupted his reverie but he dismissed it. Such thoughts were harmless enough. He had no intention of acting upon them. Inhaling deeply, he allowed his eyes to close, just for a few seconds ...

CHAPTER 6

Anna

Today I was determined to be early, no matter what. I would be super-cool, super-efficient, super-professional and I wouldn't let Josh Fielding get to me. My large rucksack, containing anything and everything I thought might be useful, including a large bottle of water, was packed. Sat at my dressing table, I inspected my face. Make up was required – not to please *him*, of course … just a bit of confidence boosting for me.

A flash of something sparkly caught my eye. It was my dragonfly hairclip, broken, one of its iridescent wings chipped, but still beautiful to me. I held it up to the light, marvelling at the shimmering blues and greens. I couldn't recall when and how I'd come to possess it but I remembered Mum had hated it. I was never allowed to wear it when we went out.

'Take that horrible thing off!' she insisted. 'I've a mind to throw it away, get rid of it once and for all.'

'No!' I protested, pulling it from my head and hiding it in my fist.

I was heartbroken when it got damaged. One morning, when I was playing outside, it had slipped unheeded from my hair and fallen on the concrete path. When I stepped back, I felt a snap beneath my foot. The edge of one of the wings had fractured.

'Oh no!' My wail came before I could stop it.

'What have you done?' Mum peered over my shoulder. 'Oh, it's only that old thing.' She snatched it from me and dropped it in the bin.

'No!' I cried, tears spilling down my cheeks.

'For goodness sake, it's only an old hairclip. We'll buy you another one.'

I'd learnt that crying only tested my mum's patience. 'Can I have another dragonfly?' I asked slyly.

'We'll see,' she replied absently, satisfied I'd already conceded the battle. I waited until she went outside and then reached into the bin to fish out the dragonfly. Like a thief in the night, I scurried upstairs to hide it in the back of my wardrobe. It stayed there until I was eight when I was given a beautiful jewellery box with a lockable compartment, perfect for hiding my dragonfly. It became my lucky charm, a talisman of my childhood. My parents had never discovered my secret. I'd always wondered why Mum had disliked it so much. Probably something to do with Dad.

Before I set off to work at The Old Rectory, I scanned the neighbourhood from the safety of an upstairs window. I hadn't forgotten that sensation of being watched as I left the house the day before. Mr Brownlow, three doors down, was cutting his front grass. Two young boys were circling the cul-de-sac on their bikes. My immediate neighbour to the right, Andy Entwhistle, was lathering up his Ford Focus. A normal Saturday. Reassured, I stepped through the front door. A brief moment of hesitation; one last check. All clear. Today there was no feeling that anyone was observing me but I walked swiftly, still on my guard, just in case.

The gravel drive of the Old Rectory crunched beneath my feet. I was a good ten minutes early. Strike one for me. Josh's black Mercedes was parked by the front door and I could hear hammering coming from within the house. I decided to head round to the back and make a start. He could not fail to be impressed.

It was a surprisingly warm day for early May and I was soon regretting my failure to apply any sunscreen lotion. Hugging the shade, I grabbed my secateurs and started cutting back the dead wood on an overgrown japonica.

'How's the hand?'

His voice surprised me and I turned quickly, catching my arm on a spiky twig. 'Ouch! Oh, hello. The hand's fine, thank you.'

I squinted up at him and saw, much to my surprise, he was actually smiling. Gosh, I'd forgotten how good-looking he was. His eyes really were the deepest brown and framed by amazingly long lashes. Once again, he was dressed in jeans and a T-shirt and looked lean and fit. I gulped, suddenly flustered.

'Don't worry – I'm only cutting the dead stuff on this japonica; I'm not doing it any harm,' I said defensively as his eyes strayed to the secateurs in my hand.

He frowned. 'Sure, but can you leave that for a bit? As I said yesterday, I haven't had a chance to cut the grass this week. Can you do that?'

'Certainly ... as long as you can provide a mower. It would take a while with these!' I laughed slightly breathlessly, tossing the secateurs to one side, and followed him to the garage.

'It's a ride-on mower so it shouldn't take too long. I'll just get it out for you.'

I waited as he started up the machine and drove it onto the lawn at the front of the house.

'Have you used one of these before?' he asked.

'No. Perhaps you could give me a quick run through of what's what?'

'Sure.' He launched into a series of instructions while I tried valiantly to focus. It was difficult when he was so close, leaning across me as I sat astride the mower, pointing things out.

'Have you got all that?'

'Um, yes, I'm sure I'll be fine.' My smile oozed a confidence I didn't feel.

'Good. I'll leave you to it then.' Another flash of dazzling white teeth and he strode back towards the house.

Oh God, what did he say again? I turned the key, sighing with relief as the engine spluttered once more into life. There had been something about increasing the revs and putting it in gear. Cautiously, I moved the controls and lowered my foot onto the accelerator as I released the brake. I was off. A glance towards the house told me he was still watching, waiting to see if I made a mistake, most likely.

No chance of that. With a burst of exhilaration, I increased the speed. I was a whizz on a ride-on mower! Soon, I was moving expertly up and down the lawn. Josh was still watching, an amused expression on his face, and I waved gaily at him as I passed.

'I'm fine,' I called out. Under my breath, I added, 'So there's no need for you to watch. I've got this.'

On my next pass, I saw Josh was making his way back towards me. Carefully, I applied the brake and cut the revs.

'Was there anything else?' I asked, trying to keep the smugness out of my voice.

'Are you *sure* you know what you're doing?'

'Absolutely,' I beamed. 'I'll have this done in no time and then I'll do the grass around the back.'

'OK. As long as you're sure ...'

'Definitely. Very sure, but thank you for taking the trouble to check,' I added politely.

'That's fine. It's just ...' He hesitated.

'Yes?' I prompted.

'It's just I've been waiting to see if you were planning to lower the cutter bar at all ... or if you had decided maybe the grass was a good length as it is!'

Oh damn. I could see he was struggling to contain his mirth. A quick glance at the grass I thought I'd mowed revealed it was exactly as before. I'd been zooming up and down the lawn without actually cutting the grass!

'Of course,' I said with as much hauteur as I could muster and pushing the lever forward to engage the cutter bar. 'I was just ... er ... getting the feel for the mower first before I ... um ... you know ... started cutting the grass. Obviously.'

'Oh, I see. Well, I'll leave you to it.'

'Thank you.' I gritted my teeth as I pulled away once more. To my dismay, I could see his shoulders were shaking as he disappeared into the house. Once again, my persona of professional efficiency lay in shreds. He must think I was a complete idiot. Still, who cared what he thought? I certainly didn't ... and, on the plus side, I now had another episode to use in *Baby Gym*.

The rest of the afternoon passed without mishap and I congratulated myself as I inspected my handiwork. The garden was looking decidedly better.

'I'm off now!' I called, poking my head around the door. Josh was in the kitchen, paintbrush in hand.

'OK. Friday next week? Same time?'

'Sure. I love that colour, by the way.' I took off my sunglasses and cast an admiring glance around the room.

He was staring openly at me now, his lips twitching with amusement.

'What is it?' I asked. 'Have I got dirt on my face or something?'

'Er ... no.' Hastily, he added, 'I've been meaning to say that you're doing a great job in the garden. I'm impressed.'

I found myself blushing. He really did seem to have undergone a personality transplant since yesterday. Rude, obnoxious Josh had been replaced by Mr Charming. 'Oh ... that's good ... thanks. I'll see you next week then.'

'I'll look forward to it.'

I strolled home, still taking a few precautionary glances over my shoulder, but feeling at ease and pretty pleased with myself. I wasn't sure what had happened but my opinion of Josh Fielding had undergone a complete revision during the afternoon and I was now looking forward, with rather more than professional anticipation, to next Friday. That *look* he'd given me as I was leaving and his parting words! Had he been flirting with me? The thought sent a frisson of excitement coursing through my veins and, upon returning home, I smiled at myself in the hallway mirror as I kicked off my trainers.

'Oh no!' I groaned the words aloud at the sight of my reflection. No wonder he had given me such an intense look. In fact, in retrospect, I had to marvel at his self-control. It was a miracle he hadn't burst out laughing when he saw me, for the horrified face staring back from the mirror was beetroot red … apart from two, sunglasses-shaped, white patches around my eyes!

CHAPTER 7

Anna

A week had passed since my last sighting of the blue Peugeot and my anxiety, although still present, was blurring around the edges, less intense than before. At least twice, I was convinced someone was watching me but nothing else had happened to send me into a tailspin. My nerves still jangled, though, every time I left the house and I found myself reluctant to go out on anything other than essential errands. My usual spin and gym sessions were forfeited as I pandered to my fears. I urged myself to relax but couldn't help remaining watchful and jumpy, suspicious of anything unusual.

Ellie had noticed and tried to reassure me. Tonight, we were treating ourselves to an evening meal at the local pub, the Hare & Hounds. It was raining so Ellie had driven. As she turned into the car park, a black Range Rover crawled by, the head of its grey-haired driver turned towards us. Once he'd passed the pub, the vehicle sped up out of sight. Goosebumps prickled my arms. I was sure I'd seen a Range Rover just like that a few times over the last week. Had my stalker changed vehicles? Biting my lip, I craned my neck to see if I could see where he was going.

'What on earth are you doing?' Ellie said as she switched off the engine. 'Have you seen something?'

'I'm not sure.' I straightened myself in my seat and undid my seatbelt. 'Did you see that Range Rover – the black one – which just passed really slowly?' She nodded. 'I'm sure I've seen him before. First time, the guy was standing by his car when I came out of Waitrose. I noticed because he seemed to be watching me and then he got into his car.'

'Not a blue Peugeot?'

'No. It was the same black Range Rover.'

'It's unlikely then that he's the same person who followed you before.'

'He might have changed vehicles after he knew I'd clocked him on the trip to Norwich,' I argued.

She raised her eyebrows. 'Mmm, well, I suppose that's possible ...' She patted my hand. 'But I honestly don't think it's very likely, Anna. The Peugeot business has spooked you. I'm sure this Range Rover is just a coincidence.'

'Yes, but then I saw him again. He was lurking outside the optician's when I went for my appointment on Monday. He went into a café when I came out but I'm sure it was the same guy.' My stomach was tensing at the thought. 'And here he is again. At least, I think it *could* be. Maybe I *am* just being paranoid.'

'Well, that would be understandable. Anyway, he's gone now. Come on. I'm starving!' She pushed her door open, dismissing my fears.

The pub was virtually empty. One other customer, a man I hadn't seen before, was slumped on a barstool, reading a newspaper and occasionally chatting with the landlady, Lucy. He was balding, in his early fifties and dressed quite smartly in grey trousers and a blue, cotton shirt. At our approach, he looked up and nodded, 'Evening,' before returning to his newspaper. A business man stopping off for a drink on his way home from work, I decided.

We both ordered diet cokes and took menus over to a round table in the corner of the bar. I peered out of the window, trying to see the car park, but it was further around the back of the building.

'*Now* what are you doing?' Ellie's voice interrupted my scrutiny.

'I was just trying to see if the Range Rover has come back and has parked up somewhere but I can't really see.' I frowned. 'If he *is* following me, that's probably what he would do.'

Ellie's shoulders sagged and she sighed. 'Would you like me to nip outside and take a look?'

'No, no. I'm sure it's fine – just my imagination working too hard again,' I replied, guilty that I was spoiling her evening.

'It won't take a minute. You wait here. I'll ninja my way to the car park and then round the front to see if anyone's parked up the road.' She winked at me and adopted a stealthy stance. I rolled my eyes as she crept to the door and poked her head round. 'All clear,' she whispered, 'at the moment.' I couldn't help myself smiling. If Madison was a spaniel, Ellie was more an exotic parrot, with flame-red hair and always dressed in vibrant colours. She was never seen in public without her false eyelashes and these fluttered dramatically as she winked again and disappeared through the door.

With only my own thoughts for company, I sipped at my drink and pretended to study the menu. I was acting like an idiot. Ellie was treating it all as a bit of a joke and I couldn't blame her. I watched out of the window as the rain outside thundered down, suddenly much heavier, grey sheets hammering the path. By the time Ellie reappeared, a few minutes later, her shoulder-length hair was plastered to her head, a sopping, red curtain. She looked askance at me and I had to laugh.

'You should've taken your coat!'

'Cheers pal.' She shook her head vigorously and droplets of water spattered my face. 'Just sharing the love. You'll be pleased to know I got drenched for nothing. There was no-one out there.'

'Sorry.' I picked up the menu, feeling embarrassed.

'It's fine, Anna. As I said, it's good you're being cautious. Whoever that guy was, he's gone now so perhaps we can relax and enjoy our evening.'

***

It was almost nine o'clock when we returned to the car. The rain had eased off but the sky was still heavy with dark clouds and the onset of dusk. The car park was devoid of vehicles apart from Ellie's VW Golf but I shivered as I slipped into the passenger seat. The feeling that someone was watching persisted.

The drive took only a few minutes and we were soon turning into Hamilton Close. Ellie swung into our driveway and turned off the ignition.

'Your turn to make coffee,' she reminded me with a grin as she headed for the front door.

'OK, I'll be there in a minute.'

I'm not sure what compelled me to walk back down the road. Perhaps I was sick of the stomach-clenching certainty someone was out there. Perhaps I felt emboldened by being on home territory. Whatever the reason, I headed cautiously into the gloom. I couldn't be imagining it. My muscles were tense, my teeth on edge. Adrenalin coursed through my body. I just wanted to have one last look, one final check. Rounding the corner and seeing only the usual ribbon of empty cars parked along the street, I almost turned back. Just a little bit further, I told myself, to be absolutely certain.

Warily, feeling darkness close around me, I walked on and reached the end of the street. I stopped, listening. A car was approaching. I slipped into the shadows, pressed against a hedge, as headlights swung into view. It was moving slowly, as if the driver was looking for something. I held my breath as it passed and watched in horror as it disappeared out of sight. It was a black Range Rover.

I stood still, my heart racing, my palms cold and clammy, not daring to move. The engine noise droned through the cool, night air, growing ever fainter. Still I waited. Could he have turned into Hamilton Close? My ears strained to hear. The sound merged into the indistinct hum of the village, no longer distinguishable. I shuddered, chilled by fear. Could he be lurking outside the house, watching Ellie close the curtains, waiting for me?

My phone suddenly burst into life, impossibly loud and I jumped, scrambling to stop the noise.

'What the hell are you doing?' It was Ellie. 'Where are you? Anna, you're freaking me out.' Her voice was shrill in my ear.

'Sorry,' I whispered. 'I'm just down the road. The Range Rover just went past. Can you take a look outside and see if … never mind.' I ended the call and pushed deeper into the shadows. A car was coming from the other direction. Dry-mouthed, I scrunched my body further into the hedge, twigs scratching my back and snagging my hair. As the lights approached, I squinted, trying to make out the vehicle. It was coming faster – a brief glimpse – then gone. The Range Rover had left the neighbourhood.

I disentangled myself from the hedge and crept out into the road, peering into the blackness, checking it was safe to move. Then I launched myself out into the open and ran.

CHAPTER 8

Jack
Tuesday 16th July, 1996

Jack's eyes snapped open. For a split second, he struggled to remember where he was. The sudden brightness was painful, fuzzing his vision and he groped for his sunglasses beneath the lounger. Maisie! He was supposed to be looking after her. Suki. The thoughts tumbled, one after the other, like a slot machine and, in a sudden panic, he jerked himself upright, scanning the pool in front of him. It was quieter now. There were just a few adults and older children on the far side, playing with a frisbee. Many of the poolside loungers had been deserted. A dark-haired woman wearing enormous sunglasses and a floppy hat sat reading a book. Beyond her, a large man with a beard was eating an ice cream. An elderly couple reclined side by side, eyes closed. On the opposite side of the pool, a young couple had moved their loungers close together and lay entwined. Two loungers beyond them, a darkly-tanned young woman in a yellow bikini was gathering up her belongings into a large straw bag. He couldn't see his daughter. His heart lurched.

Where was Maisie?

A glance at his watch. 4:05 pm. He hadn't been asleep long. Where had they gone? He stood, muscles bunched with tension, to extend the range of his vision. She definitely wasn't in the pool. The play area? An ear-splitting scream splintered the air and his head jerked towards it. Maisie? He squinted, shapes in the distance shimmering under the sun's glare. Impossible to see. He started walking, long strides towards the sea. The shapes were not moving away. As he got closer, he realised there were four of them, not two, and they seemed to be playing a game. None of them looked small enough to be his daughter.

He stopped, unsure what to do next. His eyes skimmed the beach in all directions. There were so many parasols; she could be hidden under any of them. *Come on, Jack. That's not likely. Keep calm.* He spun around, heading back to the pool. The sand scorched his feet but he barely noticed.

Then he saw her ...

CHAPTER 9

Anna

That night I had the same nightmare. I awoke clammy with panic at the moment I felt fingers closing around my ankle. I lay in bed, clinging to the duvet, curled in a foetal position, struggling to breathe. *Inhale; count to five; exhale; repeat.* My heart continued to skitter erratically but the breathing exercise did help. I forced myself to concentrate on my hands – *clench, relax, clench, relax* – then repeated the task with other parts of my body. It was an exercise I'd practised many times.

My anxiety was a familiar thing, an unwanted second skin. As a child, I'd struggled with irrational fear. Mum got really angry when I refused to get dressed and go to school. She didn't understand and I was unable to explain. How could I? I was too crushed by a feeling of dread, a voice screaming in my head, a certainty something terrible was going to happen. White-faced and trembling, I would be dragged to the car and buckled in with an exasperated snap.

Over the years, those feelings had lessened and I'd got better at hiding them but they still had a nasty habit of creeping up on me when I least expected it. And now the whole stalking thing had given them a poke, reawakening those long-suppressed fears. Last night, when I'd reached the safety of home and locked the door behind me, Ellie and I had discussed the Range Rover and Peugeot sightings. I got the impression she still thought I was over-reacting, although she was too kind to say so. Perhaps I was. I really wanted to believe my fears were just irrational flights of fancy. Deep down, though, I wasn't convinced – my nightmare was evidence of that.

I spent the day writing. That was the good thing about my work; I could submerge myself in the world of my characters and their problems. At home, I felt safe, closeted behind locked doors. It was only when I ventured out that I felt vulnerable. As I made my weekly trip to Swaffham to spend the evening with my parents, bubbles of anxiety skirted beneath my surface calm and I pulled into their driveway with a sense of relief. A small white van with the logo *DD Decorating Services* was parked on the right-hand side and I pulled up beside it.

There was no immediate sign of either of my parents so I took my usual route to the rear entrance. As I reached for the handle, the door was pushed open and a young, dark-haired man in overalls emerged, carrying a stepladder. The painter. I gave him a friendly smile and stood aside to let him pass. The man glanced up in acknowledgement and I felt my stomach reel. A flash of recognition crossed his face before he turned his head, continuing on towards his van. I closed the back door behind me and took a deep breath. *You've been leading me on all night. Bitch!* It was the man from the Norwich bar. Had he said he was a decorator? I couldn't remember. Could he be my stalker?

'Anna!' Dad greeted me with his usual hug and then held me at arm's length to scrutinise my face. 'How's my girl?' He frowned. 'You're still looking a bit washed out.'

'Thanks, Dad. Good to hear! I'm fine. How are things with you?'

He scowled. 'I'll be better when we get this decorating lark finished. It seems to go on and on as your mother decides she wants yet *another* room painted. It's driving me mad!'

'I thought I heard voices.' Mum swept into the back porch where we were standing. 'What are you doing in here? Come on through.' She ushered us into the kitchen. 'Supper's just about ready. Drinks please, Geoff.'

I waited until we were seated before asking about the decorator.

'Damien Davies,' Mum explained. 'He's the DD of DD Decorating Services. Nice, young man; very polite and punctual. He's almost finished now – hopefully by tomorrow or else he's offered to come in on Saturday to finish off.'

'Thank goodness for that!' Dad muttered.

'That's what I call good service. I have to say I've been impressed and it takes a lot to impress me these days.'

'You can say that again!' Dad whispered to me.

'That's good.' I threw Dad a complicit smile as I reached for the pepper. 'How did you get to hear about him?'

She furrowed her brows in thought. 'I think it was a leaflet through the door ... yes, that's right. That's what gave me the idea to redecorate in the first place and I do like to support local tradespeople, as you know.'

I nodded. 'So ... he lives locally?'

'I don't know, Anna. I haven't asked him for his life story!' she retorted. 'Why are you so interested? Are you and Ellie thinking of having some painting done?'

'I wouldn't have thought so. Just making conversation, that's all.'

'Well, I'm sure we can think of something more interesting to discuss than the painter. What have you been up to this past week? I hope you haven't been holed up all the time writing.'

It was never very long before the conversation became an interrogation and I was prepared for the question. I launched into a monologue about my first two sessions working in the garden at the Old Rectory, taking care to highlight all the funny moments and overlooking any references to Josh himself. When I concluded my description of the mower incident, Dad burst into noisy laughter. His laugh was very much like him, larger than life and very loud; it had the staccato quality of a pneumatic drill.

'This man, Josh ...' Mum gave Dad a strange look. 'What did you think of him?'

I felt the colour starting to creep into my cheeks. 'Seems OK,' I said dismissively. 'Before you ask, I don't know if he's single. This is delicious, by the way. Is it a new recipe?'

She ignored my clumsy attempt to change the subject, merely nodding briefly before continuing. 'Do you know what he does for a living?'

I sighed. 'No. All I know is he's been working on renovating the house. He seems to be doing it on his own ... at least, I haven't seen anyone helping him ... so perhaps he's a builder or a property developer.'

'Interesting ...' She raised her eyebrows slightly at Dad once more. Something was going on between them but I wasn't sure what. He gave her a warning look and changed the subject, embarking on a tale of his latest trip on the train down to London.

'An elderly gentleman was struggling to hear something his wife was trying to tell him on the phone. At one point, he shouted, "What? She's lost her virginity?" *That* got everyone's attention, I can tell you. You could have heard a pin drop. The whole carriage was agog, waiting for his next words, which were, "Oh, right, I see ... she's lost her *photinia*." There was a pause and then he said, "What's a *photinia*? ... Ah, yes, a shrub ... I see." That had me chuckling all the way home.'

I smiled dutifully, only half listening. The other half of my brain was mulling over the coincidence of finding someone at my parents' home with whom I'd had a bit of a run-in. Was Damien Davies following me? I recalled what Madison had said about stalkers and what I'd since learnt from searches on the internet. There were cases cited where the stalker had attempted to get close to his victim in all sorts of ways, like getting a job at the same place of employment. I wondered if he had another vehicle as well as his van. Possibly a blue Peugeot? The thought made me shudder.

'Are you cold, Anna? We could put the heating on.' My sharp-eyed mother missed nothing.

'No, no, I'm fine.' I made a determined effort to refocus my attention for the remainder of the meal and left shortly afterwards. I knew Mum was scheduled for an early start at the hospital the following day and used that as an excuse to depart early. Although it was still light, my nerves thrummed the entire journey home and, upon my return, my hands shook as I locked the front door.

CHAPTER 10

Anna

I had an early lunch and then got ready for the afternoon's gardening at Josh Fielding's, smothering myself in Factor 50 sunscreen. Which Josh would I meet *this* week? Would it be the rude, impatient tyrant of the first meeting or the other good-humoured, charming, godlike creature? Hopefully, the second one. *He* had appeared in my daydreams rather too frequently over the past seven days. I'd even found myself introducing a tall, dark, Josh-like character in the latest chapter of *Baby Gym* as a love interest for Jemima's scatty friend, Liv. I stroked mascara carefully onto my lashes. It wouldn't hurt to look my best.

The anxieties clouding my head last night seemed to have cleared like the azure perfection of the sky. It was going to be a good day. Leaving home in good time, my eyes scanned the street. No strange men, no blue Peugeots, no black Range Rovers. My spirits lifted once more and I marched to The Old Rectory fizzing with unexpected excitement. I didn't yet know if he was married, or already had a girlfriend, but my unfailing optimism was conjuring up an afternoon scenario where he said he couldn't stop thinking about me. Although I was dressed casually, ready for physical work, I knew my skinny jeans and lilac T-shirt showed my figure off to its best advantage. Today I would be cool and do nothing idiotic. He couldn't fail to fall at my feet, rather than me falling at his!

As I turned the corner leading to his driveway, my spirits plummeted. His car wasn't there; he wasn't at home. Ah well, that was what came from having an imagination schooled in romance. I'd constructed all sorts of ridiculous fantasies about the man and he'd probably not given me a second thought. Shrugging off my backpack, I made my way to the shed where I found a note pinned to the door.

Anna,
Had to go out but will be back later. Grass needs cutting again. You know where to find everything. Have left a key under the plant pot by the back door in case you need anything (like a first aid kit!)
See you later,
Josh.

I grinned, my earlier sense of anticipation right back on track. He hadn't forgotten I was coming; he would be back later. Right, I'd better get cracking and get as much done as possible before he turned up. Freshly motivated, I started up the mower and began on the grass. It was yet another beautiful day and I relaxed, enjoying the warmth of the sunshine on my skin. By the time I'd finished, the lawns looked immaculate, if I say so myself. My next task was to start work on the smaller border at the front of the house. This was less overgrown than the larger borders in the rear garden and mostly required weeding and dead-heading. It was back-aching, thirsty work and I congratulated myself on remembering a water bottle. Reaching for my rucksack, I pulled out the bottle, took the top off and put it to my dry lips. The water was warm and slightly unpleasant but at least it was wet. Just as I went to take another swig, Josh's Mercedes swung into the drive. I twisted my head slightly to give him a wave and, in the process, became unbalanced. Fortunately, I managed to prevent myself from falling on my backside and making a complete fool of myself. Unfortunately, though, the upturned bottle missed my mouth and deposited a large dollop of water down the front of my T-shirt. I looked down in dismay to see a large, wet patch spreading by the second, revealing the clear outline of my bra. Brilliant! A smiling Josh was already heading my way. Had he seen what happened? I hoped not. I knelt once more, industriously weeding, as he came to stand beside me.

'Looking good.' His voice was edged with laughter and I risked a suspicious glance over my shoulder. 'The garden, I mean. You're doing a good job.'

'Thank you. It's definitely taking shape.' I dug my fork busily into the soil, working free a small thistle.

'OK. Well, I'll leave you to it.'

I gave him an abstract nod, my attention seemingly all on the task in hand, willing him to walk away and into the house. Listening as his footsteps carried him back to his car, I offered up a prayer of thanks to the gods. Maybe, he'd seen nothing after all. I could hear him whistling to himself as he unloaded a number of items from the boot but I kept my head down. As long as I didn't draw attention to myself, my blushes would be spared.

'It's very warm, isn't it' He was calling across from his car.

'Yes, it's lovely.' Don't look up!

'I hope you remembered to apply sun lotion this week.'

I could hear the laughter bubbling in his voice for sure now. 'Yes, thank you,' I answered primly. *Just go indoors!*

'Lucky it's so warm today.'

I gave in and turned my head towards him, taking care to keep my chest still facing the ground, as if practising some strange, yoga position.

'Why is that?'

'Because that wet patch on your top will be dry in no time. If I hadn't arrived home when I did, I might have missed it!'

***

'Do *you* think it's strange for me to find that guy from the bar in Norwich round at my parents' house?'

I was drinking a cup of coffee with Ellie at the breakfast bar in the kitchen on Saturday morning, catching up on the events of the last two days. She shrugged her shoulders.

'Not really. He *is* a painter and decorator, after all … and it was your mum who contacted him because she needed some work doing – not the other way around.'

I nodded. 'I'm sure you're right and I'm being an idiot. I just hate this feeling of being watched. Everywhere I go … whatever I do.'

Ellie considered me with sympathetic eyes. 'I'm *sure* it will pass. Look, there's been no sign of the blue Peugeot for over a week. *That's* what spooked you in the first place. You wouldn't even have noticed the Range Rover without that happening and you haven't seen *that* the last two days either. I'm sure it's all just a series of coincidences.'

I shivered. I wasn't so sure. I wanted to believe her but my gut was telling me otherwise. There was something creepy about Damien Davies, something shifty in his eyes when he recognised me. A glance at Ellie's resigned face told me to change the subject.

'Enough of all of that!' I smiled apologetically. 'You haven't asked me how I got on with Josh Fielding yesterday.'

'Oooh, tell me everything!' Her eyes widened in anticipation.

I sighed. 'Well, you know how I always manage to do something stupid …'

'Goes without saying. What was it this time?' It was a long-standing joke between us and she chuckled appreciatively as I recounted the wet T-shirt incident. 'What happened after that?' she asked. 'Was Josh nice or nasty?'

'Actually, he was very nice.' I could feel my face colouring.

'Oh yes?' Ellie's tone was suggestive. 'In what way?'

'He brought me out some iced orange juice … and he said some complimentary things about my work in the garden.'

'Mmm, definitely a euphemism for something! I'd say you're making progress, kid. Did you find out anything about his personal life?'

'Yes. Actually, we chatted for quite a while. I asked how he was getting on with the work renovating the house and if he was a builder by trade. He's not. He was working for an investment bank in London but he's recently left. The Old Rectory is a project to 'clear his head.' I asked if he knew Dad and he said everyone in the city knew Dad. Small world, eh?'

'It is indeed … hey, you don't think he could be your stalker, do you? It is another coincidence, after all.'

I thought for a moment. That hadn't occurred to me. 'No …' I said slowly. 'Anyway, he drives a black Mercedes. I haven't noticed one of *them* tailing me.'

'That's good, then. Progress! Someone we can rule out! Has he been having help with the work?'

'Yes. His dad is a builder and he's been over several times apparently, mainly to give advice but also to help with some of the trickier stuff. And, of course, he's had to employ a plumber and an electrician to do all the technical stuff and to make sure he complies with building regs.'

'Well, sounds like you had quite a chat. What a change from that first week!' Ellie commented.

'Oh, he apologised for that. Apparently, he was having a really bad day and only realised afterwards how rude he'd been.'

'This gets better and better. Did you find out if he had a girlfriend?'

I blushed again. 'Don't be daft, Ellie! He was just being friendly and I was hardly going to come straight out and ask him something like that, even if I was interested.'

'You're definitely interested! I can tell. Sorry Anna, but you're an open book. Your face goes red every time you mention his name!'

'Yes well, so far it's just a job. Actually, he asked me if I was prepared to do an extra afternoon, to give him a hand with the painting.'

Ellie raised her eyebrows. 'And, of course, you said yes!'

'Don't give me that look! Yes, I'm going on Tuesday afternoon.'

'Well, I await the next instalment with interest. I remember your painting skills from when you first moved in and offered to do some decorating. Just try not to spill the paint this time!'

Before I could retort, my mobile rang and I reached to answer it.

'Hello. Am I speaking to Anna Blake?' The female voice quivered like an aspen leaf in the breeze.

'Speaking. How can I help you?'

'I ... er ...' A nervous cough. 'I saw your card in one of the cafes in Swaffham. I've recently moved in and could do with a bit of help getting sorted. You know how it is. Would you be free to pop round sometime?'

I frowned. I hated turning anyone down but I'd just agreed to do that extra afternoon for Josh. 'I *am* very busy at the moment ...'

'Oh please,' the woman pleaded. 'I don't know who else I can ask.'

I relented immediately. Her voice conjured up an image of someone old, frail and perhaps a little lonely. How could I refuse to help her? 'Tell you what, shall I pop round this morning to give you a look and see what needs doing? Then I'll have a better idea how I can fit you in. Hold on. I'll just get a piece of paper to jot down your name and address.'

'You're such a soft touch,' Ellie murmured as I rummaged for a notepad. 'You just can't say no.'

Ignoring her, I jotted down the information I needed. 'Right. Shall we say eleven o'clock? Good ... see you then.' I ended the call and gave Ellie a rueful look. 'I know ... you don't need to tell me. She sounded desperate so what could I say? Selina Matthews ...' I read the name on the pad aloud. 'At least it's not far to go; she only lives in Swaffham.'

'You're too soft-hearted for your own good.' She glanced at her watch and stood abruptly. 'Oh gosh, look at the time! I'd better run. I promised Dan I'd drop him off at the rugby ground so he can have a drink after the game. See you later.'

I pursed my lips as she rushed out of the door. She was always running around after Dan, dropping him off, picking him up, doing his shopping. It would be nice to see some of that reciprocated but that wasn't how he operated.

I put the empty mugs in the dishwasher and picked up my car keys with a prickle of disquiet. *Ignore it.* It surfaced every time I left the house. Taking a deep breath, I locked the front door behind me and headed for my car.

***

Having followed the satnav to a sprawling, modern housing estate on the outskirts of Swaffham, I located number 23 and rang the doorbell. The house was a neat, brick, detached building with a white front door. As I waited, I glanced over my shoulder but, apart from a woman pushing a buggy, there was no one about.

Then the door opened and I thrust my hand forward with a bright smile. 'Hi, I'm Anna. We spoke earlier. Pleased to meet you.'

The woman facing me wasn't at all what I'd been expecting. Selina Matthews was a slim woman in her late forties or early fifties, with short, boyish, grey hair and a tired-looking, but attractive, face. She was elegantly dressed in cream trousers, a pale pink, cashmere sweater and a patterned scarf. Her blue eyes scrutinised me with an intensity which was slightly disconcerting. Then she smiled and gave me her hand. It trembled with nervous energy. Her voice, when she spoke, had a husky edge.

'Thank you for coming. Please, come in … and please excuse the mess.' Selina waited while I slipped off my shoes before leading the way into a compact sitting room decorated in neutral shades. 'Please, take a seat. Can I fetch you a drink at all?'

I sat on one of the two matching, grey sofas and shook my head. 'No thanks, I'm fine.' I studied the older woman as she took a seat opposite me. There was something odd about her and I felt slightly ill at ease. Her manner was anxious but also brimming with emotion. I wondered what had happened to unsettle her so much.

'I see you still have a few things to unpack.' In an attempt to diffuse the tension in the room, I gestured to the boxes lining the walls. 'When did you move in?'

'Three weeks ago.' She twisted the edges of her scarf between long fingers and gave me an apologetic look. 'I know I should have got myself sorted but …' She shrugged helplessly.

'These things always take more time than you think.' My smile was sympathetic. 'Luckily, I'm great at unpacking. We could make a start now if you wish.' I leant forward.

'No, no … that is … I'm not ready,' Selina protested, prompting me to sink back against the paisley patterned cushions.

'No problem.' I waited. Perhaps some of the contents were of a personal nature. 'Is it just these boxes which need sorting? What else did you have in mind for me to do?'

'There are lots more upstairs … and there are some shelving units which need putting together and all my books to sort …'

'Do you like reading?' I asked eagerly, pleased to discover some common ground. 'What kind of books?'

She paused before answering. 'All sorts really … women's fiction, crime novels, historical fiction … anything with an interesting story, strong characters and a good ending.'

'Me too. I hate it when a book just fizzles out. It has to have a proper ending.'

A brief silence ensued and I cast about the room looking for something to say – anything to dispel this feeling of awkwardness. The bland walls offered nothing in return. There were no pictures or photographs and, apart from the sofas, the only other furniture was a worn, oak, side table covered in junk mail and free newspapers. The woman opposite was staring at me, as tightly wound as a coiled spring and I wanted to help alleviate her nervousness.

'Where did you live before?' I asked eventually.

Intense, blue eyes met mine. 'Nottingham,' she answered, 'but I'm originally from Surrey. What about you? Have you *always* lived in Norfolk?' The innocent question felt charged with importance.

'No, only the past few years,' I kept my tone light and friendly. 'I love it here though. I love the open spaces and slower pace of life. It's wonderfully peaceful after growing up in London.'

Her gaze narrowed. 'What made you decide to move here?'

'My parents. They live in Swaffham and I lived with them for a while after finishing uni. Now I live in Lewton.'

'With your husband? Are you married?'

'No, I'm single. I share a house with a friend.' I decided to put an end to the conversation. Increasingly, it felt like I was being interviewed. 'Anyway, enough about me! Would it suit you if I came on Monday afternoon for a few hours? I'm sure that between us we could make a big hole in the jobs you want doing … or you could just make a list for me if you're going to be out. I have references, if you want to see them, and my rate is £12 per hour, if that's acceptable?'

'That seems very reasonable. There's no need to show me your references. I'm sure you're perfectly trustworthy.'

We stood up and suddenly she smiled, her lips curving with a warmth which lit up her face. 'Thank you so much for coming, Anna. I'll look forward to seeing you on Monday. Shall we say one o'clock? In the meantime, I'll try and get myself into gear and make sure I'm ready for you.'

As I drove away from the house, I pondered the strangeness of that meeting. Selina was an enigma but I had warmed to her. She exuded an air of vulnerability which appealed to my caring instincts. At the very least, I should be able to help her settle in and feel comfortable in her new home.

CHAPTER 11

Jack
Tuesday 16th July, 1996

Maisie and Suki walked towards him, licking ice creams. Relief surged through him.

'Ah, looks like Daddy's awake.' He could hear the teasing note in Suki's voice.

'Daddy, you went to sleep and you were supposed to be watching,' Maisie scolded, ice cream already smearing her rosy cheeks. 'Suki bought me an ice cream.'

'Yes, I can see.' He smiled apologetically at his daughter before turning his gaze to Suki. 'That's really kind of you. Let me give you the money.'

'No way. It was my idea. I hoped you wouldn't mind.'

He watched, fascinated, as the tip of her tongue flicked across her cone. 'Of course not.' As he spoke, he realised his mouth felt like sandpaper. 'How about we all go and have a drink over at the bar? My treat this time.'

Suki gave a rueful pout. 'Sounds great. I'd love a drink but I've just promised Maisie I'll watch her on the climbing frame. She tells me she can get right to the top but I said that surely wasn't possible.'

'Yes, I can, I can,' Maisie squeaked. 'Come and see.'

'I will. Just finish your ice cream first.'

'Oh, OK.' Jack felt a little deflated and out of the loop. Then he had another idea. 'Tell you what, how about I go over there and fetch us all a drink? I'll bring them back here.'

'Perfect.' Suki's smile widened. 'May I have a can of coke, please?'

Jack gave her a little bow of acknowledgement. 'You certainly may. It'll be juice for Maisie and something long and cold in a bottle for me. I won't be long.' He gave his daughter a look of warning. 'Maisie, be a good girl while I'm gone. Do as Suki tells you.'

'Yes, Daddy,' Maisie replied obediently, cramming the remnants of her cone in her mouth.

He rolled his eyes at the sight of her sticky, cream-covered face. 'There are some wipes in that bag,' he said to Suki, nodding towards a navy, canvas holdall by his lounger.

'No problem. I'll take care of it,' Suki smiled. 'You go. We'll be fine, won't we Maisie?'

Maisie wasn't listening. She had already wandered off in the direction of the climbing frame, watching the other children scrambling over the bars.

'Wait for Suki,' Jack called to her. 'Remember, you're not to go on there without a grown-up to help you.' She nodded without turning her head. 'Are you sure about this?' he asked Suki, anxious that he was over-stepping their brief acquaintance by leaving her stuck with his daughter.

'Of course. I love kids and she's completely adorable. I've got this, Jack. Now go get those drinks!'

He grinned and sucked in his stomach as he rose to his feet. 'As long as you're sure.' He pulled his wallet from the bag. 'Won't be long.' A tiny hesitation as he pondered the wisdom of leaving his daughter with a stranger once more. His earlier panic had shaken him more than he cared to imagine. For a moment, he stopped to watch the beautiful woman and his daughter, laughing together, holding hands. It was fine. Suki had already proved herself a reliable childminder.

It was further to the bar than it looked and Jack soon regretted his bare feet. He almost went back for his flip-flops but decided against it. He didn't want to appear a wuss. As he walked, his thoughts were all of Suki. Was she here with someone? When did she get here? He was sure he would have noticed if she'd been around the pool earlier in the week so maybe she *had* only recently arrived. Another time, another life and he would definitely be trying to get to know her better. That image of her in the bikini pulsated through his mind and body. It would be very easy to be distracted by her.

He reached the bar just after a crowd of German tourists and settled into the queue behind them. From his viewpoint, he could just about make out the loungers by the pool but, from this angle, couldn't see the play area where the climbing frame was situated. Maisie was a bit clumsy and he hoped Suki was keeping a careful eye on her. Anxiety seized his gut as he wished he'd told Suki that his daughter would need reminders to go slowly. He wasn't used to looking after his children. Selina usually did that. As a dad, he liked to think of himself as the fun parent, rather than the responsible one. He adored his children though; he would never forgive himself should anything happen to them.

He glanced at his watch. Selina and Harry should be back soon. Hopefully, their trip would have been successful. Harry had taken the small camera they'd given him for his birthday and he'd been desperate to get some pictures of dolphins. No doubt he'd hear all about it when they returned. Harry could talk for England!

At long last, he made it to the front of the queue and ordered the drinks. His bottle of lager, straight from the fridge, was glistening with condensation and he drank it thirstily, straight down. Another one? Why not? He was on holiday!

With his bottle and Maisie's carton of drink in one hand and Suki's can in the other, he headed back to the loungers. The sense of anticipation grew as he got closer and he found himself planning some witty interaction in his head. It wouldn't hurt to impress her with his repartee. So far, he had the horrible feeling he'd come across as a bit of a dork.

The loungers were empty. Everything was gone, even the holdall. That was strange. He suppressed the twinge of anxiety in his chest. Suki had probably taken their things over to the play area to keep an eye on them. Still carrying the drinks and composing his face into a relaxed smile, he walked across. It was busy. The shrieks of children filled his ears and his eyes searched for his daughter's blonde head. He couldn't see her. The twinges in his chest became a full-blown ache as he circled the play park. Still no sign of Maisie or Suki. He started asking other adults if they had seen a dark-haired woman with a little girl. No-one had.

Still his brain tried to find an explanation. Probably Maisie had wanted the toilet. That would be it! He exhaled, instantly relieved. They would be back any minute.

He waited. They didn't return. He circled the area once more and then returned to the pool. Most of the loungers were now unoccupied but there were a few people still enjoying the late afternoon sunshine. The dark-haired woman with the floppy hat had seen nothing. 'Sorry. I had my eyes closed.' The young couple had seen the woman and girl in the pool earlier but hadn't seen them since. It was the third person he asked, a burly man with a beard sitting on the edge of the pool, cooling his feet, who gave him the information he'd been dreading.

'They packed up and left some while ago. They headed that way.' He pointed in the opposite direction to the bar. 'They've probably gone back to the hotel, mate.'

'Thanks.' Jack headed in the same direction, panic now clawing at his throat. His steps were urgent but he wasn't sure what to do. As the man had suggested, he entered the hotel and asked the young woman manning Reception if she'd seen a dark-haired, American woman with a little girl with fair, curly hair.

The woman frowned and shook her head. 'But I've only just come on duty,' she said. Her English was excellent but she spoke with a Spanish accent. 'Stay, please while I check with my colleague.'

Once more, Jack waited. The seconds were ticking by. If his daughter really was missing, he needed to contact the police. Oh God!

She returned with an apologetic smile. 'I'm sorry but no. No-one here has seen them.'

He turned and ran frantically from the building back to the pool and then on to the play area. They weren't there. Suki had taken his daughter.

CHAPTER 12

Anna

always enjoyed Monday mornings. Over the weekend, my laptop remained closed while I immersed myself in the real world. Secretly though, it was with a sense of relief that I returned to the fantasy world of my novel. There I felt calm and in control. Nothing happened that I didn't expect. That was the joy of being a writer – I was in charge. I could gently steer my characters through the mire of difficult circumstances and towards an inevitable, happy ending. My own life had never been so easy to keep on an upward curve. For that matter, it was difficult enough keeping on an even keel. Just when I felt I had a steady hand on the rudder, something would happen to tip me up, to submerge me once again in murky waters, like catching a glimpse of a blue Peugeot or a black Range Rover. I don't think I would ever again see those two types of car without a lurch of recognition. Here, though, sitting at my desk, with the morning sun slanting through the window and the radio playing a background soundtrack, I could relax and lose myself in a world of my own making.

Jemima waddled laboriously down the aisle, scanning the supermarket shelves for the cereal she craved. Cocopops. Triumphantly, she grabbed a packet and put it in her trolley. Might as well get two packets. She reached up and winced at the sudden twinge in her back. God, it was such a pain being nine months pregnant.

'Are you alright, love?' An anxious voice accosted her and Jemima turned to see an elderly man, his face creased in concern.

'I'm fine, thanks,' she replied, rubbing her back ruefully and depositing the second box into her trolley. That was strange. Her legs suddenly felt wet and uncomfortable.

'It's just ...' the man persisted.

Jemima looked down to see her lightweight summer dress clinging damply to her bare legs. 'Oh God,' she thought, 'my waters have broken in the cereal aisle!'

The intrusion of the doorbell was unwelcome, even more so when I peered out of the window and recognised my father's car parked by the pavement. Much as I loved him, he had an annoying habit of calling in when I was working. Sometimes I felt like pointing out that I would never interrupt him when he was at work. But I never did. Reluctantly, I hit the 'save' button and lowered my laptop lid. One time, when I'd left my work open to view, I'd caught him reading it. 'I'm sure there's a market for this kind of stuff,' he said with a grimace of distaste, 'but I'm afraid it's not my cup of tea. Don't you think you're wasting your talent? This is hardly the next George Eliot!' I wasn't going to make that mistake again.

'Dad!' I pasted a welcome smile on my face as I opened the door. 'What a lovely surprise! Are you stopping or just passing by?'

He reached forward to give me a hug before stepping across the threshold. He smelt of pinecones. 'I'm hoping I've timed it right for your coffee break.'

'As always.' I led the way through to the kitchen and filled the kettle with water while he lowered his tall frame onto one of the stools by the breakfast bar. His presence, always powerful and imposing, seemed especially large in the small kitchen.

'How's the book coming along?' he asked pleasantly.

'Good, thanks,' I replied.

He frowned. 'You mean *well*. The book's coming along well – not good. The sentence requires an adverb, not an adjective. I'm sure I've told you this before.'

'Yes, sorry.' I tried to keep my irritation out of my voice. I was used to him policing my grammar. 'I'm out of proper coffee. Is instant alright?'

His flicker of disapproval was quickly masked but, sensitive to the nuances of his face, I saw it. 'Sorry,' I said again.

'Darling, please stop apologising. Instant is fine.' He smiled as I passed him his *Best Dad in the World* mug, kept for such visits.

'You're looking well ... very tanned and fit,' I said, appraising his pale blue, open-necked shirt and beige, cotton trousers.

His brown eyes crinkled in pleasure. 'Thank you, darling. I try my best. I have the golf to thank for it. That's what I tell your mother .... I have to play for the sake of my health!' He laughed loudly, a rapid burst of staccato filling the confined space. 'How about you?' His eyes narrowed as he openly assessed my face. 'At least you're looking a bit better. The last few times I saw you, you looked like death warmed up!'

'I'm fine thank you. I had been feeling a bit out of sorts but today I'm good ... er, well.'

He raised his eyebrows but let my last-minute correction pass without comment. 'I have to say that I thought there was something else troubling you. I wanted to mention it but your mother told me not to interfere. You know how I worry about you, darling. I wish you would tell me if there was something the matter.' He took hold of my hand and squeezed it in his large, brown one, his eyes imploring me tell him the truth.

I bowed to his will and, reluctantly, told him about the blue Peugeot. 'But I haven't seen it now for well over a week so I'm sure it was nothing to be upset about.' I squashed the uneasy feeling still lurking at the pit of my stomach.

His brow furrowed in concern. 'A blue Peugeot, you say? Did you get the licence number? Have you told the police? This could be serious, Anna. You really shouldn't be compromising your safety like this!' His voice was getting louder. 'In fact, I think you should move back in with us, at least for a few weeks. Just until we're sure there really is no-one following you.'

'I *am* sure,' I said with as much conviction as I could muster. I definitely wasn't mentioning the black Range Rover. 'I've not managed to get the registration number so, no, I haven't contacted the police. Anyway, the situation seems to have resolved itself – if there ever was a situation in the first place. I might well have imagined the whole thing. Please try not to worry. This was why I didn't want to say anything at the time.'

He shook his head. 'Well, if you see it again, you are to contact me immediately. It bothers me that you've been keeping this from me. What else are you hiding? How have I failed as a parent that you feel the need to keep secrets from me? I'm your dad, Anna. You should know that I would move heaven and earth to help you if you were in any kind of trouble ... anything at all.'

I could hear the hurt in his voice and my heart went out to him. 'Oh, Dad!' I reached forward and hugged him, inhaling his warmth and the familiar scent of his aftershave. 'I know that. I love you more than anyone else in the world ... and Mum, of course. If I don't tell you something, it's only because I don't want you to worry ... and because there was never really anything to worry about.'

He held me close and I felt his chest heave. 'It worried *you* and that's what matters. Anything that bothers you – anything at all – I want to know about. Do you hear me, Anna? No more secrets. You're my world. I couldn't bear it should anything happen to you.'

'Nothing's going to happen. As I said, I haven't seen the Peugeot for over a week. If I see it again, I'll let you know. I'm pretty convinced, though that it was nothing. You know what my imagination is like. Do you remember that time I had you and Mum convinced someone was trying to get in my window when I was little? It was just the clanging of the heating pipes but I was certain someone was trying to get into my room ... trying to steal me away from you.'

His grip tightened and then he released me. 'I remember.' His face was solemn. 'I remember promising you that no-one was ever going to take you away from us. Even though you're all grown up, that's still the case, Anna. I would *never* let anyone come between us.'

The fervour in his voice melted my fears, just as it had always done when I was a little girl. He was my hero and protector. Nothing bad would happen while he was looking out for me. I should have told him earlier about the Peugeot. Maybe I should tell him about the Range Rover ... I opened my mouth but Dad turned the conversation to the subject of Mum's birthday the following day. He'd booked her favourite restaurant for dinner in the evening so I offered to pick them both up.

'Marvellous, darling. Thank you. I've booked for seven so be at our house by half six.' He put down his empty coffee mug and stood up. 'I'll let you go back to work. I can see myself out.' As he stepped forward to give me a farewell hug, he murmured against my hair. 'And remember what I've said. No more secrets.' I nodded. 'I meant what I said earlier. I won't let anyone or anything *ever* come between us.'

*****

Despite the usual twinges of anxiety as I left the house, I felt in good spirits as I headed towards Swaffham to help Selina Matthews. The sun was shining; it was a beautiful Spring day; gardens were resplendent with colour; no-one was following me. I was looking forward to getting stuck into some physical work after my sedentary morning. It would be satisfying to help Selina get her house sorted. There was something about her which struck a chord within me. She had seemed so nervous, so vulnerable, at our first meeting and I was eager to help her.

She appeared at the front door as I slowed my Fiesta to a halt outside the house. The driveway was empty, I noticed. Did she not have a car? Without one, she must feel isolated, having moved away from Nottingham only recently. It all seemed very strange. I suspected something must have happened to send her fleeing from her home. That would explain her demeanour. She had seemed abnormally emotional talking to me. I wondered if she had any friends or family living locally and made a mental note to ask her, circumstances permitting.

'Anna! Lovely to see you. Come in,' Selina called. She was smiling and looking much more relaxed than on my previous visit.

I smiled warmly back. 'Good to see you. How's the unpacking been going?'

'Slowly, but it's going, at any rate. Can I offer you a cup of tea or coffee?' Her voice was stronger, less hesitant, more confident.

'Thank you. That would be lovely but not just yet. I feel I should get started on some of the jobs you've got for me before I stop for a break.'

'In that case, let's go upstairs to the room I'm going to use as my study. I think I mentioned the bookcase which needs putting together. I'm keen to unpack all my books and get them back out onto some shelves where they belong. I don't like to think of them all shut away in dusty, old boxes. Stupid, I know.'

'It's not stupid at all. I'd feel the same way.'

She led the way to a small room, painted a pale yellow, at the top of the stairs. Lined neatly, along the right-hand wall, was a row of boxes and another, much larger, flatter box lay in the middle of the floor. A small window overlooked the compact, rear garden and in front of it was an oak desk and padded, grey chair.

'When I ordered it online, I had no idea that it was going to come flat-packed. Who knows what I was thinking! My husband always took care of this kind of thing but now he's not around, I don't have anyone I could ask to help me.' There was a pause. 'We're divorced,' she added.

'Oh, I'm sorry.' I wasn't quite sure what to say.

'No need to be. It happened three years ago and he's now with someone else.' There was no disguising the flash of pain in her eyes and she turned away, heading out of the room. A moment later, she turned back, her face composed once more. 'Oh, are you going to need any tools, do you suppose?'

'I've brought a few with me, in case, but I'll know better when I've opened the box and found the instructions. If I need anything, I'll give you a shout.'

The next hour passed contentedly. Although I wasn't naturally a practical person, I'd always enjoyed assembling flat-packed items and found they were usually straightforward as long as there were clear instructions. Fortunately, in this case, they proved easy to follow and I only needed to screw the pieces together. As I worked, more questions about Selina chased around my brain. She was certainly an enigma, so different today from the nervy, fidgety woman of two days ago. I stood up, pleased with my handiwork, and returned downstairs. She was standing by the sink in the spacious, recently renovated kitchen.

'I was just putting the kettle on. How have you got on?'

'Good, thanks ... er ... I mean well.' Dad's voice reverberated in my ear. 'It's all done. Do you want to come and have a look? Then maybe together we can move it to where it needs to go.'

'Oh, well done, Anna. You are clever,' Selina exclaimed upon inspecting the bookcase. 'I'm really pleased. I thought I would just put it here, in this corner.' She gestured to a space beyond the boxes and together we slid it into position. 'Now, I insist you stop for a drink and maybe a piece of my homemade shortbread.'

'That sounds heavenly.' I sensed she was keen to have some company. Back downstairs, I sat on a stool by the central island in the kitchen while Selina made a pot of tea. 'This is a lovely kitchen,' I said, running an appreciative finger along the smooth, granite worktop.

'I know. That's what attracted me to the house. That and the location.'

'Do you have family nearby?'

There was a pause, a play of confused emotions across her face, sadness, maybe, but also a flash of panic. However, when she answered, her voice was calm. 'No. My son Harry lives and works in London so I suppose you could say I'm a bit nearer. He came and looked at the house when I was considering buying it but has been too busy with work to visit since. He's an architect.'

'If you don't mind me asking, why *did* you choose to move to Swaffham? Was it to do with work?'

'Not exactly.' Her face took on a shuttered look and she busied herself arranging shortbread triangles on a plate before placing them in front of me. 'Do try one of these. Although I made them, I can't claim any credit. The recipe was my great aunt's closely guarded secret and was passed down to me by my mother.'

I took one of the triangles and bit into it. It was delicious – crisp and buttery but with a mouth-wateringly soft centre. 'Wow. This is incredible. Are you allowed to pass on the recipe or has it been entrusted to family only?' Another silence and I watched a cloud hover fleetingly across her face. 'Sorry. Is that a difficult subject?'

'No. My great aunt died a number of years ago but I still miss her. She was such a wonderful person.' The cloud disappeared and Selina smiled. 'I'd be delighted to give you the recipe. It's incredibly simple. The best things always are, aren't they? I'll write it out for you before you leave.'

'Oh, I don't want to put you to any trouble,' I said politely.

'It's no trouble. It won't take me a minute. Now, tell me a bit more about yourself. In fact, there was something I wanted to ask you.'

'Go right ahead.'

'It's about your name, Anna Blake. It's come to me that I recently read a book written by someone with the same name. I can't remember the title but it was about a girl who was a fitness instructor.'

'Really?' My heart skipped with joy. '*Love on a Treadmill.* That was my very first novel. How cool to meet someone who's actually read it without me having to twist their arm first. I hope you liked it?' I asked, suddenly anxious.

'I loved it,' she beamed back. 'So much that I've been looking out for your next one.'

'*Dumb Belles.* It's a sequel. It's due out this autumn. Oh, I'm so pleased you liked it.'

'It made me laugh out loud and that doesn't happen very often these days. You're very talented.'

'Thank you.' I felt my cheeks redden with embarrassment; I was unused to receiving such genuine and wholehearted praise. It had happened only rarely growing up and I felt self-conscious, unsure how to react. Hiding behind my teacup provided a moment's respite and I put it down with a clatter of finality. Conversation over. I loved finding out about other people but was reticent talking about myself. 'I guess I'd better get back to work. What would you like me to do next?'

I spent the rest of the afternoon unpacking Selina's best glasses and crockery, carefully washing them by hand and transferring them to the large, cream dresser in the dining room. When I'd finished, I found her upstairs surrounded by piles of books.

'Oh heavens, look at the time. I was just putting them all into alphabetical order ready to organise them on the bookshelf but I'm afraid I've been off task. I found your book,' she admitted sheepishly, 'and have been re-reading it. It really is a tonic.'

I smiled. 'Maybe I could get you an advance copy of my next book.'

Her face lit up. 'Could you? That would be wonderful.' She scrambled to her feet. 'Are you all finished? I'll just write out that recipe before you leave. It won't take a minute.'

Back downstairs, I waited patiently while Selina rifled through the pages of a hand-written, loose-leaf cooking diary. 'I'm sure it's here somewhere. I had it only yesterday when I made a batch. Oh, here it is; now I just need to find a pen and some paper. That's the trouble when you move house – you can't find anything.'

'Do you have a car, Selina?' I suddenly remembered the empty driveway. 'If not, I could go and fetch anything you needed while I'm here.'

'That's kind but I do have a car. I keep it in the garage – very old-fashioned, I know. Thank you for offering, though. You're obviously a very thoughtful girl.' Her eyes, intense with some unidentifiable emotion, met mine. The air felt charged with something I didn't understand.

'I really should be going,' I said apologetically. 'Would you like me to come again? If so, you could give me the recipe then.'

'Definitely. It's been lovely having you here, getting to know you ...' Selina's voice cracked and she turned to open a kitchen drawer, her back to me. 'Could you come back on Thursday afternoon? There's still plenty to do.'

I considered her request. Could I spare the time in my already busy week? The vulnerability in her voice caught at something in my chest and I replied, 'Thursday's fine. I can see myself out.'

She spun around. 'Oh, but I haven't even paid you yet.' She seemed to be crumbling before my eyes, a sad, lonely woman.

'You can do that on Thursday.' I hesitated. 'Did you need me to stay a little longer?'

'No, no, you need to get on and I will get back to my books. You are a very sweet girl.' She stepped forward quickly and clasped me in her thin arms. She smelt of gardenias. 'I'm sorry. There are times when I'm a bit wobbly but I'm fine now, honestly.'

'Well, if you're sure ...' I felt as if I was abandoning an orphaned kitten.

'Bye, Anna. Thank you.' She had turned back to the sink, her voice thin and reedy, like it had sounded on the phone. 'I'll see you on Thursday.'

I shut the front door behind me and unlocked my car. That was weird. Clearly, there was a shadow in Selina's past but there was something else also – a neediness in the way her eyes sought mine. She was forging an emotional connection between us which felt a bit claustrophobic, like being confined in an airless cupboard. Somehow, in the space of a few hours, I'd come to feel responsible for her. It was all very strange. I turned the key in the ignition and drove to Waitrose, still pondering. Selina had spoken of a son and an ex-husband but had evaded the question about her move to Swaffham.

Swinging into the supermarket car park, my mind turned to more prosaic matters. It was my turn to cook tonight and Ellie had also asked me to pick up a few items. Grabbing my purse and a bag for life, I headed into the shop and quickly found what I was looking for, some chicken breasts, a lemon and some crème fraiche plus the hand cream and shampoo Ellie wanted. I took a short detour down the cereal aisle, picturing my fictional Jemima standing, horrified, in a puddle, surrounded by well-meaning shoppers.

*'Er, I think I'd better get home,' Jemima squeaked, slightly breathlessly. 'I think the baby's coming.'
She realised she was still clutching her trolley and pushed it awkwardly to one side.*

'Do you need any help, love? Can I call anyone for you?' the old man asked worriedly.

*'Are you alright, dear? Oh my goodness, have your waters broken?' A shop assistant bustled her
way to Jemima's side. 'It's OK, I'll take care of this,' she muttered officiously to the old man. 'Thank
you but you go back to your shopping.'*

The old man was reluctant to leave...

My mind was on a roll. Maybe the baby could be born in the supermarket, a surprise shopping
delivery! As I stood daydreaming by the cornflakes, I envisaged the scene. Jemima would be half
sitting on the old man's coat next to her forgotten shopping trolley while the shop assistant, in charge
by virtue of the number of times she had watched the TV show *One Born Every Minute*, oversaw
proceedings.

*'When I say the word, I want you to push!' instructed the shop assistant, her pink curls trembling
with excitement.*

*'Right you are, love,' replied the old man, grimly clutching the handlebar of the trolley in
anticipation.*

'Not you!' The shop assistant threw him an exasperated look ...

I smiled to myself. The scene had potential. The itch to fire up my laptop was strong but it would
have to wait until later that evening. Ellie was seeing Dan after dinner so I'd have an opportunity then.
More ideas peppered my thoughts as I stood at the express checkout queue and unloaded my items.
The checkout girl was discussing her recent holiday to Crete with the woman in front of me and I
wondered if it would be quicker to swap to a different till. As I turned to look, I was assailed by the
feeling of being watched. I stiffened, all senses on full alert; pins and needles pricked my skin. I looked
behind, right and left but no-one was looking my way. Still the sensation remained. The checkout girl
had begun sliding my shopping across the scanner. I gave myself a mental shake and started loading
my few items into my bag. Another quick look round ... was that a flash of movement in my peripheral
vision? I wasn't sure.

Thanking the checkout girl, I strode out of the store and towards my car. Was someone waiting
there? I recalled watching a crime drama where a victim slid heedlessly into the front seat of her car
while a man with dead eyes crouched behind her in the back. My steps slowed and I approached the
car with caution, walking all the way around it and peering into all the hidden spaces before I
unlocked the door. Nothing. One quick, final check around the car park. There was no blue Peugeot
but there was a black Range Rover, parked some distance away. I stared across at it, unable to see if
anyone was inside. *There are lots of black Range Rovers. It's not the same one.*

My fingers gripped the steering wheel as I pulled out of the car park, watching for the Range Rover
to follow. It didn't move. My shoulders relaxed and I headed out of Swaffham. Traffic was light and, a
few minutes later, I reached the A47 roundabout. I checked my mirror, indicated and checked my
mirror again. A spasm of fear stabbed my chest. The Range Rover was behind me, still a few hundred
metres away. I turned right at the roundabout and accelerated away from it. A few moments later, the

Range Rover did the same. *Was this it? Was this the prelude to an attack?* Nerves like ants crawled in my stomach.

Minutes dragged by and I ploughed on, heart pounding, eyes restless between the road in front and the vehicles behind. Shortly, I'd be taking a left-hand turn towards the village of Lewton. *Would he follow?* Dry-mouthed, I pressed the accelerator pedal harder. The turning was coming up now. A panicky glance in the mirror. Indicator on. Slowing down. I held my breath …

The Range Rover sped past, still travelling along the A47 towards Norwich. I exhaled, exhausted with relief.

Nothing to worry about after all.

CHAPTER 13

Anna

I sat staring into space, wondering if I was losing my mind. My fears were irrational. When I considered everything in the cold light of day, there was no actual evidence I was being watched or followed. My anxiety was escalating but it was being fuelled by thoughts in my own head. The fears were my own projections.

Was I having some kind of breakdown? It wasn't normal to turn into a quivering wreck every time I saw a certain model of vehicle. After Ellie had gone out with Dan last night, I had googled 'paranoia' and the definition was horrifyingly akin to what I was experiencing. Yes, I thought and felt that I was under threat, despite minimal evidence that I was. Yes, my fears had grown and I was becoming suspicious of people I met. That was definitely true of the decorator, Damien Davies. I clicked on the link to read about the causes of paranoia but could find nothing there to which I could relate. I wasn't lonely and had never suffered from depression or a previous trauma. The section offering guidance and support was more helpful. It advised talking about my thoughts with someone I trusted. However, I wasn't good at talking about my thoughts. They were too private; I would be left exposed.

Restlessly, I pushed the laptop aside, unable to concentrate on my work. I needed fresh air and some activity. Usually, I would go for a run but the thought of it sent my nerves tingling afresh. Instead, I slipped on my old gardening trainers and headed outside. Although we only had a small garden, there was always weeding to be done. Little green shoots were peeping mischievously above the soil, enjoying the Spring sunshine. It was amazing how quickly they sprung up and how ferociously they would claim their territory, just like my groundless worries. I needed to get rid of them. With that in mind, I set to work with a vengeance. While I forked over the soil, I tried to focus on my main character, Jemima, giving birth in the supermarket aisle. There would need to be bollards, I decided, to stop random shoppers from joining in the fun. 'Bollards.' I said the word aloud; it was such a great word. There had to be some comedy potential there. I pictured a young woman, face heavy with make-up, wearing inexplicably high heels, moving the bollard and teetering down the aisle.

'Hey, what do you think you're doing?' the bossy shop assistant shouted as she tried to intercept the intruder.

'I need Cocopops,' the young woman pouted. 'Look – they're only just there.'

I was feeling better. The rear border was now weed-free and my creative juices were flowing again. It was time to get back to the laptop. As I swung around, I was briefly dazzled by a flash of light coming from the small copse beyond the garden fence and the field of beans which stretched in between. I stood motionless, watching. There was no movement, nothing out of the ordinary. The sun was bright and I shielded my eyes as I stared towards the trees. Nothing.

I headed indoors. *Paranoia. Just my imagination playing tricks.* Even if there was a flash, there would be a straightforward explanation. I sat back down in front of my laptop, my fingers moving across the keys, trying to ignore the only explanation I could think of. Was the flash the light of the sun reflecting off a pair of binoculars, watching me ...?

***

An afternoon to be spent with Josh Fielding brought jitters of a different kind. I couldn't deny the attraction I felt for him and dressed with particular care. As yet, the burgeoning relationship I sensed between us was fragile. It would be easy to mess it up, especially with a paintbrush or, even worse, a roller in my hand. Hopefully, I wouldn't be expected to do any high-level decorating and would only be entrusted with something easy. A paint pot combined with a ladder would be a recipe for disaster.

I'd chosen a flattering pair of beige, cotton cut-offs and a white T-shirt, brushed my hair until it shone and spent ages applying make-up to achieve a natural look. As I finished dabbing my lips with some clear gloss, I realised it was time to leave the house. The thought gave me an uncomfortable jolt at the pit of my stomach. It was ridiculous. Even walking through the village in the middle of the day was enough to raise my anxiety levels. Taking a deep breath, I grabbed the holdall I'd already packed with a pair of overalls, an assortment of tools which might prove useful and a bottle of water. As an afterthought, I added my hairbrush and make-up bag. It wouldn't hurt to be prepared.

Outside, everything was reassuringly normal. Sunshine had brought many of the retired residents out into their gardens and the air hummed with the sound of busy lawnmowers. In the distance, I could hear the cacophony of schoolchildren enjoying their lunchtime break. Brenda Jones gave me a wave as I walked past number ten and stood up from behind a wheelbarrow.

'Lovely day, isn't it?' she called, clearly hoping to waylay me for a chat.

'Gorgeous,' I replied. 'Sorry Brenda, I can't stop. I'm running late for an appointment.'

'Don't worry, dear. You get on. I won't hold you up. I was just going to mention ...'

Her voice receded as I walked on. Poor woman. I'd look out for her on my return journey and let myself be talked into a cup of tea if she was about. The world was full of lonely people. An image of Selina flickered before my eyes. It made my heart ache. I knew what it was to be lonely.

As the sweeping drive of the Old Rectory came into view, I tucked a stray wisp of blonde hair behind my ear and moistened my lips. Josh's black Mercedes was parked in the drive and I skirted around it, wondering whether to go around to the back or to ring the front doorbell. I was spared making a decision, though, as the front door opened and Josh appeared, carrying a document wallet and his car keys. He was dressed in an open-necked, olive green shirt and dark brown trousers and had a jacket slung over his arm. My first thought – dark colours really suit him – set my pulse racing; my second – he's on his way out – filled me with disappointment.

'Afternoon, Josh.' I gave my best imitation of a cool, professional smile. 'I'm here for some painting duties,' I added, in case he'd forgotten.

'Yes, come in.' He stood aside, allowing me to pass and I caught the musky scent of his aftershave as I brushed by him into a hallway covered in dust sheets. 'Let me just put these in the car. Won't be a minute.' I waited patiently, wrinkling my nose at the particles of dust visibly swirling as sunlight shafted through the open doorway. 'Sorry – it is a bit dusty in here.' Josh had returned and seen my expression. 'I've been sanding walls ready for painting.' He looked doubtfully at my attire – not quite the impression I'd hoped to make. 'You might want to cover yourself up a bit. I probably have an old shirt somewhere ...'

'No, that's fine. I've brought overalls.' I patted my holdall. 'I like to be prepared.'

'Good. Well, you can start in here.' He gestured to a room to the right of the hallway. 'This is the lounge. It was originally two rooms but I knocked through and put in some French windows to take advantage of the light.' I could immediately see where the split had been as the two original rooms had been painted contrasting colours – one purple and one orange. 'I think it's going to take quite a few coats to cover those awful colours, I'm afraid.'

'No problem,' I said confidently. 'I'd better get cracking.'

'OK, I'll leave you to it. I'm afraid I've got to go out for a bit. I'm not sure when I'll be back so let yourself out when you need to go. Anything you get done will be a bonus, to be honest. I think I've left everything you need.' He waved a hand towards a step ladder, large paint pots and an assortment of brushes and rollers. 'Do you have any questions?'

I shook my head, casting around for something intelligent to ask. 'I'm sure I'll be fine.'

'Good.' He gave me a distracted smile. 'I'm sure you'll do a great job. You've got my number if you have any problems. I'd better run.'

'Bye,' I called to his retreating back. Well, *that* was disappointing. I walked over to inspect the range of equipment on offer. The room was slightly misshapen with a few nooks and crannies but there were large, flat expanses of wall so I decided to risk a roller and use a medium-sized brush to cut in round the edges. My attention turned to the paint. Josh had left a screwdriver to lever the tins open and I was curious to see what colour he had chosen. Kneeling down on the floor, I found the notch in the lid and pushed down. Nothing happened. I pushed a little harder; still nothing. With visions of spending the entire afternoon trying to prise the paint lid off, I applied all the force I could muster. This time, the lid burst free. However, instead of opening with a satisfying pop, it came off entirely, catapulted into the air and landed squarely in my lap. With dismay, I peeled it from my newly washed and ironed cut-offs. Both thighs were now adorned with pale grey splodges. Thank goodness Josh had already left and not witnessed the spectacle! Rummaging in my holdall, I extracted my overalls. I didn't much fancy spending the afternoon with wet thighs so, with a quick glance round to make sure no-one could see, I slipped my trousers off, hung them over the stepladder and hauled myself into the overalls. Sorted. Josh would have no idea I was in just my knickers beneath the baggy, navy trousers should he happen to return before I left.

I set to work and soon got into a rhythm with the roller. The paint was good quality and covered the walls well, with none of the dripping I'd experienced previously. Josh had left a radio which I turned up nice and loud bellowing out the songs on Radio Two at the top of my admittedly out-of-tune voice, confident in the knowledge no-one could hear. The afternoon passed rapidly and surprisingly mishap-free. I'd just started on a second coat and was belting out 'I'm too Sexy' by Right Said Fred, wiggling my bottom vigorously to accompany the lyrics, when I became aware that I was no longer alone.

'Very nice,' Josh drawled.

I spun around to see him standing in the doorway, grinning appreciatively. I flushed. 'That's *not* something many people say about my singing,' I said, returning his grin.

'I was talking about the walls! What a difference a coat of paint makes!' His face was deadpan. Then he winked. 'Mind you, the singing and dancing were also … er … very entertaining. I hadn't realised how talented you are.'

'Glad you noticed. There's a lot more going on beneath these overalls than most people realise!' The words were no sooner out of my mouth when I realised how suggestive they sounded – especially as my cut-offs were still waving merrily from the stepladder by the open window. Hopefully, he wouldn't notice.

He raised his eyebrows and shot me an amused look. 'I'm sure.' His tone was definitely flirtatious and I could feel goosebumps tingling my bare legs. 'Looks like you're doing a great job,' he continued. 'I wasn't sure if you'd still be here as it's gone five o'clock.'

'Oh gosh, is it that late?' I turned my wrist to look at my watch. 'I hadn't realised the time. I'd just started on a second coat but actually, I'd better be off. I've got something on tonight. I'll just quickly wash the brush and the roller.'

'Don't worry about that. I'll get changed out of these clothes and then I'll take over. It would be good to get the second coat finished.'

'Great. I'll just get packed up then.' I picked up my water bottle and threw it in my bag. 'Don't let me keep you if you want to be getting on. I can see myself out.' Casually, I stood up and waited for him to leave so I could retrieve my now-dry, paint-spattered trousers.

'OK. See you on Friday?'

I nodded and began to sidle towards the stepladder. As he disappeared from view, I grabbed the cut-offs, shoved them in my bag and made a dash for the front door.

'Anna?' Josh called from upstairs.

'Yes.'

'Make sure you don't forget your trousers! They were hanging by the window.'

Dammit. He *had* seen, after all. 'Got them. Bye,' I called back breezily. *Classy, Anna.*

***

Once again, I drove to Swaffham on tenterhooks, eyes watchful, hands tense on the steering wheel. I reached my parents' house just a few minutes late and forced myself to relax and smile as Mum appeared at the door, cool, slim and elegant in a simple, fitted dress which would have cost a fortune.

'Happy birthday!' I said, proffering my gift. 'You look fabulous, Mum. I love that dress.'

'Thank you, Anna.' I was enveloped in a cloud of Dior as she presented a smooth cheek and kissed the air by my left ear. 'How kind! Shall I open this now? You'd better come inside.'

Dutifully, I followed her into the freshly-painted, hallway and looked around at the pale green walls. 'This looks really nice. Has the decorator finished now?'

'Almost. He's coming back tomorrow because I *really* don't like the colour I chose for the sitting room. It's too dark. I should have stuck to this colour throughout. Still, no harm done. Oh look!' She opened the tissue paper surrounding her present. 'How lovely! A scarf. It's beautiful – such gorgeous colours. And it's a Salvatore Ferragamo too. How thoughtful. Thank you, Anna.'

'You're welcome. Where's dad? We'd better get going.'

'I'm right here.' He appeared on cue, tall and handsome in a dark Savile Row suit and claret red, silk tie. 'How's my girl?' He gave me a warm hug. 'Beautiful as ever.' He cast an approving eye over the midnight blue Karen Millen dress I'd purchased in a sale when shopping with Madison. It was not the style of dress I would have chosen for myself but I knew my parents would like it and had bought it for occasions such as these. 'Have there been any more instances of being followed?' He studied my face anxiously. 'Mum and I have been so worried about you.'

'No, nothing, Dad. Please try not to worry.' I wasn't going to mention my recent panics. Instead, I smiled at Mum. 'Now I really think we should take this beautiful lady for her birthday dinner.'

'Well, alright.' He allowed himself to be mollified. 'That's something, at least. I'm ready if you are. I'll just set the alarm.'

A few minutes later, we were on our way. I drove with exaggerated care when transporting my parents anywhere. Dad was a terrible passenger and highly critical when anyone else was at the wheel. My driving wasn't too bad but I took extra measures so as not to offend him. Today, however, he didn't even notice when I clipped a pothole. He was in a jovial mood, regaling us with his exploits earlier that day.

'I had a meeting this afternoon and my colleagues and I were waiting for the lift. The doors opened and in we went, unaware that a previous occupant had clearly passed wind. The smell was terrible! Ever practical, Justine produced a perfume spritzer and squirted it into the air. Unfortunately, she managed to hit poor old Nigel right in the eye and the two smells combined was hardly an improvement! Meanwhile, the lift headed up to the second floor; the doors opened and there was a large party of Chinese businessmen waiting to go in. Obviously, they would think we were responsible for the stench so I gave Nigel a nudge. He nodded politely and said, 'Pardon me!' We were laughing about that for most of the meeting.'

'You're supposed to be retired! What's with all these meetings?' I scolded gently.

'They keep him happy. You know your father. He was never going to give up work completely,' Mum interjected.

'Quite right. I'm very happy for you to fuss over me, darling, but I'm fitter than I've been in years and I need to keep busy. Anyway, did I tell you what happened yesterday when I was playing golf ...?'

I allowed my mind to drift. Both parents seemed in good spirits so perhaps I could relax this evening. I glanced automatically in my rear-view mirror at the blue Toyota behind. It had been following us for the last five minutes but, on this occasion, I felt completely calm. That was because Dad was in the car with me. From my earliest recollection, I'd always felt nothing bad would happen when he was with me. He had the sort of steam-roller personality that exuded confidence and I had every faith in him to keep me safe. As a child, all of my firsts had come with his encouragement – going down a slide, learning to swim, mastering riding a bike – but also because I couldn't bear to disappoint him. For him, I would take risks I would otherwise have avoided; he'd always been my safety net. I indicated to turn right into the restaurant's car park and watched the blue Toyota continue on its journey.

The restaurant, Chez Pierre, a chic, modern French restaurant with a Michelin star, was always busy and tonight was no exception. Already, the hum of conversation and the clatter of cutlery gave it a vibrant feel and we were shown to our table by the maitre d' who greeted my parents by name and wished Mum a happy birthday.

'My best table for the beautiful lady,' he murmured as he showed us to a spot overlooking a lake and ushered us respectfully into our seats. I regarded the place settings with surprise and an unwelcome flutter of disquiet.

'Are there six of us tonight?' I asked. 'I thought it was just us.'

'Oh, didn't Dad mention it? We've invited some friends along,' Mum replied airily. 'You don't mind, do you darling? George and Louise Jacobs. You've met them before. George is a work colleague of mine. Do you remember?'

I nodded, recalling a tall, bespectacled, balding man with a serious face and a stout wife with dark curls and a ready smile. I remembered them, particularly, as their son was Ewan Jacobs whom I'd dated for a while the previous year. The uncomfortable sensations in my stomach grew as I regarded the extra place at the table. 'And the third person?' I asked, already knowing the answer. I looked up and intercepted the arch look Mum was directing towards Dad.

'Their son Ewan is coming along. Darling, don't look like that!' He patted my hand and bestowed his most charming smile. 'I know you two were a bit of an item for a while. At the time, your mother and I were rather concerned. He did seem to be a bit wild and irresponsible – not that we would have dreamt of interfering.'

I snorted at that. From my earliest memory, my parents had sought to orchestrate every aspect of my life and boyfriends had been no exception. Over the past ten years, I'd lost count of the number of nice, young men – usually sons of acquaintances – to whom they had introduced me. When I met Ewan, it had been at a friend of a friend's party and I didn't, for a while, make the connection between the good-looking, long-haired youth with devil-may-care eyes and the very staid, respectable George and Louise Jacobs. In retrospect, that was part of his appeal. He wasn't someone selected for me nor someone of whom my parents would approve.

'Anyway,' Dad continued, still smiling benignly. 'He's turned himself around and has become a bit of an entrepreneur. He specialises in security systems and he's being doing a bit of work for me recently. He asked after you, you'll be pleased to know, and I thought that maybe it was worth giving him a second chance. Oh look – here they are now!' He stood up, giving me no opportunity to reply. Instead, I watched Ewan as he approached our table. He had certainly changed, I conceded. His dark hair had been cut short and he had filled out a little. In his immaculately, tailored suit, he looked very much the young businessman and rather boring. The thought made me a little sad; he resembled a tamed Johnny Depp, undoubtedly good-looking but without the old spark of excitement.

'Anna, lovely to see you again. You look beautiful!' He pressed a shaven cheek against mine. Literally *all* his rough edges had been smoothed.

'You too.' I smiled politely at George and Louise and exchanged greetings. Then attention was focused upon Mariella and her birthday and I was able to retreat to the side-lines, inwardly seething about the way I'd been set up. Another birthday gift – Mum's favourite perfume – was duly unwrapped, drinks were ordered and menu items were discussed. I sipped my sparkling water and responded to the questions I was asked but contributed little to the conversation otherwise. Ewan tried several times to engage me in talk but I felt stubbornly disinclined to give him any encouragement and eventually he got the message, contenting himself with giving me meaningful, intense looks across the table. Dad frowned at one particularly curt response I gave but, for once, I didn't care.

By the time the main courses appeared, however, my resentment had simmered down to the level of irritated resignation. The attraction I'd previously felt towards Ewan had gone but I did enjoy his company. I found myself smiling at his jokes and, in the end, joining in with some of my own wit and sparkle. It was Mum's birthday after all. When, at the end of the evening, Ewan gave me a farewell hug and whispered in a voice loud enough for everyone to hear that he would text the next day, I merely nodded and smiled. My parents, wearing smug, knowing expressions, looked on.

'Well, *that* all went rather well,' Dad declared on the journey home. When I failed to respond, Mum added, 'George and Louise are always good company and I have to say that for once I agree with you, Geoff, about Ewan. What a charming young man! What did you think, Anna?'

'You're right, of course,' I said quietly. 'You always are.'

CHAPTER 14

Anna

The drumming of rain on my bedroom window was a welcome relief after the heat of the past few days. I lay in bed, listening to Ellie moving about downstairs, getting ready to go to work and picked up my phone when a message pinged. It was from Madison. She was on holiday in the Algarve with a friend, Jo, from work but had been texting regularly. In her last text, she'd fallen madly in love with a Portuguese waiter and I scanned the message, eager to hear the latest.

It's over. NEVER trust a holiday romance. Turns out he's also been seeing another girl staying at the hotel. I know – you did warn me and so did Jo. Still, fun while it lasted. At least I got plenty of free sangria out of it. Last day today so we're going to give our suntans some serious work and then party hard tonight. How are you? Any cars following you? Xx

Poor Madison. This was not the first time. Just like Ellie and me, she'd not had much luck with men. I tapped out my reply.

Poor you. Hope you're not too heartbroken. Give him a kick where it hurts from me. V envious of your tans by the way. You both looked fab in that latest pic. All fine here. Enjoy your last day xx

Instantly, another message popped up, this time from Ewan. That was fast work.

Great seeing you last night. Made me realise what I'd been missing. Please say you'll have dinner with me tonight. Alone this time so we can catch up properly x

Although he'd promised to contact me, I hadn't really expected to hear from him and certainly not so soon. Probably trying to impress my parents. My fingers hesitated as I contemplated my reply.

What should I say? My initial reaction was to turn him down. I didn't want to give him any false hopes. However, it seemed a little unkind to turn him down flat; better to do those things in person. By the time I'd showered and dressed, I'd decided to meet him for a drink, rather than dinner, at the village local. More casual and non-committal. As I sent my reply, my phone started ringing. Dad.

'Hello darling!' he boomed, his voice reverberating in my ear. 'Hope I haven't got you out of bed?' This was said with a gleeful chuckle. Without waiting for a response, he ploughed on. 'Your mother left her bag in your car last night with her phone. She's at work today in King's Lynn and is in a right panic about it. I could come and collect it but I'm off on a golf day today in Norwich. Alan Horner is picking me up in about ten minutes. I don't suppose you could find time today to drop it off. I know you're very busy ...' His voice tailed off expectantly.

'No problem. I'll bring it round later. I still have a key so it won't matter if you're not there.'

'Thank you darling. You're an angel. That blasted painter is here again so you probably won't need your key. Have a good day.'

'You too.'

My mind froze at the mention of Damien Davies. I didn't trust him; I hadn't totally dismissed him as my Peugeot stalker. It was too much of a coincidence to find him decorating my parents' house. Despite assurances to my friends and parents, I remained convinced I was being watched. There was still no tangible evidence, yet the whole fabric of my being was constantly on high alert, sensitive to the merest shift in the air or whisper in the breeze. It was the way the hairs on my arms quivered and trembled every time I left the house. It was the dance of shadows quickly disappearing from view and the burning in my neck as I envisaged eyes boring into me.

Get a grip. The rational part of my brain forced me back on an even keel. Damien Davies would be working; there was no need for him to see me. It would only take a couple of moments to slip into the house unnoticed and leave the bag. *Breathe.*

After a quick breakfast, I settled down to work. My aim had been to finish Chapter Eighteen by lunchtime but, after an hour of typing, deleting and retyping, I gave in to my restlessness. It was impossible to concentrate with my mind stubbornly fretting over the task ahead. With a sigh, I picked up my car keys. Better to get it over with.

The rain was still falling heavily, splashing up from the pavement as I made the dash to my car. As I neared my parents' house, I slowed and approached with caution. The white van emblazoned with 'DD Decorating Services' sat squarely in the driveway. I pulled in, willing the gravel not to crunch beneath my wheels, and turned a semi-circle, parking so my car was facing in the right direction to leave. Clutching Mum's lilac Gucci bag in my hand, I edged my body out of the car. No signs of activity were visible through the front windows but I rejected using the front door, deciding it would be easiest to sneak around the back and leave the bag in the utility room. As I ventured nearer to the house, I deciphered the strains of ACDC. Even better. If he was listening to loud music, there would be no problem getting in and out undetected. Feeling like a cat burglar, I tiptoed around the side of the house. The volume of the music was increasing and I hesitated. I wished I'd asked which room was being painted. Was it the utility room? Maybe I'd be better going in through the front after all. I chuckled nervously to myself at the thought Dad may have installed CCTV cameras without telling me. How would I explain my furtive behaviour? Actually, hadn't he said only last night that Ewan had been helping him with some security issues? Horrified, I looked up, trying to spot any hidden cameras and, just at that moment, Damien Davies walked out of the back door, his phone clutched to his ear.

'Er, I'll call you back,' he said as he eyed me warily. There was a moment's silence, during which he slipped his phone into his pocket. He was wearing overalls spattered in green-coloured paint and his long, brown hair was pulled back in a ponytail. 'Er, Alice, isn't it?'

'Anna.' I stood rooted to the spot, slow-witted with shock.

He nodded. 'I thought I recognised you when I saw you the other week. You were that girl in Norwich – was it in the King's Head?'

'Yes.' Regaining my senses, I waved Mum's bag at him. 'I'm just returning this. Don't let me keep you.' I strode past him to reach the back door.

'Wait!' He snaked an arm out to stop me. 'I want to say I'm sorry. I don't think I behaved very well that night. I'd had a bit of a skin full and, to be honest, I wasn't in a very good place.'

'That's fine. Apology accepted.' I flashed him a smile. 'No hard feelings.' I made to move on but the hand on my arm remained and its grip tightened fractionally.

'No, wait.'

I turned back towards him, my eyes questioning, scanning his face. He was wearing a discomfited expression.

'Yes?'

'Well ... I was ... er ... wondering if you'd like to do it again some time ... meet up for a drink, that is?' His dark eyes were black pebbles staring at me.

'Oh.' I smiled again, apologetically this time. 'That's a very kind offer but, I think I mentioned before, I already have a boyfriend, Jeff – he's in the Marines. Thank you though. I'd better get on.' Once again, I tried to move forward but his hand restrained me.

'Not so fast.' His dark eyes glittered dangerously. 'You don't have a boyfriend in the Marines. I mentioned him to your old lady and she didn't know what I was talking about. You're lying.' His lips curled in a snarl and, worried by the sudden change in mood, I shook my arm free.

'I'm sorry.' I was full of contrition, anxious to placate him. 'You're right. I just didn't want to hurt your feelings. Now, if you'll excuse me ...'

'Not good enough for you? Is that it? Rich bitch,' he sneered. 'Yeah ... hurry along now,' he called as I scurried into the house. 'Get back to your ...'

I didn't hear his last words. I'd flown into the utility room, dodged past the step-ladder and tray of paint, sped into the kitchen, tucked the bag next to a pile of recipe books and rushed to the front door. It was locked. *Damn.* Heart thudding, I rummaged in my pocket. My trembling fingers located the leather key fob and I shoved the correct key in the lock. I didn't dare turn around to see if he had followed. Instead, I slammed the door and dashed to my car. The engine roared into life and I flew out of the drive in a hail of gravel. I was still shaking as I headed back along the familiar route. Nothing was following and I willed my taut body to relax. But it wasn't until I reached Lewton that I realised how foolishly I was behaving.

***

The grey-haired man in the black Range Rover, hidden in the trees, had watched as the Fiesta tore past. He saw a set face, shoulders hunched over the steering wheel, a flash of long, blonde hair and then she was out of sight. Patiently, he pulled out behind her.

CHAPTER 15

Anna

I phoned Ellie, who was on her lunch break, for some reassurance. 'I definitely overreacted. This whole stalker thing is playing havoc with my mind. I seriously thought he was going to attack me!'

'Well ...' Ellie's response was cautious. 'It wasn't a good situation, whichever way you look at it. You ought to tell your parents.'

'God, no, imagine that! Dad would probably put him out of business and run him out of Norfolk. Then he'd have an even bigger grudge against me. No, it's best to let things lie. He's almost finished the work he was doing in their house and then he'll be gone for good. Don't you go saying anything either. You know what Dad's like. He'll only make it worse.'

'If you say so. Listen, I've got to go but we can talk later if you like. Dan's away – a work thing, he said – so I'll cook if you like.'

'Great but can you make it early? I'm meeting someone for a drink at eight.'

'Oooh, do tell ... damn, I've gotta go!'

The phone went dead. Poor Ellie. She deserved so much better than Dan. My skin crawled as I recalled the evening he'd come around to the house when Ellie was out. He'd stood on the doorstep with his American college boy good looks and artlessly tousled, chestnut hair, grinning at me.

'Oh,' I'd said, surprised by his appearance. 'Ellie's out. Didn't she tell you?'

'Yeah, yeah.' He'd nodded and his face had assumed a sombre expression. 'Look, Anna, I need to talk to you. Can I come in?'

'Of course.' I'd been concerned. 'Is it about Ellie?'

'Kind of ....' He'd followed me through to the kitchen.

'Is something wrong?'

He'd sighed heavily, a sound full of regret. 'You could say that.' Troubled, blue eyes met mine. I'd made him a coffee and sat listening as he told me Ellie was a great girl but very possessive and he felt hemmed in.

'Have you told her how you feel?' I'd asked.

'How can I? I don't want to hurt her feelings.'

I could empathise with that. 'I know but you need to be honest and tell her if something between you isn't right. You can't keep stringing her along.'

He'd nodded. 'You're right ... of course you are. Thanks, Anna. You're a great girl. Can I have a hug for luck?'

He'd stood up and taken a step towards me. Naïve as I was, I'd opened my arms and stepped into his embrace. The hug was not unpleasant. He was tall and smelt of citrus aftershave. His arms had tightened around me and I'd squeezed him back. Then he'd kissed me, warm lips pressing against mine, his tongue pushing against my mouth. Ugh, the memory made me gag. Shocked and furious, I'd struggled free.

'What the hell are you doing?' Rage boiled in my chest.

'I'd have thought that was obvious,' he'd responded, a sly smile playing round his mouth. 'I knew I could turn on Ellie's ice maiden friend.'

'You've got to be joking!' I'd spluttered, stepping back out of his reach and folding my arms protectively across my chest. 'You need to leave ... NOW.'

'Are you *sure* that's what you want?' He'd raised his eyebrows and let his eyes skim my body suggestively. 'That's not what your lovely body was telling me. I'll finish with Ellie first, if that's what you want. I'm sure you'd be worth it.'

'Get out.' I'd glared at him with all the disgust I could muster.

A careless shrug and a parting shot. 'Your loss.'

Afterwards, I'd been wracked by loathing for Dan, pity for Ellie and guilt that I'd somehow allowed the situation to develop. Ellie would be devastated when he finished with her but she'd have had a lucky escape. However, to my complete amazement, three months later the relationship had continued, apparently unchanged. I'd waited for something to happen. When it didn't, I wished I'd said something straight away. As time went on, it had become increasingly difficult to broach the subject. I knew what she would say.

'If there was nothing in it, why didn't you tell me at the time?'

Life, sometimes, was horribly complicated.

***

Over an early dinner of spaghetti bolognaise, I told Ellie about seeing Ewan the previous evening.

'I had no idea he'd be there last night. It was embarrassing to be honest, especially as my parents seemed to be pushing him at me. I felt like I'd been set up.'

She wrinkled her nose. 'I know he's good looking,' she said slowly, 'but I didn't like him, to tell you the truth. I thought he was arrogant ... and a bit out of control.'

'I know ... but I do think he's changed. He was completely charming last night – not at all like the old Ewan. Don't worry though.' I smiled at the look of concern on Ellie's face. 'I'm not planning on getting involved. That's why I'm meeting up with him tonight – to make it clear we'll just be friends. Maybe that's what he wants too.'

'Didn't sound like it in the text he sent you,' Ellie commented. 'You want to be careful, Anna. He might not react well when you tell him. You know what he's like. What Ewan wants, Ewan gets. I can't see him taking no for an answer. Oh!' she gasped suddenly as a thought occurred to her.

'What?' I asked.

'Well, he could be your stalker. Strange how he's turned up again, out of the blue, a few weeks after you feel you're being followed.' She shook her head. 'I don't like it, Anna. I think you should cancel.'

I frowned. 'Really? I don't think there's anything to worry about, Ell. I just can't see something like that would be his style. As you say, he's the type who only has to click his fingers to get what he wants. Anyway, we're meeting at the Hare and Hounds. There'll be other people around. I'll be perfectly safe.'

'OK. How are you getting there?'

'I was going to walk – it's stopped raining now. Why? Do you think I should take the car?'

'I don't think you should go at all. Tell you what, I'll go with you. Dan wanted me to stop by at the garage tonight and pick up his sunglasses, his new ones. He left them there and he's worried they'll get nicked while he's away.' She smiled fondly. 'He's always forgetting things – got a mind like a sieve.'

'Well, he's lucky he's got you to put things right,' I said tartly.

She gave me a puzzled look. 'I don't mind. Anyway, here's my plan. I'll drive you to the pub and wait with you until Ewan turns up – *if* he shows up, that is. Then I'll pop into Swaffham, pick up Dan's sunglasses and pick you up on the way back. That would give you half an hour to … you know … do your stuff.'

I nodded. 'Sounds good. It'll be nice to have some company while I wait for Ewan. Punctuality was never his strong suit.'

***

As it turned out, Ewan was already waiting at a table near the bar and stood up, smiling, when we walked in.

'Whoa, two for the price of one!' He reached forward to give me a chaste peck on the cheek and grinned at Ellie. 'Good to see you again, Ellie. What can I get you two ladies to drink?'

'Oh, I'm not stopping, but thank you anyway,' Ellie blushed. 'I was just giving Anna a lift and I'm picking her up later.' She gave me a look. 'See you in a bit.'

Ewan nodded. 'I get it. I'm happy to drive you home, Anna, but whatever you feel comfortable with is fine with me.'

I could tell Ellie was surprised. Her bemused expression said it all. I gave her a look which said, 'I told you he'd changed,' and turned to smile at Ewan. 'A small, dry, white wine, please. See you later, Ell.'

'You look stunning, as always,' he said as sat next to me at the small, round table.

'Thank you. You too.' It was true – he was very good to look at. Tonight, he was dressed casually in jeans and a black T-shirt tight enough to show off his impressive biceps. With his dark hair slightly ruffled, rather than smoothed down like the previous evening, and the stubble on his chin, he looked much more like the Ewan I'd found attractive. I swallowed as I met his eyes. Sticking to my resolve was going to be harder than I'd thought.

'First of all, I wanted to apologise for last night,' he began.

'What for?'

'It was clear from your expression you weren't expecting to see me and that you weren't exactly thrilled when you did.'

I pulled a face. 'Sorry. I'm hopeless at hiding my feelings. It was a …' I searched for the right word, '… surprise and you're right, I *was* a bit irritated. Luckily though, we all had a good evening despite my bad mood.'

His teeth flashed white. 'I'm glad I didn't spoil your night. I had the advantage of knowing beforehand you were going to be there and I was looking forward to seeing you again.' He turned to me, his face serious. 'Listen Anna, I wanted to apologise for the other stuff too. When we were going out, I didn't behave well. I was too selfish, wrapped up in my own wants and needs. But I wanted you to see that I'd changed.' His blue eyes glowed with a sincerity which left me feeling slightly breathless. 'When we were together, I was in a bad place … but things are better now.'

I returned his smile. 'I *did* notice the change,' I said wryly. 'What happened?' There was a pause. 'Sorry. You don't have to answer that. It's none of my business.'

'No, I want to tell you … be honest with you. I was working for a security company and, to cut a long story short, I nicked some money and got caught. I had a lifestyle I couldn't afford and couldn't give up so it seemed the only answer at the time. I'd already borrowed thousands from my parents and they'd refused to stump up any more cash. They'd realised, you see, I was taking drugs.'

'Gosh,' I sucked in my breath, taken aback by his honesty. 'I *did* wonder.'

'I know.' He looked away, his face full of shame. 'Anyway, when it all kicked off, my parents spoke to your dad about it. Asked him what they could do to save me from prison. He was amazing. The chairman of the company was a golfing mate of his and he put in a word for me. I was incredibly fortunate. They agreed I'd pay the money back, or rather my parents would, and I'd go into rehab. When I came out, your dad offered me a job and eventually, with his support, I started up my own security business. I've worked hard and I'm now in a position to start paying back. I have so much to thank them all for. I'm not going to let anyone down ever again, not if I can help it.'

'Wow, that's admirable … and very brave of you to tell me. I'm really pleased things have worked out for you.'

'I've been damned lucky and I know it.' Purposefully, he reached across the table and took my hand in his. 'I know it's too much to expect you'll want to have anything to do with me, especially after what I've told you, but I just hope we can be friends.'

I smiled warmly at him. 'I'd be very happy for us to be friends. To be honest, I'm not in the market for anything more and I got the vibe last night everyone was expecting us to get back together.'

'I know. They were a bit obvious.' He released my hand and sat back in his chair. 'That's parents for you. Still, I can't knock them. I owe them everything. Hey, watch out. Here comes the cavalry!'

I turned my head to see Ellie rushing through the door, her face flushed with excitement. She grabbed my arm. 'We need to go. I've got something to tell you!' I stared at her. The urgency in her voice was unmistakeable.

'What? Straight away?'

She nodded, lips clamped shut, and shot Ewan a dismissive glance. He took the hint and stood up. 'No need for you both to rush away. You finish your drink, Anna.' He nodded at the almost full glass of wine at the table. 'It's been lovely catching up with you. Hopefully, I'll see you soon.' He gave me a brief hug and I felt his stubble lightly graze my cheek. Then he was gone.

Ellie immediately flung herself into Ewan's chair. 'That was a bit rude,' I said. 'This had better be good.'

'It is.' Ellie spoke in a breathless whisper. 'I've seen the blue Peugeot!'

My heart lurched. All my fears flooded back in an instant.

'What? Where? Is it here?' I looked around wildly, surveying the near empty bar with new suspicion.

'No. Don't panic.' Ellie laid a reassuring hand on my arm. 'It was parked up on the forecourt of Glandford's Garage … you know, where Dan works. There's a great big dent in the front bumper, just as you described. It *must* be the same one … but perhaps you need to take a look too, to be sure.'

'I … I guess that would make sense.' My head reeled with questions. Was it the one? Was it there for repair? Did it belong to someone who worked there? What should I do now? Confronting the man who had followed me filled me with dread but, on the other hand, I wanted to get my life back. I hated the feeling that someone was following my every move, the niggle of anxiety every time I stepped out of the house. 'Do you mind going with me?'

'Course I will. I wasn't planning on letting you go alone. I asked the guy manning the petrol kiosk if he knew who it belonged to but he had no idea so it must be someone who's brought it in for some work. Probably to get that bumper repaired. It's a bit of a mess. Hey, I wonder if Dan knows. I'll give him a ring.'

I took the opportunity to take a confidence-inducing gulp of wine while I watched her make the phone call. She shook her head as she dropped her phone into her bag. 'No reply. It went straight to voicemail. I didn't bother leaving a message; I'll try him again in a bit. Shall we go or do you want to finish your wine first?'

I put the glass down firmly. 'No, let's go – get it done.'

It was still light outside although overcast, dark grey clouds threatening more rain. As she drove, Ellie chattered about Dan. He'd originally said he was going away for a few days for work and she'd thought he was on a training course of some description, especially as two colleagues from work were going with him. When she'd questioned him further, he'd become increasingly vague. Now she was wondering if the trip was actually work-related at all, especially as he had seemed quite excited about it before he left.

'But why would he lie to me?' she asked. 'If he's off on a jolly, why wouldn't he just tell me? I wouldn't have minded, he knows that. He knows I trust him.'

I shifted uncomfortably in my seat. How could I tell her *I* wouldn't trust her boyfriend as far as I could throw him? 'Who knows what goes on in a man's mind?' I sympathised. 'Anyway, you don't know for sure he isn't on some course with Tom and Justin. I wouldn't worry about why he lied until you definitely know he has.'

'Good advice,' Ellie nodded, visibly relaxing her shoulders. 'You're right of course. I don't know why I always think the worst.'

Because he's let you down in the past and it's only a matter of time before he does so again. The words remained unspoken. Maybe I *should* say something … I took a deep breath. 'Ellie, I …'

'This is it,' she interrupted and swung left into the premises of Glandford's Motor Sales and Servicing Centre. The garage forecourt was empty except for three cars parked side by side nearest to the workshop. There, in the middle, was the electric blue Peugeot. It looked innocuous, standing there, locked and empty, and I relaxed. Without its driver, the car posed no threat. I walked closer, the click of my heels on the pavement eerily loud, and stood by the driver's door. Stooping, I peered through the window to look inside. The grey upholstery was worn and clean but the car was empty. No clues to the owner's identity lay on the seats.

'I've written down the registration number.' Ellie held up her phone. 'Now we'll be able to track down the bastard who's been following you, even if it means going to the police.'

I straightened up. 'Good work, detective,' I said in an American drawl. 'Now let's get the hell out of here!'

On the way home, we agreed to see if Dan knew who the owner was before contacting the police.

'We might have to wait until next week when he's back at work, even if I manage to get hold of him,' Ellie frowned. Although she'd tried to call Dan a number of times, he hadn't responded. 'He might not remember the name, even if he booked the car in.'

'I can wait,' I said. 'I think I'd rather do that than make a fuss at the police station. After all, the whole thing may yet prove to be a total misunderstanding.'

'I'm sure it's not but you're right. You can always go to the police, if you need to, when you know who it is ... and anyway, you might not have to wait. Dan might surprise us both and come up with a name by the end of the evening.'

However, despite repeated attempts, Ellie was unable to get hold of her boyfriend that night. She left four voicemail messages and was fuming by the time she decided to give up and go to bed. 'He's obviously having a right session with his mates and hasn't even bothered to check his phone! So much for missing *me*! Sorry hon, I'm sure he'll ring back in the morning.'

I gave her a hug. 'No worries. I feel so much better knowing we've actually got a lead and it's thanks to you, my eagle-eyed friend.'

'Think nothing of it,' Ellie replied airily. Then her face cracked into a wry grin. 'Although, in fairness, it would have been pretty difficult to miss!'

CHAPTER 16

Selina
Tuesday 16th July, 1996

It was almost quarter to five by the time we stepped back on to dry land and I wondered if Jack and Maisie would have already returned to the hotel. Probably not. Maisie was insatiable when it came to the pool and Jack was as soft as butter. He wouldn't have the heart to drag her away, even if he'd had enough. Anyway, we'd agreed to meet by the loungers or thereabouts. Even though the trip had been longer than we'd thought, I was pretty sure they would still be there.

It had been a good boat trip and Harry was bouncing with excitement. We'd seen the dolphins he had wanted and many other types of fish as well. Although it had been a bit pricey for our budget, it had been good value. I felt a pang of guilt. Jack and Maisie would have enjoyed it too but there was no way we could have afforded tickets for four people. Hopefully, they'd also had a good afternoon.

It had been a lovely holiday so far. Jack worked hard and it was good for him to relax properly. Although he'd taken a lot of persuasion this year, I was pretty sure he'd be keen to book a similar holiday next year.

Harry was bounding on ahead, trying to hurry me along. 'Come on, Mum,' he called, his whole body brimming with energy. 'I want to tell Dad all about the dolphins, especially the one that took a fish from my hand. Maisie is going to be so jealous.'

'I'm going as fast as I can,' I replied, feeling my pace quicken automatically.

We walked along the promenade, a wide concourse which snaked alongside the coastline. The ocean was still, a deep, azure blue, with sailing boats bobbing like toys on its surface. Colourful parasols and loungers lined the sandy beach. Most were now lying unused but there were still some holidaymakers reclining on towels, swimming or playing games with children, enjoying the early evening temperature.

A police car sped past, its siren strident, interrupting the peace of the afternoon. People turned their heads, Harry amongst them, watching as it took the corner at speed and disappeared out of sight.

'Did you see the police car, Mum?' he asked as I drew level with him. 'Do you think it's on a car chase?'

'I couldn't really miss it,' I replied drily. 'I've no idea. I just hope it isn't an accident.'

Our hotel loomed into view, a high-rise, white cuboid with rows upon rows of balconied windows. I glanced up at the fourth floor and counted across to find our family room, half expecting to see Jack and Maisie waving down at us. But the balcony was deserted.

Another siren sounded, once again coming from behind us, and another police car tore past. This time we were able to see it slow slightly and swing to a dramatic halt outside our hotel. I shivered. Some poor holidaymaker staying there was involved in the drama, whatever it was.

'Come on, Harry,' I called when he'd stopped to watch once more. 'We need to get back.' All I now wanted was to find Jack and Maisie, hold them in my arms, tell them I'd missed them. That was the thing with accidents, especially when someone died – it made you value and appreciate your own loved ones.

As we headed towards our designated swimming pool, I saw a gaggle of police officers surrounding one of the loungers. I screwed up my eyes, trying to glimpse my husband and daughter, but there was no sign of them. My mouth suddenly felt dry and I broke into a run.

'Mummy, what's up? What are you doing?' I dragged Harry along with me but had no reply for his questions. My whole attention was focused on the ring of police officers. Wasn't that the lounger Jack was on when I left him to go on the trip? My heart beat faster as I glimpsed a flash of red. That could be Jack's T-shirt. *Oh, dear God!*

With a muffled scream, I ran faster. *No, no, this wasn't happening.*

The police officers turned as I approached. Their faces all looked the same, impassive but with the light of sympathy shining in their eyes.

'What's happened?' I yelled, still fifty metres away. 'Where's Maisie?'

Jack pushed himself up on to his feet, his shoulders slumped, his body swaying unsteadily. He opened his mouth to speak but there was no sound.

'Where's Maisie?' I screamed again. 'Where is she? What's happened?'

Harry sprinted past me, silent for once, his narrow face set as he launched himself into his dad's arms. 'Dad, what's happened?'

Jack shuddered and met my eyes. His face was white, streaked with tears, wracked with despair. I watched, paralysed with horror, as he swallowed, trying to form the words.

'She's … she's gone …'

CHAPTER 17

Anna

The next morning was spent revisiting and editing the previous chapter before starting on the next. Jemima's husband Conrad had arrived at the supermarket just in time to see his daughter, a 7 lb 6 oz, beautiful girl with silky, black hair, safely delivered. I found myself smiling as I typed the magical moment when Conrad held his daughter for the first time. Sitting back in my chair, I closed my eyes, conjuring up the image so I could describe it to my readers. Conrad was tall and dark and … I opened my eyes quickly … he'd somehow morphed into Josh Fielding! It was *his* eyes I pictured staring with joy and wonder at the tiny bundle in his arms. *That* was taking my fantasies too far; time for a break!

The doorbell sounded. Strange. Dad had already called so it wouldn't be him. I peered out from behind the curtain of my study. A young, slim woman with a ponytail stood on the doorstep, holding a basket of flowers. *Ooh, how lovely!* I sped downstairs, eager to know who they were from. Could it be Josh? I accepted the arrangement of roses, pinks and gypsophilia with a 'thank you' and took it inside, tearing open the note.

Thanks for being so understanding.
Love Ewan x

I smiled, suppressing a flicker of disappointment. How lovely of him! I quickly sent a text, thanking him for the beautiful flowers and telling him that the gift was welcome but unnecessary. 'That's what friends are for,' I signed off. No kisses. Best to reinforce the platonic nature of our relationship. He really had changed. It was just a shame I was no longer interested. Story of my life.

A ping from my phone signalled a message from Ellie.

Still no word from Dan. Do you think I should phone the garage to find out where he is?

A tricky question. If Dan was up to no good, then at least Ellie would know. But that had to be her decision.

Up to you. Or just wait until he contacts you xx

But what if he doesn't?

My fingers tapped out the response I was thinking …

Then good riddance.

I couldn't send that. Deleting that message, I replaced it with a platitude.

Stay cool. I'm sure he will xx

'Eventually,' I added verbally.

But what about the Peugeot?

Don't worry about that. We'll find out who owns it somehow xx

I put down my phone with another pang of guilt. I really had to tell Ellie what had transpired between me and Dan. Definitely … next time I saw her … not this evening, though, as I was expected at the weekly ritual with my parents. I had suggested giving it a miss this week, given that we'd already had a meal together on Mum's birthday but they wouldn't hear of it. As usual, I agreed without further demur. I was weak; I let people walk all over me rather than hurt their feelings. It was trying to spare Ellie's feelings that had got me into this dilemma over Dan. It was time to man up and come clean.

I worked diligently for the next hour and a half before stopping for an early lunch. I wanted to stop off in Swaffham to buy a housewarming plant for Selina Matthews, to take when I called round that afternoon. This time, I resolved, I wouldn't feel guilty spending some of the time just chatting. Having reflected on my last visit, I'd decided that Selina was looking for emotional support, as well as practical help, and that I should definitely be more prepared to listen to her story. Besides, I genuinely liked the woman. It would be no hardship. I just wasn't prepared to be paid for sitting talking; I'd keep an eye on the time and knock that off her bill.

***

Clutching a deep pink begonia I'd bought from Waitrose, I headed towards Selina's front door. Somehow, knowing the blue Peugeot was parked at Glandford's garage had restored some of my confidence. Today, there was no sensation of being watched either. Any sighting of a black Range Rover or a man with grey hair still caused a brief stab of panic but I was almost certain my previous fears were groundless. Once I knew the identity of the Peugeot driver, I could put the whole episode behind me.

Selina opened the door with a broad smile and holding a piece of paper. 'Is that for me? How terribly kind of you! You shouldn't have. Here, let's swap.' She handed me the piece of paper as she took the plant. 'It's that shortbread recipe I promised you. I didn't want to forget to give it to you.'

'Oh thanks.' I slipped it into my bag and stepped into the house. 'How have you been?'

'Very well, thank you dear. I'll give you a tour and you can see how I've been getting on. Prepare to be impressed – I've felt re-energised since your last visit.'

I slipped off my shoes and followed her through the house, making frequent comments about its tidiness and the absence of boxes. 'Wow! You *have* been busy! It doesn't look like there's anything left for me to do.'

Selina smiled. 'I wondered if you'd be able to put some pictures up for me. I wouldn't have the first clue how to go about it. Jack, my husband, or rather my ex-husband, always took care of things like that.'

'No problem, but I'd have to go home and fetch a drill, unless you have one?' Selina shook her head. 'No worries. It won't take me long. I'll need to buy some wall plugs and picture hooks too.'

'Oh dear. Now I feel really foolish. I didn't think of any of that. Tell you what – why don't you leave the picture hanging until your next visit? Then you can bring what you need with you.'

'Good plan. Tell you what – why don't we go around and you can tell me where you want the pictures and we can mark the spot? Then I'll know how many picture hooks I'll need.'

Selina fetched a box from her utility room. 'These are the smaller paintings,' she said, putting the box on the kitchen worktop. 'The larger ones are propped up against the wall in there.'

I helped her bring them through. They were all colourful, abstract paintings, clearly by the same artist. 'Hey, I really like these,' I said, holding one at arm's length. 'Who's the artist?'

'A friend of mine – Clarissa Maverick. She lives in Nottingham. I love her work. When I decided to move, I got rid of all the old prints I'd accumulated over the years and just kept her paintings. They're so bright; just looking at them always cheers me up.'

I nodded in agreement. 'You're right. There's something innocent ... and completely joyous about them.' I picked up another painting. 'This would look great above the wood stove in your sitting room.'

The next hour was spent amicably deciding upon the best spot for each painting. Selina was keen to defer to my opinion. 'You clearly have an eye for these things,' she said. 'I have no idea. It's the same with clothes. My friends often despair of me when I turn up at events wearing something totally unsuitable. Once, I went to a wedding in a yellow, tiered dress and wearing a green, feathery hat. It was only when I saw the photos that I realised I looked like a pineapple!'

I chuckled. 'That reminds me of when I was a teenager and dyed my own hair and it went this weird purple colour. It earned me the nickname 'My Little Pony!' I was devastated. Mum took me to her hairdresser and paid a fortune to repair the damage. I haven't dared colour my hair since.'

'You don't need to. You have beautiful hair.'

'Thanks.' Immediately self-conscious, I busied myself restacking the paintings. 'Now, what other jobs have you got for me? I don't feel as if I'm earning my pay.'

'Well, if you're up for it, I could use some help in the garden. I love gardening but I've got a dodgy knee at the moment which makes kneeling difficult. I've done a bit of dead-heading but I'm afraid the weeding has been a bit beyond me.'

'Of course. I love gardening too. Show me where you'd like me to start and I'll get to it.'

Selina led me outside to the shed where she kept all her gardening tools and I spent a happy hour with a trowel, digging up the weeds which had sprouted around the flowers and shrubs. The recent rain made the work relatively easy and I'd cleared almost half of the weeds in the larger of the two borders by the time Selina reappeared.

'You *have* got on well!' she exclaimed. 'Now, I insist you have a break. There's a cup of tea and a piece of cake waiting for you in the kitchen.'

I stood up, stretching my back. 'That sounds great.'

After washing my hands, I settled on a stool by the breakfast bar in the kitchen. An impressive carrot cake sat invitingly on a plate and I duly expressed my admiration as Selina handed me a mug of tea.

'I like baking.' She deftly cut two slices and transferred them to smaller plates. 'It's nice to have someone to bake for.'

I took a bite. It was heavenly. 'Mmm, it's delicious. Tastes even better than it looks, which is saying something.' I looked around the kitchen and noticed the array of photographs pinned by magnets on the fridge in the corner. I stood to get a better look.

'This is my son, Harry.' Selina indicated two prints depicting a smiling young man in his early thirties. 'They were taken earlier this year when he and I went to Italy on holiday.'

I looked politely at the pictures. One showed a grinning Harry holding up a glass of beer; in the other, he had his arm around Selina's shoulders. 'You must be very proud of him,' I said.

'I am. He's already won an award for one of his designs. Did I tell you he's an architect?'

I nodded. 'Yes, but he's obviously still got time for his mum if you went on holiday together. Is he married?'

'No, between girlfriends. There was one girl, Emily, recently. I thought she might be the one ... but it didn't last. A shame – she was lovely – but there. It wasn't to be.'

I cast my eye back to the fridge. There were a few older photos of a small girl, about two or three years old, with blonde curls and big, blue eyes. 'Who's the little girl?' I asked.

Selina lowered her head. 'That's Maisie,' she said quietly. 'My daughter.'

There was a brief pause as I filtered through the implications of that statement. Before, she'd only mentioned a son. I scanned the fridge for more recent photos of the girl but there were none. Had something happened to Maisie? I didn't like to ask. Instead, I said, 'She's very cute.'

Selina smiled wanly. She seemed about to say something but stopped and reached for an envelope instead. 'I must pay you for all the work you've done so far. It's in here.' She handed over the envelope.

'Er ... thank you.' I felt flummoxed by the abrupt change in the conversation but took my cue from Selina. Clearly, she didn't want to talk about Maisie. 'I'll just tidy up outside before I leave. When would you like me to come back to hang the paintings?'

'Would next Monday be OK for you? The afternoon?'

'No problem.'

I made short work of depositing the garden rubbish in Selina's brown bin and tidying away the garden implements in the shed. When I shouted goodbye, Selina was no longer in the kitchen. I called again and, this time, heard a muffled answering call. Poor Selina. She sounded upset and my heart ached for her. Poor, little Maisie too. How awful if she had died at such a young age.

***

The grey-haired man in the black Range Rover crouched down in his seat as he saw Anna leave. He had parked further along the road behind a large, black van. She unlocked her Fiesta and drove away without a glance in his direction.

CHAPTER 18

Anna

opened my curtains with a ripple of pleasurable anticipation; Friday meant seeing Josh Fielding. The sky was clear, washed through with pinks and yellows. It was going to be another fine day. As had been my habit in recent times, I scrutinised the scene outside. Everything was as it should be.

I watched as my neighbour on the left-hand side, Brian Groom, a solemn-faced, middle-aged man wearing a grey suit and carrying a briefcase, unlocked his silver Qashqai and slid behind the wheel. The engine roared into life and he reversed expertly out of his drive.

Downstairs, Ellie had not yet surfaced and I decided to take my toast and coffee out on to the tiny patio outside. The air was cool but the warmth of the sun was already beginning to permeate and I contemplated the day ahead. Writing this morning. I frowned. After the excitement of the birth, I felt my narrative had lulled and needed a bit of a lift. When I reread it yesterday, before switching off my laptop, it seemed a bit flat and boring. I was still pondering and discarding different options when Ellie clattered through the French doors, wearing a light blue, cotton dress patterned with daisies and clutching her phone.

'Finally!' she exclaimed, throwing herself into a chair and contemplating my toast enviously. 'Dan has finally called me back. His phone was out of battery and he's only just managed to recharge it. Anyway, I asked him about the Peugeot ...' She paused, waiting for a reaction.

'Yes?' I prompted.

'He didn't know who owns it. He didn't see it come in. He's going to ask Tom and Justin.' She patted my hand. 'We'll soon have this mystery solved, don't you worry. Now, I'd better run. No time for breakfast this morning but you enjoy yours.' She eyed the toast ruefully once more. 'Don't you worry about me. I'll let you know if I hear anything – if I haven't passed out from hunger, that is.'

I grinned as I spooned another dollop of marmalade onto my plate. 'Thanks, Ell. Have a good day.'

She grimaced. 'I'll try. You too. See you later.'

I finished my breakfast, savouring the time to myself. The mystery of the Peugeot and the identity of the driver would soon be resolved and that was a huge lift to my spirits. It was the not knowing which had caused the anxiety and paranoia. I was sure of it. Once I had some answers, I'd know best how to proceed. I could be proactive instead of reactive; I could take back control of my life.

I carried my plate and mug through to the kitchen and switched on my laptop. As yet, I had no idea how to add sparkle to the latest chapter but always found the best bet was to plough on – get words on the screen.

Two hours later, I pushed the machine away in disgust. Work was going painfully slowly and frustration levels were high. I seriously needed a break. I refilled the kettle and reached for my phone, flicking idly through the latest postings on Facebook, Twitter and Instagram. Unlike some of my friends, I'd never been obsessed with social media and preferred to keep most details of my life private. My publishers had insisted I have official author Twitter and Facebook accounts but I found them a chore. My poor followers must think my life was incredibly boring. The phone vibrated in my hand and a message from Ellie flashed on the screen.

Tom and Justin don't know who brought the Peugeot in. Told Dan it was important so he said he'd find out asap xx

Thoughts of Dan reminded me of my resolution to have a heart to heart with Ellie. Tonight, I promised myself. I glanced at my watch. Time for another couple of hours of graft before I got ready for my afternoon at the Old Rectory. I'd been trying to keep thoughts of Josh Fielding from my head. I really didn't need any more distractions. Yet, time and time again, I found myself indulging in daft, romantic fantasies which invariably ended with Josh taking me in his arms and kissing me ...

'Sorry,' he grinned unrepentantly as he released me from his strong clasp. 'I've been wanting to do that since the moment I first saw you.'

I shook myself back to reality. Life wasn't like a romantic novel. However, despite my best efforts, I found myself restlessly shifting in my seat. My mind wandered back to the previous evening when I'd had dinner with my parents. There were some things which I found odd. For a start, they hadn't mentioned the blue Peugeot at all. Instead, they'd asked about my Girl Friday work. Did I have any new clients? Briefly, I told them about Selina and how I was helping her get straight in her new home. They'd exchanged glances but then changed the subject, quizzing me about Ewan Jacobs and pulling faces when I said I had no thoughts of rekindling that romance.

'That's a shame,' Dad had said. 'I have to say I've been very impressed with that young man. I only helped him as a favour to his dad and I had no real expectation of it working out ... but he's surprised me ... he really has.'

'He's surprised me too,' I admitted. 'You have to take some of the credit, Dad. You've always done really well with your proteges.' Flattery was an effective tool for keeping on the right side of my father.

He nodded, pleased. 'Thank you, darling. I have to say I agree with you.'

Over the years, he'd helped other talented, young men with their careers, expecting unerring loyalty from them in return, treating them like the sons he'd never had. He'd been disappointed, putting it mildly, when I'd shown no desire or aptitude to follow him into business.

'It wouldn't be so bad if you showed any inclination for a career in medicine, like your mother, but writing soppy books …' he'd said at the time, his voice thick with disgust. 'I wash my hands of you.'

It was the only time I had successfully defied my father. He was stubborn, unused to being thwarted and his strategy was simple – withdraw all affection and wait for me to come to my senses. It had worked in the past. Many a time had seen me grovelling with apologies, desperate to worm myself back into his good graces. But this time, I was determined to stand firm. I knew I'd be unhappy in his banking world and totally out of my depth. Even Ellie and Madison had tried to persuade me that I was mad to turn down the offer of a high-flying career for the uncertainty of writing novels. For once, though, I'd stood firm, desperately unhappy about upsetting Dad but knowing, deep down, the career he'd envisaged for me would drain my soul.

I had tried to please him and fit into his world, I really had. Throughout school holidays, when friends were out enjoying themselves, I'd accompany him to his office and, under the direction of his personal assistant, a hard-faced woman called Julia Sharp, had attempted to be useful whilst acquiring an inkling of Dad's world of high finance. The experience had not been a success; I muddled even the most mundane of filing tasks and became used to Julia's mask of disapproval. The only thing I really learnt was that this type of work was definitely not for me. Now I was proud, I had to admit, I'd stuck to my guns, especially as my work had been published and achieved a modicum of success. In my own way, I was determined to prove I was capable of achieving in my chosen world, just as my parents had in theirs.

My reverie was interrupted by the buzz of my phone. Dan. My heart thumped against my ribcage.

'Hi Anna. How're ya doing?' There was an underlying suggestiveness in his voice which made my skin crawl.

'Fine thanks, Dan,' I replied coolly. 'How's your work trip going?'

'Yeah, great. Going well. Working hard, of course!' He laughed.

'Of course.' I waited impatiently for him to get to the purpose of his call. Presumably it was about the blue Peugeot. I tightened my grip on the phone.

'Well, anyway, I understand you wanted a favour …' He let his voice tail off, waiting for me to speak. When I remained silent, he chuckled, a low, throaty sound, before continuing. 'Ellie told me about your stalker …'

Damn Ellie! I'd been careful to tell no-one other than Ellie, Madison and then my parents. This wasn't something I wanted anyone to know, especially Dan.

'Information is power,' Dad always claimed and the maxim had been drummed into me from an early age. 'Be careful what you share with others,' he'd told me when I was upset once. 'Trust no-one.'

When I was six, my best friend at school had betrayed a secret I'd shared in confidence about wetting the bed. I'd wept bitter tears on Dad's shoulder. The cruel laughter of classmates and public humiliation had stayed with me ever since. Now I was very careful about keeping my secrets well hidden. Once again, I remained silent.

'Are you still there, Anna?' His voice was suddenly sharp.

'Yes.'

'Good. Well, listen. I *might* be able to help you out.' The teasing note was back.

'That's very kind of you, Dan,' I forced myself to say politely. *Get to the point!*

'It is, isn't it? Ellie said you thought you were being stalked by a blue Peugeot, is that correct?'

'I think you've been watching too many crime dramas, Dan!' I said lightly. 'Hardly *stalked*! I'd just noticed it a few times, that's all, and wondered who it belonged to.'

'That's not what Ellie said,' Dan argued. 'She said you were worried sick the driver might be some psycho!'

I shook my head in annoyance, before realising the gesture was wasted on Dan. 'I think that's rather overstating it but anyway ... do you know who owns it?' I asked as casually as I could.

'I do.'

I held my breath. Would it be someone I knew? Maybe Damien Davies after all? Dan let the silence eke into several seconds, stretching my composure to the limit. 'And?' I prompted.

'I just wondered what the information was worth?'

'Oh, for God's sake!' In a burst of anger, I ended the call and flipped the phone across the table. What a moron! Almost immediately, it rang again.

'Look Dan,' I exploded. 'Ellie asked you for this favour, not me. If you don't want to tell me without extracting some kind of payment, then fine. I'm not going to be blackmailed.'

'Whoa, hold your horses! Who said anything about blackmail?' Dan's voice was smooth, conciliatory. He was laughing at me. 'I was just having a little joke, that's all. I didn't mean to upset you.'

I took another deep breath. 'OK,' I said. 'Tell me then. Who is he?'

Dan laughed again. 'That's just it. Sometimes things just aren't what you expect.'

'What do you mean?' My irritation towards him was stretching to breaking point.

'I just mean it's easy to make assumptions about these things. It isn't a *he* at all; it's a *she*.'

'Really?' He was right. I wasn't expecting that. 'Do you have a name?'

'I do. It's Selina Matthews. Does that mean anything to you?'

I gasped, my mind racing. There must be some mistake. Surely *Selina* couldn't be a stalker. She wasn't capable of it ... was she? I realised Dan was still on the line, waiting for a response.

'Thanks for that, Dan. I appreciate the effort you've gone to. I guess I'll see you soon.'

'Hey, wait!' I heard him say as I ended the call, not caring that he would be annoyed.

Selina Matthews! *Really?* My brain hummed with disbelief, trying to understand something which seemed incomprehensible. Why would *Selina Matthews* want to follow me? It didn't make sense. Could someone else have been driving? Had her car been stolen? Selina hadn't said so but I hadn't seen it outside her house at any time. I wanted there to be a logical explanation, one that didn't incriminate her. Then again, perhaps she had deliberately concealed the car, aware I might have spotted it tailing my Fiesta. I shook my head, completely at a loss. I liked Selina Matthews, at least I *had* liked her; I felt sorry for her. It was difficult not to feel betrayed. And I had to wonder if her employment of me and the way she'd evoked my sympathies masked an ulterior motive ...

***

Still reeling from Dan's shock revelation, I strode up the drive to the Old Rectory. My world had somehow shifted off its axis; things were not as they seemed. The sight of Josh Fielding, however, bare chested, muscles rippling as he wielded a small chainsaw, put thoughts of Selina from my mind.

'You're a sight for sore eyes!' As I approached, Josh had switched off the chainsaw and was gazing at me with open appreciation. I felt a flush of warmth as his eyes travelled over my bare legs and up to my skimpy, lilac T-shirt. Raising my eyebrows, I stared pointedly at his semi-naked torso.

'I could say the same,' I said lightly. 'Shall I crack on with the gardening today or was there anything else you wanted?'

He grinned. 'I can think of a few things … but yes … gardening. The grass needs cutting again and, well, you can decide what needs doing.'

There was no mistaking it; he was definitely flirting with me! I felt my face suffuse with colour and scurried to the safety of the rear garden, all too conscious of his eyes following me. I needed a moment or two to regain my composure. It was an uncomfortable feeling – this helpless attraction which left me flustered in his presence. Josh Fielding discomfited me, disturbed my inner equilibrium. Could I trust him? I knew virtually nothing about him and our first encounter had shown him to have a short temper bordering on rudeness. He was definitely the sort of man a sensible girl would steer well clear of … and yet, I just couldn't help the rush of excitement I felt every time I saw him. 'Just take things slowly,' I told myself sternly. 'Play it cool.' Easy to say; not so easy to do when you had a face which flamed like a beacon at the merest hint of a compliment.

On the mower, scything smoothly through the expanse of lush grass in the back garden, my thoughts turned once more to Selina Matthews. There had to be a reasonable explanation. I just couldn't believe she wished me any harm. She'd claimed to be a fan of my first book, though. Perhaps she was one of those people who obsessed about authors, in the way that some people became infatuated with actors and singers, even to the extent of stalking them. Having met Selina, it didn't seem likely. She had seemed a thoroughly likeable, fragile, lonely woman – not a fanatic. I realised I was shaking my head as Josh strolled towards me, grinning. God, he must think I was a complete idiot. I braked and switched off the engine.

'Is everything OK?' he asked, giving me a searching look. 'You seemed a bit preoccupied.'

'No, no, everything's fine.' I managed to meet his eyes and give him a cool smile.

'Good. I was just wondering if I could get you a drink of anything? I was about to get myself one.'

My first instinct was to refuse but it was very warm and I was undeniably thirsty. 'Thanks,' I replied. 'Just water would be great.'

'Let's go into the kitchen. Most of the units are in now. You can let me know what you think.' He held out his hand to help me off the mower.

I hesitated. 'Maybe I really ought to crack on. I've only just started after all.'

'Don't worry. I intend to get my money's worth out of you!' He grinned wolfishly before withdrawing his hand, turning on his heel and striding towards the house. 'Come on,' he called over his shoulder as I continued to perch on the mower. 'I haven't got all day.'

Muttering under my breath at his highhandedness, I followed him into the house and gasped in delight as I walked into the kitchen. 'Wow! You *have* been busy. Did you do all this yourself? It's amazing!'

Light grey units lined the long wall of the kitchen, gleaming appliances had been installed and there was a central island topped with a marble work surface. Along the wall, facing out onto the rear garden, were more units, worktops and a large, Belfast sink. The walls had been painted white with the merest hint of green; the overall effect was sleek and ultra-modern.

'I love it,' I continued, running my fingers along the smooth marble. I looked across at Josh and caught him looking pleased.

'I'm not a carpenter's son for nothing,' he said as he added ice to two tumblers of water. 'Although I did have some help putting the units in. Sometimes you need more than one pair of hands.'

'Ah yes, I'd forgotten your dad's a carpenter.'

He nodded. 'Yes. He always wanted me to follow in his footsteps, join the family firm and all that. Unfortunately, when you're young, you think you know better. I thought my future lay in the bright lights of the city and the world of investment banking. The incentive of earning lots of cash was pretty strong too. Turns out, I was wrong.' He handed me a glass and gulped down half of his own water. 'I'm glad you like the kitchen. I'm pretty pleased with how it's turned out. It's satisfying to see your hard work create something good.' His eyes shone with pride.

'I know what you mean.' I agreed. 'Mind you, *anything* would be more satisfying than banking. Dad was keen for me to work with him at Sampson Blake but I knew I wasn't cut out for it. I'm much happier creating storylines and spending my days in a fantasy world ... and doing stuff like this, of course.' I took a sip of water and then asked, 'So are you going to return to banking or have you decided on a change of career?' I smiled. 'A carpenter like your dad, after all?'

The light in his eyes disappeared. He placed his empty glass in the sink and shrugged. 'I haven't decided. It's good to have a break, that's all I know at the moment.'

An awkward silence stretched between us. Unwilling to let our conversation come to an end, I pressed on. 'What prompted the break? My dad says the pressure can get too much sometimes. Was it something like that?'

I regretted the words as soon as I uttered them. I'd gone too far. The shutters came down and he turned away abruptly.

'Maybe,' he muttered brusquely and turned on his heel. 'Right. I'm going to crack on. Lots to do.'

'Sorry,' I blurted out, 'Have I put my foot in it ... again ...?' My voice faltered; I was talking to an empty room. He'd stalked off, leaving me sipping the iced water and pondering the sudden change of mood. One minute, Josh seemed to be opening up and the next, he was acting like a scalded cat. I sighed, berating myself for my lack of tact. It was looking like I'd blown my chances with Josh Fielding but, then again, if he was that moody, who cared? Dispiritedly, I returned to the mower and my own troubles. What was I going to do about Selina Matthews?

CHAPTER 19

Anna

That evening, I decided to put the mystery of Selina Matthews on hold. My secret about Dan was like a wound which wouldn't heal; I needed to tell Ellie. To smooth the way, I cooked her favourite supper of lasagne, salad and garlic bread and rehearsed lines in my head. What could go wrong?

The evening started well and an opportunity to discuss Dan arose fortuitously when Ellie, happily munching on the bread, commented how lucky it was he was away as she wouldn't have to worry about her garlicky breath. It was a moment too good to miss. Taking a deep breath, I launched straight in and told her what had happened when Dan had tried to kiss me.

It didn't go well. Ellie was at first disbelieving, her dark eyebrows knitted together as she asked question after question, trying to find a hole in my story. Then her face had crumpled, like a discarded tissue. I tried to comfort her but she grew angry, accusing me of lying, of being jealous and, finally, of betraying our friendship. Red-faced with rage, she stormed out of the house. My attempts to phone her were ignored and she didn't reply to any of my texts. In the end, I had no choice but to let her cool off and to leave it until the morning to try to mend our fractured friendship. I almost wished I hadn't said anything but knew in my heart that I'd done the right thing, even if it was belatedly. Much later, when I was in bed, I heard her return. I took that as a good sign.

In the morning, after a swift shower, I crept downstairs and made scrambled eggs for a breakfast peace offering. Ellie often joked that the way to her heart was through her stomach. Hopefully, she would have calmed down enough to eat and give me a chance to explain. As I buttered toast, my thoughts turned to Josh Fielding. After he had stalked off yesterday, I'd gone back to work, still wondering what had provoked his abrupt withdrawal. Obviously, his decision to take a break from his career in banking was complicated; there was hurt there which I'd heavy-handedly poked with a sharp stick. While I'd tidied up at the end of the afternoon, I'd deliberated how best to make amends but, when I went to say goodbye, he was talking on his phone. As I'd waited for him to finish his call, he'd given me a curt wave of dismissal before turning and heading into the house. That was that. No talk of further work. Perhaps that was the last I'd see of Josh Fielding. The thought was a depressing one. Later on, after much agonising, I'd sent him a brief text, apologising if I'd inadvertently upset him and asking if he had any further need of my services. There had been no reply.

I heard the thump of footsteps on the stairs and tensed, ready for Ellie to appear in the kitchen. Instead, there was a rattle of keys as the front door was unlocked and a forceful slam to herald her exit. Clearly, she was still angry.

I hated hurting anyone but yesterday had managed to upset two people I cared about. And today I needed to have a conversation which was likely to distress Selina Matthews. During the night, I'd resolved to have it out with her and there was no time like the present. Briefly I toyed with the idea of calling her on the phone but decided against it. This was something better handled face-to-face.

Forty minutes later, I stood outside her front door, ringing the bell. That tingly feeling, the sensation of being watched, was back and, while I waited, I couldn't help throwing panicky glances over each shoulder. No-one appeared to be taking the slightest interest in me. Probably, I was just wound up over the impending confrontation. I spotted Selina's face, anxiously peering out of an upstairs window and listened to the sound of her footsteps approaching. Deliberately, I clamped down any feelings of sympathy I'd harboured for the older woman and let my anger bubble to the surface. How dare this woman stalk me! How dare she invade my privacy like that and, more to the point, cause me anxiety to the point of paranoia!

'Anna, what a lovely surprise!' Selina threw open the door with a welcoming smile. 'Come in, come in.' She stood aside to let me pass. 'Sorry. I'm a bit untidy. I wasn't expecting company. Go through to the kitchen and I'll put the kettle on. Oh dear, sorry about the mess!' she apologised again as she whipped an empty cereal bowl from the worktop and ushered me towards a seat. 'I'd just finished breakfast. Can I get you a coffee?'

'No thanks, I've just had one.' Grimly, I plonked down on a stool and took a deep breath. 'I've come because I need to talk to you.'

'Is anything wrong?' Selina's hands, fluttering over unwashed crockery, stilled and she turned worried eyes towards me. I stared back, studying her face and watching concern turn to unease. 'Please talk to me Anna. You're frightening me!'

I snorted. 'Like you frightened me! Do you have any idea how scared I was when the same car, a blue Peugeot, kept tailing me? I thought I had a stalker. I nearly went to the police – in fact I would have done had I managed to clock the number plate.'

Silence. The blood drained from Selina's face and she slumped onto the stool opposite. 'I ... I ...'

'Don't try to deny it!' My tone was harsh. 'I know it was your car and it followed me several times over the past few weeks. It really freaked me out! What on earth were you doing?'

Selina stared back, lips trembling. 'I'm so sorry,' she said helplessly. She covered her face with her hands. 'Oh, this is terrible. I'm so sorry. I didn't think.'

'Clearly.' My indignation started to dissolve in the face of her obvious distress. 'I think you owe me an explanation.'

Slowly, she withdrew her hands from her face. Her eyes were brimming with tears. 'You have to believe, Anna, that the last thing I wanted was to upset you in any way. I can't believe I frightened you like that. I'm so unbelievably thoughtless.' She gave me a beseeching look. 'Please forgive me.'

I sighed. How could I stay angry when she was so upset? 'Don't cry, Selina. Just tell me why you were following me.'

She used a tissue to dry her eyes. 'It's a long story but I'll start at the beginning. Hold on, I won't be a minute.' She stood up and walked out of the kitchen, leaving me wondering what to expect. A few minutes later, she returned, clutching a photo album sheathed in pale pink leather. Reverently, she placed it on the counter in front of me and opened it, revealing a series of baby photographs. I watched, confused, as she slowly turned the pages. 'This is my daughter, Maisie. I think you asked about her last time you were here.'

'She's gorgeous.' *What on earth …?* I sat, completely bemused, as chubby baby pictures gave way to various images of a blonde-haired toddler.

'She is, isn't she? Sorry, I won't bore you with all the photos.' Her fingers caressed the album as she closed it. 'You see, something terrible happened …' Her voice broke off and pain-filled eyes met mine.

'Look, you don't have to tell me all this. I don't see how it's got anything to do with me.'

'No, I want to tell you about her if you don't mind listening. It's important. Hopefully, it will explain everything.'

'Fine.' I found myself giving her an encouraging smile. Inwardly, my brain was whirring, trying to find any relevance to this turn of events. I'd imagined many different, confrontational scenarios as I was driving to Swaffham; I could never have envisaged this.

'It happened twenty-three years ago. Maisie had not long had her third birthday and we were on a family holiday in Spain – a resort in Alla Mora. I never knew for sure exactly what happened; I wasn't with her at the time.' Selina's face had become rigid like an alabaster statue and she spoke in a monotone. I sat uncomfortably still, listening to her words, dread creeping through me, chilling my bones.

'On that day, it was the Tuesday, I took Harry on a boat trip. He'd been pestering us all week to go out on one of the boats and I was happy to take him. I'd got a bit bored of the beach and the pool. It was quite expensive so we agreed that Jack, my husband, would stay by the pool with Maisie. She loved the water and was happy splashing about in her armbands. We were only gone a couple of hours …'

Her voice rose suddenly, plaintive and bewildered, even after all the intervening years. I waited in silence, my heart going out to her, despite everything.

'According to Jack, he got talking to this American woman on the lounger next to his. He hadn't seen her around the pool before but she was, apparently, friendly and very admiring of Maisie. I expect, knowing Jack, she was also very attractive although he never admitted that. Her name was Suki and she was slim with long, dark hair and wearing a turquoise bikini. Anyhow, they got chatting and, before you know it, she's in the pool with Maisie. Apparently, she was great with her and started teaching her to swim without her armbands. Maisie was doing very well, Jack said, and had even managed a few strokes on her own. Then Suki said she was thirsty. She'd already bought Maisie an ice cream so Jack offered to get them all some drinks from the bar which was some way away. He just waltzed off, leaving Maisie with a complete stranger, without a second thought. That was the last anyone saw of her.'

'Oh my God. What happened?'

'We don't know. By the time he returned, both Maisie and this woman Suki had disappeared, never to be seen again.'

'She was kidnapped!' I gasped.

'Yes ... presumably but there was no demand for ransom so the police weren't convinced.' Selina's voice was husky with emotion.

'But that's terrible!' I gasped. 'Didn't anyone else around the pool see where they went?'

'There were a few witnesses but no-one thought anything of it. Many of them had seen us round the pool during the week and assumed this woman was a family friend or relative. Nobody paid much attention. Someone remembered the two of them wrapping themselves in towels. Then the woman picked up all the bags and walked off, holding Maisie by the hand. Nobody could tell us anything more. Apparently, the bar was busy that day and Jack was gone for about fifteen minutes. In that time, they could have gone anywhere. So ... that was it. On that day, my daughter was lost and never found.'

I stared at her in shock. What could I say? The silence become uncomfortable and I muttered, 'Oh Selina, I'm so terribly sorry.'

She shrugged and picked up the empty mugs. 'It wasn't long after that Harry and I got back. Jack had only just raised the alarm. To start with, he assumed Maisie must have needed the toilet and Suki had taken her. After about ten more precious minutes, he started asking the people round the pool.' Her voice was bitter. 'Eventually, he called the police. They'd just arrived when I got back. There was an investigation and a nationwide campaign to find her. Because the woman who had taken her had an American accent, the search became an international one ... but they never found her or Maisie.'

While I struggled to find words, Selina turned to the sink, shoulders hunched as if the pain was still too much to bear. By the time she turned back, her eyes were red-rimmed and her face seemed to be dissolving with grief. 'I'm sorry,' she mumbled. 'Even after all this time, I still can't bear it.'

'I'm not surprised.' I strode across the kitchen and clasped her in a hug. 'I'm so sorry,' I said again. I could feel her body shuddering in my arms.

After a few moments, she pulled away, shaking her head. 'I'll be alright in a minute. Believe it or not, I like to talk about Maisie. It helps keep her alive for me. I've never stopped hoping that one day I'll see her again.'

'There have been no sightings at all?'

'Oh, lots of supposed sightings, especially in the beginning. Lots of false hopes; lots of disappointment. Those first few years after it happened were a complete rollercoaster. We believed then that she would be found. I still think it now – I have to. I won't give up on her. Jack and Harry though, they've both moved on. They think I'm foolish, refusing to stop the search, but I'll never give up on her. Not while there's breath in my body.'

'I understand,' I said quietly. 'I can't imagine what it must be like, to lose a child like that, but I also can't imagine ever accepting that she's gone for good. Not in those circumstances. I'm sure she's out there somewhere and one day you'll find her.'

I was rewarded with a weak smile. 'Thank you.' She took a deep breath. 'And that's where you come in.'

'Me?' Now I *was* confused. 'I don't understand.'

'Sit down, Anna and I'll make us both some coffee. I definitely need some before I tell you the rest.'

Meekly, I complied with the request. My head was filled with terrible images – a little girl playing in the pool; a dark-haired woman walking off with her; Selina returning to the pool; her face when she found out what had happened. How could anyone carry on when something like that had happened? The sympathy I'd felt for Selina grew tenfold. My own anger and distress at being followed had completely melted away in the face of her story.

'You have to try to understand what it was like,' Selina said quietly as she slid a mug of coffee in front of me. 'In the days and months after Maisie disappeared, I saw her everywhere. At least, I *thought* I saw her. I was always looking out, always watching. Every little girl the right age and size and with fair hair could have been her. Sometimes parents got angry, understandably so, when I called out to their child or, sometimes, grabbed hold of them to get a closer look. It was never her but I had to check; I had to make sure. You understand, don't you?'

I nodded mutely.

'As the years passed, possible sightings of her became fewer. Obviously, she would have grown; her face would have lost its chubbiness; it was difficult to imagine what she looked like. Police artists produced reconstructions – pictures of her two years on and then five years on – but I was never convinced she looked anything like them. They missed the spark of her somehow.' She sighed and took a tentative sip of her coffee. 'I kept looking though. I was certain she was still alive, that she'd been taken for a reason. She could be with that woman, Suki, or she could have taken her for someone else, perhaps a childless couple. I had to keep believing she was growing up, happy and loved. And there you are!' She looked up and met my eyes with a searching stare. 'I'm still looking.'

'I think I would be the same,' I murmured. I leant forward to comfort her once more, still wondering where I fitted into the tragedy. 'I'm so very sorry for you.' She clasped me tightly this time, an embrace full of longing and despair. 'You'll find her,' I whispered against her hair. 'I know it. Perhaps I could help you search ...'

'That's so kind.' She released me suddenly. 'Please excuse me a moment.'

Once again, she left the kitchen. I sipped my coffee thoughtfully. Searching for a child who disappeared twenty-three years ago was surely a complete impossibility but what could I say? How could I tell Selina that the odds of finding her lost daughter were infinitesimally slim? No-one was helping her. The least I could do was to offer some support.

When she returned, she was carrying a copy of my first novel, *Love on a Treadmill*. She turned to the author's page. 'Look,' she said, pointing at my studio photograph. She turned back to the last picture of Maisie in the album. 'And now look at that. Can you see the resemblance?'

'Not really.' I gave a token glance to the photo and stared back at Selina in shock, horrible realisation flooding through me. *Surely, she couldn't be about to say ...*

'Well I can.' *Oh my God, she was!* 'When I saw that picture, I immediately thought you could be Maisie. Then I did some background research on you. I know you're twenty-six, the same age Maisie would be now. You could be her.'

'Yes, but I'm not.' My voice was gentle but firm. Poor woman! I could understand her hope, the constant search for the woman her child may have become. I put my arm around her shoulders to lessen the sting of my words. 'Is that what you thought? Is that why you were tailing me?'

'I was trying to find out more about you, about your life. I wanted to try to engineer a meeting with you. That's why I was following you. Then I had a stroke of luck. It was after following you into Norwich one day. I was worried you might have noticed me following you when you started driving a bit erratically. By that point, I'd discovered where you lived. I drove back to Lewton, hoping to come up with a plan. Anyway, I popped into the shop to pick up a few things and that's when I saw your

'Girl Friday' card pinned up on the noticeboard. I didn't follow you after that, I promise. Instead, I phoned the number and well ...' she shrugged, 'the rest you know.'

I was at a loss for words. How could Selina be convinced I was her long-lost daughter by the mere sight of my photograph in a book? It was incredible, unbelievable, the lengths to which Selina had gone to track me down. A sudden thought struck me.

'Did you move to Swaffham just because you knew I lived in West Norfolk?' I asked.

'Yes. I *had* been thinking of moving anyway. It's been hard living in Nottingham over the past twenty-three years – I had so many memories of Maisie there – and even harder once Jack and I split up. At first, I didn't want to move away. I believed, somehow, she'd find her way back to us there. I know ...' She intercepted a look on my face. 'I was being ridiculous. Maisie was far too young to remember anything of her life in Nottingham. Still, it was a superstition I clung to – if we stayed, she'd come back to us. After twenty-three years though, that particular thread of hope was wearing pretty thin. When I saw your picture, I saw it as a sign. I put my house on the market and moved here.'

'Gosh, away from your home ... all your friends?' I couldn't believe what I was hearing. The very thought of it filled me with dismay. 'I don't know what to say.'

She patted my hand, relaxed and composed now she'd got all that off her chest. 'I know all this has come as a bit of a shock. Don't say anything at the moment. Just let what I've said settle in. I was never expecting you to welcome me as your long-lost mum. I know you have parents living in Swaffham – parents with whom you appear to be very close.'

'I am.' *Oh God, what on earth would they say about all this?*

Selina carried on serenely, seemingly unaware of my inner turmoil. 'I know it's difficult for you to believe I'm your birth mother. I understand. Believe me, I've given this plenty of thought. I didn't want you to find out so soon. I hoped you'd have the chance to get to know me better first. I appreciate you've had no time to begin contemplating it.'

'I don't need to contemplate it,' I said sharply. Somehow, I needed to nip this in the bud. I felt sorry for Selina, of course I did, but she was clearly completely delusional. 'I *know* my parents are my birth parents and I love them very much. I'm sorry. I know how much you want to find Maisie but she's not me.'

She nodded, her shoulders drooping slightly. Despite her protestations, she'd been hoping I was going to believe her. 'I understand.' Her hands shook slightly as she collected up the mugs and placed them carefully in the dishwasher. Then she turned back to face me. Her skin was almost grey, etched deep with lines of pain, but her eyes gleamed with fierce determination. 'We won't discuss it any more except for the one last thing I want to say. I know you don't believe me. I know you think I'm crazy but, if you have any compassion at all for me in your heart, would you consider at some point having a DNA test? That's the only way we'll ever know for certain.'

'I don't need a DNA test to tell me what I already know,' I objected stiffly. 'I think I'd better go.'

I stood and marched to the front door but, with my fingers on the latch, found I couldn't just walk away without saying goodbye. As I turned, I realised Selina had followed me. 'I know you're angry but please think about what I've said,' she pleaded.

'Goodbye Selina,' I responded curtly and stepped outside.

***

That evening I sat in a wine bar in the heart of Norwich, two glasses of Sauvignon Blanc in front of me, waiting for Madison. The bar was busy, as was to be expected on a Saturday evening. Young men and women stood in clusters, laughing loudly, eyes scanning the room. One rowdy group of lads had cast several glances my way, trying to make eye contact. 'Hurry up, Madison,' I muttered under my breath. One tall guy, dressed in a T-shirt emblazoned 'Too hot to handle' was swaggering over towards me when she finally burst through the door.

'Sorry I'm late,' she gasped, giving T-shirt boy a puzzled look as he beat a hasty retreat. 'Was that guy bothering you?'

'Not at all.' I stood up to give her a hug. 'Thanks so much for coming. I really needed someone to talk to.'

I'd called Madison earlier, at around four o'clock, having decided my life was in a right old muddle and I needed some help to sort it out. As my relationship with Ellie was up the creek, Madison was the only person I could turn to.

'So, what's up?' She took a sip of her wine. 'Ah, that's good. I needed that after the day I've had.'

'Me too,' I agreed wryly. 'What happened to you?'

'Oh, same old, same old.' She pulled a face. 'But what about you? You sounded very serious on the phone.'

'Well, for starters, I've fallen out with Ellie.' I repeated what I'd told Ellie about Dan the night before.

'Oops, I can see why *that* didn't go down well. You should've told her when it happened,' Madison said pragmatically.

'I know that Mads but I thought the two of them were going to split up anyway. That's what Dan led me to believe. And I didn't want to cause her any more grief.'

Madison snorted. 'As if you should believe *anything* that sneaky bastard said! Honestly Anna, you of all people know he can't be trusted!'

'I know. I just didn't want to hurt her feelings,' I said helplessly. I sipped my wine. 'Anyway, it's done now. The point is, how am I going to put things right?'

'Oh, she'll come around.' With her typical insouciance, Madison shrugged her shoulders and took a speculative look around the bar. 'Hey, don't turn around but there's a guy over by the bar who's definitely giving us the once over.'

I swung round in my seat. 'Who? Perhaps I know him.'

Madison sighed. 'Anna, you're hopeless. I said *don't* turn around. Oh gosh, now he's coming over.'

'Can I buy you two gorgeous ladies a drink?' He was tall with blond, floppy hair and a confident smile. His eyes lingered on me as he spoke, waiting for a response.

'Thanks ... but no thanks.' My own smile was pleasant but dismissive. 'I'm here with my *friend.*' As I spoke, I deliberately placed my hand over Madison's and left it there. 'Sorry.'

'Oh, fair enough.' He understood my meaning. 'Enjoy your evening.'

As he walked back to his friends, Madison snatched her hand away indignantly. 'What are you doing?' she hissed. 'I don't want the entire male population of Norwich to think I'm a lesbian.'

'That's a bit of an exaggeration, Mads. There's not *that* many people in here,' I grinned. 'It just seemed like a good idea. You know, put him off without damaging his ego.'

'That's all very well for you. You can have any man you want just by clicking your fingers. It's hard enough for me anyway, without having the added drawback of guys thinking I prefer girls!'

I chuckled. 'Don't be daft. You're selling yourself short. Lots of guys would see it as a challenge!' She was clearly not amused. 'Sorry, Mads. I won't do it again. Anyway, about Ellie … I've been sending her texts, apologising and saying that I hoped she was OK but, so far, I've had nothing back. I'm a bit worried about her.'

'I'm sure she's fine. Shall I send her a message? Check she's alright?'

'Would you?'

Madison rapidly fired off a brief text and was just putting her phone away when it pinged in response. 'Has Anna told you?' she read aloud. 'Well, clearly she's still alive.' She sent another text and waited expectantly. This time there was no immediate response. 'I've told her I'm with you, that you're terribly upset by it all and just hope she's OK. The last thing you wanted to do was hurt her.' After a few minutes, she slid her phone back into her bag. 'Just give her time, Anna. I'm sure she'll come around, especially when she finally realises what a scumbag Dan is.'

'I hope so,' I said glumly. 'There was something else I need your advice on. It's about my stalker.'

'I thought there'd been no more cars following you in the past few weeks. I was hoping that was all done with.' Madison's voice rose in horror.

'It's OK. It is,' I retorted, anxious to reassure her.

'Do you know who it is?'

'Yes … and it wasn't what I thought. In fact, I could never have thought of this in a million years.' I proceeded to tell Selina's story while Madison listened, slack-jawed.

'O. M. G.' She screwed up her face. 'The woman must be crazier than a box of frogs. My advice would be to steer well clear.'

'She's not crazy.' It was ridiculous but I found myself rushing to Selina's defence. 'I just feel sorry for her. Grief has obviously made her delusional but that's not her fault.'

'It is when it affects other people,' Madison snapped. 'She was actually stalking you, for God's sake! She made your life a misery. You were terrified … in case you don't remember.'

'I know …' My voice trailed off. I was picturing the conviction in Selina's eyes when she was telling me she thought I was Maisie. 'It's just difficult to know how best to help her.'

'*Help* her?' Madison spluttered. 'It's not *your* responsibility to help her. You're *not* her daughter and that's an end to it!'

'I know. I told her that but she wouldn't have it. She wants me to have a DNA test.'

'You've *got* to be kidding!'

'That was my reaction at first but actually, maybe it would help, you know, give her some closure,' I suggested tentatively.

She took a deep breath. 'Look Anna, I think you're giving far too much credence to this woman and her demands. It's a huge invasion of your privacy to start stalking you and an even bigger one to ask for DNA testing. You know who you are. She just has to lump it. My advice – have nothing more to do with her.'

'I know.' I tried again. 'It's just …'

'Think about your parents,' Madison interrupted. 'Think how they would feel about their daughter agreeing to a test to see if she actually belongs to someone else! I seriously can't believe you're considering it.' She slammed her empty glass down on the table. 'I need another drink. What would you like?'

'Just a coke please. I'm going to drive home.'

'You know you can stay at mine. In fact, I insist. It's ages since you stayed over.' Madison had a small flat right in the heart of the city.

'That's kind Mads but I'm going to go home. I need to make things right with Ellie.'

Madison shrugged. 'Suit yourself.' I watched as she stalked to the bar, her round face creased in disapproval. Perhaps I shouldn't have told Madison. She hadn't met Selina so it was difficult for her to empathise with her situation. She did have a good point about my parents though. They would be desperately hurt if they knew about a DNA test. My first thought was not to tell them. Why upset them needlessly? The trouble was, in my heart of hearts, I knew that would be a massive deception. If they did somehow find out about it – and Dad did seem to have a way of knowing everything about me, his 'Dad telepathy', he called it – they would never forgive me. Madison was right. That was too high a price to pay for helping out someone I barely knew.

'Thanks.' I smiled as she slid a glass of coke and ice in front of me. 'You're right about my parents. There's no way I could do something as huge as taking a DNA test without telling them.'

'Good. That's the first sensible thing you've said. In fact, that would be my advice, Anna, as you asked for it. Don't do anything rash. Have a long, hard think about the consequences of it all and, if you're still considering going ahead, talk it over with your parents first. They'll be upset but at least you can explain your reasons. I'm sure *they* will be able to talk some sense into you!'

A ping from her phone signalled a text. She glanced at it and then showed me. It was from Ellie.

Tell Anna we'll talk tomorrow x

Madison grinned. 'Told you. She's coming around. It's all good.'

'I hope so.' I gasped as I caught a glimpse of something through the window.

'What's the matter now?'

I shook my head as I gazed out at the busy street, a splinter of fear, sharp and jagged, tugging at my throat. I'd seen a grey head, a swarthy face with eyes narrowed, staring straight at me from across the road. It had been a split-second moment when I'd met his eyes, a shudder of recognition and then he was gone.

'I ... it's nothing. I thought I saw someone watching me.'

Madison was immediately concerned, peering out into the night. 'Where?'

'He's gone. Probably nothing.'

'Are you sure? You've gone very pale.'

I turned back from the window. 'It's difficult to explain but there's this guy. I think he drives a black Range Rover. I've seen him a few times now and he gives me the creeps.'

Madison frowned. 'You think he's following you?'

'No, not really. It's just I'm not sure. Ever since the Peugeot thing, I seem to have become totally paranoid that I'm being watched.'

She smiled sympathetically. 'That's understandable, Anna. I'm sure it's nothing. You see, that woman has a lot to answer for, in my opinion. She's seriously spooked you. Give it a bit of time and I'm sure those feelings will pass.'

'I'm sure you're right.'

We chatted for another hour before agreeing to call it a night. Madison, bless her heart, insisted on walking back to my car with me. Seeing that man had set my nerves skittering and I was grateful for the company. The streets of Norwich were now virtually empty and, despite peering in every doorway and around every corner, I didn't see the grey-haired man.

When we reached my Fiesta, we parted ways. I turned the radio up loud for the return journey and sang along, determined to keep out any scary thoughts. Lewton was in darkness by the time I pulled into the drive and Ellie's car was there but the house was silent. Our reconciliation would have to wait until morning.

***

Madison walked briskly back to her flat. This Selina woman was going to cause problems, she could tell. And what about these delusions Anna was having, thinking she was being watched? Her fingers closed around the phone in her pocket. What was she going to do about it all?

CHAPTER 20

Anna

A small boy with a shock of curly, fair hair wearing a navy and white striped T-shirt and grey shorts was crouched on the ground digging in the sand with a stick. I watched, fascinated, as he reached a hand into the hole and poked around with his fingers.

'Let me see!' I peered in just as he withdrew something small and put it in his pocket.

'No, it's a secret. You're too little!' He grinned triumphantly.

'Not fair – let me see!' I tugged at his arm but he shrugged me off easily.

'I'll show you later ... maybe!' He laughed as he ran towards the sea.

'Wait for me!'

I tried to follow but was scooped up in a strong pair of arms. 'Not so fast, young lady ...'

I awoke slowly, trying as I'd done many times before without success, to hold the moment a little longer, to find out what the boy had in his pocket. It remained elusive, always just out of reach. I willed myself back to sleep, trying to recapture that loose thread and unravel the mystery ... but it was no use. Reluctantly, I surfaced to full consciousness. It was a dream which haunted my early childhood but I hadn't experienced it for years. It was Selina's fault; she was the one stirring up the past. The truth was, I'd always desperately longed for a brother. As a very young girl, I recalled the sense, long since faded, that the boy in the dream *was* my brother. I'd asked my parents about him.

'What brother? You don't have a brother, Anna.' Mum had given me a rare cuddle. 'What on earth makes you think you have?'

I told them. 'It's just a silly dream,' Dad had scoffed, his grin taking the edge off his words. 'We all have dreams like that. I think last night I dreamt I'd just become the new Arsenal football manager. I'd do a lot better than that Arsene Wenger, I can tell you that. I can't think what the board were doing, appointing a Frenchman.' He snorted in disgust. 'Anyway,' he said, giving my shoulders a squeeze, 'just forget all about it.'

I hadn't forgotten though and the dream recurred frequently, a persistent intruder, disturbing my thoughts as well as my slumber. On a number of occasions, I'd raised the subject again, to the point where my parents became angry and forbade me to speak of it any more.

'It's just a dream, for God's sake,' Dad had exploded. 'There is no bloody brother, I think we would know!'

'Language Geoff!' Mum had remonstrated, eyes like ice chips berating me also. 'See how you've upset your father, making accusations like that! Why would we lie to you? We're your mummy and daddy.' Her voice had then softened. 'It really would be best, Anna, if you put this silly idea completely out of your head. We don't want you to speak of it again. Is that clear?'

I'd nodded, cowed in the face of their anger, and kept my questions to myself. Yet, a stubborn kernel remained, deep down inside, a conviction that I'd once, perhaps in another life, had an older brother with thick, curly hair. I even investigated reincarnation. That *had* to be the explanation, so strong was my belief that the boy I saw in my sleep was my sibling. Gradually, the edges of the dream had blurred and the colours had faded, like an old photograph. As I grew older, I dismissed it as a childish imagining and yet, here it was again, buried in my sub-conscious but not forgotten. Even my feelings were the same. Always I awoke, trying desperately to stay asleep so I could discover what the boy was holding in his hand. I'd forgotten all about it yesterday when I was telling Selina I couldn't be her daughter. Now, a secret whisper, faint as a baby's breath, hissed in my mind. Selina also had a son …

The unmistakeable sounds of Ellie moving around downstairs wrenched me from my disturbing thoughts. Grabbing my dressing gown, I scurried from my room. The text Madison had received last night had given me hope that things between us could be resolved and I didn't want her to go out before we'd had a chance to talk. On Sundays, she often visited her parents, who lived in Cromer on the north Norfolk coast, and they liked to have a long walk on the beach, with their old spaniel Rufus, before going out for lunch.

I stepped cautiously into the kitchen to find Ellie pouring out two mugs of tea. There was a tray on the table, laid with toast, butter, marmalade and a small vase of freesias.

'Oh,' Ellie exclaimed, seeing me framed in the doorway. 'I was just about to bring you breakfast in bed! You beat me to it.'

Relief rushed through me and I gave her a wide grin. 'That's really sweet,' I murmured huskily. 'Listen Ellie, I'm so sorry …'

'Stop. I'm the one who should be apologising. You were only trying to be a good friend; I know that now.'

'Sorry for spoiling the surprise.' I sank onto a chair at the breakfast table and helped myself to toast.

Ellie shrugged. 'I was just trying to make up for acting like an idiot for the past thirty-six hours.' Her face hardened. 'Dan and I are finished.'

'Oh.' My first thought was to say how sorry I was but the hypocritical words stuck in my throat. I was pleased, not sorry. How could I say that?

'Yes. You were *so* right about him. You know he'd been away on a work thing?' I nodded. 'Well, the truth was, he was off with a mate and a couple of girls they'd picked up the first night they were away. He lied about it at first, pretended he'd been training all hours and that was why he barely had a chance to ring me. Then I told him what you'd said. Of course, he completely denied it; he said you were jealous and trying to cause trouble between us. But then he went too far – said things like you'd always had the hots for him and that you had come on to him, big time. He said you'd kissed him, not the other way around.'

'Scumbag!' I muttered.

'The more he spoke, the more he dug himself into a hole. I'm sorry Anna but he really does seem to have it in for you. Once I'd said I didn't believe him – there was *no* way you would have made a move on him – he started sneering about you, saying that you thought you were too good for him, too good for any normal bloke.'

I snorted. 'It's just sour grapes, Ell. I don't care what he thinks.'

'I know you don't but I just think you ought to watch your back, Anna. He was so angry at you; I've never seen him like that before … I even started to wonder if *he* was your stalker. If that Peugeot had been in the garage for a while, he would've had access to the keys, wouldn't he?'

I stared at her in astonishment. When Dan said the car belonged to Selina, I'd immediately assumed that she was the stalker. Could Dan have been involved? The shock disappeared as I remembered that Selina had admitted following me. 'It's not Dan,' I said firmly.

'Are you sure? He made it clear that you were, in his words, 'Going to get what was coming to you.' I can't believe I didn't see through him sooner.'

'It suited him to keep you sweet,' I said wryly. 'None of this is your fault. You trusted him, that's all, and he didn't deserve it.'

'Yeah, turned out I was a right mug. His parting shot was to tell me about the girl he'd been shacked up with for the past few days. He said he was going to finish with me anyway and that I'd struggle to find anyone who could put up with an ugly cow like me.' The last few words came out in a sob.

'Oh Ellie, you mustn't believe that. You're totally gorgeous. Any man would be lucky to have you.'

'Well, I could do with losing a few pounds …'

'Stop it! You're fabulous. Don't let that horrible bastard get to you. You are *so* much better off without him.'

Ellie nodded. 'I know.' She took a bite of toast and gave me a watery smile. 'Anyway, how do you know Dan isn't your stalker?'

'I've found out who it is and it's nothing to worry about.'

'Really?' Ellie's green eyes were wide with surprise. 'Who is it?'

Once more I recounted Selina's story, this time including Madison's take on it all.

'Oh, that's why you were with Mads last night. I have to say, Anna, I agree with her. This woman is one crazy lady. Definitely, you shouldn't even consider having a DNA test. It's like an admission that she could be right!'

'I don't agree,' I said slowly. 'I feel sorry for her, that's all. I think her life has been blighted by false hope and, if I took the test, at least she would know for sure I'm not her daughter.'

'Oh well,' Ellie said with a toss of her flame red hair. 'It's up to you in the end. At least you now know there's no weird creep following you – that's one good thing.' She yawned and stretched her arms above her head. 'Mum and Dad are away this weekend so I'm free if you are. How about heading up to the coast and having a walk? We could see if we could get in somewhere for Sunday lunch – my treat.'

'Sounds good to me.'

***

The sky was hung with iron grey clouds but the threatened rain stayed away while we strolled briskly along the beach. I was just filling Ellie in on the latest with Josh Fielding when my phone rang. It was the man himself. Taking a deep breath and pulling a face at Ellie, I answered it.

'Hi.' His voice, a verbal caress, warmed the pit of my stomach. 'Listen Anna, I owe you an apology and an explanation. I was a bit off with you on Friday.'

'Honestly, there's no need …' I began.

'I'd like to take you out to dinner tonight,' he continued, sending my pheromones into a frenzy, 'if you're available.'

'Er, yes … sure … that would be great … but there's really no need …'

'I'll pick you up at seven. See you then.' The phone went dead.

'Well!' I puffed out my cheeks. 'That was Josh. He's taking me out for dinner tonight.'

'Whoopee doo!' Ellie did a celebration dance, wiggling her hips, punching the air and almost tripping over a small boy building a sandcastle. 'Oops, sorry! A date. That's great news!'

'I'm not sure if it's a date exactly,' I demurred. 'He said he owed me an apology and an explanation.'

'He doesn't need to take you out to dinner to do that!' she insisted. 'It's defo a date. Now let's think about what you're going to wear …' Ellie loved clothes and had a bedroom heaving with everything from sparkly leggings and glittery jackets to a full-on sailor suit. 'I vote we cancel our lunch plans and stop for a sarnie somewhere on our way home. Then we can make sure you have enough time to get ready.'

'I know I need work but …' I checked my watch, 'seven hours?'

'You'd be surprised,' she replied sagely. 'It's all in the preparation. Come on, let's get going.'

As we reached Ellie's car and I stretched a hand to open the passenger door, the hairs on the back of my neck began to prickle. I spun around quickly, eyes scanning the buildings and cars lining the street. Nothing. I gave myself a mental shake; I really needed to get over this feeling of being watched. Nobody was remotely interested in what I was doing.

'Anna?' Ellie had already started the engine and was staring impatiently at me.

I slid into my seat and fastened the seatbelt, shaking my head at my foolishness. Yet, somehow, the edges of my consciousness were still quivering with unease, sensing a man's eyes, zeroing in like lasers before retreating into the shadows.

***

Ellie's enthusiasm was infectious and, before I knew it, I found myself in my bedroom trying on a succession of outfits at her critical direction.

'Too boring,' Ellie declared, not for the first time, as I twirled before her in a demure Laura Ashley number. 'Haven't you got anything a bit sexier? Honestly, you've got a great body. You need to show it off a bit more. It's a shame we're not the same size; I've got loads of stuff that would suit you.' She peered into my wardrobe and shook her head. 'What happened to that green, figure hugging, velvet dress, the one with the sweetheart neckline? That would be perfect.'

'I gave it to charity. I was never really that comfortable wearing it. Anyway, velvet would have been too hot for May.'

Ellie rolled her eyes. 'It was the only dress you owned which could be described as hot. You and I need to go shopping sometime soon. Your wardrobe needs some serious updating. Hey, how about this?' She pulled out a red jersey dress with a V-neckline. 'You could dress this up with some jewellery and red is a great colour on you. I think this is the one.'

I frowned. 'That neckline is a bit low. I don't want to look desperate.'

'Don't be daft. You're going to look gorgeous and knock his socks off.'

A few hours later, I tugged the red dress nervously, waiting for Josh to arrive. Ellie was right; it did suit me but it was a bit too clingy for my liking. Oh well, at least Ellie's reaction had given me confidence.

'Wow, Anna, you look amazing!' she gasped. 'Josh won't be able to take his eyes off you.'

I gave her a grateful smile. 'You don't think it looks as if I'm trying too hard? It isn't really a date, after all ...'

'You look fabulous,' she said firmly. 'Remember you have dressed for yourself to make *you* feel good. It's not all about the man.'

'Blimey, you've changed your tune. Dan used to say jump and you'd ask how high?'

Ellie scowled. 'A lot of good that did me.' We both jumped as the doorbell rang. 'That'll be him. Good luck. I'm sure you'll have a great evening.'

She scooted up the stairs while I opened the door. Josh stood on the doorstep, smiling with those killer brown eyes and looking totally hot in an open-necked, white shirt and beige jeans. His grin grew wider. 'You look stunning,' he said, proffering his arm. 'Shall we go?'

'You look pretty sharp yourself.' I stepped through the door and took his arm, my fingers tingling at the touch of his bare skin.

His black Mercedes was waiting by the kerb and he opened the door for me. That definitely earned him a brownie point; I appreciated good manners.

'I understand you're a novelist as well as an expert gardener and painter. Tell me about your work,' Josh said as we pulled away. Another brownie point – a guy who took an interest in me. Most of the men I'd dated seemed interested only in talking about themselves.

'I've had two books published,' I said proudly. 'Well, technically, the second one isn't actually out yet but it will be soon and I'm midway through writing my third. They're romantic comedies.' I waited for the putdown. So many people were disparaging of romantic fiction.

'What, like *Love Actually*?' he asked.

I smiled. 'A bit. Obviously not as good as that. I love that film.'

'It must be difficult to think of funny stuff to write all the time,' he mused.

'Sometimes.' I realised I was fiddling with my ear and swiftly clasped my hands in my lap. 'What I find funny isn't necessarily what other people do. I worried about that a lot with my first book. I thought my main character, Jemima, was hilarious and so did my friends. The general public are another matter entirely.'

'Presumably they *did* like it, though, or it wouldn't have been successful?'

'Thankfully, enough people did. There's nothing like the buzz of someone saying they've loved your book. I'll never tire of it.'

He nodded. 'I can imagine.' He glanced in the rear-view mirror. 'Does being a famous author have its drawbacks. Do I have to worry about the paparazzi?'

'Haha. I'm obviously not famous, at least, not yet.'

'Mm, a woman with ambition. I like it.'

'Well, you've got to have dreams. Where are we going?' I'd noticed we were heading north.

'Somewhere my sister recommended – a fish restaurant in Cromer. I hope you like fish?'

I allowed my face to fall. 'Oh no, I'm allergic to fish!'

'You're kidding!' he frowned.

I grinned. 'Sorry but whenever I have fish, I have to go and see a sturgeon.'

His lips twitched. 'I see, you're talking a load of pollocks.'

'I'm afraid you'll have to speak up.' I raised my voice and put a hand to my ear. 'I didn't quite catch that. I'm a little hard of herring!'

'Right, stop now or I'll have to let you out here.'

'Hey, there's no need to get snapper with me ... OK.' I held up my hands in mock submission. 'I've finished.'

'Is this what you do in your books? Are they punfests?'

I wrinkled my nose, considering his question. 'Not really. Most of the humour is character or situation driven. My main character, Jemima, is always getting herself into scrapes. But I confess, I do love a pun so there are always a few in there.'

'I'd never have guessed,' he replied dryly. 'So, to get back to my earlier question, you're happy about going to a fish restaurant?'

'Absolutely,' I beamed at him, 'and Cromer is just the *plaice* for it!'

***

The restaurant, *Ocean's Edge*, was a modern, brick building on the outskirts of Cromer and located on the brink of a cliff overlooking the beach. Josh ushered me inside, where we were met by a woman with short, black hair, a nose stud and a friendly smile who showed us to our table.

'Wow!' I couldn't help my sharply-indrawn breath as I gazed in wonder at the panoramic vista of the sea afforded by the full-length glass wall.

'Lucy, my sister, said the view was spectacular. Apparently, the food is equally as good.' He grinned at the black-haired woman.

She smiled back serenely. 'It will be,' she promised, handing us menus.

'Oh Josh, this is so amazing. I love it. Thank you for bringing me here,' I relaxed back in my seat and stared down at the golden sand where people were scattered, enjoying an evening stroll before the sun went down. The sea itself was silvery grey with white-tipped waves gently rolling on to the shore.

'You're welcome.' The warmth in his brown eyes was having a strange effect on my body and, hastily, I buried my head in the menu to hide my reddening cheeks. 'Apparently,' Josh continued, 'if we'd been here seven hundred years ago, we would be looking out over the village of Shipden.'

'Really?' I lowered the menu and stared out at the sea in fascination. 'What happened?'

He shrugged. 'The advancing sea eventually washed the entire village away. It makes you wonder if this place can survive another seven hundred years, or even one hundred.'

I nodded. 'I remember reading about houses on the Norfolk coast which had fallen into the sea. It's sad.'

'Sad but inevitable. Even without global warming, the sea is constantly eroding, taking back its own. The power of those waves reminds me that nothing lasts forever.'

'Very deep and not just the sea!' I quipped before noticing the solemnity of his face. 'Sorry, are you OK?'

He took a deep breath. 'I said on the phone that I owed you an explanation for my behaviour. I was rude, I know, but it's something I find difficult to talk about.' He paused and poured himself a glass of water from the jug on the table. 'I worked for a relatively small merchant bank in London ...'

'What was it called?' I asked. 'My dad may have mentioned it.'

He frowned at that. 'MNC.'

The name triggered a synapse at the back of my brain. *MNC ... where had I heard that name before?*

'I'm sure you know it's a high pressure, high stakes business. MNC had been struggling and my mate Jon and I were brought in to turn things around. At first, it looked as if we were doing just that ... but then Jon made a mistake. I won't bore you with the details. Suffice it to say, it was costly, to the tune of £3 million. I gave him a hard time; told him he was an effing idiot and not to bother coming back.' He exhaled and took another sip of water. 'And that was it. He didn't. Instead, he locked himself in his garage with a bottle of single malt whisky, connected a hose to his exhaust and never woke up.'

I gasped. 'Oh no!' Instinctively, I reached across the table to take his hand but stopped myself just in time. 'Oh Josh, I'm so sorry.'

His eyes were full of pain. 'It was my fault. I should have been a good friend. He would've been if I'd been the one making an almighty cock up. Ironically, things turned out alright for MNC in the end. The company didn't lose £3 million. Jon would still be here today if it wasn't for me.'

'You mustn't think that,' I exclaimed. 'He was an adult; he made his own decisions. It's understandable you were angry at the time but, if he was a good friend, he would have known you didn't mean what you'd said. I'm so sorry,' I said again, unsure what else I could say.

'I stayed with the company for another six months but my heart wasn't in it so I left. The day you first came around to help with the garden was the first anniversary of James' death. I was very down that day and I guess you caught the brunt of that.'

'Oh.' I felt my eyes welling with tears. 'Poor you.'

'Anyway,' he continued briskly. 'Enough doom and gloom. I promised you an explanation and an apology.' He took my hand, still resting on the table, sending currents of excitement shooting up my arm. 'I'm really sorry I was so abrupt with you, Anna.' He sat back, releasing my hand. 'Now, let's relax and enjoy the evening.'

'Of course,' I smiled but he was already studying his menu. Inwardly, my mind was racing. No wonder I had thought him rude and arrogant at our first meeting and then again when I'd asked him why he left banking. After everything that had happened, his behaviour was understandable. He wasn't really a Jekyll and Hyde after all; only time would tell if he could be my Mr Darcy.

***

As we arrived outside my house, I struggled to remember when I had enjoyed an evening as much. Everything had been perfect: the food had been sublime – buttery, seared scallops, monkfish and tiger prawn masala and a mint chocolate parfait which we'd shared; the view as the sun sank beyond the horizon in a sky swirled with ever darkening red and gold had been spectacular; most of all, Josh had been completely charming – witty, entertaining, attentive and generally knock-your-socks-off gorgeous.

Together, we ambled towards the front door. The night air felt chilly after the warmth of the car and I tugged my jacket around me as I fumbled in my clutch bag for my key.

'Would you like to come in for a coffee?' I asked, my heart beating faster as I awaited his response.

He sighed. 'I'd love to but I'd better not.' He took a step towards me and gave me an awkward hug. 'I have to be up at five tomorrow. I promised to take my dad fishing. And I think if I stay with you any longer, I'll find it impossible to leave.' His calloused fingers tilted my chin up, forcing me to meet his smouldering, brown eyes. I held my breath as he lowered his head and brushed his warm lips against mine. My whole body shivered in response. 'You're cold,' he observed. 'You'd better get inside.'

I gave him a tremulous smile. How could I tell him that it was his touch, rather than the nip in the air, making me tremble? 'Thank you so much for a fantastic evening,' I said huskily, willing him to take me in his arms once more. Instead, he took a step back.

'I really enjoyed it too. Hopefully we can do it again sometime soon?'

'I'd love that.'

'Good. Well, I'll be in touch. Night Anna.' He turned and walked briskly to his car. 'Go in,' he ordered, seeing me still standing there. 'You'll get cold.'

'OK, night then.'

Closing the door, I leaned against it and relived the kiss, savouring the deliciousness of the feelings he'd evoked. Had I *ever* felt such an attraction before? Definitely not. Already, as I opened my eyes, I was experiencing the angst of wondering if he really would want to go out with me again. I knew, right at that moment, I wanted nothing more. Tomorrow would be an agony, waiting for him to call but tonight … I smiled as I crept up the stairs … tonight, I would bask in the promise of things to come.

Much later, when I woke in the night from the most fabulous dream, in which Josh was whisking me away for a weekend in Paris, my eyes snapped open. Something odd had tumbled to the surface of my consciousness. How had he known where I lived? He hadn't asked me when he phoned to arrange the date and, as far as I knew, we had no mutual friends or acquaintances he could ask. It was a tiny thing but it kept me puzzling long into the night.

CHAPTER 21

Anna

With the advent of a new day, I dismissed the question of how Josh knew where I lived as inconsequential. There was bound to be a logical explanation; I just had to ask him. Maybe I would've done, had he phoned. By ten thirty, I'd heard nothing – disappointing, to say the least. He was my first thought this morning; obviously, I wasn't his. I wondered about taking the initiative, sending him a text reiterating how much I'd enjoyed last night but managed to restrain myself. That would look desperate.

I was mid-sentence on my computer later that morning when the sound of my ringtone sent my spirits soaring. *At last!* Giddy with anticipation, I leapt off my chair. As I leant across my desk to reach my phone, I sent my mug of coffee flying. *Damn!* I swiftly righted the mug but the damage had been done. Scalding, hot, brown liquid had flooded across the desk and was dribbling onto the carpet. I sprinted into the kitchen and grabbed the kitchen roll while the phone continued to ring, persistent and urgent. Luckily, I managed to catch most of the liquid before it reached the floor and, only then, did the phone cease its call. *Typical.* Heaving a sigh, I checked the screen and saw I'd missed Dad, not Josh. The sense of anti-climax was crushing.

Grumpily, I cleared up the rest of the mess. It was a good thing Dad wasn't here to see it. My habitual clumsiness as a child had always irritated him. He called it carelessness. Both my parents were neat and orderly, tidy to the point of obsession. I remembered an incident when I was about six or seven. I'd received some paints for my birthday from a well-meaning neighbour. Mum and Dad had refused point-blank to allow me to get them out and I had to wait for an afternoon when my childminder, a pretty girl in her twenties called Dani, was looking after me after school. I took immense care over my painting, a family portrait, and proudly showed Dani my masterpiece.

'That's lovely, Anna. What a clever girl!' Dani exclaimed, gratifyingly impressed by the three stick figures outlined in multi-coloured, broad brush strokes. 'Your mummy and daddy will love it.'

At that moment, the key had turned in the front door. *Daddy!* Excitedly, I jumped down from my stool, eager to show off my new talent. In my haste, I knocked over the muddy water in which my brush was resting. My painting, luckily, was out of harm's way and I held it aloft triumphantly as Dad appeared. I recalled his face, creased in annoyance, as he surveyed the scene.

'What the hell ... Dani,' he bellowed. 'What's all this mess?'

Dani rushed across, armed with kitchen roll. 'I'm so sorry, Mr Blake,' she apologised, mopping up the dirty water. 'Anna's been painting.'

'Jesus Christ, it's gone all over my mail!' He snatched the soggy letters from the table. 'What were you thinking? You know how clumsy Anna is. She needs close supervision at all times and then maybe accidents like these wouldn't happen. And at least have the common sense to remove important letters out of her way!'

'I'm so sorry, Mr Blake,' Dani repeated, tears in her eyes.

'Daddy, look at my picture!' Ignoring his rage, I tugged at his sleeve. I was sure, when he saw it, he would be so impressed he'd forget all about the mess. He gave it a brief glance, his eyes still boiling with anger. 'It's you, me and Mummy,' I explained, waiting for his mouth to curve in admiration and pride.

'Oh yes,' he sneered. 'I can see that; I always walk around with my arms like this ...' He stretched his arms out wide to replicate the figures in the painting. 'And, of course my head is almost as big as my body!' I watched in dismay as he crumpled the paper and threw it in the bin. 'I'd say you need to keep practising but, in this case, I think it's safer to say no more paints until you're capable of using them sensibly.' With that, he stormed upstairs.

I remembered turning to Dani, my bottom lip quivering. 'I wanted to show Mummy.'

She hugged me, upset by my distress. 'I know, lovey, but never mind. You can paint another one, even better, but we'll save that for another day.'

That was the last time I'd seen Dani. She was replaced by a stern-faced woman with a cap of short, grey hair called Mrs Hubert who watched over me with sharp eyes and endless cups of tea. There had been no more painting – or any fun – after school. Instead, I was told to practise my spellings, my handwriting and the times tables. I learned to curb my natural exuberance, to think about my movements before I made them, to be quiet and attentive and that way I earned a modicum of Dad's approval. I was still clumsy, though.

Having sorted my latest mishap, I picked up my mobile. Whilst it was lovely having a father who cared enough to phone at least once a day, it was a little exhausting. It was almost like he was checking up on me.

'Hi Dad.' He answered my return call almost instantly.

'Anna! Hello, my darling. I was just trying to ring you.' His rich, warm voice was like a cuddle down the phone.

'Yes sorry. I didn't get there in time. Is everything OK?'

There was a brief pause. 'Everything's fine, darling, but your mum and I were wondering if you could pop round this evening? She said she'd cook. Seven o'clock.'

Something was up; I wasn't usually summoned on a Monday. I hesitated. I'd been hoping my plans might include Josh. 'Of course.' I resigned myself to the inevitable. 'Is anything the matter?'

'No, no.' His voice was deliberately bluff. There was definitely something bothering him despite his protest. 'Nothing like that. We just wanted to spend a bit of time with you, that's all, and your Mum isn't working today so she offered to cook. You know how worried about you we've been, with this stalker business and everything. In fact, I'll come and pick you up.'

'There's no need, Dad. The stalker thing has been resolved. I'll explain it all to you later.'

The ensuing couple of seconds of silence were weighty with disapproval. 'And you didn't think to let us know?'

'I … it was a bit complicated. I'm sorry.' I was filled with contrition. How thoughtless to forget to reassure them!

'Right. Well, perhaps you'll take the trouble to explain yourself this evening. I won't take up any more of your time. See you later; seven o'clock.' He rang off before I had a chance to respond. Oh God! I'd completely forgotten I'd told Dad about the blue Peugeot. No wonder he was angry. I'd left them in the dark about the latest developments, worrying when there was nothing to worry about. I hated being in the wrong. There would need to be some serious grovelling tonight. My mind began spinning various excuses but they all sounded pretty lame. I'd just have to tell them the truth and do lots of apologising. Too much preoccupation with Josh Fielding.

My phone remained stubbornly silent for the rest of the morning and I immersed myself in my writing. My main character, Jemima, was struggling with lack of sleep and breast-feeding her baby girl, Freya, while her husband, Conrad, had finished his paternity leave and returned to the firm of architects, HJA, where he worked.

The crying wouldn't stop. Jemima had tried feeding Freya twice, changed her nappy, rocked her, sung to her in a quavery, off-key soprano, put her down in her cot but nothing would soothe the screaming baby. In despair, she sank down on to the carpet of the newly decorated nursery and sobbed.

The noise of the doorbell roused her and, red-eyed, she peered out from behind a curtain, resplendent with pink elephants, to see who it was. A tall figure with perfectly coiffed, auburn hair and wearing a slim-fitting, navy trouser suit, stepped back at that moment and squinted up at the very window Jemima had her nose pressed up against. Eye contact was made. Two perfectly shaped eyebrows were raised in question while Jemima's bloodshot eyes widened in horror. Oh God, it was Conrad's mother!

Scooping up the still-crying Freya and hurriedly wiping her tears with her sleeve, Jemima made her way down the stairs. This was a nightmare. Conrad's mother, Isobel, the high-flying director of a global software company, had always regarded her with disapproval. A gym instructor was in no way a suitable match for her talented son.

It was only as she opened the door and was subjected to her mother-in-law's scrutiny that the full horror of her situation hit her. Even wearing full make-up, her one and only Donna Karan dress, her Manolo shoes and with half a bottle of wine inside her, Jemima found Isobel Conrad pretty terrifying. Today she was sporting Primark pyjamas dotted with milk puke and hair like a bird's nest. Isobel was looking at her as if she was something unpleasant she might find on the bottom of her shoe.

Jemima tried for a tremulous smile but it was more of a grimace. 'Isobel, how lovely! I didn't know you were coming. Sorry about all this …' She gestured helplessly at Freya who, miraculously, had stopped the full-on screaming and was now docilely whimpering and hiccupping. Isobel had that effect on people.

'Jemima,' her mother-in-law snapped, her glossy, red lips curling in distaste. 'What on earth is going on?'

I sat back and reread the scene I'd just written. Poor Jemima. I knew how she felt. Why was it that the people who scared you the most were always the ones who would find you at your most disadvantaged? At that moment, my phone rang again. *Josh?* My heart leapt. No, it was Selina.

'Anna?' Her voice sounded anxious. 'It's Selina. Please don't hang up.'

'Yes?'

'Anna, I know what I said upset you. I'm so very sorry about that.'

I sighed. 'I know.'

'I was just wondering if you'd had any more thoughts ... you know?'

'What? About DNA testing? No, I haven't. Look Selina, there really isn't any point ...'

'Wait!' The interruption was urgent, panicky. 'Please listen. There's something else ... something I forgot to mention on Saturday.' There was a pause as if she was waiting for me to respond. 'It's ... it's something I need to show you. Would you mind very much if I popped round? Now I have my car back ...' There was another embarrassed pause. 'I wouldn't expect you to come to me.'

My instinct was to comply with the request but my friends' voices were still ringing in my ears. 'I don't think that's a very good idea. Honestly, Selina, you need to let this go. I'm not your daughter and there's nothing more you can say to persuade me.'

'Oh please!' The plea sounded desperate. '*Please* Anna, I won't ask you for anything else, I promise.'

I sighed again. I really did need to learn how to say no. 'Alright.' I glanced at my watch. 'But you don't know where I live so I'll drive to your house. I'm free now, if that suits.'

'Oh, Anna, thank you so much,' Selina gushed and then, her voice bubbling with relief, continued, 'But I'll still come to you. I know where you live. I followed you ... remember?'

***

I watched the blue Peugeot, now intact with a shiny, new front bumper, pull into the drive. Seeing the car again was a physical shock. That fear of being hunted down, along with the quickened pulse and lurch of the stomach it induced, still simmered inside me. Selina, her face drawn and pale, stepped out of the car. She had an old shoebox in her hands.

'Thank you for seeing me,' she said simply as I opened the front door.

'Come in. I've made coffee.'

'Lovely.'

Selina followed me through to the compact kitchen diner. 'This is nice,' she said, taking in the sleek, grey cabinets and the freesias from Ellie on the table. Wordlessly, I handed her a mug of coffee and gestured she should sit. I knew I was going to find it hard steeling my heart against her pitiful, brown eyes and hopeful expression.

She set the shoebox on the table. 'You're probably wondering how I could possibly convince you that you're Maisie.' She lifted the lid, revealing a jumble of old photographs. 'It occurred to me in the night, when I couldn't sleep, that I'd made a mistake just showing my album of Maisie photos. I should have shown you these.' She took out the top three and handed them across the table.

I took them, curious despite my reluctance to be drawn into Selina's story. All three were taken in the eighties, judging by the hair and clothes being worn by the young man in the pictures. He was thin-faced with smiling, blue eyes and shoulder length blond hair. My gut reaction was that he would

102

be fun to be around. Other than that, they meant absolutely nothing to me. I shook my head and handed the prints back. 'I'm sorry Selina but I'm not sure what I'm supposed to notice.'

She spread them out on the table. 'This is Jack, my husband, before we were married. He would have been about the age you are now. Don't you see the resemblance? You look *so* like him.'

I squinted more closely at the man's face. 'Really? Other than the blond hair and blue eyes, I'm afraid I don't see it.'

'Well then,' Selina removed a fourth photo from the box. 'Look at this one.'

This photograph had been taken when Jack was clearly unaware of the camera. In it, he was bent over a book, his eyes intent, his face serious and his right hand holding his right ear. An impartial observer may have been able to detect a resemblance in this picture but I couldn't. I shrugged and put it on the table with the others. 'Sorry,' I said flatly.

'Look again,' Selina persisted. 'Look at what he's doing with his ear. He was always fiddling with it, especially when he was concentrating on something, just like you are doing now.'

I snatched away my hand as if I'd been scalded. It was something I couldn't help, something which had always irritated my parents but I'd been unaware that anyone else had noticed. I shook my head. 'That doesn't mean anything Selina. I'm sure lots of people fiddle with their ear or their hair. People do all sorts of strange things when they're anxious. Just because two people happen to do something similar doesn't mean they're related.'

'But doesn't it make you wonder if you could be? To me, you are so like Jack that I am certain you are my daughter. *Please* won't you take the DNA test?'

'I *did* think about it,' I admitted, 'and if I genuinely believed there was any chance you were right, of course I would take the test. But I don't ...' I couldn't look at Selina. Instead, I picked up the photos and tucked them into a neat pile. 'You have to understand that what you're asking would cause heartache for the people I love. I'm not prepared to risk that. I'm sorry, Selina.'

She slumped back in her seat, the despair of defeat etched in the sag of her slim shoulders and the pinched line of her mouth. She took a sip of her coffee and I watched as she regrouped, preparing for her next effort. She was nothing if not persistent.

'Perhaps if you were to meet him ...' she began.

'Selina.' Gently, I took her hand. 'This has got to stop.'

'Won't you even consider meeting him? Or perhaps Harry ... your brother,' she added defiantly.

'I'm sorry.' What more could I say? To provide a distraction, I pulled out a wad of the photographs. 'Is this you?' I gasped at the image of a stunning, raven-haired woman alluringly blowing a kiss at the camera. Clearly it was as there were several photos of the woman with Jack, their arms around each other. 'Wow, Selina, you were beautiful ... well, obviously, you still are.'

She smiled sadly. 'Thank you but I know the years haven't been kind to me. The grief of losing a child has taken its toll. But I don't care about that. I would happily die tomorrow if I knew I'd found my daughter.'

I continued to rifle through the pictures, at a loss for something to say. Suddenly, my fingers stilled and I took a shocked breath.

'Anna, what's wrong?' Selina's voice, sharp with concern, jolted me out of my stupor. 'You look like you've seen a ghost.'

With a trembling hand, I drew the photo closer. I must be mistaken. This couldn't be happening. I blinked hard but the image remained the same – a small, dark-haired boy grinning triumphantly, his thin arm aloft, his fist clenched. It was the boy of whom I'd dreamt throughout my childhood.

CHAPTER 22

Anna

My head was in turmoil as I drove to my parent's house that evening. I was early but I wanted to take a look through the photo albums documenting my early childhood. I was sure, somewhere in those old photographs, I would find conclusive proof that I was not Maisie Matthews. I knew it was a coincidence that Selina's son resembled the boy in my dreams. The photo changed nothing. I had a birth certificate which proved who I was. It had shaken me though, leaving a tiny seed of doubt, like a speck of dust in my eye, rubbing against my conviction. I needed to find something, some evidence to eradicate it completely.

Selina had noticed my distraction over the photo but I'd managed to fob her off. The last thing I wanted to do was to give her something tangible she could use as evidence. As she left, a tragic figure stooped with disappointment, I'd promised to stay in touch. It was the least I could do. Deep in thought, I almost missed the black Range Rover parked at the end of my road. The sight of it ripped my already-frayed nerves and I watched for it to pull out behind me. It didn't. *Breathe, Anna.* It must belong to someone who lived locally. I had to cease imagining I was being followed. To distract myself from the rush of anxiety, I wondered exactly why I'd been summoned to my parents' home on a Monday. There would be a reason but nothing, apart from the stalker business, sprang to mind. I knew I would have to tell them Selina Matthews' story and that was not going to be easy. In fact, I was dreading it. I could predict their reactions. Mum would be icily annoyed and sharp-tongued; Dad would erupt with his usual explosive temper. I was bound to be in the crossfire, especially as I was already in bad books. My plan was to confess everything in the guise of asking for their advice. They liked to feel I was still dependent on them.

Both cars belonging to my parents were parked in front of their house but I still hoped I might be early enough to look through the photos. Mum looked up in surprise as I wandered into the kitchen.

'Anna, you're early!' It sounded like an accusation. She turned a cool cheek towards me and held up her flour-covered hands.

'I know, sorry.' I gave her a dutiful peck and peered into a saucepan simmering on the stove. 'Mm, smells great. What are you making?'

'Steak and kidney pie.' I received a frank, assessing glance. 'Well, it's lovely to see you. Why don't you help yourself to a drink? Your dad's in the shower; he won't be long.'

'I'm fine thanks. Do you mind if I go and have a rummage in the study? I've been looking for a copy of the Hanchester School year book – the one published in my last year at school. I can't find it at home so it must be here somewhere.'

'I wouldn't be surprised. The study is full of lots of your old school things. Help yourself. Dinner will be a while yet.'

I slipped out of the kitchen and over to the end of the hallway where Dad's study was situated. It was a place I'd always loved, nostalgic with scents of old leather and his distinctive, musky aftershave. A large, bay window overlooked the back garden and in front of that was an enormous, antique desk, tidy as always. Everything orderly and in its place – that was Dad. It was a large room with a giant, oak cabinet along one wall and I knelt down on the grey carpet in front of the left-hand cupboard. Swiftly, I pulled the door open and lifted out a pile of leather-bound photograph albums in various colours. This was what I was looking for. A quick flick through allowed me to put them in chronological order. Each album contained pictures of me as a child, mostly snapshots, some with my parents but mostly me engaged in various activities: pony riding, ice skating, swimming, gymnastics, ballet dancing, birthday parties, playing with other children, trampolining – the list was endless. It was like a catalogue of a perfect childhood.

I started with my baby album. It was a while since I'd looked at it but I knew what to expect. I had been born with thick, dark, wavy hair which had disappeared by the time I was four months old, leaving me chubby-faced and bald with bright, blue eyes. When my hair did return, it was blonde with cute curls which framed my face. I had been a pretty baby. The next two albums detailed my toddler phase. By seven months, I was crawling and I'd taken my first steps by the time I was one. There were lots of toys in the photos. I knew I'd been a privileged child. In the fourth album, I'd grown taller and slimmer and was pictured, smiling and happy, playing on a purpose-built, wooden castle in the garden. We'd lived in Hastings, I'd been told, before moving to London when I was three or four. I dug deep into my memory bank but couldn't remember playing on that castle. I'd been too young.

The opening pages of the next album detailed my first day at school. These were the first photos I actually remembered being taken. I had blonde plaits, a gap in my front teeth and was dressed in my school uniform, excited at the prospect of the day ahead. As an only child, I'd craved the companionship of other children and hadn't attended any nursery or playgroup. I'd looked forward to starting school with eager anticipation. Unfortunately, it was memorable for all the wrong reasons. Happily playing in the book corner, I'd ignored signs I needed the toilet until it was too late. When Mum had picked me up at the end of the day, she had been mortified. It had been drummed into me with unerring regularity after that – toilet every break time and no more wet knickers.

I frowned and turned back to the remaining albums. There seemed to be at least one album missing and, infuriatingly, that was the one I wanted to look at. At least one year, possibly two – when I was three and four – had not been documented at all. With a sinking heart, I swiftly flicked through them again. How annoying! I'd hoped I'd find something to prove beyond doubt that I wasn't Maisie somewhere in the albums.

'Looking back on the good, old days?' Dad's voice behind me made me jump, guilty in the knowledge that I wasn't doing what I'd said.

I forced a smile. 'Dad, you startled me, creeping up behind me like that!' I closed the albums and turned to face him. 'Yes. I came in here to look for my final school yearbook and got distracted. You haven't seen it, have you?'

'All your school stuff is in the middle cupboard, as I'm sure you're aware.' I looked up at him. Was that the hint of an accusation? But his face was impassive.

'Of course.' I started bundling the photo albums ready to put them away and then stopped. 'Dad, do you know if there are any albums anywhere else? It seems strange there are no pictures of me when I was about four. There are hundreds of all the other years.' I watched him carefully. An emotion flitted across his face, gone so swiftly I couldn't be sure what it was.

'No idea,' he responded nonchalantly. 'You'll have to ask your mother ... ah, wait a minute.' His brow furrowed as he thought. 'That would have been about the time we moved to London. It was a chaotic year, I can tell you that. I remember my camera broke too. You'll find it difficult to believe but, in those days, a phone was just a phone. You had to have a camera to take photographs. Yes.' His brow cleared and he gave me a genial smile. 'That would the reason. Now ...' He held his arms open. 'Aren't you going to give your old Dad a hug?'

I grinned and leapt to my feet. Even when he was cross with me – as he undoubtedly was for my neglect in reassuring him about my stalker – I didn't doubt his love.

'Now, finish what you're doing in here and come into the kitchen. Your mother and I want to know what's going on.'

I nodded obediently. It didn't take me long to locate the yearbook and put away the albums. When I entered the kitchen, Mum was sipping a glass of white wine and Dad was sifting through the mail.

'Right, come and sit down, young lady.' He pulled out a chair. 'Tell us about this stalker who's had us worried sick. We need to know *everything*.'

'I know.' I gave him my most contrite look. 'I'm sorry, I really am. I should have let you both know as soon as I found out who it was but ...' I sighed, 'it was complicated.' My apology was met with silence so I continued, admitting that my client, Selina Matthews, was the stalker.

'I *knew* this Girl Friday business was a bad idea,' Dad exclaimed vehemently. 'Have you told the police? Have they arrested this woman?'

'No.' I held up my hands. 'Like I told you, it's complicated.' I then told them the story of Maisie being snatched from a holiday resort in Spain. 'The poor woman has been searching for her ever since and well ... here's the thing ...' I hesitated before plunging on. 'She was following me because she had some crazy idea that I may be her. She thinks I could be Maisie.'

'That's ridiculous.' Mum spat the words, her face a mask of contempt. 'I hope you put her right on *that* score, Anna.'

'Of course, I did, Mum. I feel sorry for her but I told her she was mistaken. I knew you'd be really upset by this; that's why I didn't tell you straight away. It was a complete shock and I needed to process it myself first. That's also why I refused to do a DNA test – because I knew how upset you'd be.'

'A DNA test?' She stiffened, rigid with rage. 'The nerve of the woman! How dare she demand a DNA test! How dare she think she can just waltz in and try to claim *our* daughter!'

I looked across at Dad. He was strangely quiet. I'd expected him to erupt as he'd done so often in the past. Instead, he looked thoughtful, reasonable, like a man steering the moral high ground. 'The woman is clearly talking nonsense. Try not to upset yourself, darling.' His soothing tone was directed at Mum. 'Such a claim is so absurd that it's really not worth worrying about. Anna knows how ridiculous it all is.' His eyes narrowed with sudden suspicion. 'Unless that's why you were ferreting about in those photos? Good God, Anna, you're surely not tempted to believe this dreadful woman?'

'Daddy, of course not.' I squeezed his hand. 'I'm *your* daughter – end of story.' In my heart, I believed what I was saying; I just couldn't rid myself of the image of Selina's son. How could I explain that?

'What photos?' Mum snapped. 'I thought you said you were looking for a school yearbook. What's going on? Am I missing something here?'

'No, Mum. I just got distracted by my old baby albums, that's all.' I shifted uncomfortably as I felt her icy, blue eyes boring into me. She wasn't fooled. Her unerring ability to read my mind was like a guillotine cutting through paper.

'Is that the truth, Anna, or yet another lie? What were you doing exactly? And why the secrecy? Why were you looking through your baby albums, after telling me some rubbish about a school yearbook? What were you expecting to find?' Her voice had become high-pitched, the jarring squeal of a violin.

'I was just ...' I tried to answer but she'd built up a head of steam.

'After all we've done for you ...'

'Mum, please,' I wailed. 'I was looking at the photos because ...' I faltered. How was I going to explain it without upsetting them further? I folded my arms across my chest. 'Look, I told Selina she was wrong. There was one tiny thing, though, which was a bit strange ...'

'What?'

'Well, it's silly really ...' I was reluctant to tell them. 'It was just something for which there was no logical explanation. There still isn't. I don't know what I was expecting to find in the photographs. It just seemed like a good idea to look through them again, you know, just to reassure myself.'

'So, you *did* have doubts,' Mum snarled. 'Well, there you go; maybe you should have a DNA test, after all.'

Dad's head turned sharply and he fixed Mum in his stare. The air throbbed with tension. I could feel the silent communication between them as a tangible thing.

'Look,' I said, 'I've already refused a DNA test. It's not necessary, honestly.'

'No, I insist. Obviously, you need some proof that we are your parents. Clearly, the twenty-six years of love and care we have given you isn't enough.'

I winced at Mum's sarcasm. I deserved it, I realised. How stupid was I to have been caught looking through those albums when I was about to disclose Selina's bombshell! Little wonder my parents were now staring at me with suspicion and, worse, disappointment.

'You say this woman wants you to have a DNA test?' Mum repeated. 'Well, I say, why not? It will prove you're not her daughter and put paid to any doubt.'

Dad sighed loudly, a long-suffering sound I'd heard many times before. 'I have to say I feel let down, Anna. Do you *really* have so little loyalty to us that you allow your birth to be questioned by a mad woman?' He gazed at me, eyes heavy with hurt. 'How could you do this to us?'

I spread my hands like a supplicant seeking forgiveness. 'Mum, Dad, I'm so sorry. I've handled this really badly but that was because I was trying to avoid upsetting you. The last thing in the world I wanted was to hurt you guys. You know how much I love you both. I'm really sorry.' My plea was heartfelt but, when I looked up, they remained stony-faced.

'Really, Anna?' Mum's voice, frosty with contempt, swept away my apology like a snow plough cutting through a drift. 'You lie to us; you try to deceive us; yet you say you love us? Well, forgive me if I find that a little difficult to believe right now.' She stood up to peer into the oven. 'Dinner's ready. Geoff, would you mind topping up my wine glass? I'm afraid I really need another drink now.'

My stomach was in knots. Somehow, I had to do something to put things right. *Tell them about the boy. You can't make things any worse.* As Mum placed a steaming plate of perfectly-cooked steak and kidney pie, laced with thick gravy, mashed potatoes and green beans in front of me, I rehearsed the words in my mind. Eventually, though, it was Dad who broke the silence.

'Anna, you said earlier there was something which bothered you. A tiny thing, I think you described it. What was it?'

There was my opening. I lay down my cutlery and took a deep breath. 'Selina showed me pictures of her daughter, Maisie, as a baby and a toddler. I think she was hoping they might spark some memory of mine. Of course, they didn't,' I continued quickly at Mum's snort of derision. 'How could they?' I smiled tentatively. 'Obviously, they weren't pictures of me. To be polite, I looked through other photos she had from that time – the time when Maisie was abducted – and there was something a bit strange.'

My parents had both stopped eating and were staring at me intently.

'Do you remember, when I was little, I sometimes used to have dreams about a boy? It was always the same dream – this boy on the beach, teasing me, holding something in his hand and not letting me see what it was.'

'I don't remember. It was a long time ago,' Mum frowned, her tone dismissive.

However, Dad nodded slowly. 'It used to wake you up. You weren't very old. I remember it used to upset you and I used to give you a cuddle – tell you it was just a dream.' He smiled briefly. 'I couldn't bear you being upset. They didn't last very long, though. Certainly, by the time you went to school, you weren't having any more nightmares.'

'That's true, but I still dreamt about this boy – not all the time and the dreams became less frequent as I grew older. Anyway, to cut a long story short, the same boy – or one who looks very much like him – cropped up in Selina's photo album. He's her son.' A strained silence followed, charged with unspoken words. I swallowed, trying to shift the lump in my throat. I had to say something else to relieve the tension holding all three of us in its thrall and found myself spinning a white lie.

'I was thinking maybe he was someone I'd met before … when I was too young to remember it. I just wondered if perhaps you guys had met Selina and her husband all those years ago. I know it's a long shot but I thought there might be a photograph of that same boy in one of the albums. The whole thing just struck me as weird, that's all, and I was looking for an explanation.'

The lie weighed on my heart. As a child, I'd thumbed those albums countless times looking for the boy. I knew there were no photos of him or the rest of the Matthews family but I needed to set their minds at rest.

'I suppose it's possible.' Dad's shoulders relaxed and he nodded. 'I can see why you were spooked … but Anna, I really think the explanation is a lot simpler than that. This boy just happens to *resemble* someone you used to dream about. The mind can play funny tricks on you with things like that.' He shrugged. 'I suppose we might have met this family at some point … but it's hardly very likely. To me, it sounds like your mind is trying to rationalise something you've never been able to explain. If we start from the premise that you're our daughter, which we know you are, then nothing else matters. I think you can forget about the whole thing. I wish you would.'

I nodded, thankful that he was being so reasonable. 'You're right Dad, as usual.'

'Naturally.' His face assumed its habitual complacency. 'Now we've got that out of the way, let's eat this delicious food.' He picked up his cutlery and attacked his plate with relish.

'Is that the end of it?' Mum remained unmoved. 'Will you have nothing more to do with this woman, Anna?'

I hesitated. Could I be that cruel to Selina – refuse the DNA test and all further contact? It seemed so heartless. It would be tough to cut all ties. I remembered my promise to help her with her search. However, I'd hurt my parents and was reluctant to cause any further distress. Perhaps the simplest thing was to take the DNA test after all. Then a line could be drawn under the whole affair. 'Well, obviously, if that's what you want ...' I began.

'I can feel a *but* coming,' Dad interjected, chewing his food. 'Let's have it, Anna and stop shilly-shallying. What's the problem?'

'It's just that, maybe, I think the right thing to do would be to take the DNA test, as Mum suggested. Not for me,' I continued hurriedly, in case they mistook my intention, 'but for her ... Selina. For whatever reason, she's convinced I'm Maisie and *she* needs proof that I'm not. Then she can move on. Otherwise, I'm worried she'll continue to try to come between us. She's not going to let it go; I know that much about her.'

Silence descended once more as they considered my words. I could feel the unspoken communication transmitting between Mum's cool, blue eyes and Dad's hooded, brown ones. There had always been moments like this with the three of us, moments when whole conversations took place silently over my head. Although they'd never been a loving couple, they'd always presented a united front in a crisis.

Eventually, Dad spoke. 'I hate to say it but I think you're probably right, Anna,' he said solemnly. 'A DNA test may be the only way to convince this woman of her stupidity. Don't get me wrong ...' He held up a hand to stop Mum from interrupting. 'I don't like it. I think the whole thing is an abominable intrusion into our family. I can't bear the thought of this woman trying to worm her way, falsely, into your affections but she does need to be stopped and this would be a cast-iron way of doing it.'

Mum nodded, grim-faced. 'I agree. I don't care a jot for this dreadful woman but if you want to subject yourself to this DNA test, Anna, I say go ahead. Otherwise, this thing could just drag on and on. It needs nipping in the bud and this is the most effective way.'

Surprised by this turn of events, I beamed at them both. 'I love you guys. You're so cool.' The cloud of uncertainty fogging my brain had miraculously cleared with their decision. Obviously, there was no conspiracy twenty-three years ago; there was no pretence. I *was* Anna Blake; Selina was mistaken. It wasn't until this point that I actually allowed myself to frame the thoughts lurking like imposters in my head. How could I have ever doubted it?

CHAPTER 23

Selina
May, 2019

A veil of despondency clung to me like a spider's web, impossible to shake off. The visit to Anna's house had not gone to plan. I'd been so sure the photos would jog her memory but she remained unconvinced. There *had* been a moment – an infinitesimal flicker of something when she'd seen the picture of Harry – I was sure of it. Harry would have been seven years old. The picture had been taken on Hunstanton beach the year before Maisie's disappearance. Had there been a spark of recognition? Difficult to tell and Anna hadn't admitted it. Certainly, her face had paled and there had been a sharp intake of breath, quickly masked. Whatever it was, it hadn't been enough to persuade her to take a DNA test and I was at a loss as to what to try next. I knew Anna was Maisie – she had to be – but how could I prove it?

The evening sky was gloomy and it felt cooler than previously. I sat on the sofa staring unseeingly at the television. The film on Netflix hadn't grabbed my interest. Instead, I found myself lost in the past – memories good and bad. My own earliest memory had been when I was only two years old and in my grandparents' garden. I knew this because I had a photo of it, found in my mum's things when she died. The grass was long and the garden overgrown, like a jungle. My baby sister Lucinda had managed to crawl into an old, tin bath lying outside and was rocking it to and fro like a boat. With her dark curls peeking out from under her sunhat, she looked adorable; all the adults fussed and marvelled at her loveliness. I watched from the side-lines as someone fetched a camera and photographs were taken. Even now, all these years later, I remember how jealous I was of the attention bestowed on my sibling while I was ignored. There was indignation too. Earlier, I'd sat in that very bath – probably that's what gave Lucinda the idea in the first place. No-one had cooed at me. I remembered climbing back into the bath when Lucinda crawled out and calling for *my* picture to be taken but the camera had been put away and no-one was interested. Seeing the photo of Lucinda always prompted that memory. Would I have remembered the incident without it? I didn't know.

Maisie was three when she was taken. She would have grown up with no photos to spark early memories. Perhaps that was why Anna didn't remember anything.

It was past nine o'clock when my phone rang and I snatched it up, fearing the worst. Late night phone calls were always a worry. *Harry? What's happened?* But the caller ID showed Anna's name and my anxiety evaporated. Puzzled, I accepted the call.

'Hello, Anna?'

'Selina, I'm sorry to ring so late but I've just got back from Swaffham ... from seeing my parents ...' There was a pause. Her words filled me with fresh concern. What was she going to say? I remained silent. There was a muffled noise and then nothing. 'Anna, are you still there?' I asked.

'Sorry ... I just knocked some papers on the floor and I was picking them up.' Her voice sounded cheerful and I felt my shoulders relax. 'Selina, I have some good news for you. They're happy for me to take the DNA test.'

I wasn't expecting that! My pulse leapt with a rush of excitement and relief. 'Really? Oh, thank you so much, Anna. I'm ... well ... I'm overwhelmed.'

'Just don't get your hopes up too much, please Selina. When I talked to my parents, *they* suggested I take the test. You realise what this means? They *know* a test will prove I'm not the daughter you're looking for. I'm so sorry.'

I let the words sink in and settle, feeling my unfettered joy ebbing away. 'Oh, I see.'

'It won't mean your search is over, Selina. I meant what I said. I'll help in whatever way I can. Try not to be too disappointed. At least the DNA test will give you proof and then you can move on.' Her voice was full of sympathy and I felt warmed by her compassion.

'Thank you. I'll get something sorted as soon as possible and I'll be in touch. Goodnight, Anna.'

I ended the call and slumped back against a cushion, awash with a jumble of emotions. My initial elation had been overlaid by doubt and confusion. I'd been *so* certain Anna was my daughter – I still believed it, despite what the Blakes had said – but my conviction was shaken. Perhaps I *was* a silly, deluded, middle-aged woman, stubbornly persisting in a hopeless search, letting the tragedy blight my remaining years. That's what Jack said. It was the reason we split up in the end. He wanted to move on and I couldn't.

By ten o'clock, I'd given up on the film and gone to bed. I preferred books to films anyway and was currently engrossed in *A Week in Paris* by Rachel Hore. The drama unfolding on the pages proved a welcome distraction and I read for an hour before my eyelids began to droop. I lay back against the pillows and switched off the bedside lamp. Despite feeling tired, it took a while before I finally succumbed to sleep. My mind drifted, lulled by the sounds of the night, trying to invent possible reasons for the Blakes' decision other than the obvious ...

*****

Someone was coughing. I awoke with a start, immediately aware something was wrong. The room was dense with something thick and pungent, filling my nostrils, making it difficult to breathe. *Smoke!* I succumbed to another bout of coughing – wheezing, rasping, scratching for clean air. *Fire.* The realisation brought shock and horror. I pushed back the covers and stumbled from the bed. *Need air.* Lurching through the fog, I fumbled the latch on the window and leant out, sucking in greedily. It brought on another fit of coughing but I no longer felt I was suffocating. *Phone for help.* I had to find my phone. Where was it? Crazed with fear and panic, I cast wildly about the room, searching. Had I left it downstairs? The bedroom door was open and there was light coming from the stairs. *Escape.* I was aware of a dreadful noise coming from the landing, a roaring, crackling, spitting conflagration of sounds. As I moved closer, I could feel the heat, intense and searing, burning my throat. *Think.* I tried to remember facts about fires, anything useful. *A wet towel. That was it. Bathroom.* I reached the doorway and stopped, horrified. The stairs were on fire. Flames leapt and surged along the bannisters. There was no way I could get down there to safety, even with a wet towel. Fascinated, I stared, entranced by the hypnotic rhythm of the fire. Tongues of orange, yellow and blue were dancing dangerously closer. Smoke flooded my lungs and, eyes streaming, I blundered back to the window. *More air.* My gasps were painful now. I had to get help. *Siren.* I leant further out of the window. It *was* a siren. 'Please,' I prayed. 'Let it be for me.' The sound was growing louder. Then, abruptly, it stopped. Was it outside the house? My bedroom window faced the rear of the house so I had no way of knowing.

'Help!' My voice came out as a croak. 'Help!' I tried again but I couldn't seem to make my voice work properly. I needed my phone. I had to let them know I was here, before it was too late. Another breath of air and I checked my bedside table once more. It wasn't there. *Think. It must be here somewhere.* Hysteria was taking over, making coherent thought impossible. *Voices.* I could hear shouts outside. Wildly, I threw myself towards the window and waved. 'I'm here!' I rasped. 'Here!' I stumbled over something on the floor. Reaching down, I clawed at the carpet. My fingers brushed against something smooth and hard. *My phone.* I pressed the home button and the screen lit up. It was 3:14 am.

'We'll get you down. Just a few more minutes. Try not to worry.' There was a voice calling up towards the window, a man's voice, calm and confident. 'We know you're in there. Just another minute or so. You're going to be OK.' *Oh, thank God.* I leant helplessly against the wall, gasping painfully for air, weak with relief. They were going to get me out.

Mere seconds later, a helmeted head appeared at the window. The man's face was barely visible through his visor but I could see his eyes. *Kind eyes.* 'What's your name, love?' he soothed.

'Selina.' My voice was just a whisper but he nodded.

'Hold on, Selina. We're going to get you out. Now, is there a chair or something you can use to stand on?' *A stool, by the dressing table.* I nodded. 'Can you get to it? Bring it over here?' I did as he'd instructed and pushed it up against the wall by the window. 'Now, hold on to the sill and stand up on the stool. Take it easy. Good.' He was so calm and reassuring I obeyed him without question. This man could save me, *would* save me. 'You're doing brilliantly, Selina. Well done. Now I want you to stand up on the ledge. I've got you. You won't fall.' Somehow, one move at a time, I found myself, barefoot, in my old, cotton nightie, standing on the ladder in front of him, his arms tightly around me.

'Right, I'm going to walk you down. I'm right here with you.' His voice was a comforting rumble in my ear, something safe amongst all that was surreal. 'Descending!' he called down to the darkness below.

Step by step, rung by rung, he helped me down. I could feel my whole body shaking but the warm tones of his voice gave me the confidence to do as he said.

'Thank you,' I whispered as we reached the ground.

'No problem. This is Selina,' he said as other faces crowded around. I looked up, unwilling to lose my connection to the man who'd saved me, but he'd disappeared, leaving me in the care of an ambulance crew.

'Here, let me take that from you.' Fingers prised at my clenched fist and I realised I was still clutching my phone. 'We'll keep it safe, don't you worry.' A blanket was thrown around my shoulders and I was helped into the back of an ambulance. Friendly faces smiled reassuringly. 'We're just going to examine you, Selina,' said a young woman with short, dark hair. 'Just relax. You're going to be fine.'

I lay back exhausted and gave my body up to their ministrations. My befuddled brain was still trying to comprehend the night's events. *A fire. How had it happened?* I became aware the woman was talking to me once more. 'We're going to take you to hospital, Selina. You've inhaled a lot of smoke and fumes so we're going to get you checked out properly. You just take it easy.'

I nodded and closed my eyes. Sleep ... I needed to sleep. Then, maybe, this whole nightmare would disappear.

CHAPTER 24

Anna

Ellie was standing by the worktop, dressed in a pale, green shirt and a pair of black trousers which looked slightly incongruous with her Minnie Mouse slippers.

'Morning Anna. Cup of tea?'

'Thanks but I'll get it. I don't want to make you late for your hot date with Mr Pearson,' I teased.

'Ugh!' Graham Pearson was the sour-faced dentist for whom Ellie worked. 'I would never be *that* desperate! I'm glad you're up. Yesterday I saw Emily Botti in Dereham. Do you remember her? She was part of the crowd I used to hang out with a few years back when I was going out with Kieran Byers.'

I shook my head. 'The name sounds familiar but I can't place her.'

'You'd know her if you saw her. Anyway, the two of us are going to the cinema in Norwich tonight. We're going to see *A Star is Born*. Do you fancy tagging along? Emily won't mind.'

'Can I let you know?' I had still heard nothing from Josh but was holding out the forlorn hope he would want to see me. How sad was I!

'No worries.' Ellie blew me a kiss, grabbed her brown, leather tote bag and sped through the door. 'You look after yourself,' she called as she pulled on her sensible, black work shoes. 'Don't work too hard!'

'You too!'

The house seemed empty and eerily silent when she'd gone. Feeling a little uneasy, I turned on the radio for company and relocked the front door. Prickles of fear were niggling once more. *Get a grip, Anna!* From behind the curtain in the living room, I scanned the neighbourhood but saw nothing untoward. To be sure, I went back upstairs and inspected the view from all the bedroom windows. In the distance, a John Deere tractor was pulling a fertiliser spreader across a field of crops. Two doors down, old Mr Brownlow was already busy in his garden. *No-one's there; no-one's watching you.*

I wasn't hungry so took a mug of tea over to my desk. Writing would help shake these irrational anxieties. Distraction – that's what I needed. I switched on my laptop and groaned as I saw it was performing updates. While I waited, I picked up my phone. A message from Josh. My heart began a frenzied dance in my chest.

Hi Anna. Just checking you're OK for this pm? There are doors which need waxing. J

I reread the text and snorted. It couldn't be more impersonal. I replied in kind.

Fine. A

Damn him! After Sunday evening, I'd been weaving romantic fantasies but, clearly, he hadn't been doing the same! *Back to work, Anna. Move on.*

The updates had finished and my fingers hovered over the keyboard as I read the last section of my novel, written on Friday.

It had seemed like a good idea that sunny April morning to take baby Freya into the city for a spot of retail therapy. Two hours later, red-faced and flustered, Jemima sat desperately trying to console her screaming child in the Mother and Baby Room of John Lewis. 'How do other mums do it?' she wondered when, a slim, dark-haired woman dressed in figure-hugging jeans and a cream jacket calmly fed her own angelic, little darling. She watched, in awe, as she wrestled with her squalling infant who steadfastly refused to latch on to the decimated nipple of her right breast. No-one told you breast feeding was painful. No – painful was the wrong word; it was excruciating! When she tentatively mentioned this to the midwife who had visited in her first week of parenthood, she'd been assured it would get better and she just needed to persevere. Well, she had and it hadn't. Three weeks later and she still winced with pain every time. It didn't help that Freya seemed to require feeding so frequently. 'At this rate,' Jemima had wailed to Conrad, 'my boobs will be round my ankles by Christmas!'

He had been calmly reassuring and supportive – of course he had – but he didn't know what motherhood was really like. He was now back at work, blissfully unaware of the shambolic way his wife was coping with his daughter. It had been his idea to go shopping.

'It'll do you good to get out of the house,' he'd smiled encouragingly. 'You'll probably find Freya will settle better when she's out and about in all the noise and bustle of the city. And buy yourself something gorgeous,' he'd added. 'You deserve it.'

Stupidly, she'd taken his advice. In fact, she'd looked forward to it. She'd dressed Freya in a gorgeous, little, lemon dress made of super-soft, organic cotton. Then she'd packed her baby bag. That was another thing no-one told you – just how much stuff you needed to cart around with a baby. Pre-birth, she'd imagined herself drawing admiring glances as she wheeled her beautiful baby through the streets in her brand new, expensive Egg travel system. She hadn't envisaged all the other things she would need to hang on it as well: nappies, changing mat, wipes, spare clothes, pacifiers – not to mention all the extra, emergency intimate items she seemed to have acquired for herself – all jammed into a cavernous baby bag. By the time she picked Freya up from her crib, she was already running late. Then Freya was promptly sick, all over her best dress. It had been eleven o'clock by the time they made it out to the car.

I frowned. Was I overdoing it? Not according to my old school pal, Penny Johns, a mum of three children and my source of information on modern day motherhood.

'The first few months after Milo was born were absolute hell,' Penny had bellowed cheerfully down the phone in her broad Yorkshire accent.

'It can't have been *that* bad. You had two more!'

'Complete accidents,' she laughed. 'No, I'm joking. Yes, things did settle down and eventually I managed to get into some sort of routine but, oh goodness, I'd never want to go through that again. It was worse than the actual birth! Milo wouldn't sleep at all at night; I was totally exhausted and continually feeding. When I think back, it was a miracle we all survived!'

She then recounted some of the incidents she particularly remembered, one of which I planned to use next.

Jemima's stomach growled. If only she could get Freya off to sleep, she could grab a coffee and a sandwich somewhere … and maybe even do some actual shopping.

'Rock-a-by-baby,' she crooned and miraculously, Freya's head began to droop. Her eyes closed …

At that moment, the door crashed open and a young boy appeared, brandishing a toy sword with which he attacked the unoccupied furniture in the room. 'Take that! Hah!'

Freya's eyes shot open and her rosebud mouth, so perfect in repose, emitted a hearty wail.

'Oh, sorry. George, stop that! Can't you see the lady's trying to get her baby to sleep?' A harassed-looking woman pushing a buggy clattered in behind the boy. Meanwhile, George continued to put a comfy chair to the sword. 'I'm really sorry.' The woman gave Jemima an apologetic look but made no further attempts to stop her son.

'Don't worry, I was just leaving anyway,' Jemima lied as, just in time, she managed to whisk Freya's head out of reach of the flashing weapon. Awkwardly, she balanced her over her left shoulder, held the door open with her left hip and managed to drag her bag-laden buggy through with her right hand. Now standing by a row of televisions, she began the rocking process once more, this time without the singing. Her voice wasn't up to the standard of a public performance. 'Come on Freya, off to sleep,' she muttered. She was desperate for a wee. By now, shopping on her own with a small child seemed a very bad idea.

At last, Freya closed her eyes and Jemima gently lowered her into the buggy. However, by the time she reached the toilet, Freya was making ominous noises and Jemima had to perform her ablutions one-handed whilst also rocking the buggy. The strategy worked and, heading towards Costa, up the busy street and across the road, she heaved a sigh of relief. The sun was shining and she found herself relaxing, enjoying the admiring glances coming her way as she steered her way through the pedestrians. Yes – heads were definitely starting to turn. She favoured the onlookers with a confident smile; she was bossing this parenting! People were actually stopping in the street. She turned her head to see some of them were pointing, huge grins on their faces. One older woman was waving frantically at her; Jemima waved back. The woman continued to wave and marched purposefully towards her, pointing emphatically. Jemima stopped to wait, still rocking the pushchair. She'd better see what she wanted.

'Hey,' the woman wheezed as she got within speaking distance. 'You've got your dress stuck in your knickers. We can see your arse!'

When Penny recounted this incident, I exploded with laughter. 'It was months before I ventured out shopping again on my own with Milo,' she said. 'The whole experience was so traumatic. Thank goodness I didn't see anyone I knew.'

I was still smiling to myself when my phone rang. It was Ewan. 'Hello gorgeous,' he said breezily. 'How do you fancy being whisked away for a spot of lunch?'

'I'd love to but I can't. I've got a job this afternoon so there won't be time.' I glanced at my watch. 'If you're free now, we could meet for a coffee.' Indulging in a little of Ewan's charm and flattery would be a tonic for my bruised ego.

After a brief hesitation, he agreed. 'I'm out your way as it happens. I could be at yours in about fifteen minutes.'

'Great. I'll see you then.'

By the time Ewan rang the doorbell, the kettle had boiled and coffee was brewing in a cafetière. Ewan, immaculate in shirt and tie, leaned in to brush his lips against my cheek.

'Hi friend. Coffee smells good.' He stepped into the hallway.

'Through here. You know the way,' I said, my first reference to our past relationship. I felt comfortable with him. It was good to have a male friend who sought my company without any ulterior motive. 'How are things with you?'

'Good thanks. I don't deserve to be doing well but I am. Business is going great – thanks to your dad.'

'Don't be daft. It's down to your hard work, I'm sure. I'm really glad things are working out for you.' There was an awkward pause and he toyed with his coffee mug. 'Was there something particular you wanted to see me about Ewan?' I asked, giving him an encouraging smile.

'Well yes, actually.' He grimaced. 'It's a bit tricky but I think it's something you should know.'

'Yes?'

Again, he hesitated. 'There is some client confidentiality involved ...'

'Curiouser and curiouser,' I said to prompt him further.

'Well, in my work, it has come to my attention that you are in contact with someone called Selina Matthews. Has she at any point made any claims to you or about you?'

I stiffened. What was going on? What was Selina Matthews to Ewan Jacobs? 'Why do you ask?' I said, trying to read his expression.

'In my work for a client, I've found out that on at least five separate occasions, complaints about her have been filed with the police. You may or may not know that twenty-three years ago, her three-year-old daughter was snatched from a holiday resort and never found.' I nodded. 'Over the intervening years, she's made something of a habit of claiming that different children are actually her missing daughter. She's caused a lot of upset with a number of families. To my knowledge, she has a restraining order against her to stop her harassing one particular family. You would be the right age and have the right colouring. It's possible you could be her next target.'

I stared at him. 'How do you know all this?' I demanded. 'Did my Dad put you up to this?' The revelations about Selina were not a surprise. She'd hinted at them herself. More puzzling was the fact Ewan knew that I'd been doing some work for her.

He returned my stare, his eyes full of apology. 'I'm sorry, Anna, but I can't say. I can only tell you I've been working on this case for some while. The woman is a menace. I don't think she poses any actual danger but she does seem to make a habit of stalking people. Your dad *did* mention you were worried about a stalker and then your car was seen outside her property in Swaffham. I put two and two together.'

'Have you been following me, Ewan?' I asked, my eyes narrowing in suspicion.

'No, of course not. Why on earth would I?' He lowered his gaze.

'I don't know.' My shoulders sagged. 'Sorry, I guess I'm not making much sense. This is just all a bit of a shock ...' I sighed. His brown eyes were earnest with concern for me and I decided to trust him. He listened, his face serious, as I told him about the blue Peugeot, my discovery that Selina was the person following me and her claim that I was Maisie.

'I knew it! The damn woman is a serial menace. Do you want me to accompany you to the Police Station and file a complaint? That appears to be the best way of stopping her. She's always backed off when threatened with court action.'

I shook my head. 'No. At the moment, I don't know what to think.' I told him about the discussion I'd had with my parents and their agreement to a DNA test.

He raised his eyebrows. 'Really? That's incredibly tolerant and understanding of them. Maybe, they don't know her history. Perhaps you should tell them.'

'Maybe.' I decided to change the subject. 'The reason I asked if you'd been following me is because I still sometimes feel someone is watching me. It sounds daft, I know ...'

He frowned. 'Have you seen anyone?'

'Not as such ... There was this guy, stocky with grey hair, who I've now seen a number of times in the past few weeks but, oh I don't know, it's probably nothing. It might not even be the same guy all the time. Often it's just glimpses ... a feeling ...' I shook my head ruefully. 'You probably think I'm crazy.'

'Not at all.' He grabbed my hand and squeezed it hard. 'Next time, if you see this man, give me a call. I'll drop everything and come straight over. Promise me?'

'OK, thanks.' I smiled. It was nice of him to take my fears seriously.

'It is probably nothing,' he continued. 'You were stalked by Selina Matthews and that experience is going to impact on you for a while. It's only natural to feel spooked.' He stood up. 'I'd best be going.' As he hugged me, he murmured, 'You take care of yourself and make sure you call me if you're bothered or worried about anything, anything at all.'

'I will.'

After he'd gone, I thought about what he'd told me. Did it affect how I felt about things? Not really. It was easy to imagine a younger Selina, desperate for her daughter, single-minded in her efforts to locate her. I would be the same. I wouldn't let anyone or anything stand in my way if I thought I might have found my missing daughter. Yes, the stuff about the police restraining order was concerning but, in my heart, I didn't feel Selina posed a threat.

Could I rely on my instincts though? That was a more difficult question. They'd often let me down. How many times had Dad told me I was too trusting? 'Knowledge is power,' he would say when, cheeks streaked with tears, I told him of a friend's betrayal. 'Don't give people information about yourself. They will invariably use it against you.' As a child and then a teenager, my parents' seal of approval was my guide. If they said someone was OK, I then felt relaxed in their company. All my friends had been subjected to the Geoff and Mariella test – boyfriends too. They took it upon themselves to point out the flaws I'd overlooked and the few times I'd chosen to ignore their advice, I'd come a cropper.

However, things changed when I hit my twenties. I became protective of my independence, determined to make my own decisions. Yes, there were mistakes but I realised it was empowering to stand on my own two feet. I remained consultative and cautious, valuing my friends' opinions, but no longer relied on Mum and Dad to tell me what to do, much to their mortification. Dad still expected me to come running when I had a problem but I'd grown up. I didn't always want his opinion. That's why I'd been so reluctant to tell him about my stalker. I didn't want him thinking I needed his help. I had little enough confidence in my judgement as it was. As for Selina Matthews – did I trust her? I wanted to. I would give her the benefit of the doubt and carry on with the plan to take the DNA test. In my heart, I wanted certainty as much as she did.

A text from Ewan interrupted my thoughts.

Thanks for the coffee. Remember to call anytime if you need a friend.

I smiled. How kind and dependable he had become. The knowledge that he was looking out for me made my insides turn squidgy like an under-baked macaroon. He'd turned into the sort of man I *should* be falling for, not someone like Josh Fielding who was all over me one minute but couldn't be bothered with me the next. Maybe I should give Ewan a second chance …

***

The sky was moody with heavy clouds and the air felt warm and oppressive as I walked briskly through Lewton to the Old Rectory. Out in the open, I still felt strangely unsettled and the knots in my stomach had tightened as I stepped through the front door. Despite seeing nothing untoward, I was unable to relax as I scurried towards Josh's house. Some of my twitchiness was because of Josh himself. I'd dressed with care, eschewing the shapeless overalls for some worn, figure-hugging jeans; my make-up was painstakingly understated; I felt confident my appearance was OK without looking like I was trying too hard; I'd given myself a pep talk about maintaining a cool professionalism; I was ready.

Except I wasn't ready – at least, not ready for the sight of him as I turned up the drive. He was standing on a ladder, sanding the frame of an upstairs window. His top had been removed and a sheen of sweat glistened on his well-muscled, tanned back. Oh Lordy. My pulse soared into overdrive. 'Don't look,' I told myself sternly as I sauntered towards the house with as much nonchalance as I could muster but it was impossible to tear my eyes away. With hindsight, that was a mistake. At the very moment he turned his head and saw me, I was looking up and did not notice the obstruction in my path.

'Watch out!' he called.

I was too busy giving him a careless wave for his words to register fully. The first I knew of the ladder lying on the drive was when it sent me sprawling into the gravel. Although I lessened the impact of the fall with my right arm, I managed to end up with my face in the stones and my bottom in the air.

'Anna, are you OK?' He must have sprinted down his ladder and across to me because he was there before I'd managed to recover the situation with any amount of decorum.

'Fine,' I mumbled, brushing away the grit stuck to my face. 'I don't know how I managed that. I'm such a clutz.'

'As long as you're alright.' Solicitously, he helped me to my feet. Probably worried I'd sue him, I thought uncharitably, irritable at having made a fool of myself yet again. 'Let's get you indoors and check the damage. Those scrapes on your right arm could use a wash ... and on your face. Can you walk?'

I nodded but he kept an arm around my waist as I hobbled painfully into the kitchen and sank onto a stool. 'Damn, that hurt. Another episode to use in my book though. That's why I do these things really, you know – research!'

He raised his eyebrows and grinned. 'Wow, that *is* dedication. Let me get you some water and you may wish to use the bathroom.'

I nodded. It was quite difficult to breathe normally with his naked chest in such close proximity. Whilst the sensible part of my brain hoped he'd put on some clothes, the rebellious bit was itching to stroke the exposed flesh. 'That's fine; I can manage,' I said quickly, sensible Anna going into overdrive as his supporting arm slid once more around my waist. Reluctantly, I shrugged out of his grasp.

'If you're sure.' He stepped back and watched me doubtfully. I felt sore all over but, thankfully, didn't appear to have done any serious damage. My pride had suffered yet another knockback but, with a few minutes respite from his distracting presence, I would soon have my cool, dignified persona back on track. It would be fine. I'd get on with waxing the doors; he'd go back outside and finish what he was doing and by the time we next had a conversation, we'd both have completely forgotten all about it. A plan always helped me to regain control of the situation. While I washed the dirt off my hands and attended to the scratches on my arm, I decided my accident was also his fault for leaving a ladder lying in the drive. Anyone could've tripped over it! While I added that misdemeanour to my list of grievances against Josh Fielding, I looked in the mirror ...

O.M.G! Aside from the dirt which was smeared in army camouflage splodges all over my face, I'd split my top lip and bruising was already starting to appear around my right eye. Even when I'd carefully washed off the mucky debris, it was still a right mess and looked as if a black eye was developing. 'Oh bollocks,' I exclaimed aloud.

'Are you alright in there?' Josh's voice came from outside the door. 'Do you need anything?'

'No but thank you.' I swung the door open and let him survey the damage. It was either that or make an escape out of the bathroom window and, given my track record, I was pretty sure that wouldn't go well.

'Oh dear,' he grimaced. 'That looks sore. You're probably going to have a black eye.'

'Probably,' I said cheerily, limping past him to the kitchen. 'Still, no real harm done.' A glass of iced water stood on the worktop by my stool and I sipped it gratefully, willing its coldness to have an effect on my burning cheeks. He was still topless and that really didn't help my embarrassment. *Cool and dignified* wasn't going well. 'My arms are both working fine so at least I'll be able to crack on with waxing those doors like you wanted,' I said, determined to regain a professional footing.

He shook his head. 'Don't be daft. I'm not letting you do that today.' I watched as he took a bag of frozen peas from the freezer and wrapped them in a clean tea towel. 'Here. Hold this against your eye. It'll help.'

'Thanks.' I did as he'd instructed. 'Honestly, I'm fine to get on with all the jobs you have lined up for me. I expect it's a long list. I know what a taskmaster you are.'

'Absolutely not. You've had a nasty fall and you need a little bit of TLC. A good, long soak in the bath would help too. I'll drive you home.' He hesitated, his brown eyes twinkling mischievously. 'Or I could run a bath for you here … then you'd have someone to scrub your back for you.'

'Ha, bloody, ha,' I responded, flushing hotly. 'Trust you to try to take advantage of a girl when she's down.'

'I wish …' He gave me a smoky-eyed look which turned my insides molten. 'Unfortunately, though, I'm too much of a gentleman. I'm going to drive you home and then, to make amends, I'm going to cook you dinner. It's the least I can do.'

'No honestly, I don't want any fuss,' I protested, my pulse skipping like a demented bunny.

'I insist. If you can just wait while I have a quick shower, I'll run you home. Do you want a tea or coffee or anything?'

'No, water's fine, thank you.' What could I say? My spirits had soared at his show of concern for my well-being.

'No worries. Won't be long.'

He disappeared, leaving me feeling slightly bemused. It felt nice to be cosseted and his concern was welcome attention after the curt text earlier. The idea of a long soak in a hot bath was also very appealing. While I waited, I clambered painfully off my stool and wandered around the kitchen. My excuse was that I needed to keep moving but the truth was I wanted to find out more about Josh. Apart from a used, empty mug standing by the sink, the room was immaculate. The gleaming units were devoid of anything personal. Our fridge at home was plastered with post-it reminders and messages between Ellie and me which never seemed to get removed. I suddenly realised he would be going into that very kitchen and tried to remember in what state I'd left it. Not as tidy as this one. I just hoped I'd stacked the dishwasher before I left. My bedroom, though, was a complete mess. I'd tried on and discarded a number of outfits before settling on my current attire. Definitely, I'd have to tidy those away before Josh could see … God, what was I thinking? As if there was going to be a scenario with Josh ending up in my bedroom – especially when I looked like I did!

'What are you thinking about?' Josh was standing in the doorway, fresh from the shower, ridiculously sexy with damp hair.

'Mmm, nothing much,' I lied. 'Just thinking how tidy your kitchen is.'

'Really?' Josh cocked a disbelieving eyebrow. 'The thought of a tidy kitchen brought out that little, secret smile you sometimes have? I have to say I'm disappointed. I thought maybe you were fantasising about me in the shower.'

I rolled my eyes, inwardly horrified he was so close to the truth. 'You wish,' I retorted. 'Look, honestly there's no need for you to go to any trouble. I'll be …'

'I want to,' he interrupted. 'No arguments.' He picked up his car keys. 'Would you like me to help you get to the car?'

It was so tempting to say yes and to feel his arm around me once more but sensible brain kicked in. 'No. I'm fine, really.'

'Well just try not to trip over anything else on the way,' he teased.

It took barely a few minutes to drive the short distance. Josh switched off the engine and leapt out of the car as I gathered up my bag. He opened the car door with a flourish and reached out a hand to help me out.

'Quite the gentleman!'

'I can be when I want.' His brown eyes glowed warmly and I swallowed hard. 'Now, can I leave you for a few hours to have that bath while I just run a few errands and pick up some groceries for our dinner?'

'Yes, thank you,' I replied, grateful I was going to have a decent amount of time to get tidied up and to camouflage the damage to my face.

He checked his watch. 'I'll be back by six, if not before. Try to stay out of trouble in the meantime.'

I grinned. 'I'll do my best but, knowing me, expect the worst!'

***

The bath and two paracetamol tablets helped alleviate the soreness and I was ready, jangly with anticipation, by 5:30 pm. White wine was chilling in the fridge, the table was set with cutlery, glasses and condiments and I was dressed in a simple, turquoise, jersey wrap-around dress and sandals. I'd tried my best to mask the damage to my face but still looked like someone who'd been dragged through a hedge. My top lip was now swollen, giving me a lopsided trout pout, and many frustrating minutes were spent trying to hide the worst of the bruising with concealer. I looked a mess but it couldn't be helped.

Josh's motives remained a mystery. He'd definitely seemed interested in me today, as he had on Sunday evening, but his phone silence, except for the work text, gave me pause. Was he just a flirt – a case of out of sight, out of mind? Maybe he wasn't a texting kind of guy. I sighed. There was no point in agonising over it all. *Stop worrying about what might happen and just enjoy it.* I'd never had a man cook for me before and the romance of it was very seductive. 'Que sera sera …' I warbled as I plumped cushions for the third time. My optimism about the evening ahead would not be dampened and I waited with growing excitement for Josh's arrival. Ellie was not coming home before picking up Emily Botti for their cinema trip to Norwich so we would have the house to ourselves. I debated getting out some scented candles but decided against it. I didn't want to give him the wrong idea.

At a few minutes after six, he arrived, brandishing two bags of groceries and a colourful bunch of tulips.

'For you.' He leaned in to kiss my cheek as he gave me the flowers. I detected the earthy tones of sandalwood and his cheek felt slightly rough as it brushed against mine. My skin tingled in response. 'I hope you're not feeling too sore.'

'I'm fine. Thank you so much. I'd better find a vase. Come in.' I felt flustered and awkward. 'The kitchen's this way.' He followed me through and emptied his bags as I fumbled through a cupboard searching for a vase. 'This really is very nice of you,' I smiled shyly, peering at his assembled ingredients.

'Fillet steak,' he said. 'I hope that's acceptable. And I'm afraid I cheated and bought a cheesecake for dessert. I can't confess to being an expert in the kitchen. Oh, and I managed to find a bottle of that wine you liked on Sunday.' He handed me a bottle and frowned. 'I'm afraid it's not chilled though. And there's a bottle of red, in case you'd prefer that with your steak.'

'That's so thoughtful.' I put the white wine in the fridge. 'What can I get you to drink? I'm afraid I don't have any beers in.'

'Just a coke if you have it. I'd best keep a clear head if I want to impress you with my food.'

Whilst I poured two glasses of coke, he busied himself chopping vegetables and assembling a salad. His movements were quick and assured. 'I really enjoyed our meal together on Sunday,' he said. 'Sorry I wasn't able to ring you yesterday. I was with my dad fishing all day and didn't have any phone signal.'

I smiled, my spirits soaring as I ticked off my concern about his lack of contact. 'I enjoyed it too. Did you catch anything?'

'Nope. The fishing was terrible. It's my dad's thing really. I just tag along to keep him company.'

'What do *you* like to do with your spare time?'

He shrugged. 'Over the past few years, I haven't had a lot of spare time to be honest. I was busy with work and then, living in London, there are always parties to go to, people to see. I guess I got caught up in the whole craziness of that kind of lifestyle. It's taken moving away and having a break for me to see it. I don't want to go back. I like life in Norfolk. Maybe I'll take up playing rugby again and cricket.' He paused as he tipped sliced potato into a frying pan. 'I read a lot too and it's been good to have the time for that. And I *have* ordered a novel by my favourite author.' He gave me a pointed look. 'Romantic comedy is not something I normally read so I'm looking forward to that.'

'Oh God. I won't be offended if it's not your thing.'

'I'm sure I'll love it. I enjoy cooking too and DIY, I've just found out. Practical stuff. All the things I wasn't doing in my old life.' I sipped my drink contentedly, watching him frying steaks in butter and then flipping them onto a warm plate to rest as he dressed the salad. 'It's almost ready if you'd like to take a seat. Have you decided which wine you'd like?'

'Red, I think, with the steak. Will you have some too?' I picked up the bottle.

'Let me do that.' He ushered me to a chair and poured two glasses of the rioja he had brought. 'Cheers.' As we clinked glasses, our eyes met, mirroring mutual appreciation. Flustered, I lowered my gaze and took a large swig. 'How's the wine?' he asked.

'Lovely,' I replied. In truth, I'd swallowed it without even thinking how it tasted. 'Delicious. Dinner looks great too.'

It was. During the meal, Josh laughed at my attempted witticisms and told entertaining stories about his family. I discovered he had an older sister, Marie (married with three young children), his mum was half Spanish and quite fiery and his dad was the only laidback member of the family. 'Marie and I tend to take after Mum,' he said, 'so there's a tendency for fireworks when we meet up. The last time I went around to their house, Marie actually threw a glass of water at me! Luckily, her husband Ben is pretty chilled and he usually acts as peacemaker.'

'What did *you* do to provoke the water?' I asked.

'*Me*? Nothing!' he retorted in mock innocence. At my look of disbelief, he added. 'Well, I *may* have said something which upset her.'

'Yes?' I prompted.

'But I was only joking. She has no sense of humour, my sister.' He paused, a smile teasing the corners of his mouth. 'I may have suggested she was a useless cook.' At my exclamation, he continued, 'She *did* forget to put eggs in the Yorkshires and completely cremated a piece of beef. In fairness, she *is* pretty terrible in the kitchen. Thankfully for the children, Ben does most of the cooking.'

'Josh, that's terrible,' I told him sternly.

'I know. It is pretty shocking that a top flight barrister like Marie can hardly boil an egg,' he agreed, deliberately misunderstanding.

'No – you know what I meant! You're very lucky to have a sister. I was an only child, which was pretty lonely growing up. I would have loved a big sister.' His brown eyes were warm with sympathy and I felt compelled to continue. 'It would have been nice to have someone with whom to share the burden of expectation. My parents are both high achievers,' I explained. 'And whilst I always knew they loved me, I was also aware I was a disappointment. Maybe if there'd been a brother or sister, there wouldn't have been the whole weight of their ambition focused on me.' I smiled ruefully. 'Sorry. I'm sounding like the archetypal poor, little, rich girl. I had a privileged, happy childhood but you know what they say, the grass is always greener …'

He nodded in agreement. 'Much as I moan about Marie, I wouldn't be without her. I'm a typical, protective, older brother.' His eyes crinkled in amusement and his smile broadened.

'What?' I asked. 'Have I got lettuce on my teeth?'

'No.' He leaned across the table and took my hands in his. I could feel my heart thudding in anticipation. 'You look so beautiful, even with your poor battered face. I feel I want to protect you too …' His voice grew husky. 'Amongst other things.' He stood up, pulling me gently to my feet. 'Right now, I just have to kiss you.'

My body seemed to have turned to liquid and I watched, fascinated, as his lips lowered hypnotically towards mine. They brushed my face gently and then, with infinite tenderness, rested against my swollen lips. I closed my eyes and leaned against his chest, my hands fluttering and then, tentatively, touching his arms. The kiss deepened. He slid his fingers into my hair, pulling me nearer, before wrapping me in his strong arms. I responded, urgently digging my nails into his biceps, hungry for him in a way I'd never felt before.

'I want to make love to you,' he whispered, pressing his lips into the side of my neck.

I nodded. 'Me too,' I murmured breathlessly.

***

Afterwards, we lay wrapped in each other's arms on my bed. My head was resting against his chest and I could feel the thump of his heartbeat and the deep, even rhythm of his breathing. I felt safe. The thought was startling. I barely knew him but he'd connected with the emotional core I normally kept so guarded. Without even realising it, I'd allowed this man to touch my soul. I lay perfectly still, not wanting the feeling to disappear.

At that moment, a phone rang. Selina probably. I'd been expecting her call all day. However, as I sat up, self-conscious in my nakedness, wondering where I'd left my phone, Josh reached an arm down to the floor and picked his up.

He frowned when he saw the screen. 'It's my mum. Sorry.' He threw me an apologetic glance and swung his legs off the bed. 'I'd better answer it.'

He walked out of the room, gloriously nude, while I scooted for modesty under the duvet. Within a few seconds he was back, his face set as he cast about for his clothes. 'My dad's collapsed, possibly a heart attack. They're waiting for an ambulance. I'm sorry, Anna, but I've got to go.'

'Oh no! Of course. I hope he's alright.'

He nodded grimly. 'I'll call you,' he said and, just like that, he was gone. I listened to the slam of the front door and the roar of the Mercedes as he sped away. Poor Josh. Fervently, I willed everything to be OK. When he was talking about his dad, it was obvious he thought the world of him.

Inevitably, my thoughts turned to the passion we'd shared just a few moments earlier. Cocooned in the duvet, I squeezed my eyes shut and wallowed in the delicious aftermath. Every pore of my body tingled from the magic of his touch. It had been simply perfect. This was what it was all about, I mused. At last I could identify with heroines of romantic fiction who succumbed helplessly to the all-consuming desire they felt for their heroes. Up until now, my experiences of sex had been disappointing and I'd wondered if my expectations were too ridiculously high. Now I hugged the duvet around me and savoured the spine-tingling bliss of it. It was real; it had happened.

***

Later, I returned downstairs and cleared away the remnants of our meal. Restlessly, I turned on the television while I waited for Josh's call and started watching a film which involved a lot of explosions and car chases. My phone lay mute beside me and I wondered anew why I hadn't heard from Selina. Her silence was strange after her delight at my decision to go ahead with the DNA test. When yet another commercial break interrupted the mindless flow of film action, I switched the TV off and went back upstairs to collect the book I was reading instead. It was an old Regency romance by Georgette Heyer with a particularly feisty heroine. I'd just settled back on the sofa and opened it when the phone rang. It was Josh.

'How is he?' I asked breathlessly.

'We're at the hospital and they're running some tests. It looks like it was a heart attack but they don't know yet how serious. At least he's conscious – cracking jokes and chatting up the nurses, can you believe? Mum is beside herself with worry. I'm sorry but I'm going to have to stay here, at least until I know he's out of the woods.' His voice sounded tired and my heart went out to him.

'I know.' I sought words of reassurance but could only think of clichés. 'He's in the best place. They'll sort him out.'

'I hope so. I'll phone you tomorrow. Night.'

'Night,' I repeated softly.

The lights of Ellie's car lit up the window as her car pulled into the drive.

'Anna!' she cried as she burst through the door. 'You're still up. Brilliant! I can tell you about this guy I met tonight.'

She was bubbling over with excitement and I smiled inwardly. How quickly she had recovered from her break-up with Dan! I hoped this new man would prove more reliable. 'That was fast work,' I grinned.

'I know,' she beamed. 'I can't believe it, Anna. When the film had finished, we decided to get something to eat and we ended up at Nando's. There were these two guys sitting at the table next to ours, you know how it is. We ended up sitting together. One of them seemed interested in Emily and, well, the best looking one seemed to like me. He has his own business and he wants to take me out for a drink tomorrow night, just the two of us.'

'That's great. I'm really pleased for you Ellie.'

'Thanks. Obvs it's early days but I've got a good vibe about this one. He lives in Swaffham so that's convenient – not far to travel to meet up with him.'

I nodded. 'Handy. So … what's his business? Does he work in Swaffham?'

'He offers a range of services but mostly painting and decorating. His name is Damien Davies …'

CHAPTER 25

Anna

Josh called early next morning to say his dad was doing well. 'It was a very mild heart attack, thank God. They're keeping him in today for observation but hopefully he'll be allowed home tomorrow.'

His voice triggered a bout of butterflies in my stomach. 'Thank goodness. You must be so relieved.'

'I am. Anna, I'm so sorry I had to leave you last night, especially just … well, you know.' He cleared his throat. 'Anyway, I'm hoping you'll let me make it up to you this evening? Obviously, I'll have to wait and see how dad is doing …'

He sounded unsure of himself which helped to alleviate my own insecurities. 'Yes please … as long as your dad is OK.'

'Great. I'll pick you up at five. As it's a lovely day, I was thinking of driving up to Wells for a picnic?'

'Sounds great. Can I bring anything?'

'Just your gorgeous self. See you later, all being well.' He hung up and I was left smiling at my phone. It was going to be a good day. He was right – the sun was already filtering through the wispy, early morning haze and a warm day had been forecast. A picnic would be perfect. All was right with the world.

I'd woken earlier with a sense of foreboding, a seeping niggle of worry, tickling and teasing the edges of my mind. Now I'd heard from Josh, though, I could relax. His dad was going to be fine and things were going well.

Except I couldn't relax completely. Ellie's announcement about Damien Davies last night had completely blindsided me. Over the last few days, I'd not given him a thought and had never expected to see him again. Was he genuinely interested in Ellie? He must be. The fact that Ellie was my housemate was a complete coincidence … just as it twas that he happened to be the person painting my parents' house.

Did I believe in two coincidences? Maybe but, given the fact I still felt I was being watched, I wasn't convinced. Time would tell. In the meantime, I would have to tell Ellie that Damien was the guy with whom I'd had the run-ins. Thinking back to the last incident, I realised I'd never mentioned his name to Ellie. Then, last night, I'd been too shocked and my thoughts too disordered to do anything other than mumble a token interest and plead tiredness.

I switched on my laptop and reviewed my latest piece of writing. Things were going to get even trickier for Jemima when husband Conrad announced he was going to be away in Dubai for the next week meeting some prospective clients for a new development. That was bad enough – abandoning Jemima when she was barely coping with parenthood – but then she was going to find out that he wasn't travelling alone; his ex-girlfriend, the ultra-clever, ultra-beautiful and ultra-untrustworthy Samira Goodman, was going with him. Sparks were going to fly when she found out.

I was mulling over the wording of my first sentence of the day when I received a text. This time it *was* Selina and I read the words with mounting concern.

Sorry I haven't been in touch. Am in hospital in Kings Lynn. There was a fire at my house Monday night. Speak soon.

A fire? Dismay clutched at my heart. I had seen burns victims on TV documentaries. My fingers sped over the keys as I replied.

Oh my God, are you alright?

I stared at the screen, waiting for the reply.

Yes. I was very lucky. Am suffering from the effects of smoke inhalation. Hopefully allowed out tomorrow.

Poor Selina but thank God it wasn't more serious.

Would you like me to come and visit?

Mentally, I started rearranging my day.

No point. I'm not allowed to talk. Perhaps tomorrow, if you were able? Could you bring me something to wear and give me a lift back to Swaffham, please? Only if it's not too much trouble.

I sent her another message, confirming that of course I'd do as she'd asked and put the phone down. Poor Selina ...

***

Later that day, I waited for Josh to pick me up. If anything, my face looked worse, my right eye now a spectacular mass of purple bruising. My attempt to blend it in with some mauve eyeshadow had merely emphasised it, achieving the look of a purple-eyed panda and I'd quickly scrubbed it off. I'd just have to be an eyesore – literally. In the scheme of things, though, it was very little to put up with – certainly compared to Selina. Thoughts of her, lying in hospital, had not been far from my mind all day. What a terrible thing to have happened! I dreaded to think what state her house may be in. Presumably, she'd have to find somewhere to stay. Maybe I could help with that.

I dressed for the evening in lilac jeans, converse trainers and a long-sleeved, white, cotton top and carried a pale pink sweater to combat any evening chill. Physically I was ready; emotionally I wasn't so sure. The roiling in my stomach as I waited for Josh's arrival made me feel a bit panicky and out of control, like the time I went on a rollercoaster ride and hadn't realised it was going to loop the loop. Part of me was telling me to get off before it was too late; the other part was advising me to enjoy the ride.

My thoughts turned to Ellie and Damien Davies. There had been no chance to have a discussion with her as she'd texted earlier to say she was seeing Damien that evening. Probably I was worrying over nothing but my reply reflected my concern.

Have fun but be careful. You don't know anything about this guy. Make sure you meet in a public place and ring me if you're at all worried. Am seeing Josh tonight but we can be there if you need us xx

Her reply was almost instant.

Oh yes? Seeing Josh? Will make sure I'm up when you return. Want to know everything! Xx

I had no idea if she'd heeded the warning and didn't want to repeat it for fear of alarming her unduly. The doorbell announced Josh's arrival and the sight of him standing on the doorstep, tall, dark and carelessly sexy, sent my pulse racing.

'Hi,' I smiled shyly. 'How's your ...?'

I got no further as he swept me into his arms and kissed me thoroughly. 'Mm,' his voice rumbled against my hair. 'You smell gorgeous. I've been desperate to kiss you all day.'

'Me too,' I answered breathlessly, leaning into him and initiating my own kiss. 'Do you want to come in?'

'Of course I do ... but we have a picnic waiting.' He released me and stepped back. 'I know you're just after my body,' he grinned, 'but I want to convince you I'm fantastic in other ways too.'

'Sounds good. I'll be interested to see what you've got, Fielding.' Grabbing my sweater, I stepped outside and locked the door. 'I'm expecting great things.' I waited until we were in the car before asking about his dad.

'They think he might need a stent but otherwise he's on good form. He's now back home with orders to rest and being waited on hand and foot. My poor Mum! I really feel for her – he's always been a terrible patient.'

'Sounds like my dad,' I sympathised. 'He's so active, he's like a bear with a sore head if he's ill. Maybe it's a dad thing.'

We passed the next few miles in a companionable silence. It really was a beautiful evening, still and warm, the blue sky bathed in golden sunlight. I loved this time of the year when gardens were colourful and lawns were verdant. I relaxed back into the black leather seat, enjoying the drive.

'I really like that about you,' Josh said suddenly.

'What?'

'You don't need to fill the silence with inane chatter. You only speak when you have something to say.'

'Thank you.' I felt ridiculously pleased by the small compliment.

'You look beautiful tonight, despite the eye ... and the lip ... and all the bruising,' he grinned. 'How are you? Have there been any ill effects from the fall yesterday?'

'No, just my pride. I'll try not to fall over or drop anything this evening. You must think I'm a complete dork.'

'Not at all.' He flashed me a quick smile. 'I find it very endearing. It makes me feel all protective over you ... although, just so you know, please no accidents anywhere near my car. I wouldn't be happy if she got damaged. She's my pride and joy.'

'Point taken. It *is* a very lovely car ... such a shame about that terrible scratch all down the passenger side.'

'What?'

I giggled at his look of horror. 'Sorry. Just joking. I couldn't resist.'

He relaxed and favoured me with a mock glare. 'Also, jokes like that about my car are off limits.'

'Understood ... although I really don't get this obsession some people have with cars. As far as I'm concerned, as long as they're reliable and get you to where you want to go, then I'm happy.'

'Well, you're a girl. I suppose that's to be expected!' came his amused retort.

'Ooh!' I arched my brows. 'A chauvinist as well as a petrol head. You *are* going down in my estimation. And there you were promising to impress me with your fabulousness.' I shook my head sadly. 'I feel I'm in for a disappointing evening.'

'Me too,' he nodded, his voice echoing my feigned dismay. Then he grinned. 'Perhaps we'd better stay off the subject of cars. What have you been up to today?'

'Just writing. I did have a bit of a shock though ...' I told him about Selina and the fire at her house. As Josh questioned me further, I found myself telling him the whole story – the blue Peugeot following me, Maisie's abduction and Selina's claim that I was her kidnapped daughter. Josh listened intently, his frown turning to a look of incredulity as I concluded the story.

'Really? That all sounds daft, if you ask me. What on earth makes this woman think you might be her daughter?'

I shrugged. As I recounted my dealings with Selina, I realised how far-fetched it all sounded. 'Just a number of little things really – the way I look, I'm the right age, I twiddle my ear which is something her husband does ...' I hesitated, unwilling to mention my dreams and the photo of Maisie's brother, Harry.

'All sounds a bit tenuous to me. I'm surprised you're taking it seriously.'

'I'm not really.' His doubts made me defensive. 'I just feel sorry for Selina, that's all. Taking a DNA test will allow her to move on, put her mind at rest that I'm not Maisie. My parents were actually very understanding about it and gave me the go-ahead.'

Josh raised his eyebrows. 'Wow. If you were my daughter, I'd be furious. You realise what this woman is suggesting, don't you? Her claim is tantamount to accusing your parents of being kidnappers!'

'I know.' A wave of guilt resurfaced. 'It was difficult but I had to tell them about Selina. They were worried sick because I'd thought someone was following me so I had to reassure them when I found out who it was. Then, they wanted me to report her to the police so I had to tell them the whole story. They were pretty angry at first but then Mum insisted I took the DNA test. She agreed that was the only proof which would convince Selina and the quickest way of getting rid of her.' I chose not to tell him that Mum had also sensed my own ambivalence about Selina's claim. I felt bad enough about it without confessing it aloud.

'Wasn't your dad angry?'

I pondered his reaction, frowning a little. It *had* been strange, now I came to think of it. He was volatile at the best of times and thwarting him always provoked an explosive response. Yet, when I'd told him, he'd said very little, leaving Mum to take the stance of righteous indignation. He'd been almost unnaturally calm, not like himself at all. At the time, I'd been relieved that he'd taken it so well; it hadn't occurred to me that his response was completely out of character.

'I expect he was,' I said eventually, 'but he was actually pretty cool about the whole thing. Maybe he's mellowing in his old age.'

'Must be,' Josh said shortly.

'Anyway, the DNA test will have to be postponed for a while, I expect, with Selina recovering in hospital.'

As we approached Wells-next-the-Sea, I scanned the horizon until I spotted a ribbon of grey. 'Oooh, I can see the sea!' I declared triumphantly.

He smiled indulgently. 'Is there a prize for that?' he asked.

'Absolutely. Don't you know that the first person to spot the sea gets to make a wish?' I closed my eyes tightly. 'There, I've wished.' My cheeks turned pink.

'And what did you wish for?'

'I can't tell you that. You can't reveal a wish or it won't come true,' I said glibly. There was no way I could tell him that my silent plea to the wish-fairy had been about him.

***

Sometimes wishes *do* come true. The evening was completely magical. We chose an isolated spot tucked in the dunes to have the picnic and watched the hues of the sky gradually redden and darken. Josh had poured chilled champagne and solemnly raised his glass.

'To us,' he smiled, his brown eyes molten.

'To us,' I repeated, taking a fortifying sip to cover my self-consciousness. 'I like the sound of that.'

We feasted on smoked salmon parcels, crusty rolls, chicken and strawberries and chatted about good pubs in the area, holidays, books and Game of Thrones. I found out he was a huge Game of Thrones fan and had been wading through the box set since moving into the Old Rectory. He discovered I'd never watched an episode and promised he would have to remedy that. As the sun dipped lower and the air grew cooler, he put his arm around me and I nestled into the warmth of his chest. He wrapped his other arm around me and we lay entwined, listening to the gentle lapping of distant waves.

'This is nice,' I murmured, snuggling into him, savouring the hardness and the earthy scent of him.

'Better than nice,' he replied huskily, sliding a hand to cup my breast and seeking out my lips. Passion flared between us and, within seconds, we were tugging at each other's clothes, each desperate for the other.

Afterwards, he wrapped the rug around our bodies as we cuddled.

'That was nice,' I whispered.

'Better than nice.' I could feel his smile.

'God, I hope nobody could see us.'

'No chance. Why do you think I picked this spot?'

I leaned back, resting on my elbows to study his face. 'It sounds like you make a habit of bringing girls here.'

'Mm.' He considered my words. 'That's not a bad idea.'

'Hey,' I pouted. 'You'd better not!'

He grinned and pulled me against him. 'Only you,' he whispered against my hair. 'Only you.'

***

It was completely dark by the time his car stopped outside the house.

'Do you want to come in?' I asked.

He leaned across to kiss me softly, a feather touch against my lips. 'I would,' he said, 'but then I wouldn't want to leave.'

'Then don't.' I tugged him into my arms and deepened the kiss.

'I can't.' Regretfully, he pulled away. 'I have to go to London first thing tomorrow.'

'London?' I queried. 'Work or pleasure?'

'Work. Come on gorgeous. I'll walk you to your door.'

Before I could respond, he'd sprung out of the car and was opening my door. As I walked with him towards the house, a sudden thought occurred. 'Hey, how did you know where I live?'

He turned his face away. 'Didn't *you* tell me?' he asked.

'No.'

He shrugged, his body language suddenly off-kilter.

'So how did you know the address?' I persisted, niggled by his response.

'I don't know, Anna' His voice was brusque, laced with impatience and he pulled me into his arms. 'Does it matter?'

'Not really,' I replied, distracted by his proximity. 'I just wondered, that's all.'

'OK then.' He kissed me firmly and led me to the front door. 'I'll call you tomorrow.' His face softened and he dipped his head to kiss me once more. 'Sleep tight.'

'You too.'

Quietly, so as not to wake Ellie, I stepped inside, locked the door behind me and slipped off my shoes.

'There you are!' Ellie appeared in her dressing gown at the top of the stairs. 'I can tell by your face that you've had a good evening. I want all the details,' she said dramatically, scooting down the stairs.

'Sure but first tell me about *your* evening.'

We sat down in the sitting room, feet curled up on the sofa and told each other about our respective dates. Ellie was clearly blissfully happy about her evening with Damien Davies.

'I wasn't sure what to expect because he had suggested we meet for a drink in the pub but then he insisted on buying me dinner. He was a perfect gentleman … and a great kisser,' she added happily. 'Tomorrow, he's taking me to Norwich to see a film.'

'He sounds keen,' I said warily. 'Ellie, did he ask you anything about me?'

'No.' Ellie was surprised by the question. 'Does he know you?'

Reluctantly, I confessed that he was the painter who'd scared me at my parents' house and told her about our previous encounter in Norwich. 'I'm sorry I didn't mention it last night but I couldn't face it. You were so full of how great he was. It's probably a coincidence, you know, that he's the same guy,' I finished lamely.

'Must be.' She frowned. 'He hasn't been like that with me at all. He's had a difficult past and had to fight for everything he's achieved. Definitely, he's got a bit of a chip on his shoulder.' She regarded me thoughtfully. 'When you turned him down, he was probably upset that you thought he wasn't good enough for you.'

'I'm sure you're right.' Truthfully, I wasn't sure what to think. It was like we'd met two different versions of Damien Davies.

'Now, tell me all about Josh,' Ellie demanded. 'The last I knew, you weren't quite sure what to make of him. Wasn't he really rude to you the first time you met or have I got him muddled up with someone else?'

'No, that was Josh,' I admitted. Already that seemed so long ago. Half-smiling, I recounted everything that had happened since then, finishing with the picnic that evening.'

'Anna Blake, you're not telling me that you had sex on the beach?' Ellie's eyes were round with delight. 'You devil! Go on girl, I didn't think you had it in you!'

'Me neither,' I grinned. 'Now I need to go and have a shower to get rid of all that sand. See you in the morning.'

I headed up the stairs, still tingling and buzzing from the evening with Josh. It was only when I stood luxuriating beneath hot jets of water, reliving every second of the evening, my mind reached the moment when I'd asked him how he knew my address. I pictured his face, a snapshot beneath the streetlight, turning away from me, trying to conceal the guilt in his eyes. With a cold blast of clarity, I knew he was lying. He was hiding something.

CHAPTER 26

Selina

*S*omeone had tried to kill me.

I lay in a hospital bed, hidden behind a magazine, turbulent thoughts churning whilst the bay's other occupants chatted with their visitors. I should've closed my curtains before visiting began. It was too late now – relatives of the invalids had arrived and it would look like I had something to hide. The group opposite was especially noisy, clearly ignoring the two visitors at a time maximum and congregated around the bed like baying cattle at a food trough.

'Are you using this?' I lowered the magazine to see a young woman with a nose stud and tattooed arms, her hands already grasping the chair by my bed.

'No, no,' I croaked, my throat still painfully scratchy. I gestured at her to take it. 'Try not to speak,' the doctor had said.

I raised the magazine once more. It was an old copy of House & Gardens, fetched for me earlier by a kind, auxiliary nurse, but the glossy photos failed to capture my attention. There were too many other things, worrying things, to fret over. The more I thought about it, the more convinced I became that the fire wasn't an accident … and if it *was* deliberate … maybe it had something to do with my conviction that Anna was Maisie. Were Anna's parents capable of murder? Surely not … so perhaps it was an accident after all … but then there were too many things which didn't add up. My head ached with trying to figure it out.

At least I was going home today. The doctor had been round, listened to my chest, checked my notes and declared me fit to leave. I'd sent a text to Anna who had responded instantly. Bless her; she said she would come straight away. While I waited, I also fretted about what I'd find when I returned home. A fire safety officer had visited yesterday and informed me that the ground floor had sustained considerable damage. That sounded bad. I'd probably have to stay in hotel or bed and breakfast accommodation for the foreseeable future. It was the fire officer who'd triggered the fears now consuming my thoughts. He'd arrived armed with leaflets and given me a kindly but stern pep talk about the importance of smoke alarms. Until that moment, I hadn't given a thought to the fact that my house had been full of smoke and yet not one of the alarms had gone off.

Later, in the afternoon, two police officers, a middle-aged man and a younger woman, had arrived. As I'd been told to avoid talking, I'd written answers to their questions on a notepad they had provided. They wanted my account of events on Monday night and I gave them the facts they requested. I'd then sought my own answers and written a sequence of questions.

Who called the fire brigade?

The man had responded. 'One of your neighbours. He works shifts and saw the smoke when he returned home. When he looked closer, he realised the house was on fire and dialled 999.'

How did the fire start?

'We can't be certain. The fire officer said it started in the kitchen. Possibly something flammable had been left lying near a hotplate which had been left on.' He shrugged. 'We'll probably never know for certain.'

Why didn't the smoke alarms go off?

He frowned and consulted his notes. 'It says here there were no batteries in the smoke alarms.' His face took on a patronising demeanour. 'You won't forget that again in a hurry.'
Furiously, my pen scrawled across the page.

But they all had batteries in. I'm sure of it. My son put them in and tested them all when I moved in about six weeks ago.

The officer shook his head. 'Well, there were no batteries when the fire crew checked. Probably you thought your son had done so but he hadn't got around to it. I have a son myself. He's not very reliable either.' His voice acquired a stern note. 'It could have cost you your life. You're very lucky to have survived.'

I watched him put the batteries in.

Seeing the pitying expression on his face, I let the pad drop on the bedsheets. It was no use. He didn't believe me. Another thought struck and I grabbed the pen once more.

I know I didn't leave a hotplate on. I had salad for tea.

He frowned again. 'What are you suggesting?'

Could someone have started the fire deliberately? Was someone trying to kill me?

He exchanged a glance with the female officer and raised his eyebrows. 'Now what makes you think that? Have you had threats against you?'

No.

'There was no sign of a forced entry at the property and all the doors were locked so, unless there is any evidence to the contrary, we're treating it as a very unfortunate accident.' He stood up and held out a hand. It was soft and slightly puffy. 'I'll take the notepad. Your responses will be needed for my report. Your concerns will be recorded, of course, and we'll be in touch should it become necessary.'

After they left, I asked for a pen and paper and rewrote my account of events ready for Anna's arrival. She was certain to have questions. So absorbed was I in the task, I failed to notice visitors arriving and only gradually became aware of their curious glances my way. They made me feel vulnerable and I was grateful for the screen provided by the magazine.

'Selina?' It was Anna's voice.

I forced a smile and held out my hand in greeting. Anna took it gently, as if it might be injured, and perched beside me on the bed, her face pale and anxious.

'Selina, how are you feeling?'

I handed her the paper, now covered with my spidery handwriting.

I'm suffering from smoke inhalation and have some damage to my vocal chords. I've been told to avoid speaking so have written down what happened.

I went to bed on Monday night at around ten o'clock and read for about an hour. I'm not sure exactly what time I fell asleep but I think it must have been shortly after eleven. When I woke up, my bedroom was full of smoke and I could barely breathe. It was 3:14 a.m. I realised the house was on fire. I tried to escape downstairs but the flames blocked my path. Then I heard a siren. Thankfully, it was a fire engine. I tried to shout but all I could do was cough. However, someone saw me because, within a few minutes, a fireman was on a ladder outside my window and I was helped down to safety. I was brought here by ambulance and have been told I'm very lucky to be alive.

Anna put the paper down and grabbed my hand again, more fervently this time. 'Thank goodness the fire brigade arrived when they did. Who called them?'

I picked up the pen.

A neighbour who works shifts. He saw the flames through a downstairs window.

'Thank God for him and for shift work. And for those amazing firefighters.'

I nodded, my eyes grim at the thought of what might have been.

'Do they know yet what caused the fire?'

The police came yesterday. They said it started in the kitchen – probably a hotplate left on caused something to catch fire.

I frowned as I wrote.

That can't be right though. The hotplate was definitely off. I had a salad for my tea. There was another thing I don't understand. Apparently, the smoke alarms didn't go off because there were no batteries in them. That's NOT true. I know there were new batteries in there. Harry put them in and checked them when I moved in. That wasn't many months ago. Even if the batteries had gone dead, they should still have been there.

I laid the paper down, my eyes trying to convey the confusion I felt.

'Try not to worry about it at the moment.' Anna patted my shoulder consolingly. 'You just need to concentrate on getting better. Have you had other visitors?'

I shook my head.

Harry is away on holiday – 6 weeks travelling around Australia. There's no-one else.

The stark words resonated in my heart and I swallowed the lump of self-pity sticking in my throat.

Anna's face was sympathetic. 'Well, I'm here. You're not alone.' I squeezed her hand. 'How much damage did the fire do to your house?' she asked.

Not sure. A lot of internal damage downstairs, I've been told.

'You'll need somewhere to stay. I can help you sort that and I've brought you some clothes.' She gestured towards the holdall lying by her feet. 'Hopefully you'll find something here to fit. I stopped by the chemist as well, to pick up some bits and pieces for you. My clothes will probably be baggy but I didn't think that would matter too much. I didn't know your shoe size so I've brought some of my flip flops – I thought that would be easiest.'

Thank you so much. I don't know what I'd have done without you. I'll pay you for the things you've bought.

'Please don't worry about that now. I'm happy to help.' Anna gently disengaged her hand and pulled the privacy curtain around the bed. 'Do you want me to stay and give you a hand or can you manage?'

I'll manage. I'll try not to keep you waiting too long.

'Take all the time you need. I'll wait outside, just in case.'

Thank you. And then you can tell me what happened to your face!

***

Within a few minutes, I pulled back the curtain, feeling self-conscious in grey sweat pants with the bottoms rolled up, a baggy, blue T-shirt and a pair of black flip-flops. The carrier bag of toiletries was in my hand and I pointed to a nearby bathroom. At Anna's nod of comprehension, I shuffled away, head bowed, trying to attract as little attention as possible. Once in the bathroom, I balanced the bag on the sink and stared at my reflection in the mirror. I looked awful, my hair lank and my face washed-out and stern with frown lines. What was I going to do? The future, which had been looking brighter with Anna's acquiescence to the DNA test, now felt troubled and uncertain. Rubbing face cream on my pallid skin, I wondered if I should take steps to protect myself, even go back to Nottingham. At least I had friends there.

No! My gut issued an instant denial. I couldn't give up on this chance to discover if I'd found my daughter, no matter what the consequences. If I left, I could lose her all over again. I couldn't take the chance. If Anna's parents were responsible for the fire at my house, it proved they were the ones who took Maisie all those years ago. Mind you, it was a very big if. The police believed the fire was accidental. Maybe I was weaving a fantasy from the threads of events to suit my own beliefs. Maybe I *was* what everyone believed – a silly, delusional, old woman.

Anna had also bought me some face powder and lipstick. She was such a sweet girl. I'd never been one for much make-up but a little colour on my cheeks and lips would improve my ghostly pallor. I applied both with a burst of renewed determination. It was time to stop behaving like a victim. Mentally, I scrolled through my to-do list: find somewhere to stay; phone the insurance company; get the house repaired; find answers. One step at a time. Today, I would achieve the first and most pressing item; the rest could wait. I added a final point – stay safe.

'Have you thought where you might stay?' Anna asked as we headed to the car park. 'Sorry; silly of me to ask questions when you can't speak. I'll do the talking and you just nod or shake your head.' A nod. 'Right. I think we should go to your house first and see what we're dealing with. Then we'll organise somewhere to stay?' Another nod. 'Good we have a plan.' She gave me an encouraging smile.

***

As Anna drove, she told me, in a light, self-deprecating way, about her fall at Josh's house the day before. 'I was *so* embarrassed, especially after I saw myself in the mirror. It's a wonder he didn't fall about laughing but actually he was very nice about it.' Her cheeks grew pink, I noticed, when she spoke of Josh. Clearly, she had feelings for him. I hoped he would prove worthy of her affections.

Her eyes constantly flicked to her rear-view mirror and she gave an embarrassed look when she saw I'd noticed.

'There's a silver BMW a few cars back behind us,' she said. 'I was wondering if it belonged to a friend of mine, Ewan Jacobs.'

We drove the rest of the way in silence and pulled up outside my house. I stared hopefully at the façade. The downstairs windows were blackened but, outwardly, the house looked normal. That was good news. My Peugeot stood in the driveway, covered in dust but otherwise unblemished.

'Do you have a key?' Anna asked.

A nod. The police had brought one to the hospital. Apparently, the fire crew had to break down the door to gain entry and a locksmith had been called the next day to repair the damage and secure the house.

I eased myself out of the car, unwilling to go inside and face the damage. Perhaps, it wouldn't be as bad as I was imagining. The picture of flames devouring the staircase was vivid in my memory and

I could smell smoke, even from outside. I shivered. The fear of choking to death or being consumed by the fire had haunted me since it had happened. Going inside was about more than seeing what remained.

We entered the house in silence. Downstairs was a charred, blackened mess. The acrid smell of burnt plastic filled my nostrils.

'Oh!' I couldn't help an involuntary gasp as my eyes travelled over the walls, streaked with soot, and the ruined furnishings. My paintings! They were still hanging, tarnished and forlorn, their frames almost melted away, layered with black.

'They may still be OK. I think the frames have borne the worst of it.' Anna saw where my gaze had centred and laid a comforting hand on my arm. We stood for a few moments, just taking it all in. It was horrible. I wondered if I'd ever be able to bring myself to move back in.

We shuffled through to the kitchen. It was even worse. The room was gutted. I choked back a small sob and covered my face with my hands.

'It can all be replaced,' Anna reassured me.

I shook my head. Not my photos. My favourite photo of Maisie had been on the fridge. *Oh God, all my other photos were upstairs.* I needed to check ... I spun around and picked a route up the charred staircase. Anna followed as I headed for the spare room and pushed open the door. *Oh, thank goodness.* Apart from the all-pervasive smell of smoke, the room remained intact. The metal strongbox, containing all my personal papers, photographs, certificates and insurance documents, was where I'd last left it, completely undamaged. At least I'd be able to start getting everything sorted. Weak with relief, I closed my eyes. It wasn't the end of the world. I hadn't lost everything.

Silently, we retraced our steps and entered my bedroom. That too was virtually untouched.

'It's lucky the fire crew got here so quickly,' Anna observed. 'Look, I'll wait for you in the car. I can check out availability of bed and breakfast places in Swaffham, if that's what you'd like?'

I nodded absently, my head swirling with memories and feelings – panic, fear, thick smoke burning my throat, stinging my eyes. The stool was still by the window, specked with flakes of soot. I remembered how terror made me shake uncontrollably as I clambered up and into the firefighter's comforting arms. I could hear his soothing voice encouraging me, telling me I was doing brilliantly, making me believe I *could* climb out of the window and down the ladder. Could I find out his name? I wanted to write to him, thank him properly.

'Good news,' Anna smiled at me as I clambered, a short while later, into the passenger seat. 'I've found somewhere for the next few nights at least. It's in Swaffham. We can go there now if you like and see if it's suitable. The lady on the phone, Sue Fawley-Green, sounded lovely. The place is called Oak Cottage. Is that OK with you?'

I nodded and gave her a smile of thanks. Anna truly was a lovely girl – the sort of compassionate, caring woman I always knew Maisie would grow up to become.

CHAPTER 27

Anna

I took a sip of water and watched my mother through the window. She was pacing outside, on the phone to a colleague, immaculately dressed as usual in tailored trousers and a beautifully cut, patterned shirt which enhanced her slim figure. Her features were creased in annoyance and I imagined her giving some junior doctor a hard time over something which had met with her disapproval earlier. That was Mum – a tough, uncompromising, impatient perfectionist. She'd never been the world's most loving parent but she was fiercely possessive and protective and I'd never doubted she loved me in her own way. She hadn't given up trying to mould me into the woman she wished me to be – her recent machinations concerning Ewan Jacobs were proof of that. Some things would never change. My phone buzzed and I smiled when I saw the caller's ID.

'Hi Ewan. I was just thinking of you.'

He chuckled, a deep, throaty sound. 'That sounds promising. Were you thinking good thoughts?'

'Of course.'

'Maybe some naughty thoughts?' he asked hopefully.

'Ewan.' I injected a note of censure to my voice. 'We're just friends, remember?'

'Yes, yes. Anyway, I was thinking of you too and wanted to check you were alright.'

'Fine thanks. Hey,' I said as a thought occurred to me. 'Were you in Swaffham this afternoon? It looked like your car following me.'

There was a heartbeat of silence. 'Not me I'm afraid. I've been tied up with a client all day.'

'Oh dear. Was it something you said?'

'What?' Ewan's voice now sounded unnaturally sharp.

'Sorry. Just a joke. Obviously not a very good one.'

'Oh, I see.' His voice relaxed once more. 'Seriously though Anna, did you think someone was following you again?'

'No, no. Nothing like that. It was a silver BMW and it looked like yours, that's all.'

'Not guilty.' There was another brief pause and then he added, 'OK, I was just checking how things were. Don't forget to call me if you're bothered by anything or anyone.'

'I will. Thanks. You're a pal.'

***

As usual, the meal was delicious and both my parents seemed to be making an unexpected effort to please me. Dad was light-hearted and witty, entertaining us with a funny article he'd read in *The Independent* and then his latest golf exploits. Mum asked me about my latest book and seemed genuinely interested when I told her what I'd planned for Jemima and Conrad. That was a first.

'I remember a time when your father always had a glamorous PA by his side on business trips so I can sympathise with your character, Jemima. I soon put a stop to that, I can tell you,' she said drily. She gave Dad a cool, superior smile. 'I found him the indispensable and incomparable Julia Sharp. Then I could rest easy when he went away.'

Dad smiled benignly. 'That's what you thought!' he joked.

She raised her perfectly arched eyebrows but let the comment pass and turned back to me. 'What about your love life?' she asked bluntly. 'You write about all this romance but never seem to have one yourself. I had high hopes for Ewan Jacobs but ... I know.' She held up a hand when I threatened to interrupt her. 'You're just good friends.'

'Actually, I *am* seeing someone ...' I began cautiously, my cheeks reddening.

'Really?'

'Yes.' My natural reluctance to share too much information meant the words felt uncomfortable on my tongue. So many times, I had revealed details about a boyfriend, only to have my excitement crushed by damning disapproval. 'His name is Josh Fielding,' I admitted at last. 'He used to work in banking so you might know him, Dad.' I held my breath, waiting for his response.

'Josh Fielding ...' He mulled over the name slowly as if trawling through a personnel database. 'I'm sure I *do* remember that name.' He rubbed his chin thoughtfully. 'Why yes, I believe I do recall him. Very clever young man. Disappeared from the City almost overnight after a colleague committed suicide. Terribly sad. Is that him?'

'Yes.' I scrutinised his face. His voice sounded slightly unnatural, like an actor in a play, trying too hard to recite his lines with conviction.

'He seemed a good chap. What's he doing now?'

'He lives in the Old Rectory in Lewton. He's been doing it up and I've been helping out, mainly in the garden.'

'Excellent,' he beamed, his face a picture of congeniality. 'We'll look forward to meeting him properly. Maybe you could bring him here for supper next Thursday?'

'Well ...' Things were moving a little too fast for my liking and I wanted to sound a note of caution. 'Obviously, it's still very early days. I'll have to let you know about next Thursday.'

'Of course, of course.' Dad reached across the table and patted my hand. 'There's no rush. We're happy as long as you're happy.'

Yes, and as long as I'm doing what you want. The words came unbidden to my mind and I rebuked myself. I was being unfair.

'So,' Mum spoke with brittle brightness, 'how are things progressing with the DNA test?' Her grey eyes were expressionless as she looked at me. It was so hard to know what she was thinking; Dad was easier to read.

I waited a moment before replying. Having asked me to avoid Selina, they wouldn't be happy to know how I'd been helping her. 'Nothing's happening at the moment,' I replied, watching their reactions. 'Selina Matthews had a fire at her house on Monday night.'

'Oh goodness. Was there much damage? Was she hurt?' Mum's face was a model of concern, slightly at odds with the flinty greyness of her eyes.

'Yes and no. The house was quite badly damaged and no, apart from suffering the effects of smoke inhalation, Selina wasn't seriously hurt.'

'You've seen the house then?' Dad's voice was sharp, challenging and sounded as if he already knew the answer to his question. I hesitated before responding. It was like he was testing me, seeing if I was going to lie. But how could he know I'd been to the house?

'Just briefly,' I said at last. 'I picked Selina up from the hospital. She asked me. There was no-one else.' I hated that I sounded so apologetic.

'Really?' Disdain dripped from Mum's voice. 'I've said it before and I'll say it again, Anna – that woman is trying to get her hooks into you and you're letting her. We agreed to the DNA test because we thought that would be the end of the matter and yet here we are – no test and a fire which conveniently makes her even more dependent on you.' She paused for breath and began clearing plates, the cutlery clattering angrily against the china. 'I wouldn't be surprised if she started the fire herself, had you thought of that? *She* doesn't actually want a DNA test because that would prove you're not her daughter. In the meantime, she's doing whatever she can to play upon your sympathies. You mustn't trust her.'

'Your mother's right.' Dad's voice was surprisingly measured and sombre. His hazel eyes bored into me, mesmerising me with the force of his will. 'The woman is clearly a lunatic. This is serious, Anna.' He grabbed my hand to emphasise his point. 'She could even be dangerous. Promise me you'll have nothing more to do with her.'

'There's no proof that Selina started the fire herself,' I said gently. 'I know you're concerned but I don't think you have anything to worry about. I feel sorry for her, that's all.' I looked across at Mum, stacking plates into the dishwasher with smooth precision. 'She's not *getting her hooks* into me, as you describe it. She's the victim here. The fire was a terrible accident and she's in need of a friend. End of story.'

'Hmph,' Mum snorted. 'You've always been far too trusting for your own good. Look how many times you've been hurt in the past and how many times your Dad and I have had to pick up the pieces.'

'I know.' I took a deep breath and kept my voice calm but assertive. 'But I have to make my own decisions, make my own mistakes. I'm twenty-six years old and this is my life, not yours.'

'I don't like your tone, Anna.' Dad pushed his chair back sharply, its legs scraping across the tiled floor like nails on slate. He stood up, nostrils flaring and eyes narrowed. 'I want you to promise me you will have nothing more to do with that woman. It's for your own good.' His sudden anger was oppressive, prodding old anxieties. I'd gone too far and I sought words to pacify him without backing down. In the past, so often, I'd agreed to his demands and basked in his approval. 'Good girl,' he'd say at my acquiescence, bathing me in his golden glow. He still expected me to submit to his demands, march to the beat of his drum.

I stood up too, my hand twisting my right earlobe nervously before reaching out to clear condiments from the table. 'I can't promise that, Dad,' I said at last, avoiding his gaze. 'Selina is dependent upon me at the moment. When everything settles down, I will try and keep a bit of distance between us. Will that do?' I glanced up anxiously. He was shaking his head, his face taut with anger.

'Not good enough. For pity's sake, Anna ...' he shouted, all attempts at self-control abandoned. 'After all we've done for you ... We ask you to do one thing but you refuse. I can't believe you're so ungrateful, so uncaring of our feelings and our wishes. Why can't you let us look after you and keep you safe? Why do you persist in defying me when I know what's best for you?'

'Dad, please ...' My attempt to interrupt, to deflect his escalating rage was like trying to stop an articulated lorry thundering downhill with no brakes.

'Listen to what we're telling you. If you persist in seeing this woman, you're running the risk of tearing this family apart, had you thought of that?'

'Geoff!' Mum's icy voice snapped through his tirade. She was shaking her head in warning, her body tensed, poised to intervene.

'Yes, well ...' His voice was still belligerent but back under control. 'I've told you how I feel about all this. If you care for us at all, you'll take our advice.' With a final glare, he stalked out of the room, slamming the door behind him.

'I'm sorry, Mum.' I turned towards her, beseeching her to understand. 'You know how much I love you guys but Dad has to realise that I must make my own choices.'

'Even if they're wrong?' she replied.

I sighed and sat down. 'I *do* listen to what you say and take notice of your advice. I know you want what's best for me.'

'Yes, well, I hope for your sake that you heed what we're saying this time. Look, sit down again for a minute, will you?' Her tone had become more conciliatory and I eyed her with suspicion. She was up to something. We faced each other across the table and her lips curved slightly in a complicit smile. 'I have to admit I'm secretly pleased to see you standing up for yourself, asserting yourself like that. You've grown up to become a beautiful, independent woman and, although you might not believe it, I'm proud of your success as a writer. I support the fact that you want to make your own decisions. That shouldn't change. Your father's full of bluster and threats but, ultimately, he loves you more than life itself. He only wants to protect you ... and in this instance, I think he's right.' Her voice had become soothingly persuasive, lulling me with her reasonableness. 'Let me finish,' she said when I tried to interrupt. 'Just hear me out and then make up your mind.'

I nodded. I was still fiddling with my earlobe, I realised, and made a conscious effort to keep my hands clasped in my lap.

'I'm worried about this woman,' she continued, her face serious. 'I think she could be one of those insidious people you hear about on the news every now and again, someone who twists and winds their way into another person's life, taking it over, suppressing the other person entirely and cutting them off from their friends and family, like some religious sects do. I don't think this Selina ...' She spat out the name with contempt. 'In fact, I'm pretty certain she's only pretending you could be her long-lost daughter. It's how people like her operate.' Her thin lips curled in disgust. 'Tell me, how much has she told you about her life since her daughter disappeared?'

'Not much but ...'

'Exactly. I'm not surprised. Wait there for a moment.' She stood up and strode from the room, leaving me wondering what was coming next. She returned, clutching an A4, white envelope and sat down, withdrawing a thin sheaf of papers. 'Now, let's see ...' She put on her reading glasses and flicked through the first few pages until she found what she was looking for. 'Here we are. In July 1996, Maisie Matthews was kidnapped. Then, in October 1998, the police were called to an attempted kidnapping in Derby and Selina Matthews was arrested. Charges were eventually dropped. The police were called and Selina Matthews was questioned about a number of minor offences after that, all concerning young children, but parents were apparently persuaded not to press charges. In January, 2007, she was once again arrested, this time in Nottingham. Apparently, she'd made repeated contact with a fifteen-year-old girl claiming she was her real mother. Eventually, the family took out a restraining order to keep her away.' She looked up from the papers. 'You see, Anna, you're not the first person she has targeted.'

I stared at her in dismay. 'How did you get all this information?'

'Oh ...' It was her turn to look evasive. 'Never you mind. Dad thought it would be a good idea to make some enquiries about her. He was very troubled by what you told us.'

I raised my eyebrows. 'That's pretty fast work. Who found this out?' Realisation dawned. 'Was it Ewan? He said he was helping Dad with some security issues.'

Mum shook her head. 'It doesn't matter. The important thing here is that this woman causes trouble. *That's* the reason, the *only* reason, your Dad and I want you to avoid her.'

I was thinking hard. It felt like pieces of a puzzle were jumbled in front of me and I just needed to grab the pieces in the right order to make sense of them. 'Ewan told me on Tuesday that Selina had had a court order issued against her,' I mused aloud. 'He texted me that morning and we met for a coffee. He warned me about Selina then. He said he's been working for a client on another case and her name had cropped up. That must have been before I told you and Dad anything about Selina ...' I gave my mother a searching look. 'Mum, tell me the truth. Did you both already know about Selina, about her following me in her blue Peugeot, before I told you?'

Her eyes widened in innocence. 'Of course not. How could we possibly know something like that?'

I shook my head in confusion. 'I don't know. It just doesn't make any sense.'

'What doesn't make sense? Like I said, your Dad and I were pretty worried on Monday and first thing the next morning, your Dad called someone he knew to see if he could find out anything about this Selina Matthews. This is what he found out.' She held up the sheaf of papers. 'I don't know what Ewan told you but what I've given you are the facts. We were hoping you'd agree to stay away from her without knowing what we'd found out. But, well, needs must. If you won't listen to us, then listen to the facts. Selina Matthews is trouble and will only bring you grief.' She shuffled the papers back into a neat pile and slipped them back into the envelope.

My mind whirred with the information I'd been told. Mum's explanation seemed reasonable but where did Ewan fit into all this? I thought back to the silver BMW following my car that very morning and the way Ewan had hesitated when I asked him about it. Had he been lying? I was finding it difficult to think straight under my mum's piercing scrutiny and stood up abruptly.

'There's a lot to take in,' I murmured, keeping my face impassive. 'I promise I'll think carefully about what you've told me. Thank you for dinner.' I leant forward to kiss her smooth cheek. 'Say goodnight to Dad for me.'

I walked to my car puzzling the things bothering me. Was it *really* a coincidence that Ewan and my parents had independently sought information about Selina Matthews? There were just too many coincidences but my parents wouldn't lie to me. I thought back to the things they'd said about Selina, that she was deceiving me, that she'd played upon my sympathies and was trying to drive a wedge between me and my family. Could that be true? The image of Selina's white face as she lay in her hospital bed defied that accusation. They hadn't met her and were judging her by the crude facts they'd read in a report. I didn't believe she had any motive other than trying to find her missing daughter.

Other things were tingling my consciousness, sending prickles of disquiet through my body. Who *was* the person they employed to dig into Selina's past? Was it Ewan? Had *he* been lying to me and, if so, why? Throughout the evening, I'd had the vibe my parents knew more than they were letting on. Before Dad had become angry, I'd definitely felt there was something off about his dialogue, that he was putting on an act. Again, why? Things weren't adding up. Their approval of the DNA test also bothered me. It was far too understanding. Dad never backed down from confrontation, not in business nor in his personal life. The idea of him agreeing, even when it was Mum's suggestion, was out of character and yet he had. I thought back to their reaction when I told them about the fire. Dad had said nothing until I mentioned the damage to the house. When he'd challenged me about seeing it myself, that was truer to form – when he was feeling defensive about anything, he'd always go on the attack. Perhaps I was reading too much into everything; perhaps I *should* just take them at their word. It seemed disloyal to do otherwise. The cyclical debate rotated on as I drove home, spinning an ever-increasing web of confusion and second guessing. I would speak to Selina tomorrow, make sure she was OK and get the DNA test sorted. That would resolve everything.

***

Mariella watched her daughter's departure through narrowed eyes, silently cursing her stubbornness. As she heard the car engine start up and wheels grinding through gravel, she picked up her phone.

CHAPTER 28

Anna

Friday was heralded with dour, drizzly clouds and no further answers. I sent Selina a text suggesting I pick her up at ten o'clock for a coffee while we planned next steps and received a prompt, affirmative reply. Then I reread a text Josh had sent earlier. He was staying in London until Saturday but his words gave me the kind of warm, fuzzy feeling I'd never tire of. He hadn't said he loved me, but he made it clear he was missing me. Closing my eyes for a moment, I allowed myself to imagine his lips on mine, his hands sensuously stroking my body ...

Enough romanticising – time to write the phone conversation between Jemima and Conrad when he was away on his business trip. It would start well but then Conrad would divulge he was with Samira, his ex-girlfriend.

'Samira? Samira bloody Goodman is on this trip with you?' Jemima was incredulous. 'And you didn't think to tell me?'

'I'm telling you now, aren't I?' Conrad's voice held a mixture of dismay and defensiveness. How stupid was he to let that one slip! He knew Jemima would go off on one. She had a thing about Samira still working for the same company as him.

'Only by accident!' she scoffed. 'No ... don't try to deny it!' she continued belligerently when Conrad tried to intervene. 'You weren't going to tell me at all! How do you think that makes me feel?'

'Jemima, you know I love you. I didn't want to upset ...'

*'Ha, so you **admit** you had no intention of letting me know that you are away on a jolly in a nice hotel with your ex-girlfriend,' she declared triumphantly. 'I knew it!'*

I worked for an hour and then drove into Swaffham. No-one was following and I was able to relax. Selina was waiting when I pulled up outside Oak Cottage.

'How are you feeling?' I asked as she got in the car.

'Better.' Her voice was a rasping whisper. 'At least I can speak.' She managed a wan smile.

'Just don't overdo it.'

I parked on the market place and we sat down inside a small café in the centre of town. With coffees in front of us, I asked her more about the fire.

'I was asleep, dreaming that I couldn't breathe – something was suffocating me and someone was coughing. Then I realised my bedroom was full of smoke and I was the one coughing. I knew there must be a fire and I had to get out. My bedroom door was open and I stumbled to the top of the stairs. They were on fire ...' She choked back a sob. 'That's when I really started to panic ... when I knew I couldn't get out.'

'Oh God, it must have been awful. What did you do?'

'I went back into my bedroom and looked for my phone. I usually keep it on my bedside table but it wasn't there! I opened the bedroom window to get some air. Then I heard the fire engine. I tried to shout out of the window but I couldn't stop coughing. Luckily someone saw me. They put a ladder up to the window and a firefighter helped me down. He was wonderful, so calm and reassuring. He saved my life – well, he and the person who phoned 999. Otherwise, I'd have been a goner for sure.' She paused, angst in her face, reliving the ordeal. 'Then they put me in an ambulance and carted me off to hospital. The police visited the next day and told me a fire investigation team had been to the house to determine the cause of the fire. Apparently, it started in the kitchen; they said a hotplate on the hob had been left turned on. Something – they suggested a tea towel or some paper – must've been close enough to catch fire ... but that's what I don't understand. I didn't use the hob at all that evening; I just had a salad for my tea. Surely it hadn't been left on for a whole day without me noticing?'

'I've done that more than once – left a plate on, that is. Once it was a couple of hours before I noticed so it's possible,' I replied.

Selina sighed, twisting her hands in her lap. 'I suppose so ... but then they asked me about the smoke alarms and gave me a bit of a telling-off that not one contained a battery. I told you that yesterday, didn't I? Well, I know for a fact that Harry had put batteries in and tested them when I moved in. That was only a few months ago. I don't understand how they could have disappeared. It doesn't make any sense.'

I was silent for a few moments. 'Moving house *is* a very stressful time,' I offered. 'It's possible that you *thought* Harry had installed batteries in the smoke alarms ... maybe he told you he was going to do so but didn't get around to it.'

'No.' Selina was emphatic. 'He definitely did. I watched him do it. He showed me how to test the battery was still working and told me I had to remember to check them – not that I did, of course,' she said guiltily. 'I wish I had now. Clearly the police and the fire investigation team think I'm a stupid, forgetful, old woman. They left information leaflets with me at the hospital about keeping your house safe from fire.'

'What happens now?' I asked.

'Nothing. They're not treating the fire as suspicious and told me to contact my insurance company. That's it.' Frustration was evident in her voice.

'Surely you don't think someone started the fire *deliberately*?'

'That's exactly what I think,' she said forcefully. Her eyes were lit with the same light of conviction as when she'd told me I was Maisie. 'Things just don't add up. I think someone *must* have started the fire. Whoever it was removed the batteries so the smoke alarms wouldn't activate.'

I stared at her in shock. 'But why?' I said at last, trying to keep my voice calm and soothing. 'It makes no sense that someone would want to harm you. There must be another explanation.'

'Believe me, I've spent some time thinking about it and I can't come up with one. It's the only answer. But there ... I can see you think I'm as silly as the police did.'

'Not at all. But you have been through a lot the past few days ...'

'That doesn't make me an idiot,' Selina snorted. 'I told the police I thought someone was trying to kill me and they said there was no evidence of that – no sign of a forced entry. They went away and, later on, a nurse gave me a leaflet about mental health issues. That says it all. They didn't take anything I said seriously.'

'Well ...' I said cautiously, 'if there was no sign of a forced entry ...'

'That means I must be wrong,' Selina interrupted. 'That's what you're going to say, isn't it?'

'Not wrong as such but ...' I hedged, 'you have to admit that if someone was going to break into your home, remove the batteries in your smoke alarms and start a fire, there would have to be a motive.'

'But there is ...' Selina croaked, '... you!'

I felt my jaw drop. 'What on earth do you mean?'

'Well ...' Selina shifted uncomfortably in her seat. 'I probably shouldn't have said that out loud.'

I stared at her in horror. 'Are you saying you think someone's trying to kill you because of me? Because you think I may be your daughter? That's ridiculous.'

'I know,' Selina's shoulders sagged and she nervously plucked at a thread hanging off the oversized T-shirt she was wearing. 'I just ... well ... I wondered if maybe I'd gotten too close to the truth. I'm sorry, Anna. I know you don't want to hear something like this about your parents.'

'My parents?' The words erupted as an incredulous snort. 'Are you saying my *parents* want you dead? Are you out of your mind?' I was angry now, boiling with indignation.

'I knew I shouldn't have said anything,' Selina whispered miserably.

'No.'

She stared at me helplessly. 'I'm sorry.'

'You should be. I can't believe you are actually suggesting my parents are capable of murder.' Conscious of curious looks from other customers in the café, my voice was a furious hiss. 'It was bad enough you questioning my identity.'

Selina pushed back her chair with a clatter and began fumbling in her bag for her purse. 'Perhaps I'd better go.'

I watched her with cold eyes and said nothing.

'Anna, really ... I'm truly sorry.' She looked down at me, her face drawn, her eyes begging for understanding.

I shrugged, deliberately closing my heart to the silent plea of those tear-filled eyes. 'Goodbye Selina.'

Afterwards, I wondered if I'd treated her too harshly. She'd been through a terrible trauma and had to cope with the emotional aftermath all alone – not to mention enduring the perpetual horror of not knowing what happened to her three-year-old daughter. No wonder she was delusional. My heart ached for all she was going through but this showed my parents were right. I would keep my distance from her in future. She'd crossed a line with her wild accusation. How dare she suggest what she did! Nevertheless, I could've controlled my anger better. As I drove home, I clamped down on the part of my brain still trying to unravel the chain of events – the grey-haired man, Ewan investigating Selina, my parents hiring an investigator, their evasiveness, the fire ... They weren't connected.

Back at my desk, I phoned Madison to invite her over that evening. I needed someone to talk to, someone who could help me get things in perspective. If Ellie was there as well ... even better.

Madison jumped at my offer of wine, food and a chat. 'I'll be there,' she declared. 'That's perfect actually. A group of people from work have been trying to persuade me to go to a lingerie party one of the girls is hosting ... as if, with the state of *my* love life, I need to be buying sexy underwear! This gives me an out – my friend *needs* me. Obviously, I *am* the queen of agony aunts so I can understand why you want my help,' she joked. 'The course of my *own* life is always problem-free and I *never* get in a muddle – not with men or anything else. Perhaps I should start up my own YouTube channel as a lifestyle guru.'

I chuckled. 'First of all, you should be buying nice lingerie for yourself, not to impress a man, and secondly, you need to stop putting yourself down. You're a lovely friend and a wonderful person. I'm so pleased you can come over this evening.'

'Yes, well, pot, kettle and black is all I need to say to that and I'm looking forward to seeing you too. I'll be round by eight.'

Shortly after midday, Mum phoned, briskly reminding me about a long-planned, local charity function which I'd agreed to attend in two weeks' time. There was no mention of the previous evening but I could feel the residual tension between us in her clipped consonants and my terse replies. I heard nothing from Dad.

During the afternoon, Josh sent a number of texts which had me reaching for the phone, smiling with anticipation. I'd also heard from Ellie who'd sounded strangely subdued after her night out with Damien.

'Count me in,' she said when I asked if she could join Madison and me. 'I could use a bit of advice too,' she added cryptically, 'but I won't go into details now. See you later.'

By five o'clock, I was done with writing for the day. In terms of productivity, it had been a good session and I reread the chapter I'd written. Some of the dialogue between Conrad and Jemima seemed to jump at me from the screen.

'Of course, I'm angry,' Jemima muttered through gritted teeth. 'What do you expect? You're in Dubai, in a hotel, with your ex-girlfriend!'

'It's a business trip! Samira is with me because she's an architect. We work for the same firm. The fact that we used to see each other is completely irrelevant.' Conrad was trying to sound calm and reasonable but frustration was edging his words with anger.

'I know that. I wouldn't have minded if you'd been upfront and honest about it but you didn't tell me!' Those last words came out as a wail.

Conrad sighed. 'I didn't tell you because I didn't want you to worry.'

'Oh, I see,' Jemima pounced on the words, 'because clearly there was something for me to worry about.'

'No! Not at all!' he exploded. 'Look Jemima, any romance between Samira and me is just in your head. You should trust me, just as I trust you. I'm annoyed that you don't.'

She hated when he managed to do that, turn things around so it seemed like it was her fault. 'I do trust you,' she mumbled defensively, 'but I don't trust her.'

Quite right too. Samira was definitely going to use this opportunity to try to get her hooks back into Conrad. He just didn't know it yet. I pushed my chair back and tucked a stray wisp of hair behind my ear. That was the great thing about writing; as the author, you knew what your characters were secretly thinking and plotting; you knew who could be trusted and who couldn't. If only real life was that straightforward; if only *I* knew who I could trust.

***

Mellow with wine, I watched my friends piling rice, noodles and spoonfuls from various meat dishes onto their plates. The takeaway had been delivered and wine had been consumed; cheeks were flushed and all three of us were a bit tipsy. Madison was laughing at something Ellie had just said, her curly, brown, shoulder length hair bobbing in unison with her chuckles. Ellie was looking striking as always with her flame-red hair, porcelain skin and the ever-present false eyelashes. My heart swelled with affection for them both. I'd updated Madison on developments with Josh and then Ellie had admitted her brief relationship with Damien was over.

'I'm rubbish at choosing men,' she moaned. 'I only stayed over at Damien's last night because I'd had too much to drink but nothing happened between us. He's not a very nice person.'

'Really?' Madison raised an eyebrow.

Ellie bit her lip and lowered her eyes. 'I hate to admit it but you were right about him, Anna. After a couple of beers, he knew it all – in fact, he was full of crap – and then he became pretty mean.'

'Wow, he sounds pretty terrible, even by your low standards,' Madison teased. 'I'm surprised you were remotely interested in him.'

'Yeah well,' Ellie shrugged. 'He started out being totally cool and charming. It was just last night things went downhill.'

She was studiously avoiding my gaze. 'Was it anything to do with me?' I asked.

'Typical Anna!' Madison rolled her eyes. 'It's not always about you, you know.'

But Ellie was nodding. 'He … er … said some pretty horrible things about you. I'm not going to put up with someone who's rude about one of my closest friends!'

'Good for you. Sounds like you're well rid of him,' Madison said. 'Do either of you want this last prawn ball?'

I shook my head and set down my knife and fork. 'I'm sorry Ellie.'

She shrugged. 'It's not your fault. You did warn me after all. Anyway, what's up with you? You've been very quiet.'

'As you both know, I'm in a bit of a quandary …' I began. Twirling the stem of my wine glass between my fingers, I told them about the fire at Selina's house, the accusation Selina had made and the conversations I'd had with my parents and Ewan Jacobs. Then I shared all the silly things niggling me. They listened in silence, totally immersed in my story.

'Blimey!' Madison was the first to speak. 'This has all the ingredients of a psychological thriller. Honestly, Anna, you're talking as if there must be a villain and you're not sure who it is. But what if there are no villains here? Selina is mistaken, both in thinking you could be her daughter and in thinking that someone deliberately started the fire. End of story. Your parents hired an investigator but so what? They have the money and they only want to protect you. I can't say I blame them.'

'I agree,' Ellie chipped in, her green eyes serious. 'I think you're taking this woman far too seriously, Anna. Just remember the whole thing started with her scaring you witless by tailing you in that blue Peugeot of hers. How can you trust anything she says after that?'

'You're right,' I sighed 'but there are still some things I'm struggling with ... the photo of the boy, for instance.'

'What boy?' Madison interrupted.

I told them about the recurrent dream I'd had as a child which had resurfaced recently. 'The photo really freaked me out,' I admitted. 'That boy was identical to the one I'd had all those dreams about. How could that happen?'

My two friends exchanged glances. 'You could be mistaken, Anna,' Madison said gently. 'You've been under a lot of stress recently. Maybe all of this is just your brain trying to impose some sort of order to everything you've been experiencing.' She gave a self-deprecating laugh. 'I've no idea what I'm talking about here. Obviously, I'm no expert on the physiology of the brain but I do know it's pretty powerful and can make you believe things which aren't real.'

'You think I'm delusional.' My tone was flat as Madison's words hung in the air. I inhaled deeply and let my breath puff out as a self-pitying grunt. As I cleared the plates to hide my disappointment with Madison's response, I muttered, 'You're probably right.'

'Don't get upset.' Madison knew me too well. 'As I said, stress can wreak havoc with the human brain. It would be understandable for a creative mind like yours to come up with all sorts of conspiracy theories in trying to make sense of your emotions.'

I sat down again, considering what she had said. 'But the theory wasn't mine – it was Selina's,' I protested.

Ellie snorted. 'At the risk of repeating myself ...' she began.

'That doesn't usually stop you,' Madison interjected, trying to lighten the atmosphere.

'This Selina has a lot to answer for,' Ellie ploughed on, giving Madison a dismissive scowl. 'All the stress you've been experiencing is down to her. If she hadn't freaked you out by stalking you, then you wouldn't have had all those other scary moments when you thought someone was following you or that you were being watched.'

'You're saying I imagined all of that?'

'Maybe ...' Ellie's face creased into a concerned smile. 'Look Anna, we both love you dearly but we've been quite worried about you.'

I shook my head, a gesture of defeat. Then something else occurred to me. 'But why would my parents conceal things from me? I definitely think they knew all about Selina before I told them. They must have done. Dad's reaction especially was so weird.'

Ellie looked across at Madison who imperceptibly shook her head.

'What? What is it? What are you not telling me?'

'Well we can't keep tiptoeing around it,' Ellie directed a defiant glare at Madison. 'It doesn't feel right that Anna doesn't know. No wonder she's so confused!'

'Doesn't know what?' I looked intently at Ellie. 'Come on Ell, what is it?'

'Well ...' She took my hand and squeezed it. 'Yes, your mum and dad *did* know about the blue Peugeot following you and then all about Selina because ...' she took a deep breath, 'we told them.'

'What?' It was as if I'd been punched in the stomach. I stared at my friends in confusion. 'Why?'

'Because we care about you … and so do your parents,' Madison said softly, moving around the table to give me a hug.

I shrugged her off. The sense of betrayal was a physical ache in my heart. 'How *could* you? I told you that stuff in confidence. Why on earth do you both think you have the right to go behind my back like that?'

'Look, Anna, we can see you're upset.' She glared at Ellie. 'This is your fault. You'd better try to put things right.'

'I'm listening.' My voice was cold.

Ellie grimaced. 'Your dad approached us when we were at uni. He was worried about you coping and asked us to let him know about anything out of the ordinary, that's all.'

'My dad asked you to spy on me?' I spluttered. This was beyond belief! 'And you *agreed*? I thought you were my friends!'

'We only agreed for your own good.' Madison tried once more to put her arm around me; once again I pushed her away.

'I keep hearing this, that *it's for my own good*. Why don't I get to decide what's good for me?' I wanted to rage and cry at the same time. Another unpleasant thought surfaced. 'Did he pay you?' I asked. 'Did my father give you money to spy on me and to report back to him?' When they remained uncomfortably silent, I erupted with fury. 'Oh my God, he did, didn't he!'

'No, not exactly,' Madison replied, her cheeks pink with embarrassment. 'He offered to pay us but we both refused. Honestly, it wasn't about money. But then, once a year, your dad would send us each a very generous cheque. He insisted we kept it, that it was a gift and he'd be offended if we didn't. I'm really sorry, Anna. I can understand how you feel but we really do love you and care about you. That's the only reason we did it. We didn't want you to have another breakdown.'

The world seemed to tilt on its axis and I felt sick. 'What do you mean?' I asked weakly. 'What breakdown?'

'The breakdown you had when you were fifteen when you tried to take your own life. Your dad said you didn't want to talk about it and that we shouldn't mention it to you but it meant they were always on eggshells, worrying if you might try again. He explained that the pressures of university may leave you struggling to cope and he told us to let him know immediately if anything happened or if you met anyone who upset your equilibrium. Don't you remember the breakdown, Anna?' Madison was studying my face, confusion wrinkling her features at my expression of incredulity.

'No.' I was emphatic. 'I never had a breakdown of any kind and I've never tried to commit suicide. I *do* have anxiety issues – I'll admit that – but nothing like you're suggesting.'

'I don't understand.' It was Ellie's turn to look puzzled. 'Why would your dad tell us that and get us to watch out for you if it wasn't true? Are you sure you haven't just blocked it out of your mind, Anna?'

'I'm positive.'

'But why would your father lie to us?'

'I don't know,' I replied grimly. 'But I'm going to find out.'

***

What do you do when those you trust let you down? I sat at my desk the following day, alone once more, staring unseeing at the computer screen and struggling with that question. My world had fallen apart. I'd trusted my parents and my two best friends and they'd deceived me, treachery which seared my soul. The previous evening, we'd talked long into the night. My anger had gradually dissipated and I'd accepted they'd acted in good faith. They'd been misled by my father and were only trying to look out for me. I believed that. It would take longer for the fractured trust between us to heal.

'No more secrets – promise me!' I insisted.

'Absolutely,' they chorused, eager with relief.

Madison advised confronting Dad to find out why he'd lied about the whole breakdown thing. Ellie, on the other hand, remained a little more sympathetic towards him.

'I think he's just hopelessly over-protective of you, Anna,' she argued. 'You're the centre of his world and, when you went off to university, he couldn't bear to let you go. He still wanted to keep an eye on his little girl ... Yes, I know he shouldn't have done it,' she'd continued at my cynical laugh, 'but I'm just saying I can understand it, that's all.'

They were both in agreement that Selina's assertions were ridiculous and I should disentangle myself from her life.

'She's either deranged with grief or downright malicious,' Madison declared, her nostrils flaring emphatically. 'Either way, you need to move on from her, Anna. She's brought you nothing but trouble and worry.'

Ellie nodded. 'Your dad is a good person, Anna, despite what he's done. The things Selina has suggested are completely outrageous. Think about it! She's insinuated that your parents kidnapped you when you were three years old and then tried to set fire to her house to get rid of her, presumably to keep their previous crime hidden. The whole thing is ridiculous! Do you really think your parents would be capable of such terrible things?'

I listened, guarding my own thoughts. My hurt was too raw to share more confidences. It would take time for me to confess anything to either of them again.

I slept surprisingly well and the kitchen was a flurry of activity when I finally surfaced at half past eight. Ellie and Madison were bickering good-naturedly as they cooked breakfast. By the smoky aroma, I deduced they were crisping bacon to within an inch of its life.

'I like it like that.' Madison gestured at the burnt offering.

'Mm, nothing like a bit of charcoal to set you up for the day,' Ellie remarked, taking a noisy crunch.

After breakfast, Ellie disappeared up to her bedroom. She was catching a train to Perth that morning for a family Christening on Sunday and then staying up there for a week's holiday. Madison also left promptly.

'I've got loads of stuff I need to catch up on. You know how it is for us girls with a proper job – oh sorry, you don't,' she teased.

'I *have* got a proper job.' I couldn't stop myself from taking the bait.

'I know.' Madison hugged me fervently. 'And I'm really sorry about everything. Please call me if you need me. I won't let you down again.'

She left, Ellie following soon afterwards and I plonked myself in front of my laptop. My aim was to overhaul my website and post a long-overdue update on my Facebook author page but instead I sat and stared unblinking at the screen. *Knowledge is power.* I needed to ascertain the truth about my birth, once and for all. Picking up the phone, I scrolled through until I reached Selina's name.

'Hello, Anna.' She answered on the second ring, her voice sounding stronger but tinged with wariness.

'Hi Selina. How's it all going?'

'Fine, thank you. The landlady here, Sue, is lovely – nothing is too much trouble – and yesterday I met an insurance assessor at the house. He gave me numbers of clean-up companies he recommended so that's what I'm trying to sort at the moment. As it's Saturday, though, I haven't managed to get through to anyone yet. How are you?'

'Well, thanks. Look Selina, I was wondering if you'd done anything about that DNA test yet?'

'No ...' she answered cautiously. 'I ... I wasn't sure if you still wanted to go ahead with it.'

'I do.'

'Oh ... fantastic. Thank you, Anna. I was so worried I'd upset you too much by what I said.'

'You did upset me but I'm sick of people lying to me. In the end, it's the truth that matters.'

There was a moment of silence as my words settled. 'Right. Well, I'll get online and organise something straight away. Can I use your address? It's just that I've only got one more night here and then I've got to find somewhere else to stay. Sue only has one room and it's booked up after that.'

'That's fine. Take care, Selina.'

I looked out of the window. Grey clouds scudded across the sky and next door's washing flapped furiously on the line. The frenzy outside stirred a need to expend some energy. I would go for a run – something I hadn't done since I first suspected someone was watching me. Before my anxieties could take hold and I changed my mind, I sped upstairs and rummaged through a drawer for my running gear. It felt good to be doing something active, something positive. I hadn't decided what to do about Dad but that could wait. At the moment, I really didn't feel like talking to him.

***

Josh was home. At just after four o'clock that afternoon, I received a text saying he couldn't wait to see me. I hugged his words to myself like a security blanket, the anticipation of our reunion filling me with giddy excitement.

I'll be round as soon as I can. Probably about 6pm xx

Hmm. I wondered what could possibly be so important as to keep him away for a whole two hours. I would've been racing around immediately to fall into his arms, travel weary or not. I scolded myself for my impatience; his father had recently suffered a heart attack, after all. Perhaps he was going to see him first. The image of his face, his eyes averted when I'd quizzed him over his knowledge of my address, crowded in, crushing my initial joy at seeing him. It bothered me. With last night's revelations still ringing in my ears, I knew I needed to be cautious. As yet, I didn't know if I could trust him.

CHAPTER 29

Selina

It was as if I knew something else was going to happen that day. I sensed the danger, lurking like a predator. I knew he'd be coming back to finish the job.

Ever since the night of the fire, I'd been on edge, taut, like a bow pulled too tight, threatening to snap at any moment. The strain was taking its toll. Oak Cottage was beautiful; Sue, the landlady, was lovely; my room was comfortable. But it was impossible to relax. I was alert to every sound, jumpy with fear. It was worse when I went outside. There I was in the open, vulnerable. If anyone wished me harm, I'd be powerless to prevent it. The conversation I'd had with Anna the day before also preyed on my mind. If only I could have that time again. How foolish to voice my suspicions! I didn't blame Anna at all for her reaction. It was my own fault.

I sat in my room, listening to the wind rattling the window, trying to pluck up the courage to move. I needed to go back to my house. There were a couple of things I'd forgotten when I was there yesterday with the insurance assessor. *Just get it done.* I peered out of the window to the driveway bordered with rose bushes. My car stood alone; Sue had gone out. A woman pushing a buggy walked along the pathway. *There's nothing there.* It was easier yesterday. Then I'd waited by the front door until I saw Anna's car. Today I would be on my own.

I glanced at my watch. Almost two o'clock. I couldn't keep putting it off. *What could happen in broad daylight?* Grimly, I checked my bag one more time. Car keys; house keys; key for Oak Cottage; purse; phone. With a small sob, I rose unsteadily from the chair. I hated feeling like this. It was ironic really. So many times after Maisie had been taken, I'd wished I was dead. Now I was fearful for my life, I realised just how precious it was, how much I wanted to live. I couldn't die without finding my daughter. And that wasn't going to happen if I stayed hiding in my room. Inhaling sharply, I opened the door and stepped onto the grey-carpeted landing. The house was quiet; no-one was about. The stairs were old and steep and I took them carefully, watching where I put my feet. They creaked and groaned beneath my step like aching joints.

A gust of wind whipped my hair as I opened the front door. It was cooler than the past few days and I pulled my thin, lilac cardigan protectively around me. Beneath my beige loafers, the tarmac drive made no sound and, in the distance, I heard the rumble of traffic crawling through the town. I kept my eyes fixed on my car, parked in one corner behind a hedge which shielded it from the road. The thought was reassuring. My car was hidden; no-one other than Anna knew where I was. I was safe here. The danger would be at my own house. Maybe there, someone would be hiding, waiting to pounce …

A surge of fear swamped my body and I squeezed the car keys, hearing the pop of the doors unlocking. I wouldn't stay long – just a quick visit to pick up some more clothes and my reading glasses. As my hand stretched forward towards the door handle, I felt the air shift behind me. Someone was there. I began to turn my head. Hands grabbed me, smothering my arms and I was jerked backwards out of sight from the road. As the scream formed in my throat, I felt something sharp, a knife, held precariously at my neck. My eyes widened with horror and I choked back my cry for help. The cold metal, the viciousness of the blade, pressing against my skin made me squirm. I couldn't help my small yelp of terror. He pressed a gloved hand against my mouth.

'Be quiet,' he hissed, his face against my ear. 'If you make another sound, it will be your last.'

He pushed me towards the boot of the car and demanded the keys. Paralysed with fear, I tried to pull my right arm free.

'In my hand,' I whispered. He loosened his grip and I contorted my arm backwards, trying to do as he wanted. My hand shook and the keys slipped from my grasp. 'Sorry,' I gasped, again trying to wriggle free, to see his face.

He swore and pressed the blade harder against my throat. I hardly dared breathe.

'Reach down and pick them up.' His voice was quiet and deadly, his intent unmistakable.

Slowly, gingerly, I leaned forward. The keys had skimmed across the tarmac and were lying behind one of the rear tyres. 'I can't reach,' I croaked.

'Dammit. Stand still.' I felt him move the knife and release his grip as he reached down to pick them up himself. I glimpsed short, grey hair, a black, leather jacket, a gloved hand reaching to the ground and realised, suddenly, this was my chance. Wrenching my body from his loosened grasp, I staggered away from him and towards the road, my ear-piercing screams swirling in the breeze. A car was indicating to turn into the drive and I threw myself at the driver's door. It was Sue, my landlady, staring at me as if I'd gone mad.

She lowered her window. 'Selina love, what's wrong?'

'A man … there's a man …' I pointed to the drive. 'In there. He has a knife.'

Her eyes widened. 'Have you called the police?'

'Not yet. I've only just got away. He had the knife at my throat.' I clutched my neck and glanced round nervously but there was no sign of the man. He had disappeared. 'I … I think he's gone.'

'Well, we're not taking any chances,' Sue said. 'Get in the car. I'm calling the police. We'll wait here, in plain view of anybody passing, until they arrive. You poor love. You'd never think something like this could happen in Swaffham.' She rummaged in her bag for her phone while I sat trembling beside her.

It was difficult to remember exactly what happened after that. Two police officers had arrived promptly, two men in their twenties, and had walked several times around the house. There was no sign of the man. I was asked to get out of the car and re-enact events as they had occurred.

'Did you get a look at the man at all? Can you give us a description?' one of them asked.

'Not really. It was more of a glimpse, an impression. He was white and quite thickset … stocky. His voice was gravelly. I'm not good with accents but he may have had a Norfolk accent. He was wearing a black, leather jacket and black gloves.' I paused, thinking. 'Oh, he had grey hair but I didn't see his face.'

They asked if I felt able to accompany them to the station to give a statement and I nodded. Still numb with shock, I was helped into the back of a police car and, a few minutes later, escorted into a small room at the police station. I waited. Eventually, a round-faced, young woman in uniform appeared and I found myself repeating everything I'd previously said while she recorded it. I tried to keep my emotions at bay and focus solely on the facts but terror still had me in its stranglehold. I couldn't stop my voice cracking as I answered her questions and I must've sounded very unconvincing. It was difficult to recall exact details; it had all happened so quickly.

At last, it was over. With a sympathetic smile, the officer switched off the recording device and told me to wait where I was. The interview room had windows along one side and I could see the people beyond it. The shorter man appeared to be the one in charge. He was doing most of the talking and the others were nodding.

All three officers returned. The shorter man told me a forensic team was currently at the scene but they didn't expect to find anything.

'Your keys were lying by the car where you dropped them. He must have run as soon as you started screaming.' He spoke in a flat monotone. 'Can you think of any reason why you may have been targeted?'

His face grew more concerned as I told them about the fire and why I was convinced that too was an attempt on my life. They left the room and I watched them talking once more. The female police officer returned and my statement was read back to me. In it, I'd talked about Maisie and my twenty-three-year search to find her. I hadn't mentioned Anna. I just couldn't. It would destroy any hope I had of re-establishing a relationship with her.

After I'd signed my statement, I was told any knife attack was treated with the utmost seriousness, even if the victim was uninjured. My case would be a priority. The woman then gently handed me some leaflets and told me about counselling and victim support groups. I let the words float over me, not listening. I had an overwhelming urge to cry. How could strangers help me? I needed my family.

Reaching in my bag, I pulled out my phone. When the young woman offered to drive me home, I shook my head. I would call Anna.

CHAPTER 30

Anna

My phone rang and I tutted with annoyance. Dad had already called once that afternoon and I hadn't answered; it was probably him again. The phone was lying on my desk and had stopped ringing by the time I reached it. To my surprise though, it was Selina who was trying to reach me. Briefly, I toyed with the idea of ignoring her but my conscience wouldn't allow it. Whatever she wanted would only take a few minutes.

'Selina, hi. Sorry I missed your call. I didn't make it to the phone in time.'

'Oh Anna, thank goodness!' Her voice sounded suspiciously tearful.

'What's wrong? What's the matter?'

There was a sob and then the trembling voice once more. 'I'm sorry, Anna but I need your help again. I wouldn't trouble you but ...'

'Just tell me what's wrong,' I demanded. 'You're worrying me.'

'I ... well ... can you come and fetch me?'

'Where are you?' Impatience was creeping into my tone.

'I'm ... I'm at Swaffham police station.'

'What?' I couldn't hide my shock. 'Why? What's happened?'

'I ...' Selina was crying openly now. 'There was a man. He ... he tried to grab me. I got away.'

Horror flooded through me. 'Oh Selina, that's terrible. Are you OK?'

'Not really.' There was a noisy gulp and then a wail. 'Anna, I'm scared.'

'I'll be right there. Try not to worry, Selina. You're safe now.'

Thoughts raced through my mind as I grabbed my car keys and dashed through the front door. Who was the man who had tried to grab Selina? Was it a mugger? A random attack? Or was it a deliberate attempt on Selina's life? Clamping a lid on where those thoughts were taking me, I sped towards Swaffham. There was no point in trying to second guess what had happened; I would have to wait until I got there.

At the police station, Selina was sitting, head bowed, in the waiting area. Her back was bent and she looked brittle enough to snap at the slightest puff of wind. I felt a surge of pity and rushed to sit beside her.

'Selina.' I slipped a tentative arm around her thin shoulders. 'I'm here.'

She started, the anxiety in her lined face melting into relief. 'Oh, thank goodness.' She rose unsteadily to her feet.

'Take your time. There's no rush. Tell me what happened.'

She shook her head. 'Not now, not here. Later.'

As I escorted her through the door, Selina stopped and peered nervously down the street.

'My car's just along here.' I encouraged her forward. 'You've had a nasty shock but you're safe now. No-one's going to hurt you.'

She allowed herself to be ushered into the front passenger seat of my Fiesta. With trembling fingers, she snapped her seatbelt into place and turned to face me. 'You're so kind,' she muttered.

'Nonsense. I'm just being your friend. Where do you want me to take you?'

She gave me a frightened look. 'Back to Oak Cottage, I suppose ... but ... that's where it happened.'

'What? You were attacked at the B & B?'

'Yes, well, just outside. I was walking towards my car ... Anna, I'm sorry but I don't want to stay there, even if it's just for one night. I don't feel safe. He knows where I am ... and he ... he might come back.' Tears filled her eyes and her hand was shaking as she wiped them away. The poor woman was clearly terrified.

'That's no problem. You can stay with me.' The words were emitted from my mouth before I could think about the wisdom of such a statement.

'Are ... are you sure?' The hope etched on her face was piteous to behold.

'Of course,' I replied firmly. 'But I suggest we go and pick up your things and to tell your landlady. She needs to know that a man has been lurking around her premises.'

'Oh, she already knows,' Selina said, her voice already sounding stronger. 'She was the one who called the police for me.'

'What happened?' I asked as she started the engine and pulled away from the kerb.

'Oh ...' She sighed heavily and her shoulders slumped. 'Can we wait until we get back to your house?'

***

While Selina packed her things at Oak Cottage, I called Josh. I didn't give him all the details, just that a friend needed me so we couldn't meet up after all. He was gratifyingly disappointed.

'You're not serious,' he exclaimed, dismay reverberating through the phone.

'I'm really sorry. I was so looking forward to seeing you. I just can't leave my friend alone this evening, not after what she's been through.'

He sighed. 'OK, I understand. How about tomorrow?'

'I'm sure that will be fine.' At least, I hoped it would.

'I'll be round at ten to pick you up, as long as you think you can leave your friend.'

'I can't wait.'

'Me neither.'

Ellie had not been quite so understanding when I phoned to tell her. 'You've agreed to let her stay in the spare room? After everything Mads and I said? You must be mad.'

'I know.' I bit my lip ruefully. 'But you should see her, Ell. She's a nervous wreck. There's no way she could stay where she was attacked so … I offered.'

'That's because you have a heart of putty. Well, it's done now. I just hope you don't regret it.'

That too was my niggling concern. If Selina was the person my parents thought she was, this could all be another act to garner my sympathy. Her distress seemed genuine but, the way I was feeling, I no longer trusted my judgement about anyone.

It was half past five by the time we pulled up outside my house. 'This really is terribly kind of you,' Selina mumbled.

'Not at all.' I sprang out of the car and unlocked the front door. 'You go on in,' I told her. 'I'll bring your bags.'

Once Selina was unpacking in the spare room, I put the kettle on and opened the fridge to see what I could rustle up for dinner. There were some bacon and eggs left over from breakfast time and half a packet of spaghetti in the cupboard so maybe a carbonara. I also put a bottle of wine in the fridge to chill. I had a feeling I was going to need it. My phone rang and I picked it up without thinking. *Dad.* My stomach churned and I was tempted to let the call go to voicemail once more. The trouble was, if I failed to pick up, there was always the danger he could turn up here. With the current situation, that was a definite no. Squaring my shoulders, I hit the button. Knowledge is power, I reminded myself. Don't give it away.

'Darling, I've been trying to get hold of you.' My senses were on full alert, listening for the undertone in his voice, hearing only his usual bluff tone tinged with exasperation.

'Sorry,' I answered coolly. 'It's been a busy day.'

A pause. He was waiting for me to elaborate further. When I didn't, he continued, this time with a touch more asperity. 'Yes, well, you know how I worry about you.'

The sentence triggered annoyance. Worrying about me didn't give him the right to interfere in my life. I took a deep breath and bit back the retort forming on my lips. 'There's no need.'

'I think there is. You're my little girl; I'll never stop worrying about you.' His voice had softened now as he switched on his renowned charm. 'Listen Anna, I've been thinking. Why don't you come home, stay with us for a few weeks? I feel like we've grown apart recently – don't say it, it's probably my fault – and then with all this stuff going on with *that woman* … Anna, it's doing my head in. You mustn't trust her, darling. You don't know what she's capable of …'

I listened dispassionately to his words. How could I believe anything he said? Yet, he sounded so worried that I felt the hairs on the back of my neck begin to prickle. What on earth would he say if he knew Selina was now camping out in my house?

'Anna, are you still there?'

'Yes, Dad, sorry.' A pause, while I collected my thoughts. There was still a small part of me wanting to do as he asked; go home, let him take care of everything. But I no longer trusted him. *Don't let him control you. He may love you but he's trying to stifle you. He has to let go.*

'I was just thinking things through,' I continued. 'Thank you for the offer but I don't think I can come home at the moment. As I said, I've got a lot going on.'

'Ah … your young man … Josh, isn't it? I hope you're out with him tonight. It was today he was coming back from London, wasn't it?' *Had I told him Josh was going to London?* I didn't think so. *Maybe Ellie or Madison had told him.*

'Yes, we did have plans,' I said simply. There was no need to tell him they had been cancelled.

'Oh.' He sounded surprised. 'Well, have a good time. I'll phone you in the morning.'

I closed my eyes, relieved the call was over but feeling disturbed by things he'd said. How did he know about Josh going to London? I fired off a text to my friends.

Did either of you tell Dad that Josh was going to London and would be back Saturday?

They'd agreed, last night, to tell him nothing more about my life, no matter what, but one of them may have mentioned it beforehand.

'I've unpacked.' Selina was framed in the doorway, a wan smile pasted on her face. She looked so frail, so helpless and hopeless. How could such a person be capable of the things my Dad was suggesting?

'Well done. I'll make some tea and then you'd better tell me what happened earlier today,' I said firmly.

Selina nodded and slid into a seat at the table. 'A cup of tea would be lovely,' she agreed.

I carried two mugs across the kitchen and sat down opposite her. 'Just take your time. I know it's going to be difficult to talk about it.'

Selina drew in a shuddering breath. 'I still can't believe it happened …'

CHAPTER 31

Anna

Since my conversation with Selina the previous evening when, with a tremor in her voice, she'd described the attack, I'd been unable to think of anything else. It sounded far-fetched. Was the man with the knife real or had she made him up? How cynical I'd become, I realised. I no longer accepted anything at face value. I'd watched Selina carefully when she told me what had happened. Her face was ashen; her hand trembled. Surely no-one could fake that kind of reaction.

If it *was* true and she was being targeted, her life was in danger – mine too, by harbouring her. I was extra vigilant, locking all the windows and doors last night and making frequent checks through the window this morning, making sure no-one was there. My blood had run cold when Selina had revealed details of her attacker. The man I thought was following me, watching me, fitted that description. My brow furrowed as I tried to recall when I'd last seen him. Not since I'd mentioned him to Ewan. Could it be the same man?

'What did the police say?' I asked.

Selina shrugged. 'Not much. They sent a forensic team to the scene and are treating the case as a priority. They asked if I had any reason to believe someone had it in for me.' She paused and looked at me with tremulous eyes. My blood froze. 'I told them about Maisie and the fire at my house. They said they'd look into it.'

'Did you mention me … or my parents?' I had to ask.

She looked me in the eye. 'No.'

I exhaled, swamped with relief. 'Thank you,' I said. I took her hand. 'Whatever's going on, I'm sure my parents have nothing to do with it. I know the DNA test will prove that so I'm so glad you didn't say anything.'

Selina was upstairs when Josh arrived promptly at ten o'clock and I fell into his arms. So much for treading warily!

'Mm, nice welcome,' he murmured huskily into my hair, hugging me tightly. 'It was almost worth going away … although you've still got to make it up to me for putting me off last night.'

'I know. Sorry about that.' I grabbed my bag and stepped outside, locking the door behind me.

'You said it was an emergency? A friend needed you?' he queried.

'Yes.' I shared no further details. Despite my feelings for Josh, I was determined to be cautious. The less people who knew Selina was staying at my house the better.

We headed for the coast once more, this time to Holkham, for a walk on the beach and Sunday lunch. I'd fretted about leaving Selina on her own but she had insisted.

'I'll be fine here,' she said firmly when I offered to postpone my plans. 'I'll lock all the doors and spend the day reading, if you don't mind me borrowing one of your books. I noticed you have a Jill Mansell novel I haven't read. She's one of my favourite authors, apart from you, of course. You can't stay at home babysitting me all the time and no-one knows I'm here.'

'OK, if you're sure.' I allowed myself to be persuaded. 'Help yourself to whatever you need. I've ordered a grocery delivery between six and seven tonight and I'll be back by then.'

As we neared the coast, the mists started to gather, casting a fuzzy, grey shroud over the trees lining the road. I shivered, suddenly cold in my thin, cotton shirt. Claustrophobia was closing in …

I was sobbing … just a small child … restrained in a car seat … travelling through thick fog … unable to escape …

What had triggered that memory? I dug my finger nails into my thighs, an attempt at distraction from the creeping anxiety seeping into my bones. The sense of panic was gaining momentum, taking hold. *Not now, please. Think of something else.*

'Do you want the heating up?' Josh asked. 'Are you alright? You look as if you've seen a ghost.'

'I … I am a bit cold,' I admitted.

He shook his head, dismayed at his thoughtlessness. 'Sorry. I tend to forget that not everyone likes the air-conditioning on full blast. You should've said.'

I rubbed my palms against my legs, trying to disperse the fright/flight adrenalin coursing through my body. It wasn't working. I had to get out of the car. The blackness was threatening to overwhelm me.

'Anna, are you OK?' Dimly, in the distance, I heard Josh's voice.

'Stop the car!' It took all my energy and focus to get the words out.

'What?' Josh glanced across, his face furrowed with concern. He flicked the indicator switch and pulled onto a verge by the side of the road. Even before the car had stopped, I was fumbling the catch on my seat belt and pushing the door open. 'Wait!' he called but I'd already tumbled out of the car, my breaths coming in shallow gasps. I stumbled forward. The verge was shadowed by trees and I headed for the nearest, a large oak. Numbly, I leant against the gnarled bark and focused on slowing my breathing. Away from the car, the panic was beginning to recede and the blackness was fading. I took a deep breath and fumbled a tissue from my pocket to wipe my clammy forehead.

'Anna, what's wrong?'

Josh was bending over me and I looked up, bracing myself for scorn or impatience. 'I'm sorry. I felt a bit queasy.'

He put his arm around me. 'Don't apologise. You poor thing! I think there's a bottle of water in the car. Shall I get it?'

I nodded gratefully. 'Thanks.' As I watched him rummaging in the boot of his Mercedes, I tried to unpick my childhood recollection of the car journey which had distressed me. At the far edges of my memory, there was something teasing, just out of reach, but the more I tried to grasp it, the more elusive it became.

'There you go.' Josh handed me a bottle, his brown eyes soft with concern. 'How are you feeling now?'

'Much better, thanks.' I smiled weakly. 'The fresh air has helped.'

He frowned. 'Perhaps I'd better take you home.'

'No.' The panic had gone. I was safe; I was with Josh who wasn't going to hurt me. 'It was just a moment. It could have been car sickness. I'm not good on winding country roads.'

'Well, take all the time you need. There's no rush. I'll give you a bit of space. At least we haven't got much further to go.'

He headed back to the car and I felt a rush of warmth towards him. His kindness and solicitude made my heart glow. Idly, I watched as he retrieved his phone, his face serious as he scrolled through his messages. My own phone vibrated in my pocket and I glanced at the screen in case it was Selina. In fact, it was Madison, saying she'd told Dad nothing at all about Josh. I'd received the same response from Ellie last night. Another mystery; how did Dad know Josh was in London and returning on Saturday?

I looked across to Josh who was now engaged in a phone conversation, his back to me. Was he also in cahoots with my father? My mind trawled back to the conversation we'd exchanged in his kitchen, when he'd talked about his career in banking. My mention of Dad's name had met with a non-committal response and he'd changed the subject. It occurred to me that Geoff Blake was very well known in the City community; Josh had to be aware of him. So why the evasion? Perhaps Josh had a reason to dislike him – that would explain it. But Dad had described Josh in glowing terms. What was going on? Already smarting from the Ellie and Madison's revelation, I watched Josh with narrowed eyes. *Ask him.*

He put his phone away and returned to my side.

'Josh, how well do you know my father?' I could see the question took him by surprise but was there also a flash of panic in his eyes, quickly hidden, as his features settled into a look of polite curiosity?

'Why do you ask?'

'Because my father hasn't been entirely honest with me recently,' I replied drily. 'And a number of things haven't been adding up.'

'Such as?'

'Both of you suggested to me that you barely knew each other and yet, somehow, my dad knew you were away in London the past few days. Not only that, he informed me when you were returning. How did he know?' I tried to keep my voice calm but couldn't hide the accusatory note, evident in the rise in pitch at the end of the question.

He shrugged. 'How should I know? Perhaps you should ask him.'

'And another thing ... you knew where I lived but I hadn't told you the address. I'm very careful about things like that. How did you know where I lived?'

'Damned if I can remember.' He shook his head. 'Look Anna, are you accusing me of something here?'

'No ... it's not that.' At his direct question, I halted my interrogation. There was no proof he'd done anything wrong and I didn't want to upset him needlessly. 'Last night, I found out my two best friends had been tricked by my father into reporting back information about me. It's left me feeling betrayed, like I don't know who I can trust.'

'That's terrible!' He took me in his arms. 'Why on earth would he do such a thing?'

I pulled away and searched his eyes, seeing compassion and something else ... I couldn't be sure. His reaction wasn't straightforward. 'Who knows. He's always been over-protective and, I guess, once I'd moved away from home, he still felt the need to keep tabs on me.'

He nodded thoughtfully. 'I suppose I can understand that.' He grinned suddenly. 'If we had a daughter, I think I'd find it difficult to let her out of my sight.'

My heart leapt. 'If we had a daughter,' I repeated. 'Aren't you jumping the gun a bit?'

'Maybe.' He pulled me once again into his arms. 'But when you've found the one, you know.' His lips found mine, warm and urgent, and all coherent thought deserted me.

It was only much later I realised he hadn't answered the question about my father.

***

I tossed and turned in my bed, alternately pushing the duvet off and then hauling it back over me. Sleep was elusive and my mind picked over recent events, seeking answers to questions which remained unfathomable. Having tackled Josh about his relationship with Dad, I'd shelved the issue, allowing myself the uncomplicated pleasure of his company. The hours passed all too quickly and I was home by six o'clock, as I'd promised Selina. He'd tried to persuade me to check in on my friend and return with him to the Old Rectory. The offer was tempting but my conscience wouldn't allow me to accept. 'Soon,' I promised with a parting kiss.

Selina was endearingly pleased to see me. She'd spent part of her day scouring the contents of cupboards, fridge and freezer and a mouth-watering aroma was emanating from the kitchen. A chocolate cake took pride of place on the worktop.

'Wow, that looks amazing. You *have* been busy.'

'Not really.' Her smile was self-conscious. 'I love cooking and wanted to do something to repay you for taking me in like this. Which reminds me, I want to pay you rent, like I was paying at Oak Cottage. It'll be covered by the insurance and it wouldn't be right for you to be out of pocket.'

After our evening meal of chicken fricassee and cake, we talked long into the night, mostly about me. Selina seemed to have an endless thirst for knowledge about my childhood and I was happy to answer her questions. We both avoided any conversation about the past few days and what would happen in the future. For a few hours, we existed in a bubble, impenetrable from the outside world.

However, having got into bed at around midnight, I twisted restlessly, trying to shut out all the unwelcome visitors, all the 'what-ifs,' crowding in on my mind. It was impossible to relax sufficiently for sleep and eventually, exasperated with myself, I decided to get up. An hour's writing would hopefully make me sleepy. Stealthily, so as not to wake Selina, I tiptoed down the stairs in the dark and groped through to my study before flicking the light switch. The glare felt too bright, too invasive. I switched it off again and turned on my desk lamp. My computer was in sleep mode – I'd forgotten to shut it down yesterday in my dash to Swaffham police station – and I reread the paragraph I'd been writing. It wasn't great but editing would have to wait; I needed the soothing effect of my fingers skipping over the keys as the words flowed out.

Jemima stared at the photograph in horror. It couldn't have been any more blatant. There was her husband, looking totally gorgeous, the cheating bastard, his arm casually draped around a stunning-looking woman who was reaching up to kiss him. He was smiling affectionately down at her; he certainly wasn't trying to fend her off. Worse still, the woman in the photo was his ex-girlfriend and (clearly still very close) work colleague, the manipulative, scheming Samira Goodman. It was she who had deliberately tagged Jemima in the post on Facebook which read 'Please don't be jealous, Jemima darling. You have him all the time. At work, it's my turn.'

What was she saying? Was she suggesting that she and Conrad were having an affair but that it was OK because it was work? No, she wouldn't believe it; she **couldn't** *believe it.*

I screwed my face up, pondering what Jemima would do next. She'd phone Conrad, I decided, but her call would go to voicemail.

I sat back and heard a tiny click, the noise magnified by the silence. It sounded like the lock on the front door. I held my breath, listening, my body stiff with tension, my stomach spasming with fear.

Nothing.

I swallowed and stood up. Suddenly, the darkness in the hallway loomed as a threat and I switched the main light back on. *No-one's there; it's just your imagination playing tricks on you.* My eyes swept the contents of the small study, searching for a possible weapon and fastened on an umbrella standing in one corner. I tiptoed over and grasped it firmly, brandishing it like a truncheon. The weight of it in my hand provided some small reassurance – it wasn't much but it was better than nothing.

I stood there for a few minutes, waiting, listening for another sound. In the distance, I heard a car engine start up. Outside the window, the breeze had picked up, rustling the leaves. Nothing else. I imagined an intruder, standing by the doorway, waiting for me to step out, waiting to pounce. For a moment, I even thought I could hear his breathing but, when I strained a little closer, there was no sound.

I can't stand here like this all night. Flexing my fingers on the umbrella handle, I inched forward towards the door. Fear of the unknown, that's all it was. Sweat trickled down the back of my neck. I reached the doorway and lifted the umbrella higher. A deep breath and I peered around the corner, heart pounding.

The hallway was empty.

My fear abated ... then I wondered if the intruder could be hiding somewhere. There was nothing for it; I needed to make sure. Like a ninja, constantly spinning around to check behind, I moved towards the front door. It was locked. *This really is just my imagination. Thank goodness no-one can see me. I'm behaving like an idiot.* I crept around the rest of the house, switching on the lights, looking for anything untoward. Again, nothing.

Shaking my head at myself, I returned the umbrella to the study and shut down the laptop. The thought of sitting alone, enveloped by the dark, had lost its appeal. I headed upstairs to the safety of my bed, exhausted by my own nervous energy. Wrapping myself in the comfort of my duvet, I reached out to turn off the bedside light and then hesitated. Maybe I'd leave it on ...

***

A few miles away, the grey-haired man in a white Audi was driving at speed towards Norwich. He'd been clocked in the Range Rover – a dent in his professional pride – and had switched vehicles. His craggy face was outwardly calm but inside he seethed with frustration.

Who would have thought the girl would be up at 2 am? His plans would now have to wait until tomorrow. Then there would be no more mistakes.

CHAPTER 32

Anna

The sunshine filtering through the curtains the following morning felt warm on my face. With my bedroom bathed in golden light, my night-time fears seemed absurd. Today was a new day. Downstairs, Selina was making pancakes, humming tunelessly as she worked.

'Wow, what a treat!' I exclaimed, 'Although I'm not sure my waistline would agree.'

'Nonsense. You're slim and beautiful. A pancake's not going to change that.'

I slid into a chair, the compliment lifting my spirits. The thought of Mum scolding me as a child for wanting a second slice of cake came unbidden. It was at a children's party. There were all sorts of unhealthy goodies on offer and I tucked in greedily, enjoying foods forbidden at home. The birthday cake was an enormous dinosaur, resplendent with lurid, green icing. It was delicious; I savoured every crumb. More cake was offered and I extended a chubby hand to take another slice. I remembered the hand on my wrist, nails biting into my skin, pulling my arm back. Mum's voice, glacial with disapproval, hissed in my ear. 'Greedy child. You'll be as fat as a Teletubby if you eat like that. Time to go home.' I remembered my cheeks burning with shame as I was escorted from the party. She then lectured me all the way home. 'I'm not saying you can't eat cake, Anna. You just have to learn moderation. I don't want you growing up fat and ugly. That's why we don't have things like cake and biscuits at home.' I learnt right there that I'd only attain her approval if I was slim and pretty. Often, growing up, I stared anxiously at the mirror, horrified at my gap-toothed smile, knowing I wasn't good enough for my glamorous parents.

'Come on, eat up. Don't let it get cold,' Selina scolded gently as I sat staring into space, lost in childhood angst.

I bit into the pancake, sweet with a dusting of sugar and sharp with lemon. 'Mm, I could definitely get used to this.' Suddenly hungry, I forked in another mouthful. 'This is sublime.'

'I've made another one, if you'd like it.'

'Do you know, Selina, I think I will. I can't remember the last time I had home-made pancakes.' Who cared about moderation! 'What are your plans for today?'

She pulled a face. 'I need to phone these specialist house cleaning companies recommended by the insurance company and get things moving there. At some point, I have to get my car. It's still at the B & B. I know Sue said I could leave it there as long as I liked but I'm going to need it for showing people the house. I can't stay holed up here for ever.' She bit her lip and lowered her fork, leaving half a pancake uneaten.

'One step at a time,' I said gently. 'Make your calls this morning and we'll sort your car when we need to. I don't think you should go anywhere on your own at the moment – not while the lunatic who tried to abduct you is still out there. Hopefully, the police will discover something useful soon.'

'Thanks Anna.' She squeezed my shoulder as she rose to clear the plates. 'I realise I can't stay here indefinitely but it's so nice spending time with you.' Her eyes filmed with tears and she blinked them away.

'There's no rush.' I stood to give her a hug. 'You can stay as long as you need. Ellie's fine with it and, anyway, she's not back until the weekend. Hopefully, by then, this man will be in custody. That's when you can worry about moving out.'

Selina turned away, her shoulders shaking with silent sobs. 'Thank you. You don't know what that means,' she gulped. 'I've been so worried ...' She grabbed a handful of tissues from the box on the worktop. 'I'm scared, Anna. I think it's only a matter of time before I ...' She groped for words. 'I've been lucky but how long can that last?'

I watched, helpless in the face of her distress. What could I say? She was convinced there had been two attempts on her life. I was beginning to believe it too. 'Come on,' I said. 'I'll make you a coffee and then you can get started on those phone calls. You'll feel better when you're busy doing something.'

As I filled the kettle and stood staring out of the window, waiting for the water to boil, I wondered if I was being naive. Could I trust her? I knew exactly what Dad would say.

'How convenient that no-one else managed to see this attacker! And, if this woman is so fearful for her life, what is she doing hanging around with you? Why hasn't she gone back to where she comes from where she'd be safe?'

He had a point, this imaginary voice. I believed her distress was genuine. Nobody was that good an actress. But why had she remained here? That was something which didn't make sense.

'Listen,' I said, 'you're obviously still very frightened, understandably so. Is it sensible to stay in this area, do you think? Would you be safer back in Nottingham?'

Selina sipped her coffee and sighed. 'Probably. I have to admit I've thought about it. If my life's in danger, it's daft to stay ... I suppose I ... oh, you're going to think I'm ridiculous!'

'Go on. I promise I won't.'

'It's just that this all started when you agreed to the DNA test which makes me believe I'm truly on to something at last. I may have finally found my daughter.' She gave me an apologetic smile. 'I know you don't agree but I'm just being honest. I guess I'm banking everything on this DNA test. It should arrive today, we'll do it and send it off. Then, maybe I'll consider heading for the hills.'

I nodded slowly. 'I think that would be wise until the police arrest someone. Thank goodness no-one else knows where you are – just you, me and my friend Ellie ... and she won't say anything.'

***

Ewan phoned as I sat at my desk. His name on my screen evoked all my recent suspicions.

'Hi Ewan.' I kept my voice neutral.

'Hi Gorgeous. What are you up to this lovely morning?'

'The usual. Trying to write. How about you?'

'That's why I'm calling. I have an appointment in Swaffham later this morning. A client wants a quote for the installation of an alarm system so I was wondering if we could meet up for lunch afterwards at the Hare & Hounds. If not, maybe I could pop round this morning?'

'Lunch sounds great,' I said quickly. I definitely didn't want him turning up at the house when Selina was there. 'Shall we say one o'clock?'

'Perfect. See you then. I'll be the one wearing a purple wig and a false moustache.'

Smiling, I laid the phone down. Almost immediately, it rang again. This time it was Josh calling from his car.

'I've got a few things to do this morning but I thought maybe we could have lunch?'

'Oh.' Although my relationship with Ewan was platonic, I couldn't help squirming with guilt. 'I'm sorry I can't. I've just agreed to meet up with a friend.'

'The same one who has been keeping you from me the past few days?' He didn't wait for my reply. 'That's a shame. I have a family get together tonight – it's my mum's birthday – so I won't be able to see you ... unless you'd like to come along?'

'Er ...' The thought of meeting all his family induced a flurry of anxiety. It was too soon; I wasn't ready. Then there was Selina to consider. 'I'm really sorry but that might be tricky. You enjoy your evening with your family and I'll hopefully see you tomorrow.'

'OK, will do.' He didn't sound offended. 'Tomorrow's Tuesday. Are you still planning on coming around as usual in the afternoon?' he continued. 'There's a paintbrush at home with your name on it.'

'How could I refuse such an enticing offer?' I replied. 'Can't wait.'

'Me neither. I've missed you.'

'Me too.'

I ended the call, savouring the giddy excitement, fizzing like champagne bubbles, that speaking to Josh always brought. As it faded, disappointment followed. If only I hadn't agreed to meet Ewan, I could've had lunch with Josh instead, enjoying the charge of sexual chemistry as my eyes met his across the table and the secret touches beneath it. Heat flooded my face as I realised Selina was staring at me curiously.

'Sorry to interrupt you, Anna,' she said, 'but the DNA test has arrived.'

***

Ewan was already waiting by the bar, darkly handsome in a crisp, open-necked shirt and tan chinos, a glass of orange juice in front of him, when I rushed in.

'I'm so sorry I'm late.' I leaned towards him for a friendly peck on the cheek. By the time Selina and I had unwrapped the fat package containing the DNA testing kit, read the instructions, completed the mouth swabs and sealed them as directed, time was pressing on. Selina wanted to post the return package immediately and was intent on walking to the post office on the other side of the village. A brief argument over the wisdom of such action had been resolved when I offered to post it myself on the way to meet Ewan. I had no time to get changed and was running late by the time I reached the post office. Then I was forced to queue, outwardly serene but tapping my foot irritably, for what seemed like an age but was probably only a few minutes. I hated being late. Tardiness had never been acceptable when I was growing up and was panic-inducing now.

'No worries. I've only just got here myself,' Ewan smiled warmly. 'Drink?'

I settled on the stool next to him, letting my eyes slide casually around the bar to check out the clientele. An older couple were seated by the bay window, both intent on the plates of food in front of them, and a craggy-faced, old man with shoulder-length, white hair was reading a newspaper at the end of the bar; otherwise the pub was empty. I relaxed and smiled back at my companion. 'I'll have a diet coke, thanks. So,' I continued as the barman slid a glass in front of me, 'to what do I owe this honour?'

Ewan shrugged. 'No particular reason. As I told you, I was in the area and thought I'd give you a call. Ever since you told me you thought you were being followed, I've been worrying about you.'

'Really?' I was touched by his concern.

'Well, not much,' he said with a grin, 'just a tiny bit. Anyway, I wanted to check how you were doing.'

'Fine, thanks,' I replied smoothly. My budding suspicion that he could be working for my parents meant that, despite his charm, I needed to keep my guard up. 'Since I last saw you, I haven't seen grey-haired guy, as I think of him, at all. It was probably just my imagination.'

'That's good.' The lines of concern etched on his brow dissolved and I felt a stab of guilt for doubting him. His eyes, framed by those long lashes, were as guileless as a Labrador puppy's. I would've liked to trust him as the friend he claimed to be but there were too many unanswered questions holding me back. I needed to find out first exactly why he was investigating Selina Matthews and what he was doing for my father. Having both ordered the 'house' sandwiches, we made our way over to the table by the other bay window.

'How's the business going?' I asked conversationally.

'Great, thanks. Very busy.'

I took a deep breath. 'Are you still doing work for my father?'

His open countenance hardened, just fractionally, but I saw it. 'I can't really discuss that with you – client confidentiality and all that. You'd need to talk to him.'

I nodded but was determined to dig deeper, even if that meant some subterfuge of my own. 'I understand. He said he'd asked you to look into Selina Matthews' background.' He'd admitted no such thing but I was hoping to prompt an indiscretion. 'Is that still ongoing? I think, given the circumstances, you should be able to tell me *everything* you know about her. Did he tell you about the DNA test?'

He hesitated, his eyes shifting away from mine. 'I've already told you why you should stay away from Selina Matthews,' he said eventually. 'Your parents agree with me. Hopefully, between us, we've convinced you.' He took a sip from his drink and directed his gaze to my face once more. 'Have we?'

This time, it was my turn to hesitate and lower my eyes. Taking my cue from him, I took a long swig of coke while I formed my response. *The best form of defence is attack.* 'When did Dad ask you to investigate Selina Matthews?'

He thought for a moment and this time took the bait. 'A couple of weeks ago maybe. Now I've answered your question. How about you answer mine?'

A couple of weeks ago ... Ewan had been employed by my father to investigate Selina Matthews at least a week before I'd ever mentioned her name to him. How did he know about her?

'Anna?' Ewan prompted.

'I haven't decided,' I said flatly. 'I still feel there's a lot going on that I don't know about.' That was an understatement.

He took my hand, the weight of his fingers hot against my skin. 'But Anna, surely you trust me? Surely you trust your father? He knows what's best for you?'

'My Dad knows what's best for *him*,' I replied coolly, pulling my hand from his grasp. 'I'm the best judge of what's right for me.'

'But Anna, he's just trying to protect you. You have to admit, you're very vulnerable where someone like Selina Matthews is concerned.'

'What do you mean – *vulnerable*?'

'Well ...' His cheeks coloured. 'You know ... because of your past.'

'I see ... and what *past* would that be?'

'I'm sorry, Anna.' He reached for my hand once more and, instinctively, I snatched it under the table, beyond his reach. 'Your dad told me about your breakdown. Honestly, it's nothing to be ashamed of. Look at my past!'

A rush of anger surged through me. Another one! My father had a lot of questions to answer. What on earth was he playing at? 'You shouldn't believe everything he tells you,' I snapped. 'He is quite capable of playing fast and loose with the truth to get what he wants.'

Ewan stared at me and raised his eyebrows. 'Aren't we all? I know your dad thinks the world of you and would do anything in his power to protect you. He believes this woman poses a threat and I'm inclined to agree. Not necessarily a physical threat,' he continued at my expression of scepticism, 'but a threat to your emotional wellbeing. He's a good guy, Anna. I owe him everything and trust his judgement completely. You should too.'

The arrival of the landlady carrying two plates of food provided a welcome lull in the conversation and gave me a moment to gather my thoughts. Ewan's passionate defence of my father sounded so genuine I found myself acknowledging his point of view. An imposter was claiming Geoff Blake's daughter as her own. No wonder he was using all the resources in his possession to keep her away from me. But was he capable of violence against Selina? I wouldn't believe that; I *couldn't* believe it. Whatever the truth, I needed to cut Ewan some slack.

'This looks good,' I smiled, a placatory gesture, indicating the plates piled high with club sandwiches, a smattering of thick-cut chips and salad garnish. 'Look Ewan, you're probably right. I'll think about what you've said.'

'Good,' he replied.

***

That night, my eyes closed almost as soon as my head hit the pillow but sleep didn't bring the oblivion I craved. My dreams were a continuation of the emotional turbulence in which I was embroiled. I feared there would be no answers until I confronted my father but was reluctant to do so until I'd received the results of the DNA test. Ewan's words had forced me to face the fact I may be letting my natural liking for Selina cloud my judgement. The police seemed to be no further forward in their investigation of the alleged attempted abduction and I couldn't be certain it had actually happened. It *was* possible that Selina had made the whole thing up.

A scream shattered the silence of the night, cutting through a nightmare where a grey-haired man held me by the throat. My eyes flickered open. *Did I dream it?* Another cry pierced the darkness. Selina! I flung back the duvet and leapt out of bed ...

CHAPTER 33

Selina

It was pitch black when I woke. I fumbled for my phone on the bedside table to check the time. 2:43 am. What woke me? A tiny thunk. It sounded like the click of a door lock. An intruder? Or had I dreamt it? I lay really still, holding my breath, listening. Nothing. It was so quiet I could almost imagine the darkness ticking. Heart thudding, I reached out once more, groping for the bedside lamp. The light snapped on and I blinked furiously, orientating myself. My eyes sought the shadows. Nothing there. I lay still, the pale glow of the lamp comforting my fears. *Silly woman.* I really wanted to close my eyes and allow sleep to claim me once more but my bladder had other ideas. Such a nuisance but I was going to have to use the bathroom.

I pushed back the covers and slid my feet onto the carpet. The pile felt soft between my toes as I crept noiselessly to the door. The bathroom was just across from my bedroom and I resisted the temptation to switch on the landing light. I didn't want to wake Anna.

As quietly as I could, I pulled the bathroom door shut behind me and slid the latch across. The sudden screech of an owl sent my pulse skittering and I shook my head at my nervousness. One of the stairs creaked, a mournful, echoey sound. Terror seized me once more. It was the fifth step; I'd noticed earlier that it was the only one which made a noise. *Relax; it's probably Anna going downstairs. I must have disturbed her.* My heart was thudding like hammer in my chest as I stood, stiff as wire, listening intently, ear to the door. A rustle – the minutest of sounds but I heard it. Someone was there. I could feel his breath the other side of the wood. Horrified, I watched the door handle descend with excruciating slowness. In a stupor, I stared at the silver metal, seeing its stealthy return to its normal position. *What should I do? Stay here?* I was safe there … or was I? In a burst of panic, I stepped back away from the door. He may have a gun; he may be planning to break the door down. My breathing was shallow, my skin clammy. Leaning against the bathroom wall, I cast desperately for options. *Shampoo; soap; towels; nothing useful. Bathroom cabinet.* With shaking fingers, I pulled it open and looked inside. More toiletries but also a can of hairspray. I pulled the cold, metal tube from the shelf and popped the plastic lid off. My thumb rested on the button and I pushed gently to test it. The tiny hiss sounded loud in the small space. I inched towards the bathroom door, my ears straining for a sound. I could no longer feel his presence on the landing – I sensed only empty space where there had been menace – but I couldn't be sure. Where had he gone? The hollowing in my chest intensified. *Anna!* She could be in danger. I had to warn her! Before I could stop myself, I slid back the bolt and pushed the door open, holding the hairspray ready. No one was there. The landing was a dark void. I stepped forward, my mouth dry. Anna's bedroom door was closed but mine was cracked open. With a jerk of realisation, I saw my room was shrouded in blackness. I was sure I'd left the lamp on; someone had switched it off. He was in there. My mind worked furiously. What did he plan to do? How could I thwart him? He wouldn't realise I knew he was there. Maybe that would work in my favour. I returned to the bathroom, flushed the toilet and washed my hands noisily, humming to myself. Let him think I was oblivious to his presence. Concealing the hairspray under my arm, I pushed the bedroom door wide open and marched across to the bed. With a sleepy sigh, I pulled up the duvet, holding the hairspray ready. My eyes desperately tried to make out the shapes in the darkness and then I saw it, a shifting of the space, a shadow looming. I pulled the covers higher – enough to conceal my face but still allowing me to see. As he approached, blood roared through my veins. My heart was drumming so loudly I thought he must hear it. He drew nearer, coming stealthily, his breathing light and even. I waited until I could bear it no longer, until the moment he was towering over me, gloved hands stretching towards my neck. Then I shot upright, screamed as loudly as I could and blasted the hairspray directly in his face.

He cursed and fell back, spluttering and coughing, clutching at his eyes. I screamed again and shouted. 'Run Anna, run!' I watched as he stumbled sightlessly around the room. He was dressed all in black, a balaclava covering his head. As he neared the bed once more, I gave him another blast, full in the face, straight into red-rimmed eyes. He screamed and lurched away. Then I saw Anna standing in the doorway, eyes wide with shock.

'Selina, are you ...?'

'Run!' I screamed again. 'Get out of here!'

Ignoring me, she leapt into the room and grabbed the bedside lamp, brandishing it like a club. As the man staggered unsteadily towards her, she swung and landed a blow on the back of his head. He grunted, turned and headed out through the door. I shot out of bed and towards the landing, just in time to see his figure pulling open the front door and disappearing into the night.

'Selina, are you alright?'

I turned to see Anna still holding the lamp and collapsed weakly against her. 'Yes, I'm fine. Why didn't you run? I was screaming at you to run.'

'What ... and leave you alone with him? How could I do that?'

I shook my head. The can of hairspray slipped from my grasp and rolled along the carpet. I suddenly felt deathly cold, shivering uncontrollably despite the warm night air.

'You're in shock.' Anna steered me downstairs and towards the kitchen. You need a hot, sugary drink.'

'I need to call the police,' I replied grimly, sinking into a chair.

Anna shuddered. She took my hand and gripped it firmly. 'We'll do it together,' she said.

***

At 4:25 am, there was sharp knock on the front door. I'd watched the police vehicle pull up outside from behind the curtain of the sitting room window. The two people striding purposefully towards the house, a tall, pasty-looking man in his thirties with a long, pointy chin and a younger, black woman with short, dark hair slicked back and a wide mouth, were not the officers who had previously interviewed me. It was to be expected but it irritated me. I would have to start afresh, tell them everything all over again. The thought filled me with leaden weariness. I heard the wobble in Anna's voice as she invited them in and stood up as they entered the room. Their uniforms, their air of authority, felt like an invasion, another violation, reminding me of other occasions when I'd let the police into my home in Nottingham, desperate for answers but receiving only platitudes. Always they had let me down.

'Now, tell us what happened?' said the woman, who had identified herself as DS Thorncroft. She stared at me with assessing brown eyes. The man, PC Flook, pulled out a notebook.

I took a breath. 'I heard a noise. It sounded like the front door clicking open so I lay really still, listening. There were no more noises.' I could hear my voice sounded timid and cleared my throat. As I spoke, I forced myself to maintain eye contact with the two police officers, especially the woman. 'I decided there wasn't anything to worry about and I got out of bed to use the bathroom. I switched on my bedside lamp but left the landing light off because I didn't want to wake Anna. The bathroom is just across from my bedroom and I went in. Then I heard one of the stairs creaking. The fifth step does that. I held my breath and listened really carefully. I wondered if it might be Anna going downstairs but then I heard a rustle outside the bathroom door. It's difficult to explain but I just knew someone was there.' I shrugged my shoulders, my fingers twitching around my mug. 'I just felt it.' I paused, struggling to maintain my equilibrium. Reliving this wasn't easy. The room was quiet as everyone waited patiently for me to continue. I leant forward to put my mug down on the coffee table, conscious of my shaky hands. It rattled, almost toppling over, and I had to leap forward again to save it.

'I wanted to stay locked in the bathroom but I was worried about Anna. It was terrible; I just didn't know what to do.' I wrung my hands together in my lap.

'Just take your time,' DS Thorncroft's voice was breathily soft, almost a whisper, and she gave me an encouraging smile. 'You're doing really well.'

'All the time I was looking around for something to use, you know, to protect myself. There was a can of hairspray in the cabinet so I took that. I was so terrified I could barely stand when I opened the bathroom door. Then I noticed my bedside light had been switched off. I knew I'd left it on. I guessed he was in there, waiting. It probably sounds daft but I decided to pretend I didn't know he was there. I went back into the bathroom, flushed the toilet, made a show of washing my hands. I did wonder about creeping across to Anna's room and waking her but then I thought he'd follow me there and that would put Anna in danger. There was nothing for it; I was going to have to confront him myself. I didn't hold out a lot of hope but I thought if I made enough noise, Anna could escape.'

'Oh Selina!' Anna exhaled, a plaintive sigh. 'How could you risk your life like that? You should have got out while you could and phoned the police.'

I shook my head. 'I couldn't leave you – I just couldn't. Anyway, I got back into bed, held the hairspray ready and waited until he was in front of me.' I drew a shuddering breath. 'It was dark so I couldn't see very well. I think he was dressed all in black: a hoodie; trousers; a balaclava over his head. He was reaching towards my neck, as if he was planning on strangling me, and I blasted him with hairspray, right in the face. I remember screaming, shouting at Anna to get out. He was staggering about, holding his eyes. Then Anna appeared. I managed to give him another dose of hairspray and Anna hit him on the back of the head with the lamp. That's when he left. By the time I'd reached the top of the stairs, he was heading out through the front door.'

'Did you see if he was carrying a weapon?' DS Thorncraft asked.

I shook my head. 'I didn't see anything.'

'Can either of you give us a description of this man?'

'He was stocky, quite broad and medium height,' Anna replied. 'Other than that, he was completely covered up. He was wearing gloves,' she added after a pause, 'so I don't suppose you'll find any fingerprints.'

DS Thorncraft looked at me. 'You said he swore. Can you tell me anything about his voice or his accent?'

'Not really.' My whole body was drooping; I was exhausted. 'I can't even remember what he said. I'm sorry.'

'That's fine.' The policewoman stood up. 'We'll just go and have a look around – see where he got in.'

The two police officers left the room leaving us alone. For a while, there was silence as each of us struggled to come to terms with what had happened. Eventually, Anna spoke.

'I can't believe how brave you were. And quite mad. What on earth were you thinking? You could have been killed.'

'I didn't know what else to do,' I replied simply. I shivered and wrapped my arms around my body. 'I have to admit, though, it makes me feel quite sick to think of it now.'

'Well, you can't stay here, not while this man is out there. Do you think it's the same man who tried to abduct you?'

I shrugged. 'Could be. Probably. It would make sense.'

'You need to tell the police about the other attacks.'

'What other attacks?' The two police officers had returned and DS Thorncroft was looking sharply at me. 'Has this happened before.'

Here we go again. Numb with fatigue, I told her about the attempted abduction in Swaffham and then about the fire. DS Thorncroft listened intently, her face serious, while her colleague made notes.

'Well, I have to say, this changes things. There was no sign of a forced entry here. I was going to say you possibly forgot to lock the front door and the intruder walked straight in. Tonight's incident looks like it could be an attempted burglary which was interrupted by you getting up to use the bathroom. However, in the light of the previous incidents, we'll consult with our colleagues and treat all three as related. Do you know of anyone who would wish you harm?'

I looked across at Anna whose body was suddenly as taut as a bowstring. My lips quivered as I answered. 'Not as such. You'll also discover that my daughter was abducted twenty-three years ago when we were on holiday in Spain. Despite an intensive police investigation, she was never found. Recently, I have suspected that Anna here could be that child. As yet we have no evidence – we have done a DNA test and sent it off today. Things have got a bit hairy for me since I voiced that suspicion publicly so it's possible there's a link.'

DS Thorncroft drilled her gaze at Anna. 'What about you? What do you think?'

'I ... I don't know.' I could hear the tremble of panic in her voice. The officer turned to me once more.

'Can you give me any names … anyone at all you suspect may be behind this?'

Anna's panic throbbed invisibly between us and I hesitated. I should've realised it would come to this but it didn't make things any easier.

'Please,' the policewoman insisted. 'There have possibly been three attempts on your life in a matter of days. This is extremely serious. You need to tell me anything which may help, even if it turns out to be a false alarm. Eliminating suspects will be crucial if we're to find your attacker so please don't hold back.'

Still I remained mute, mulling my options, eyes squeezed shut as I searched for a way to avoid saying the names at the forefront of my mind. Seconds ticked past, heavy with portent. The weight of my indecision, the agony of it, was drowning me. I couldn't bear it. Sucking in a deep breath, I opened my mouth but still I couldn't say the words.

Then, as the silence stretched to breaking point, Anna exhaled in a puff of resignation. 'Selina is struggling to say the names because she suspects my parents may be involved. I think she's wrong but …' she shrugged. 'there you are.'

'Names?'

'Geoff and Mariella Blake. They live in Swaffham, The Causeway, Brandon Road.' Anna's voice was flat, expressionless as she recited the postcode. 'Please eliminate them from your enquiries so you can catch the real culprit.'

'Thank you. Anyone else?' DS Thorncraft continued, her tone neutral, pragmatic.

'I suppose whoever abducted Maisie, my daughter, all those years ago would have reason to wish me dead. You see, I can't give up looking for her. Eventually, I'll find her, I know I will,' I said. 'There have been others I've suspected, over the years. None of them would agree to a DNA test – why would they? Some of them even went so far as to secure a court order against me, forbidding me from pursuing them. I know all this makes me sound like a crazy woman …' A small, wry smile. 'But anyway … you should have those names too, in case they may be involved. Heidi Foster. She's an American living in the Nottingham area. She has a daughter, Jessica, who would be the same age as Maisie. Then there's Tom and Tracy Egerton. They lived in Nottingham for a time but I think they moved away. Their daughter is called Emily. Jane and Martin Lucas live in Surrey. I think they still live there. Their daughter, Alicia, was on a TV talent contest a few years back – Britain's Got Talent. As soon as I saw her, I thought she could be Maisie. Now I don't think so but, at the time, I wasn't sure. They were the ones who got the court order.' I looked up and caught the two police officers exchanging a brief glance. 'See, I told you you'd think I was a madwoman. Maybe I am …' I waved my hands impatiently. 'I just want to find my daughter. It's all I've ever wanted.'

'I understand,' DS Thorncroft said kindly. 'In the meantime, your life is in danger. Do you have somewhere safe you could stay? Or we could organise for you to stay somewhere while we pursue our investigations.'

I threw a panicky look at Anna. 'I … I don't know. Maybe … but I've still got to get people in to clean up my house, you know, after the fire … and there's the DNA test …'

'I think your safety is more important than any of that, don't you?' DS Thorncroft said firmly. 'Look, give it some thought and give me a ring.' She handed a card to Selina. 'We'll leave you now and confer with our colleagues in Swaffham. In the meantime, don't go anywhere alone and make sure the house is locked. Call if you think of anything else or if you notice anything suspicious. We'll be in touch.'

CHAPTER 34

Anna

In the end, after considerable persuasion, Selina agreed to go and stay in a police safe house. DS Thorncroft had returned, this time accompanied by a brisk, no nonsense woman in her forties who introduced herself as DI Green. Both Selina and I had been subjected to a barrage of questions and then informed that a team of detectives were not only investigating the suspected attacks on Selina but were working with detectives in Spain and in Nottingham with regard to Maisie's disappearance twenty-three years ago. As yet, they had not established a connection between that and recent incidents but DI Green had assured them, in her nasal, Yorkshire accent, they were making sure they covered all the bases. She insisted that the police couldn't guarantee Selina's safety unless she moved to 'a secure location.' Selina was stubbornly reluctant and at first refused. However, once the police had left, I managed to convince her she should do as they advised.

'But what about the DNA test? How will I get in touch with you?' Selina pleaded, having been told she'd need to leave her phone behind in case it had been compromised. To pacify her, I'd been out and bought two pay-as-you-go phones and programmed in our numbers.

'Only you and I will know we've got these,' I assured her.

Once she'd gone, I felt tense and edgy. The events of the early hours loomed large in my mind, making it impossible to settle. When Josh had called and I'd told him about the night-time intruder, he'd come around straight away and taken charge.

'It's not safe for you to stay here on your own. This lunatic could return at any time. You need to come back to my house.'

I bristled at his high-handed tone. I was sick of people telling me what to do.

'I'd already decided I wasn't going to stay here alone,' I retorted, thrusting my chin forward in annoyance. 'But I don't want *you* or anyone else telling me where I should go. That's *my* decision.'

'You're right.' He held up his hands in a placatory gesture. 'I'm sorry. I'm just worried about you, that's all. I would love it if you'd consider staying at mine for a few days ... or longer, if necessary.' His brown eyes were pleading and tugged at my heartstrings.

'Thank you.' I relented, secretly relieved the issue was resolved and, deep down, happy to be spending more time with Josh. 'Just for a few days … that would be great.'

Now, two days on, I couldn't imagine wanting to stay anywhere else. Josh was great company and we soon fell into a comfortable existence at the Old Rectory. We discovered a shared love of animals and bantered good-naturedly about music, books and sport. In the evenings, we stayed in, talking, watching TV and playing cards. We cooked food together and washed it down with white wine and beer. But the majority of the time was spent in each other's arms. We just couldn't seem to get enough of each other. Despite the worry about Selina and the ongoing investigation, it was a magical time. Everything was put on hold, as if the outside world didn't exist. When I left home, I switched off my phone. I'd sent my parents, Madison and Ellie texts to say I was going away for a few days. It was strangely liberating to be off the radar, undetectable and non-contactable. I decided to do this more often, when all this was over.

The enforced proximity with Josh had deepened our relationship and last night, lying in his bed, he'd told me he loved me. Since then, I'd been glowing with happiness. There was still a tiny kernel of my heart sounding caution – it was too soon – but I *was* beginning to believe he was the one. Everything about being with Josh was perfect. I loved the way he teased me and made me laugh but never made me feel inferior. He encouraged me to voice my opinions – something I'd always avoided – and respected my viewpoint, even when he disagreed with it. Despite everything, despite all the mistrust and uncertainty, I'd never been so happy and I was determined to make the most of it. We'd even made plans together. Josh had suggested a holiday 'when all this is over', asked my opinion on furnishings for the Old Rectory and we'd even discussed names for the rescue dog we would adopt sometime in the future. The idyll of the past two days held the promise of a lifetime together.

Even so, an insidious whisper persisted, telling me it couldn't last. I couldn't help myself mentally preparing for things to go wrong. Every moment with him was wrapped into a delicious parcel and carefully stored in my memory bank … just in case.

Thoughts of my parents were never far from my mind. The police would have interviewed them by now. I imagined their shock and distress at being questioned. Then there would be anger. I was certain I'd have countless missed calls from them on my phone. The guilt at my part in that was a nagging pain in my chest. When I'd given their names to DS Thorncroft, tears had been dangerously close, burning the back of my eyelids. Surely, I'd just committed the ultimate betrayal?

A text from Selina on my secret phone reminded me the DNA test results were due to arrive via post at my home address that day.

What time does your post usually arrive? Will it be safe, do you think, for you to collect it?

My stomach clenched into a tight knot of panic at the thought of it. It had been easy to forget the masked intruder when I was wrapped safe in Josh's arms. I stared at the screen, chewing my lip and fighting back the tide of anxiety rolling in.

'Hey? What's up?' Josh appeared, fresh and tousled from the shower. 'You've gone as white as a sheet.' He frowned. 'I thought you'd switched your phone off.'

Belatedly, I tried to smuggle it under the covers. 'I have.'

'So why are you staring at the screen and looking as if something terrible is about to happen?'

'I ...' Reluctantly, I pulled out the phone, like a guilty child caught shoplifting. 'It's not my phone ... well, it is but not my normal one ...' I sighed. I was going to have to tell Josh; I was going to have to trust him. If we were to have any kind of future together, I had to be willing to share at least some of my secrets. 'It's a burner phone. I bought two so I could keep in contact with Selina. She's currently staying in a police safe house. She was with me on Monday night when ... you know.'

'Selina?' His brow crinkled in puzzlement.

'Selina Matthews. I told you about her after she had the fire at her house.'

'Ah, *that* woman. The one who thought you were her long-lost daughter. I'd forgotten all about her.'

'Yes, well, I'd been trying not to think about it all.' He sat on the bed beside me, holding my hand, stroking my skin with his thumb as I recounted everything that had happened since the fire. I left out all my thoughts and suspicions and just stuck to the facts – simpler, that way. 'The police think there could be a connection between Maisie's disappearance and the recent attacks so they have re-opened the investigation into her disappearance.'

Josh listened intently, his face serious. 'So that's how you're involved? Because Selina thinks you may be her daughter?'

'Yes and because I was there and saw the man who broke into my house on Monday night.'

'This DNA test is quite important then,' Josh mused. 'Why didn't the police do their own test? Surely they do that sort of thing all the time.'

'I asked them that. They said they were focusing their inquiry on finding the man who attacked Selina in Swaffham and broke into my house. They were examining CCTV and interviewing residents near the guest house in Swaffham to try to get some leads on him. They were also interviewing everyone connected with Selina's search for Maisie, mainly for elimination purposes. As a DNA test had already been done, they were happy to wait for the results. I don't think they thought there was any possibility that I could be Maisie, especially because I told them I had records of my birth and photographs of myself as a baby.'

'They've probably interviewed your parents as well,' Josh pondered. 'That must have been difficult for them?'

I looked sharply at his face. 'What do you mean?' Was it my imagination or was that shifty look back in his eyes? There was only a glimpse before he averted his face so it was hard to tell.

He shrugged. 'It must have been bad enough having some crazy woman claiming they had stolen her daughter. Then having the police involved, asking questions ... That would be upsetting for anyone.' His tone was light but the flush on his cheek was unmistakeable. He was lying.

Dread seeped into my bones, chilling my skin 'Josh, is there something you're not telling me? Look at me,' I commanded.

Slowly, he raised his eyes. There was apology there, I could see it now. And guilt – yes, definitely guilt.

'Tell me.'

He remained silent, breathing deeply, rubbing a calloused hand through his wet hair. Finally, he shook his head. 'It's difficult,' he began. 'I promised ...'

'Tell me,' I insisted.

He squared his shoulders and faced me properly, taking both my hands in his. 'I haven't been entirely honest with you,' he admitted. I held my breath, anxiety clawing at my throat. So much depended upon what he said next.

'I know your parents,' he said. 'In fact, I know your father very well. I worked for him at Sampson Blake for five years. You could say I was his protégé. We parted company when I went to work for MNC but we remained in close touch. He's a fine man.'

I exhaled. 'Why didn't you tell me? I asked if you knew him. You could have told me then.'

'I couldn't. You see, it's more complicated than that. When Jon committed suicide, I basically went to pieces. My family were great – I don't know what I'd have done without them – and so was your dad. When he heard what had happened to Jon, he got in touch and we spoke a lot. He was retired by then but he was obviously trying to entice me back to Sampson Blake. At least, that's what I thought to start with but actually he was just being a really good friend. When I said I needed a break from banking and was thinking of working for my dad, doing up old houses, he said there was the perfect property here in Lewton. I looked at it and decided, right there and then, to buy it, do it up myself. It would be a project to put my heart and soul into and a distraction from everything that had gone before. The location was great too – closer to my family and to Geoff. I would be near people I cared about and who cared about me.'

'I still don't understand why you couldn't just tell me all this.'

'Your dad asked me not to. Shortly after I moved in and began work on the house, he told me about you, all about your writing and your part-time Girl Friday work. That worried him, I could tell. He felt you were vulnerable and people might take advantage of you. The upshot was he wanted me to give you a job, to help keep an eye on you and to keep you busy so you didn't end up working for strangers.' He paused, his face heavy with resignation. 'You're not going to like this but I feel I owe you the *whole* truth. Your dad also suggested you were in the market for some romance and he'd be very happy were I to become his son-in-law.'

I dropped his hands, horrified. 'What? All of this,' I waved my arms at nothing in particular. 'All of this ...' I repeated. 'Everything that's happened between us is just because my father *told* you to?' I stared at him aghast.

'No,' he said emphatically. 'Not at all. Listen, to start with, I refused. The last thing I needed was to look after some rich man's daughter and I certainly wasn't looking for a girlfriend. But you know your dad; he doesn't take no for an answer. He told me a little bit about you, that you'd had a breakdown when you were fifteen and how worried he was it may happen again. He explained he had to watch you like a hawk and it would be doing him a huge favour if I could help in any way with that. He said to forget the romance thing – that was just the pipedream of an old man who wanted to see his daughter happy and settled before he died. What could I say? When I agreed, he said not to say anything to you, that you were very sensitive about accepting any kind of help from him and liked to think you were independent. I'm sorry, Anna. I wasn't happy about it, I can tell you that. If you remember, the first time you came here, I was in a foul mood. Yes, it was the anniversary of Jon's death but that wasn't the only reason. I'd decided to help your dad by employing you, as he'd requested, but I wasn't going to make it easy for you. Then, hopefully, you'd decide to stop coming. The trouble was, you turned up and took my breath away. That made me even angrier. I certainly didn't want to be attracted to you so I was as vile as I could possibly be. By the time you left, I decided I'd done enough to persuade you not to return. But I couldn't stop thinking about you. You were even in my dreams that night. The next day, I was on complete tenterhooks, expecting you to cancel right up until the moment you appeared. The rest is history.' He took my hands again, his eyes fervent with sincerity. 'I love you, Anna. I didn't expect it to happen but it did. I love you despite your father, not because of him. Already I know, you're the woman I want to marry, to be the mother of my children.' I felt myself melting at his words and allowed him to take my unresisting body into his arms. 'I'm so sorry I haven't been entirely honest with you but I have in all the ways that matter.'

I let him hold me, feeling the tension seep from my muscles. I wanted to believe him. Desperately. But could I?

'Have you been spying on me for my father? Does he know I'm here now?'

'Yes.' Instantly, I pulled from his embrace. 'He was desperately worried about you,' he pleaded, raking his hand once more through his hair. 'He was horrified when he knew a man had broken into your house. I told him you were with me and you were safe. At least that stopped him from charging round here and carting you off to his house. I'm sorry,' he said again. 'I won't tell him anything else. I should have stopped once I'd got to know you but it seemed such a small thing – to keep his mind at rest.'

'But what about my privacy?' I said tightly.

'I know.' He shook his head in disgust. 'Your dad was very persuasive and I guess I felt I owed him.' He hunched his shoulders. 'I understand if you feel you can no longer trust me. I expect I'd be the same in your situation but, when I started to care for you, I was worried too. Knowing that you'd had a breakdown, that you were fragile, I was willing to do anything I could to protect you. You scared me rigid the other day when we were on our way to the coast, when I had to stop the car.'

I sighed, my breath an audible puncturing of the tension. 'There was no breakdown,' I said quietly. 'That appears to be something Dad made up to encourage my friends to tell him stuff about me – anything amiss, you know, so he was always one step ahead of me. You're not the only one he lied to.'

'But why on earth would he say something like that if it wasn't true?' Josh's face was full of confusion.

I shrugged. 'To keep tabs on me, I guess. A misguided attempt to look after me when I was out of his sight. Who knows? I haven't asked him yet. I've only recently found out about it and, as yet, I haven't decided what to do.'

'I still don't understand. What happened the other day ... the car thing?'

I looked him in the eye. 'I have anxiety issues,' I told him. 'Sometimes full-blown panic attacks. I've had them since I was a child. You're the first person to whom I've admitted that.'

'Didn't your parents know?'

'My parents were part of the problem. They're both high-achieving individuals who despise weakness. I hid it from them.'

'You haven't tried any medication, any therapy? I'm sure you could get help with it.' His eyes had softened with sympathy.

'You're probably right.' I swung my legs off the bed, unwilling to discuss the subject any more. 'Now I need to go and collect the results of the DNA test from my house. Remember, I told you last night that they'd be delivered this morning.' I looked at my watch. 'They're probably already there. The post is usually early, before eight and it's already half-past.'

'Before you do ...' Gently, he stopped me and gathered me close. 'Are we OK? Can you forgive me?'

I hugged him tightly in response, eyes closed, inhaling the shower-fresh scent of him. 'My dad had us all fooled,' I replied. 'I only hope there are no more surprises ...'

***

Josh offered to pick up the mail and bring it back. I was tempted but, in the end, thought it was too important to delegate to anyone else. I needed to go.

'Would you like me to come with you? I'll wait outside the door, keeping guard. I don't like to think of you going there alone. Someone could be there, watching the house, lying in wait. Anything could happen.'

'Yeah, I could end up with another black eye,' I quipped, pointing to my face.

'Exactly. We both know what you're like,' he smiled back. 'So, is that a yes?'

'Fine. Thank you.'

It was reassuring to hold his hand as we walked together the short distance to my house. The thought of returning, alone, had set my heart pounding and I was relieved he was with me. Not that I'd told him that; old habits die hard.

When we reached the house, Josh insisted on going inside first to check the house was empty. 'You wait here,' he said as he unlocked the front door. I did as he asked, my eyes alert for any movement nearby, any unwelcome visitors. I could just detect the strains of next door's radio but otherwise the cul-de-sac was silent. A few minutes later, Josh was back. 'All clear,' he said. 'Do you want me to come in with you?'

'No. I think I'd rather be on my own.'

I pushed the front door and stepped inside, my eyes devouring the pile of mail scattered across the doormat. My heart leapt at the sight of a brown envelope, A4 size, with my name printed on the front and the word 'CONFIDENTIAL.' It had arrived.

Nausea welled inside me as I scooped up the letters and took them through to the kitchen. I pictured Selina, sitting alone in a room somewhere, waiting for my call and, with trembling fingers, grasped the brown envelope. In the next few seconds, my life could change forever. It was a terrifying thought. *It's not going to happen. Just open the envelope; get it over with.*

I pulled open the sticky flap and withdrew the sheets of paper inside. My eyes swept over the figures, the rows of data listed, scanning the first page until I found what I was looking for. My heart leapt. There was the proof, in black and white, at the bottom of the page. I made myself reread the sentence in case I'd made a mistake. I hadn't. The words were stark and clear.

'There is a 99.87% probability that the two samples are NOT related.'

CHAPTER 35

Anna

I phoned Selina. The call was answered before the second ring.

'Yes?' Her voice was breathless with hope.

'I'm sorry, Selina,' I said gently. 'We're not a match. I'm not your daughter.'

'Oh.' It was the almost inaudible gasp of a dying sigh. The ensuing silence of pain and disappointment throbbed through the phone.

'This was always the likely outcome,' I continued. 'I'm sorry, I know that's not very helpful.' There was no reply – just a muffled sound which may have been a sob. 'I'm going to go now – give you a bit of time to process all of this. We'll talk later.'

I ended the call and sat for a long while, staring blankly out of the window, thinking, trying to come to terms with the result myself. My feelings were complicated. I'd been bracing myself for the news my parents had lied, that I was not who I thought I was, and that reaction shocked me. I was swamped with remorse for even considering the possibility I was Selina's child. It was the photo of the boy. Since the moment Selina had told me he was her son, Maisie's brother, I'd secretly doubted my own parents, the people who loved me. Not only that, I'd actively looked for signs they were deceiving me – trawling through old photo albums, questioning them about the information they'd obtained about Selina, trying to catch them out by quizzing Ewan Jacobs. And all the time, they were just trying to protect me from the delusions of a distraught woman. Now, in the guilt-ridden aftermath of it all, I could even view the lies my father had told in a more positive light. Granted, he shouldn't have done it; he *had* crossed the line and he needed to be told. But he'd always been over-possessive and over-protective. I shouldn't have been surprised.

My thoughts turned back to Selina and the ongoing police investigation. Her conspiracy theory about my parents was now dead in the water. I should phone DS Thorncroft with the results of the DNA test, I realised. They wouldn't be surprised though. With luck, they'd unearth fresh leads about what really happened to Maisie all those years ago. I desperately hoped so, for Selina's sake.

I switched on my normal phone and keyed in the number on the card I'd been given. The call went straight through to voicemail so I left a message.

My third call was to Mum. Usually, I'd call Dad but I wasn't in the mood for his inevitable smugness, his 'I told you so.'

'Anna, thank goodness. We've been *so* worried. Are you alright?'

'I'm fine, Mum. How are you?'

A long-suffering sigh. 'Holding up. I can't deny it's been pretty awful. The police have been round here, questioning *us*. Can you believe it? That *woman* has a lot to answer for.' Her voice bristled with indignation.

'I know, Mum. I'm sorry you've had to go through all that. Anyway, listen. I have good news.'

'Yes?' Expectation vibrated through the single word.

'The results from the DNA test are back and they confirm I'm not related to Selina. Of course, you knew that anyway.' I pictured her nodding, holding back the long-suffering, accusatory diatribe going through her head.

'We did but now *you* know it too.' There it was, the implicit, deliberate pricking of my conscience. 'Thank heavens this whole nightmare is over. Now we can get back to normal.'

'Yes.'

'Well, I think this calls for a bit of a celebration. Are you coming for dinner tonight? It is *Thursday*, after all.'

I hesitated. I really didn't feel like facing them so soon but, on the other hand, I owed it to them to get things back on an even keel as soon as possible. 'That would be lovely,' I replied with forced brightness.

'Bring that young man of yours – Josh, isn't it? We've been looking forward to meeting him.'

They were *both* in on the lie. Of course, they would be. They always had each other's backs.

'I'll ask him,' I said. 'See you later.'

***

I was quiet as Josh drove me to Swaffham that evening. In my mind, I was rehearsing what I might say to my father. Having Josh by my side would help; he'd back me up. I glanced across at him, admiring the way his dark hair curled across his forehead and the endearing way he squinted in concentration as he drove. During a day in which my life had resettled and stabilised following the DNA news, I'd allowed myself to consider a future with Josh. Yes, he hadn't been entirely honest with me but I'd forgiven Ellie and Madison and this was no different. All of them had been taken in by my father. My fists clenched in my lap. I was about to confront Dad and put a stop to his meddling once and for all.

As we approached the house, a white Audi was coming from the opposite direction. My stomach dipped as I caught a glimpse of the driver. It was the grey-haired man, the same man I'd thought was watching me. I hadn't seen him since I'd spoken to Ewan and had pretty much convinced myself I'd been imagining things all along. Now, my old suspicions were instantly revived. Was Ewan somehow involved with the grey-haired man? Had he told him to back off ... change vehicles ...? He was coming from the direction of my parents' house. Could they *all* be involved in following me – Ewan, grey-haired man and my parents? I clamped a lid on my doubts. *Stop it. You're doing it again.*

My parents stood in the doorway, smug with delight, as we walked, hand in hand, across the drive towards them. Dad stepped forward, holding out his hand to Josh. 'Geoff Blake,' he said, 'Delighted to meet you.'

The pretence was a prod of irritation. I was sick of the veil of lies poisoning our relationship. 'Dad.' I gave him a disappointed stare. 'I know Josh worked for you at Sampson Blake. What I don't know is why you wanted him to lie to me about it, why *you* lied about it?'

He smiled genially and clasped me in a warm hug. 'Lovely to see you, darling. Let's go in, shall we? Let's not discuss this on the doorstep.'

The reprimand was clear. *Attack is the best form of defence.* I knew how he operated. Well, two could play at that game.

'Let's discuss it now,' I said, as we walked into the open-plan kitchen. 'Dad?' I felt emboldened by Josh's presence and was determined to confront Dad before my confidence crumbled.

He responded with a look of intense hurt, as if I was accusing him of a crime he hadn't committed. 'It makes me so sad, Anna,' he said quietly, 'when you don't trust me. What happened to that small girl who used to put her hand in mine and believe in me without question?'

'She grew up,' I replied coldly, angry at his blatant attempt to belittle me. 'And she doesn't trust people who tell lies.'

He shook his head, sighing to emphasise his displeasure at the way I was disappointing him. 'I haven't lied to you; I just haven't told you the whole truth – there's a difference. I didn't tell you Josh had worked for me, just as I asked him to avoid telling you, because I love you both dearly and nothing makes me happier than to see you together as a couple, as you are now.' He nodded pointedly at my left hand clasped in Josh's right. 'However, I knew nothing would put you off more than thinking I was matchmaking. I have noticed,' he added drily, 'you resent any intrusion from me into your life. It's better that you make the decisions for yourself. I was just doing what I could to help you make the right decision – that's all.'

I hesitated. Much as I hated to admit it, he was right about that. Had I known he was trying to set me up with Josh, I would've avoided him like the proverbial bargepole. Another wave of anger surfaced as I remembered the bigger lie – my imaginary breakdown.

'You say you haven't lied, yet you told Josh and my friends I was fragile, that I'd had a breakdown and you used that to get them to spy on me. That's unforgivable.'

'Oh darling,' he said, shaking his head sadly. 'Spying? That's such an ugly word. I didn't tell anyone that you'd had a breakdown. That *would* be a lie. I admit I told them you had issues, that you were fragile. That's true enough, isn't it, darling?' His velvety voice smoothed his deeds with a coating of honey. 'I told them about the panic attacks which you tried to hide. I told them how, when you were fifteen, we had all sorts of problems with you. Do you remember? You refused to go to school. Your mother had to give you hypnotherapy sessions like you had when you were little. That's all true or do you now deny it?'

'That's not the same as having a breakdown,' I insisted. 'And you told Madison and Ellie I'd tried to take my own life.'

He looked confused at that. 'I'm sure I didn't. They must've misunderstood. Maybe I said I was worried you might try to take your own life. That must be it. I can't remember my exact words. Look … maybe I shouldn't have said anything,' he continued, his tone edged with belligerence, 'but I'm just a father trying to look out for his little girl. I'm not going to make excuses for that. I'd do the same again in a heartbeat.'

I slumped into a chair, feeling defeated. My dad was like a steamroller, squashing all resistance to his path. He sounded so plausible and I so much wanted to believe him. 'You overstepped the mark,' I said wearily. 'Whatever your reasons, and I don't doubt they sprung from a good place, you went too far. It made me feel betrayed.'

'Anna, that's enough,' Mum stepped in, her voice sharp with rebuke. 'It's all in the past and there's no real harm done. You need to accept that your dad and I care about you, maybe too much, and we'll always want to prevent anything bad happening to you. You've always been secretive so no wonder we had to enlist help in looking out for you. But from now on, we just need to trust each other. No more secrets.'

I looked up and gave her a hard stare of my own. 'And no more interference in my life. I'm not a little girl anymore. I need to make my own mistakes.'

'Hmph, like you did with Selina Matthews.' Her retort was a knife twisting in a wound.

Before I could respond, Dad patted my arm. 'That's fine, darling, as long as you promise to ask us for help if you need it. Keep us in the loop, hey?' He headed towards the fridge. 'Now, I think it's time for a celebratory drink. At last, we can put all that Selina Matthews nonsense behind us.'

Mum shuddered. 'Thank goodness. Can you believe, the police even came here, asking us questions? It made us feel like criminals.'

'It must have been quite an ordeal for you.' Josh spoke for the first time.

She shrugged her slim shoulders. 'It was a farce, that's what it was.' Her gold bracelet jangled heavily on her wrist as she waved her hands in disgust. 'That woman has a lot to answer for but there ...' She glanced across at Dad and gave him a tight smile. 'Now it's all over. Hopefully, she'll go back where she came from?' Her questioning gaze turned towards me.

'I've no idea what she'll do,' I replied. 'Thanks.' I accepted a glass of champagne and took a fortifying sip.

'I propose a toast ...' Dad began when a shrill ringtone interrupted him. The noise was coming from my bag. *Damn.* It was my secret phone. I'd forgotten to switch it off.

'Sorry,' I said, grabbing my bag and walking a few steps away.

'That doesn't sound like your phone,' Mum said, her eyes narrowing.

I ended the call, switched the phone mode to silent and smuggled it back into my bag before anyone could get a good look at it. 'I changed my ringtone,' I said, the lie spawning more guilt. 'Awful, isn't it? I need to get around to changing it back.' The phone continued to vibrate from inside my bag and I pushed it away, under the table. Poor Selina was clearly anxious to speak and I regretted not calling her back before heading to Swaffham. I would have to remember to ring her later.

The champagne helped ease the tension and Josh lightened the atmosphere further by launching into a story about the Old Rectory. 'When I first moved in, the main bedroom was something to behold,' he chuckled. 'It was completely purple, even the ceiling and there were various gadgets attached to the wall. Apparently, the previous owner, a retired doctor in his eighties, used to have regular visits from scantily dressed women. He died of a heart attack, in bed, I was told. I can imagine he died happy.'

Dad's laugh sounded unnaturally loud. 'Good on him. What better way to go!'

'It must have taken forever to paint over the purple,' Mum interjected, frowning at Dad.

'Oh no, I've left it as it is. The gadgets too. I like it!' Josh grinned. Dad spluttered into his glass at Mum's look of shock.

'He's joking,' I smiled. 'It's now pale grey and very tasteful. You'd approve.'

Her face cleared and she arched an eyebrow at Josh. 'Very funny,' she said in a tone which made it clear she didn't find it remotely amusing. 'Right, shall we sit down? Food is ready.'

Before anyone could move, the doorbell sounded. Dad stood up, the light of battle in his eye. 'Whoever that is, they're going to regret choosing now to call round.'

'Probably a nuisance call.' Mum picked up her oven gloves. 'You two sit yourselves down. Dad won't be long.'

We dutifully headed towards the dining table. There was a murmur of voices at the front door and then Dad's voice raised in anger.

'What on *earth* is going on?' Mum slid two dishes, potatoes and green beans, onto the table and turned her head crossly towards the noise.

'Someone obviously won't take no for an answer.' Josh pushed his chair back again. 'Shall I go and lend some support?'

'No, no. I'm sure Geoff can handle it.'

'This is beyond ridiculous. I'm really sorry about this, everyone.' My father, red-faced and incandescent with anger, marched back into the kitchen, closely followed by DI Green and DS Thorncroft. 'These police officers have insisted on coming in. I told them it wasn't convenient.'

'Good evening, officers,' Mum said smoothly, as if she entertained the local constabulary on a regular basis. 'I'm sure this won't take long.' She turned a warning glance towards her husband. 'How can we help you?'

'I apologise for the intrusion.' DI Green looked directly at me before turning her attention back to Dad. 'Geoffrey Blake, I am arresting you on a charge of the abduction of a minor. You do not have to say anything but it may harm your defence if you do not mention, when questioned, something which you later rely on in court. Anything you do say may be given in evidence.'

The ensuing silence in the room was palpable with shock and disbelief. I stared open-mouthed at the two police officers, blood pounding in my ears. Josh was the first to recover.

'I fear you have made a mistake,' he said politely.

'There's no mistake.' DI Green shot him a look which said 'be quiet.'

'This is outrageous.' Mum's voice, strident and commanding, cut through the air. 'What abduction?'

'We'll discuss it at the station.' DS Thorncroft stepped forward in front of her, blocking her path. 'Mariella Blake, I am arresting you on a charge of the abduction of a minor. You do not have to say anything but it may ...'

'Oh, for God's sake,' Dad spluttered, his face now puce with rage. 'Is this anything to do with Selina Matthews? If so, you're making a grave mistake. We have a DNA test result confirming that Anna is our daughter and nothing to do with that woman. If you persist with this farce, I warn you that I will have the two of you hauled before a disciplinary committee and booted off the force.'

'Are you threatening us, sir?' DI Green asked coldly. 'I suggest you think again before you say anything else.'

I stared, speechless with dismay, as DS Thorncroft completed the Miranda rights and took Mum by the arm. 'This way, please.'

Still protesting vehemently, my parents were escorted from the house. We followed and watched numbly as they were directed into two, separate cars.

'I don't believe this,' I muttered as the cars pulled away.

'It's obviously a mistake.' Josh put his arm around me, hugging me against him. 'I'm sure it'll all be cleared up soon enough.'

'But I don't understand. I rang the police this morning and told them about the DNA test. What's going on?' I stood rooted to the spot, surveying the empty road. 'I need to do something.'

'You can't do anything,' Josh said gently, ushering me back inside the house. 'We just have to wait.'

'I can't just wait. There must be something ...' I snapped; my eyes widened, 'Selina,' I breathed. 'She was trying to phone me ...'

My bag was still slung under the table and I tugged out the phone. Four missed calls.

'Selina,' I gasped as soon as she answered. 'What's going on?'

'Oh Anna.' Her voice throbbed with emotion. 'I'm so sorry.'

'Sorry about what? Selina, my parents have just been *arrested*. What's going on?' I was shouting now, desperate for an explanation and yet terrified to hear what she was going to say.

'Oh gosh, I don't know if I should tell you this over the phone ...'

'Selina, just tell me!' The sense of panic was crushing me, making it difficult to breathe.

'They did it, Anna.' Her voice was almost a whisper. 'They took you all those years ago. You're Maisie.'

'No!'

The phone slipped from my fingers and clattered on the tiled floor. She was lying; she had to be. It couldn't be true ...

Yet, in my heart, I knew it was. My parents were not my parents. I was a girl who'd been ripped from her world twenty-three years ago. They had fabricated my entire existence. Even while my mind was still screaming denials, I knew I'd been on a collision course with this moment. There had been an inevitability about it. I could feel my past disintegrating around me and my heart shredding, pieces of confetti carelessly tossed upon the breeze. My life was a lie.

The next few minutes passed in a blur. I was vaguely aware of Josh picking up the phone and arranging to meet Selina back at my house where she would explain everything. At some point after that, police officers, who had a warrant to search the property, told us we needed to leave and Josh steered my stupefied body to his car.

CHAPTER 36

Selina

I waited outside Anna's house, every cell in my body charged with a mixture of emotions. Incredible excitement and ecstasy were laced with overwhelming concern for my daughter. The aftermath of this was bound to be agonising for Anna. I'd need to tread carefully. Our reunion could not be the joyous occasion I'd always imagined.

It had been a rollercoaster day. I'd been floored by the phone call that morning, so sure was I that Anna was my daughter. I'd clung to that certainty like a drowning woman to a lifebelt. Without it, I was cut adrift. I'd sunk down onto the mottled brown carpet, alone in a featureless semi on the outskirts of Thetford, and wept. Who knows how long I'd sat there, feeling sorry for myself, but eventually tears were replaced with renewed determination. It was a mistake; somehow, the results were wrong. I was convinced; I had to do something about it …

My thoughts were interrupted by the appearance of Josh's Mercedes. Eagerly, I rushed to greet them but my steps slowed as I approached the car. Anna's face was an alabaster sculpture, cold and white. I watched as Josh helped her from the car, solicitous and supportive. It was difficult to contain the love brimming through me but I knew I had to walk on eggshells. Stepping forward, I wrapped my arms around my daughter – my *daughter*. I allowed myself a moment of pure joy as I clasped Anna's unresponsive body to my chest, our beating hearts reunited after twenty-three tortuous years. Then I let her go.

'Anna, are you alright?'

'She's in shock.' Josh's voice was curt. 'Let's get her inside.'

'Of course.' I hovered nervously. 'I'll make tea,' I said as he helped Anna onto a kitchen stool. 'Plenty of sugar.'

'Thank you,' Anna said. She wouldn't look at me. A painful silence ensued as I boiled the kettle and poured tea into three mugs.

'What's going on?' she asked suddenly, regarding me with eyes of stone.

I bit my bottom lip, wondering how best to frame the words. 'There's no easy way to tell you this,' I began. 'When you rang me to tell me the results of the DNA test, I just didn't believe it. I was so certain you were my daughter. It's difficult to explain.'

'Try,' Josh said, impatience etched in his frown.

'Yes, well ...' My hands fluttered at his tone. He was angry; I could understand that; I'd turned Anna's life upside down. I hurried on. 'I rang the company directly and asked them to email me the results themselves. You see, I thought if someone had been trying to kill me to stop me from finding the truth, it was certainly possible that the results could have been intercepted somehow ... or doctored.'

'That's a bit far-fetched, don't you think?' Josh interrupted.

'Maybe, but I thought it was worth a try. Anyway, it turns out I was right. The company refused to email the results to me. They said it was a data protection issue. So, then I phoned DS Thorncroft and asked her to intervene. She took a lot of persuading but finally agreed. I think they'd no other leads. Apparently, the CCTV cameras had turned up nothing of value and they were fast running out of options. The police obtained a warrant to access the results and they rang me immediately. The two samples *were* related; the information you'd been sent was false.'

Anna shook her head angrily. 'No!'

'I'm sorry, Anna, but I'm telling you the truth. Things moved quite quickly after that. I wasn't told anything about the decision to arrest your parents but I was told not to contact you before 7pm. That's when I tried to ring but you didn't pick up. You know the rest.'

Silence descended once more. A fly settled on the rim of my mug and I flicked it away. We all watched as it boldly circled and settled once more, this time on the handle of Josh's mug. He brushed it away and took a sip of tea.

'All this sounds unbelievable,' he said at last, turning accusing eyes upon me. 'You'd better be right. If, after all this, it's another mistake ...'

For a horrible moment, I wondered if I *had* got it wrong. I'd wished for this for so long, maybe my fantasy was obscuring reality. No – the police had confirmed it. The proof was there.

'I'm sorry,' I said again. 'I know this is horrible for you but I'm telling you the truth.'

Anna exhaled loudly. 'I just can't get my head around all this,' she muttered. 'If my parents took Maisie, what happened to the baby – the little girl – they had before? It doesn't make any sense.'

I shrugged, wishing I knew how to comfort her. 'I don't know. Only *they* know that.'

'What happens now?' Josh asked.

'The police want me to return to the safe house for the time being while they attempt to tie up all the loose ends. The man who attacked me is probably still at large so my life remains in danger, they said. Will you continue to stay with Josh, Anna?' I gave him a tremulous smile. 'He'll take care of you.'

He responded with a curt nod. She remained silent, staring at the floor. I watched as Josh put his arms around her. 'I still think this will all prove to be a huge cock-up, Anna. Don't give up hope on your parents yet,' he said.

'I just don't know what to think,' she croaked.

'That's understandable.' I leant across and squeezed her hand. 'I really am sorry, Anna – not that you're my daughter, obviously, but that you're having to endure all this. It's a terrible ordeal for you.'

Her face was closed to me and I decided to leave it there. It would take time for her to come to terms with it all. I remembered how it was after I'd lost her. I'd blamed Jack in the beginning and then

I'd blamed myself for leaving her with him. Grief and anger made me push away the people closest to me. As much as I loved Anna and wanted to stay close to her, I knew she'd resent it.

I stood up. 'I know you won't want to be around me right now. I understand. I'm going to leave. But remember you can call me if you want to talk.' I ached to give my beautiful daughter another hug, to hold her close and never let her go, but now was not the time. Instead, I walked away without a backward glance.

As I drove back to Thetford, I wondered for the first time if I'd done the right thing. Had I been selfish insisting on a DNA test, questioning Anna's parentage? I was putting my daughter through hell and causing her immeasurable pain. How would she cope? A cloak of depression settled on my tired shoulders. Perhaps I should've put Anna first – left things alone. It was too late now. All I could hope was that, one day, my daughter would forgive me.

CHAPTER 37

Anna

I relived that moment when Selina told me I was her daughter over and over but the outcome was always the same. My world collapsed around me like bits of flotsam tossing on the ocean. As fast as I tried to gather the pieces in, they bobbed away once more, leaving me bereft and anchorless.

My life was a lie. Thoughts hardened and crystallised into nuggets of certainty. My parents were imposters. I hated them and I mourned my lost life. All those years of anguish, blaming myself for not fitting in; all the loneliness of my cloistered existence, years spent missing my brother.

After Selina had left, Josh had studied me, his face taut with anxiety. He was waiting for me to react but I couldn't; I didn't know how. I no longer knew who I was.

'Anna?' His voice was soft, tentative, as if I was a fragile piece of glass about to shatter. 'Are you ready to leave?'

He held my hand as we walked to his car. I slumped into the passenger seat and closed my eyes, trying to mute the thoughts crowding in, overwhelming me. My jaw ached with the weariness of it.

'Take me home,' I said. With a nod, he started the engine and his car purred into life. It was only as we took the road heading for Swaffham that I realised I didn't know where home was.

***

Back in Lewton, Josh continued to protest on behalf of my parents. 'The police may yet realise they've made a mistake,' he argued. 'I'm sure things will sort themselves out in time.'

Cocooned in his arms, I railed and sobbed while he continued to utter comforting reassurances. It was tempting to believe him, dismiss the whole scenario, pretend nothing had changed.

But it *had* changed. In my heart, I knew the truth of it, the hot, hard certainty. It explained so much. The more I thought back to my childhood, in the light of everything that had happened, the more I was convinced.

The next morning only brought a continuation of the nightmare in the form of another visit from DS Thorncroft. My parents' house had been searched, she informed me, and several items were being closely examined. She wouldn't tell me what they were. My parents remained under arrest and both had consulted with their lawyers. She recommended, in light of the situation, that I didn't attempt to visit. Not that I'd thought to do so. It hadn't even crossed my mind. Everything was too raw and I was too consumed by my own misery.

After she'd gone, I tried to block it all out, lose myself in my writing. But focus and concentration eluded me. It didn't help that I was trying to write about the rift between Jemima and Conrad, caused by the machinations of the devious Samira Goodman and Jemima's lack of faith in her husband. Faith ... trust ... how could I resolve issues like those when they had failed me in my own life. How could Jemima regain the trust she'd lost when I felt I'd never trust anyone again?

I gave up and spent the day helping Josh with jobs at the Old Rectory. Expending energy with physical work provided more of a distraction and I somehow got through the day. *It's out of your hands. Put it out of your mind until you know all the facts.* Easier said than done but it was pointless trying to understand what was going on when I wasn't party to any of the evidence. Selina had sent a couple of texts throughout the day, reiterating her availability should I wish to contact her and hoping I was OK. At least she didn't try to phone me; I was grateful for that. My feelings towards her were confused. I couldn't help blaming her for everything but knew, deep down, it wasn't her fault. However, I wasn't ready to speak to her and I certainly wasn't ready to acknowledge she could be my real mother.

At around six o'clock that evening, I still felt unbearably restless and decided to go for a run to stretch off my aching muscles. Having spent a large part of the day on my hands and knees, first painting and then in the garden, I felt the stiffness of overused limbs but not the physical exhaustion I craved. Somehow, I needed to blank out all the questions buzzing my brain like angry flies.

It was ironic, I thought as I pulled on my trainers, how the devastating shock seemed to have eradicated my previous anxieties. My attitude towards personal safety had morphed into a cavalier lack of concern. A day ago, I would've been too worried, fearful that someone might be watching me, wishing me harm. Such fears were now irrelevant. With a recklessness I hadn't shown in weeks, I shrugged off Josh's concern. He was three quarters of the way through staining a skirting board when I told him my intention.

'Is that wise?' He looked up, his liquid, brown eyes searching my face. 'If you give me a few minutes to finish up here, I'll come with you.'

'It's fine.' I gave him a small smile. 'It's kind of you to offer but I want to run by myself – clear my head. I'll just do a loop around the village. I'll be back before you know it.'

I set off briskly, letting the warmth of the evening sunshine soothe me. Exercise had always proved a balm to my soul and I'd missed it. Breathing heavily after the first mile, I slowed my pace. The lack of exercise over the past month had played havoc with my fitness and I still had the final uphill stretch to complete. *Pace yourself.* I gave myself up to the steady rhythm of my feet, oblivious of everything but the road ahead and my rasping breaths as I struggled to get more oxygen to my lungs. It felt good to be pushing myself. My heart was pounding by the time I reached the crest of the hill and rounded the final bend. *Time for the final sprint.*

Then I saw the police cars. There were three of them, parked across Josh's driveway.

My pace slowed. *Three* police vehicles? Why? As I ran towards them, prickles of apprehension tingling my spine, I saw Josh, accompanied by a man in uniform, getting into the back of one of the cars. *What the hell …?* I ran faster but I was too late. The car pulled away just before I reached it. I caught a glimpse of Josh's face, stonily impassive, as he turned his head but he didn't see me.

Panting hard, I was staring in confusion at the open front door when DS Thorncroft emerged.

'Anna,' she called. 'This way, please.' Her face was serious and I was seized by waves of fresh dread.

'What's going on? Why have you taken Josh?'

'Come inside. I just need to ask you a few questions.' DS Thorncroft gave a brief, encouraging smile but it was laced with something else. Sympathy?

'Why? What's happened?'

I was ushered inside to a seat in the living room. Another officer, a tall, spotty, young man who looked scarcely old enough to be out of school, handed me a glass of water.

'You'll be needing that after your run,' he said kindly in a broad Norfolk accent.

I sipped the water gratefully. My mind was reeling with questions but I wasn't sure I wanted to hear the answers.

'Why have you taken Josh?' I repeated, staring at each of the police officers in turn, trying to detect clues from their body language. Above, I could hear footsteps and other voices. 'Why are people upstairs?'

'We'll get to that,' DS Thorncroft said briskly. 'First we just need to ask you a few questions. Can you tell us who knew that you and Mrs Matthews had taken a DNA test to determine the exact nature of your relationship?'

I thought hard. Who had I told? 'Josh.' I replied. 'I think that's it. I'd told other people that was my intention but I hadn't told them when we did it.'

'Names?' DS Thorncroft prompted.

'My housemate Ellie Peterson – she's away on holiday at the moment. My friend, Madison Grey. She lives in Norwich and I haven't seen her since Saturday. And my p … parents.' My tongue caught on the word.

'You didn't mention it on the phone, text, social media?'

'No, definitely not. I may have told Ewan Jacobs. He's another friend and also does a bit of work for my dad … but I can't remember.'

Was it my imagination or did DS Thorncroft's gaze sharpen at the mention of Ewan's name?

'Right, just to clarify, only Mrs Matthews, Josh Fielding and yourself knew when and where the DNA results were expected?'

'Yes.'

'Did you tell Josh Fielding what time you were expecting the post to arrive yesterday morning?'

I frowned. 'Josh asked me. We were talking about it the night before.'

'Can you describe what happened when you went to the house to collect the results?'

'Josh offered to pick them up for me but I said I'd go. He volunteered to come with me and we both walked round to my house.' I wrinkled my nose, trying to remember the exact details. 'I guess it was about half ten, maybe a little later. Josh went into the house first, to check it out … you know, to ensure no-one else was in there … and I waited outside.'

'How long was he alone in the house?'

'I don't know. It felt like forever but it was probably just a few minutes.'

DS Thorncroft nodded. 'After that …?'

'Then I went in. There was a pile of post but I could see the envelope with the results was there. I picked everything up and went into the kitchen. Then I opened it and skimmed through to find the result. It was negative.'

'Do you still have the envelope?'

'Yes, it's upstairs.'

'We'll be needing that.'

'Of course.' I went to get up but DS Thorncroft gestured for me to stay seated.

'Did anything give you cause to believe the results had been tampered with?'

'No. I believed them. They were a relief. I phoned Selina and later on, I phoned my mum. She was pleased, obviously, that it was all over. This had been quite an ordeal for both my parents. She suggested Josh and I went over for dinner that evening which we did.'

'If it was, as you suggest, an ordeal for your parents, what made you agree to the DNA test in the first place? Did you have suspicions you may not be their natural child?'

'No, nothing like that.' I was feeling increasingly defensive. Nervously, I twiddled my ear lobe. 'I'd met Selina through my part-time Girl Friday work.' I wondered briefly about mentioning the fact that Selina had been following me prior to that but decided against it. It would probably be a distraction. 'Eventually, she told me about Maisie and said she had a very strong suspicion that I could be her child. I thought that was ridiculous and told her so. When I informed my parents, they were understandably upset and angry. It was my mum who suggested the DNA test – to set my mind at rest, she said.'

DS Thorncroft nodded thoughtfully. 'And she expected you to go through with it, do you think?'

'I've no idea. I thought the suggestion was genuine. Then, as you know, Selina had the fire at her house and things developed from there.'

'Tell me about your relationship with Josh Fielding.' DS Thorncroft suddenly changed tack. 'How did you meet him?'

'He contacted me about helping out with the garden. It was very overgrown when he moved in and started renovating the house. It was a professional relationship which started about a month ago.'

'Were you aware that your father asked Josh Fielding to employ you?'

'Yes, but not at the time. I only found out recently.' My brow creased in puzzlement. 'How do you know that?' I asked.

DS Thorncroft turned a direct stare upon me. 'Yesterday, as you know, we obtained a warrant to search your parents' property. In the course of our search, we found email communications between your father and Josh Fielding pertaining to yourself.'

I swallowed hard. I felt I was going to be sick.

DS Thorncroft withdrew a sheet of paper from a plastic wallet. 'April 25th,' she read aloud. 'Geoff Blake asked how the repairs to the Old Rectory were going. Fielding replied to the effect that they were coming along slowly. Blake asked him, as a favour, to employ his daughter on a casual basis to help out. Fielding said he was too busy to be babysitting. Blake then invited him to his house for a meeting. Did you know all this?'

'Yes ... well ... not all the details but yes, I knew.' I sighed. 'My dad has always been very over-protective of me. He told Josh he was worried about me. That's why Josh agreed ... and because he felt he owed my dad. He worked for him at Sampson Blake; I expect you know that.'

The detective nodded. 'There were further emails, asking how things were going. Do you think your father asked Josh Fielding to pursue a personal relationship with you to keep tabs on what was happening with Selina Matthews?'

'No,' I protested immediately. 'Josh wouldn't do that!'

DS Thorncroft was relentless. 'I'm sorry,' she said, 'but in one email, Geoff Blake suggested it would make him and Mariella very happy if your relationship was to become more personal. Fielding didn't reply.'

I shrugged. 'That doesn't mean he took any notice of that.'

'No,' DS Thorncroft agreed, 'but it is true that your relationship became more personal, isn't it?'

'Yes, but ...'

'We found other evidence,' DS Thorncroft interrupted. 'In your father's safe, we found a phone. There were only three numbers listed in this phone. One belonged to Ewan Jacobs. I believe you mentioned him earlier. Texts were exchanged relating to the surveillance of Selina Matthews and also regarding the surveillance of yourself. Were you aware of this?'

My jaw dropped. 'No!' I exclaimed. 'I thought I was being followed and I spoke to Ewan about it. I thought it was just my imagination but Ewan took me seriously. After that, the feeling disappeared.'

'You didn't report this to the police?'

'No. As I said, I thought I was imagining it.'

'Can you describe the person you thought was following you?'

'A man in his forties or fifties. Grey hair. Quite stocky. I just kept noticing him in random places ... or thought I did. I wasn't sure it was always the same man. Initially, he was driving a black Range Rover; later, he was in a white Audi but I couldn't be sure it was the same person.'

'Is this the man?' DS Thorncroft pulled out another piece of paper and handed it to me. The face was instantly recognisable and I shuddered.

'Yes,' I answered, passing the photo back, anxious to be rid of it.

'His name is Kevin Docherty. Have you ever heard your father mention him?'

'No, why? What's he got to do with my father?'

'His name was the second one in his list of contacts on his phone. We believe he is also the man who attempted to abduct Selina Matthews in Swaffham.'

'Oh my God!' I was horrified. 'Are you saying you have evidence my dad was involved in that?'

DS Thorncroft just looked at me.

'Oh my God,' I said again. This was my dad we were talking about – the man who had told me bedtime stories, who had hugged me when I was hurt, who had listened when I told him I was being bullied at school. He'd always been there for me, loved me, if anything, too much. I shook my head vehemently. It wasn't possible.

'The investigation is ongoing,' DS Thorncroft said at last. 'We'll know more shortly.'

This nightmare was assuming phantasmagoric proportions. I recalled Selina hinting my parents may have been behind the fire too but I'd dismissed her comment out of hand. I knew my parents. Dad was a ruthless businessman but he was also funny, kind, charismatic and fiercely loyal. He wasn't a murderer.

'You've got it wrong.' I looked helplessly at the detectives sitting with me. 'It's not true.'

'That's always possible, of course.' DS Thorncroft's face had softened with compassion.

The room was silent apart from the echoing of footsteps above. I was reminded of my earlier questions.

'What's going on upstairs? And you still haven't told me why you've arrested Josh.'

'As yet, Mr Fielding is helping us with our enquiries,' DS Thorncroft replied formally. 'He hasn't been charged. In the meantime, we have a warrant to search this property.'

'Oh.' I thought for a moment. I was obviously missing something. So far, there was nothing to suggest that Josh was involved in any of this. 'Why?' Even as I asked, I realised, with sickening clarity, what she was going to say.

'I'm sorry,' DS Thorncroft said quietly,' but the third person listed on your father's phone was Josh Fielding.'

CHAPTER 38

Anna
Three months later.

hadn't seen Josh since that day. Eventually, he'd been released by the police without charge but my faith in him was shattered, a broken ornament, beyond repair. He'd begged me to see him, via text, email and, when I didn't respond, through Ellie, Madison and even Selina. He could explain everything; he was innocent. I remained hardened to his pleas. Still, I received regular texts from him – I couldn't quite bring myself to block his number – telling me he loved me, how it was breaking his heart to be apart from me. He understood, he said, I needed time to come to terms with everything. He would wait; what we had together was worth waiting for. Since then I'd received no further messages. As the edges of my heartbreak began to soften, I wondered if I was being too hard on him. The truth was I'd been avoiding him because I didn't trust myself to remain immune to his charms. Perhaps I was being unfair by refusing him an opportunity to defend himself. As I wavered to the brink of calling him, I asked DS Thorncroft what she thought about his innocence or otherwise.

'I can't answer that,' she replied tersely.

'But you must have an idea ...' I pleaded.

'Look, if you're asking me if I think he can be trusted, then the answer is no. There's no proof he was involved in the deception with the results, but I think he was. He had the opportunity to switch the envelopes when he entered the property alone. And there's something else which doesn't make sense. If he was genuinely concerned about your safety, why did he leave you outside on your own while he went inside?' She noticed my look of dismay. 'Look, this is just my opinion. I could be wrong.'

I could tell she didn't think so. Her words tore my wounds afresh and I wept once more. Despite everything, up until this point, I'd hoped for a different outcome. It wasn't going to happen.

In the meantime, I'd got to know the Matthews family. My relationship with Selina was still awkward. I was polite but distant; her transparent longing for a mother/daughter closeness felt cloying, claustrophobic. How could I think of her as Mum? It was too soon. She'd driven me to meet

Jack Matthews, my real father, with whom I'd immediately felt a connection. Since then, I'd met him twice more and loved him already.

'It sounds cheesy to say it,' I'd told Ellie and Madison, 'but when he hugged me, it really felt like coming home.'

'You were always Daddy's little girl,' Selina remarked, seeing our instant bond. 'You took after him in every respect, whilst Harry was more like me.' It was true we looked similar. We both had the same tall, athletic build and fair colouring, although the small amount of hair Jack retained was mainly grey. I watched him closely, fascinated by the mannerisms which were so familiar to me. 'There you are,' Selina said, pointing as Jack fiddled with his earlobe. 'I knew you were Maisie as soon as I saw you do that.'

No-one called me Maisie. That would have been too weird. They all accepted me as Anna and welcomed me whole-heartedly into their family. Jack had remarried, to a small, dark-haired woman called Lou who bore more than a passing resemblance to Selina. She had two children of her own and I found myself suddenly with two stepsisters, slightly older than me but loud, gregarious and instantly likeable.

I'd also met my brother, Harry. It had been nerve-wracking; the memory of him was the only one I owned from our past as a family and so the meeting took on special significance.

'Sis!' Harry, dark and wiry, eyes damp with tears, hugged me as if he would never let me go. 'I can't believe we have you back.'

I clung to him, unable to speak. All those years I'd missed him desperately without even realising he existed. The loneliness I'd felt throughout my childhood was because of him, because deep down I'd always known I had a brother, even when it seemed impossible.

Then, when I found my voice, it was as if I couldn't stop. The two of us sat for hours, talking about our lives, both hungry for every detail. Being three years older, Harry was able to tell me about our life before the abduction.

'I always teased you terribly,' he said apologetically. 'I felt so guilty about that after you disappeared.'

I, in turn, told him about my recurrent dream. 'Hopefully you can put me out of my misery,' I smiled. 'What was it you were holding in your hand, that day on the beach? You'd run off with it and wouldn't let me see.'

'I'm sorry, Anna but I don't remember,' he replied sadly. 'I was always doing stuff like that. It could have been anything. A shell, maybe? A fossil?'

'No, I'm sure it was something else,' I said, 'something you'd found and you knew I would want. Oh well,' I continued when there was no response, 'it doesn't matter now.'

I'd met up with Harry since then and had a riotous time with him, his new girlfriend Kate and his circle of friends. He lived in London and had invited me to stay with him for the weekend. Madison and Ellie had encouraged me to go when I was at first reluctant.

'It's a bit soon,' I demurred. 'We've only met the once. A weekend seems a bit much.'

'It'll be fun,' Ellie urged. 'You have to go.'

And it was. I couldn't remember when I'd laughed so much. Their easy acceptance allowed me to relax and it wasn't long before I was cracking jokes along with them. Harry and I shared the same sense of humour and I loved joining in with the kind of wisecracks I usually reserved for my writing.

In the middle of a discussion about my novels, Harry announced, 'I'm reading a book about anti-gravity. I can't put it down!'

'Hilarious,' I retorted. 'I like reading sitting at the back of my wardrobe.'

'Why?'

'That's Narnia business.'

There was a collective groan. 'Oh no,' Kate wailed. 'Now there are two of them. Pun doubles!'

'I once wrote a book about wind systems.' I was on a roll. 'It's saved in my drafts.'

'Haha,' Harry replied. 'You ought to write one about a tornado. It would have a twist at the end.'

The weekend was a welcome respite and I felt re-energised as I headed back home on the Sunday evening. My life may be in turmoil but the pain would pass – it was passing.

I tried not to think of my parents – well, the people who purported to be my parents all those years. Geoff and Mariella were still in prison awaiting trial, both charged with abduction and conspiracy to commit murder. The police had, as yet, failed to apprehend Ewan Jacobs and Kevin Docherty who had disappeared without trace. The search, I was told, had been extended to Europe and Interpol were now involved.

'It's only a matter of time before we have them locked up,' DS Thorncroft insisted.

Strangely enough, I didn't blame Ewan. He was weak, I decided, easily manipulated by a powerful man like my father. Probably, he hadn't realised what he was involved with until he was in too deep to extricate himself. That was what I liked to think, anyway.

The trial was looming, a black hole of awfulness where everything would become painfully public. The evidence, DS Thorncroft said, was overwhelming and, recently, Geoff Blake had changed his plea to 'guilty.' Currently, he was assisting the police with details of the abduction. He had also written me a long letter, explaining many things and asking for forgiveness. It was a letter which left me with a dilemma I had yet to resolve.

My dearest Anna,

I love you, my darling girl, I will always love you. Please hold that in your heart and don't forget it.

You deserve an explanation and you shall have it – not some sanitised version from the police but the real story, from the horse's mouth – so here goes.

Your mum and I came to Alla Mora on holiday in June 1996 with our three-year-old daughter Anna. We stayed in a private villa, up in the hills overlooking the bay. It belonged to a friend of mine. We enjoyed three idyllic days of sunshine, lazing by the pool, swimming when we got too hot and then tragedy struck. The villa had a balcony and, while we were in the bedroom, Anna wandered out onto it without us realising. She was always an adventurous, little thing. Anyway, the worst possible thing happened – she fell over the balcony and crashed on to the rocks below. I am weeping now as I think of it. She was killed instantly. We were totally devastated. For a day, we did nothing other than cradle her poor, broken body. I guess we were in shock. When I suggested calling the authorities, your mother refused. It was bad enough, she said, that we had lost our child. She just couldn't bear a police investigation. 'We will probably be blamed,' she said. 'I may lose my licence to practise.' She had a point. It was possible the authorities would accuse us of negligence and that could blight her career as a paediatrician. She came up with a plan. It was totally ridiculous, I told her so, but she insisted it would work. There was another reason for her confidence, for the whole plan, but more of that later.

We would bury our daughter, privately, there at the villa. No one but us would ever know. And we would take a little girl from the hundreds playing at the resort – one who looked like Anna's passport picture. We would return home and relocate, somewhere far away from friends and family. For at least a year, we would see no one we had previously known. I know, with hindsight, this was a terrible thing to do and I'm sorry for the grief we caused. Anyway, Mariella did it. She wore a wig, put on an American accent and pulled it off. I couldn't believe it when she returned to the villa with you. It was incredible. You looked so much like Anna too. After that, it was easy. Obviously, there was a huge amount of publicity about the missing girl but no-one suspected us. They were looking for an American woman. It was a masterstroke – I had to hand it to her. Your mum gave you a sleeping tablet for the flight home so you wouldn't say anything to give the game away. The rest you know. I was worried you would remember what had happened to you, your previous life, as you got older, but your mum took care of that too. She had some experience in hypnotherapy and specialised in treating traumatised children. You had several sessions with her to help wipe away those memories.

Yes, we were over-protective of you. Now you know why. There was always the chance we could lose you or we could be found out. While you were living at home, we could influence your decisions, lessen the risks but you insisted on going to university. We needed a way of keeping an eye on you, keeping you safe from a distance. That's where your friends, Ellie and Madison, came in, not to spy on you but to look after you. Madison told me you were being followed by someone in a blue Peugeot and that was when I got Ewan involved. He arranged for someone to follow you, to keep you safe while he investigated the driver of the Peugeot. When I found out it belonged to Selina Matthews, my blood ran cold. How could she have found you? We upped the surveillance and knew when she made contact with you. Most of the rest you know. It was your mother's idea to arrange an 'accident' for her – not that I'm trying to absolve myself from blame. We just wanted to scare her off. Despite what the police claim, we didn't wish her dead, just out of the picture. That's why your mother was confident about agreeing to the DNA test; we both thought Selina wouldn't be around to follow it through. I knew a man who would organise the 'accident' – the same man who'd been following you, Kevin Docherty. Unfortunately for us, he proved particularly inept. Selina Matthews is a lucky woman. Perhaps it was just meant to be.

As I said earlier, that's not quite the whole story. There's something else, something I haven't yet told the police. I'd love you to come and visit me so I can tell you myself. Then the whole sordid business will be laid bare and ghosts can be laid to rest. Please come.

I've done some bad things, I realise that now, and I deserve to go to jail but I did them in the name of love, for your mother and for you. Please can you find it in your heart to forgive me?

Your forever-loving

Dad x

I'd reread the letter several times. It was so typical of Geoff – I now refused to think of him as Dad. He was still trying to pull my strings, the puppet master he'd always been. Deliberately, he was dangling one final secret in front of me as bait and it irritated the hell out of me. If I chose to go and see him, I decided, it would be on my terms. It was also typical he was managing to pass all the blame onto Mariella whilst still protesting he accepted responsibility for everything. I couldn't envisage a time when I would ever forgive either of them. Questions, though, still taunted me. I needed to know everything ... but was that worth the pain of facing Geoff Blake once more?

It was a difficult decision and I continued to postpone making it in the race to meet the deadline for finishing my latest book. Prompted by phone calls and emails from my agent and publisher, I'd knuckled down and written the happy ending my readers would want, that I wanted.

When Conrad phoned to say he was going to be away for another week, Jemima had responded in typical fashion by booking flights for her and baby Freya and they'd flown out to Dubai to confront him. Once there, she'd realised that her husband loved only her and her worries about his relationship with Samira Goodman were unfounded. Of course, there had to be a few mishaps along the way – an incident on the plane involving a pompous businessman and vomit (Freya's, not Jemima's); a shopping bag containing sexy lingerie she'd bought as a surprise for Conrad accidentally upended in a lift she was sharing with some of his male colleagues; an embarrassing faux pas when she mistook the CEO of the company Conrad was working with for a waiter and asked him for a glass of sauvignon (well he *was* very casually dressed) – but the story concluded with the triumph of Conrad's architectural plans and a celebratory return home.

On the train to London to meet my agent, I was already thinking of ideas for the next book in the series – a move for Conrad, Jemima and Freya to Japan perhaps. I would enjoy doing the research for that one.

'Anna, how's things?' My agent, Helen Barton-Thomas, a slim woman in her thirties sporting a dark bob and a wide smile, greeted me with a brisk embrace. 'Water?'

I returned the smile and sat down at the table. 'Hi Helen, yes please,' I said, ignoring the first question. 'This is lovely.' I looked around, admiring the crisp, minimalist décor of the restaurant she'd chosen for our meeting.

'Well, you *are* one of my favourite authors.'

I chuckled as I sipped my water. I knew Helen said that to everyone she represented.

'I *loved* this latest book, *Baby Gym*,' Helen continued. 'It's with Juliet now.' Juliet was an editor. 'She's working her magic as we speak – but I've no doubt it's going to be a best-seller. Well done you.'

'Thank you. You know I couldn't have done it without your help.'

Helen smiled modestly. 'It's a team effort but you're the star. You'd have made it, even without your father's backing. Oops,' she pulled a face. 'Sorry, I shouldn't have said that. Just erase that last comment please. Me and my big mouth.'

'What do you mean?' It was like being doused with ice water. 'My father's backing? Are you saying that he's been behind my books all along … or rather, his money has?'

'Oh Anna, I'm so sorry. I was sworn to secrecy and now I've gone and blown it.'

Upon further questioning, Helen admitted that Geoff Blake had contacted her shortly after she'd received my first submission and before she'd had a chance to read it through. He'd promised a significant financial contribution should she sign me up and funding for all publishing and publicity costs to ensure the book was a success.

'How could I refuse?' Helen threw up her hands in apology. 'Of course, I would have, had the book been rubbish,' she continued hastily, 'but it wasn't. You write like a dream, Anna. As I said before I put my foot in it, you would've been a success anyway.'

'Would you have signed me without that incentive?' My voice was cold, my heart heavy.

She hesitated for a split second, enough to send my spirits plummeting even lower. 'Of *course*, I would,' she gushed. 'I can spot success when I see it. Anyway, he only put up money for the first book. Remember, the publishers were keen to sign you up for a subsequent, two-book deal. People like your novel. You have good reviews. Please don't let it bother you. I wish I had a dad who could put money behind me.'

Having lost my appetite for lunch, I left as soon as I could politely get away. I'd been so proud of my success as a writer, so happy I'd accomplished what so many only aspire to on my own merits. But I hadn't. My joy in writing was tainted, my self-belief undermined.

On the train home, I sat staring out of the window, feeling sorry for myself, when my thoughts were interrupted by a voice in my right ear.

'Excuse me, I'm sorry to disturb you but are you Anna Blake?' The voice belonged to a girl, possibly in her late teens, wearing glasses with purple frames and supporting herself awkwardly on two crutches. As I looked up, the train lurched around a corner and the girl fell into the seat beside me. 'Oops, sorry, I guess I'll sit down then, if that's OK with you?'

I smiled despite my self-absorbed gloom. 'Go for it,' I said, 'and yes I am.'

'That's amazing. I absolutely love your book. I've just pre-ordered the second one – it's due out any day now isn't it? I can't wait.'

'Thank you. That's kind.' Warmth spread through me. The girl was regarding me with unadulterated hero-worship, as if I were a rock star.

'I'm Lucia.' She started rummaging in a canvas bag.' I can't believe I'm sitting next to Anna Blake. Emmy – she's my bestie – will be *so* jealous when I tell her. Can I have a selfie?' A phone emerged from the bag and I duly smiled for the photo. Lucia's fingers flew over the keys as she talked. 'I'm putting this on Insta straight away,' she grinned happily. 'It was worth having a boring old hospital appointment just to meet you.'

'Thanks.' I grinned back. Lucia's irrepressible good humour was infectious. 'Have you injured your leg?' I looked at the crutches now resting by the seat.

'No. I've got MS,' she replied cheerfully. 'It's a bloody nuisance but I don't let it bother me. There are lots of people worse off than me. I miss playing tennis – I used to play for Essex – but that's about it. I can still get about, do stuff I want to do. I don't let it define me. Anyway, I don't want to talk about me. Do you mind telling me how you became a writer? I'd love to become an author so any tips would be appreciated.'

I told her all about the creative writing course I'd taken at university, about my attempts, soon abandoned, to write literary fiction and Lucia pulled a face.

'Thank God you gave that up and decided to write proper books,' she said fervently. I laughed aloud. I was enjoying telling my writing story.

'Anyway, I've just finished writing the third book in the series and today I've been to London to meet with my agent.'

'An agent,' Lucia breathed, her eyes wide. 'How cool – to have an agent!'

'Yes, well, today wasn't quite so cool,' I said drily. I wasn't quite sure how it happened but there was something about this girl which invited confidence. Before I knew it, I was telling Lucia about my recent discovery. 'There you go,' I said, cynical with self-deprecation. 'Without my father's money, I probably wouldn't be sitting here now.'

'Oh, you mustn't think that,' she gasped. 'So what if you had a bit of help! That doesn't disguise the fact that your book made me wee myself laughing.'

'The ultimate accolade! Can I quote that on my next book cover?'

'Ooh would you?' Lucia's eyes shone. 'My surname is Fox. Lucia Fox. You'll need that for the quote.'

I realised she was serious and made an instant decision. 'Definitely,' I said making a note of it on my phone. 'It's my new, favourite comment about my writing. I'll insist it goes on the third book. Give me your address too so I can send you a copy.'

'Oh, this is just so brilliant.' Lucia's face flooded with joy. 'This is fast becoming my best day ever. I wish I could stay on the train but this is my stop.' She flung her arms around me and squeezed me hard. 'Thank you so much.'

'No, thank *you*,' I replied as the young girl struggled to her feet and gave me a wobbly wave goodbye.

The rest of the journey seemed especially quiet after that but Lucia's words lingered. 'I don't let it define me,' she'd said about her MS, a debilitating illness which must have had a huge impact on her life. I felt humbled by the encounter and resolved there and then I wasn't going to let anything that had happened in the past define me either. I was a successful author and proud of it. I was also the author of my future. I would determine its course. I would listen to others but make my own decisions – no regrets, no more wallowing in self-pity, no more letting others put me down.

I knew what I had to do.

***

I parked my car in the free car park and stared up at the large, red-bricked, rectangular building in front of me. Wayland Prison. It was not as imposing as I'd expected, three storeys high and with lots of windows, but then I hadn't been sure what to expect. I glanced at my watch. 1:26 pm. I'd been allotted a visiting slot of 2-3 pm so I was in good time but I also knew there would be security checks to endure first. Grabbing my phone and bag, I marched to the entrance. I felt apprehensive but also determined. I wanted answers.

Having endured the identity checks and searches, I was directed to the Visitor Centre where I was told to leave my bag and phone in one of the lockers. Then I waited.

At 2:02 pm, I was directed to the Visitors Hall. Immediately, I spotted Geoff. He was wearing a navy polo shirt with a green bib over the top. Other prisoners were also wearing brightly coloured bibs, generally over light blue T-shirts. All the men were sitting on chairs behind individual tables. I took a deep breath and headed his way. At my approach, he smiled broadly and I could feel my muscles tensing.

In my head, I had practised how our meeting would be. I would be cool, emotionless, give him nothing … and yet, I managed to blow all that with my very first words.

'Hello Dad.'

CHAPTER 39

Geoff
HM Prison Wayland

It was tough being in prison but he'd been in worse places. The trick, he'd discovered, to securing a comfortable existence, was to recreate the illusion of himself as a powerful man. That was easy enough. It was a front he'd used all his life. Politics in prison were no different from those in business: sort out the pecking order; deal with those at the top; demand respect; bullshit like hell; give no quarter. He'd been there only three months but, already, he was established as one of the big players. His lawyer, Charlotte Greatwood, an ambitious, young woman with a pleasingly shapely figure and sharp brain, had told him he was going to do some time – no question about it – so it was worth the effort. He would do OK.

The next thing was to ensure his sentence was kept to a minimum. He had no intention of leaving jail an old man. He'd listened to Charlotte's advice and changed his plea to guilty. From that standpoint, he could work on the mitigating circumstances, make sure he came across to the jury as a victim rather than a criminal. Mariella, he'd been told, was working out her own deal. It would be interesting to see how she was going to spin it.

When he did get out, his main aim would be to pick up as many of the threads of his old life as he could. He couldn't lose Anna. If he did, it would all be for nothing. Smiling broadly, he studied her face as she strode purposefully to his table. She was very pale and looked as if she had lost weight but there was a glint of steely determination which hadn't been there before.

'Hello Dad.' He knew the greeting had slipped out automatically and that she was inwardly cursing herself. His grin widened.

'Darling. Thank you so much for coming.' He held out his hand across the table to her. She hesitated and then took it, giving it a brief squeeze before releasing it. Old habits die hard. Already he could see her weakening. She felt sorry for him, he realised. A good start. He could play on that.

'I have questions,' she said as she sat in front of him.

'I'm sure you do. Fire away.' His smile was contrite. He tried to engage eye contact with her but she refused to look at his face, staring instead at his ridiculous bib.

'Why on earth are you wearing that?'

He laughed. 'I wasn't expecting that. Apparently, it's for identification purposes. Otherwise, as a prisoner on remand, I'm allowed to wear my own clothes. Any other sartorial questions?'

She smiled in spite of herself. 'No. I guess I'll start with the DNA test results. How did you switch them?'

'It was pretty easy. I have a key to your house, remember. I made sure I had all the information I needed and went there myself to switch the envelopes. I burnt the original.'

'What information did you need?'

'The name of the company doing the test. What time the post arrived. Things like that.'

'And how did you obtain that information?'

'Josh told me.' He could see that disappointed her. She'd always been an open book to him.

'Josh was involved?'

Geoff frowned and looked slightly puzzled. 'Not really. You already know I'd been in contact with him, keeping an eye on what was going on. He told me the name of the company because I said I wanted to ensure a reputable company was employed. I told him I needed the time of the postal delivery because I wanted to know the approximate time I could expect your call. He knew I was anxious about the whole thing so he was happy to help.'

'Josh didn't switch the envelope?' Geoff watched as she began fiddling with her left earlobe. She always did that when she was anxious about something. Clearly, this was an important question.

'No. I've already told you. I did. What on earth makes you think he did?'

'That's what the police told me.'

He rolled his eyes and snorted. 'Yes, well, I should take no notice of them. Useless bunch.'

'They managed to put you in here,' she retorted.

'True but that was complete luck. Who would believe that Matthews woman would manage to find you after all these years? We were just unlucky but there you go ...' He shrugged. 'As they say in the movies, it's a fair cop.'

'Why are you now helping the police? Why have you changed your plea to a guilty one?'

'The truth?' She nodded. 'I'm a pragmatist. I know they have irrefutable evidence against me. My lawyer has advised it will mean a significant reduction to my sentence. I'm also pleading extenuating circumstances. Yes, I'll have to do time but, with my co-operation and good behaviour, I could serve as little as five years. Better than the rest of my life, don't you think?'

Her lips tightened but she made no comment. He allowed the silence to drift between them. Let her think she was in charge.

'To clarify,' she said at last, 'you employed Ewan and Kevin Docherty to keep tabs on me and Selina and then you told Docherty to get rid of Selina but make it look like an accident.'

'Not to get rid of her. To scare her off. As I said in the letter, it was your mother's idea. She persuaded me we had no choice. Of course, I regret that now.'

'Was there anyone else involved? Damien Davies, for instance?'

Geoff's face creased in bewilderment. 'Who on earth is he?'

'Damien Davies. He was decorating your house?'

His brow cleared. 'Oh him. No, of course not. He only ever had dealings with your mother. Nothing to do with me.'

'OK, and to be absolutely clear, Josh didn't know what was going on?'

'No. I don't know why you keep asking me about him.' He knew all too well.

'The police found the phone in your safe. Three people were listed in the contacts. Josh was one of them.'

'Oh, that!' He pretended to think for a moment. 'I needed to speak to Josh and my usual phone had no signal. I told Josh I'd borrowed a colleague's phone. That's all it was.'

She remained suspicious. 'How did you know his number?'

He gave her a look. 'I'm good with numbers. I remember them. It's how I am.'

The information pleased her. Her face relaxed slightly, losing its chilly demeanour. 'OK,' she said. 'Now what was it you wanted to tell me?' She met his eyes for the first time – a small thing but for him a major triumph. He reached again for her hand but she snatched it away under the table. One step at a time.

'Yes, well, I wanted to tell you first, before I told the police. It's how it all started. It's time the story was told.' He could see she was intrigued. He'd always known how to tell a story.

'Our daughter was born in the Royal Edinburgh hospital on November 13th, 2002. We called her Anna Mary Blake and she weighed 7lbs 6oz. She was absolutely perfect in every way. I fell in love with her immediately. It was more difficult for your mother. There were complications with the birth and she had to have emergency surgery. Afterwards, she was told she could have no more children. We were both devastated but Mariella took it especially hard. Then, she suffered from post-natal depression. It was a tough time for her. Anyway, we managed to get through the first few months and I'd gone back to work. At that time, I was working for a bank in Edinburgh but I was away in London when it happened ...' He paused, tears filming his eyes.

'What happened?'

'She died. Our beautiful baby girl – gone. Just like that. Cot death. Sudden Infant Death Syndrome it's called now. Mariella found her dead in her crib.' He shook his head, remembering. 'She was already fragile, after the surgery and with her depression. This tipped her over the edge. She told me she sat all day, cradling Anna in her arms. She told no-one, not even me. I phoned from London that evening. I tried several times but she didn't pick up. Anyway, that night she went back to the hospital. She was working there before the birth as a junior doctor so she had access to the wards. She walked into the maternity unit and took a baby girl. Just like that. When I got home the following evening, Anna was lying dead, still in her crib, and your mother was bottle feeding another baby, calling her Anna, pretending that nothing had happened.'

She stared at him open-mouthed. He could see the horror and shock in her eyes. There was something else too. He was pretty sure it was sympathy.

'It was a terrible shock,' Geoff continued. 'Eventually, she told me what she'd done. When I said we needed to return the baby, explain the situation, she went berserk. She refused to let me take the baby from her. I was so afraid for her mental state that I did nothing. I always planned to return the baby but, at that time, I couldn't refuse Mariella. I thought, in time, she'd come to terms with the tragedy and be prepared to give the baby up herself. I loved her you see. I would've done anything to see her smile again. But it never happened. In the meantime, it was all over the news – the family pleading for their baby's return. Awful.' He shuddered. 'Anyway, time passed and the baby became

Anna. We buried the body of our own baby in the garden and moved to Kent. No one knew us there you see; no one would put two and two together.'

'What about your friends … family? Surely someone realised the truth?'

'No-one. You have to remember it was a different time. Nowadays, photos are posted all the time on social media but there was nothing like that then. A few friends had visited after the baby was born and moving away made it easy to avoid them. If you recall, my parents were killed in a car accident when I was eighteen and I was an only child. Mariella's elder brother was living in Canada and she'd never really got on with her parents so we only ever saw them occasionally. We moved to Kent and I got a transfer with the same bank in London. Mariella didn't return to work for a while. She was such a devoted mother.' His face softened briefly. 'But then tragedy struck a second time, as I told you in my letter …' He paused and his eyes hollowed with pain. 'Mariella was hysterical with grief. There was no reasoning with her. Then, of course, there were other complications, like the chance of the authorities discovering she wasn't really our child. Mariella had accomplished an abduction successfully before; she said she could do it again. The real driving force here, though, was her desire for a child. She'd been obsessed with Anna; she wasn't prepared to let her go.'

He paused, watching her as she processed the information. Around them, the whispered hubbub of voices filled the void.

'I don't believe you,' she said at last. 'The Mariella you're talking about is not the same woman who raised me. *She* could hardly be described as a loving mum.'

He looked at her sadly. 'I know. I'll come to that in a minute. We travelled back to England with no difficulty but that's when our problems really started. The picture of the child who'd gone missing in Spain, Maisie Matthews, was all over the papers. You *did* look remarkably alike, you and our Anna, but it was only going to be a matter of time before people asked questions. So, we headed back to Scotland and from there, took a ferry to Mull where we stayed, keeping ourselves to ourselves, for six months. As I'm sure you remember, my parents had left me a substantial sum of money when they died and I'd invested it well. I was fascinated from an early age by the stock markets and, by that time, my inheritance had doubled. It was relatively easy to give up my job and disappear for a while. Mariella cut your hair while we were there and dyed it. Nobody recognised you and life in Mull was very removed from the life we'd left behind. In the end, that became a problem. We both were going stir crazy living in such isolation so we returned to England, this time to the anonymity of London. In the meantime, we'd been taking precautions with you and your memory. Mariella had used hypnotherapy before with children and conducted several such sessions with you.' He gave her a wry smile. 'You were very resistant. Hardly surprising really. You cried endlessly and woke us night after night with nightmares. You may have looked like Anna but, in personality, you couldn't have been more different. Anna had adored Mariella, followed her everywhere, and you didn't. It was as simple as that. Instead, you always turned to me and that made things worse. Mariella tried to make you love her but you never did and that's why she changed. She became cold and withdrawn. When we returned to London, you were enrolled at nursery and she got a job at Great Ormond Street Hospital. Her work became her life. And she resented you. You were not the real Anna; you could never match up. I loved both of you and did my best to mediate between you but it was never enough, I realise that.'

He looked at her with compassion, allowing his words time to sink in, to take effect. A fat, black beetle scuttled along the edge of the table. He resisted the urge to crush it with his fist. 'That's about it. The whole truth. I'm so pleased you agreed to see me, Anna. I wanted you to hear the story before I told anyone else. You mean everything to me. I hope and pray that, in time, you'll be able to forgive me.' His eyes searched hers, begging, brimming with all the love and sincerity he could muster.

'Thank you for telling me,' she mumbled. He could see the emotions playing across her face, threatening to overwhelm her. Abruptly, she pushed back her chair and stood up.

He stood too. 'I'm not a monster, Anna,' he pleaded.

'I know,' she whispered and she walked away.

CHAPTER 40

Anna

It had been completely surreal, sitting there, in prison, surrounded by people I didn't know, listening to a man I thought I knew. It had helped, hearing what he had to say. Things I'd fretted over for years now made sense. I'd always known, in my heart, that Mariella didn't really love me. I'd always thought it was my fault – I was never clever enough or pretty enough; I liked the wrong sort of things, making up stories rather than excelling in subjects like maths and science. Today had explained so much and left me feeling incredibly sad. I'd never stood a chance.

The whole story was a Greek tragedy. The Mariella whom Geoff had painted was a woman devoted to her child, crazed by grief, out of her mind at the loss of not one but *two* baby girls. I tried to picture that woman, understand what she went through but the image kept jarring, going out of focus. My own memories – of hurt and rejection – got in the way. Did I feel sorry for her, for both of them? Fleetingly, yes. The way Geoff had spun it, they too were victims of a chain of events beyond their control. Then I remembered what they'd done, what they'd planned to do, and jettisoned any fledgling sympathy. How could Geoff expect forgiveness? Driving home from the prison, in a spurt of anger, I put my foot down hard on the accelerator pedal, feeling the rush, speeding along the open road, enjoying the sense of control. Maybe one day I'd be able to forgive them. Not yet. Everything was too painful, an open wound refusing to heal.

I slowed down as a Volvo towing a caravan blocked my path. My thoughts turned inevitably to Josh. The way I'd heard it, he was a bystander, involved only at Geoff's direction and innocent of everything else. Had I judged him too harshly? Possibly. Was it too late to do anything about it? Probably. I'd heard nothing from him for two months now. Was he still waiting, as he said he would? Whenever I'd driven past The Old Rectory over the past months, my eyes had swung involuntarily in that direction, but I hadn't seen him. It was just as well. Perhaps the best thing would be to close that chapter in my life and move on afresh.

***

It had been Selina's idea to get away from it all, to take a week's holiday abroad, somewhere warm. I'd been stunned at her suggestion, though, to return to Spain, to Alla Mora.

'It might help us both to find some sort of closure,' she said. 'And it will be nice to spend some time together, away from here.'

I was unsure; my feelings towards her had thawed but were still complicated. In the end, reluctantly, I relented. She was my real mum and I owed it to her to find a way forward in our relationship. Maybe, away from Lewton and thoughts of the ever-looming trial, we might stand a chance. I was also procrastinating about Josh. My conscience insisted it was unfair to leave things as they were, like a fragment of wool dangling from an unfinished scarf. At some point, I'd need to see him but had no idea what I'd say. My feelings about him veered between fatalism – it was never meant to be – and regret. Above all, I struggled with the idea of trusting him. That bond between us had been snapped. Like a broken chain, the links could be soldered back together but would it ever be as strong as before? Possibly not. Selina was right. I needed closure.

We spent our week in Alla Mora chasing shade and air-conditioned bars, watching the world go by, shunning all things touristy. For us, there were no day trips out, no ocean boat rides, no sessions snorkelling beneath the calm, blue water. Instead, we read by the hotel pool, under striped umbrellas, during the heat of the day; we went for early morning and late evening walks when it was cooler and we talked. Our conversations were studiously undemanding. We avoided discussing anything too personal or about the future and slowly, hour by hour, minute by minute, we grew closer.

As we sat drinking cocktails in a seafront bar festooned with brightly-coloured sunshades on the final evening before our departure, I felt relaxed and happy. Selina looked well. The sun had given her a golden glow and her face had smoothed out as the strain of the past twenty-three years had lifted. Wearing a floral-patterned, fitted sundress, she looked twenty years younger than the woman I'd first met. By contrast, I felt twenty years older. The past three months had been an ordeal but I'd survived and grown tougher. At Selina's suggestion, I'd been seeing a hypnotherapist. The panic attacks had receded; old fears and anxieties still threaded through my veins but, having acknowledged them, I'd clung back more self-control.

'Was this bar here when you came with Jack back in 1996?' I asked.

'To be honest, I don't remember. After you disappeared, everything was such a blur. It's been really strange coming back here and finding that it's not at all as I recall.'

'How do you mean?'

'It's much brighter, livelier. In my head, it was a terrible place – a place where your worst nightmare came true. I couldn't even hear the name Alla Mora without coming out in a cold sweat. This week has really helped.' Her lips curved. 'Thank you. I hope it's helped you too.'

I returned the smile. 'It has. You were right; I needed to get away. And now I don't want to go back.'

It was then I told her what had transpired at Wayland prison. She listened, her jaw slack with incredulity, and then she cried. She was weeping for the other mother, she said, the one whose child was snatched from the hospital. 'I'm sorry,' she sobbed into a tissue. 'That poor woman! She'd just given birth to a beautiful, healthy baby girl, she went to sleep and when she awoke, her baby was gone. Never seen again. All those years, wondering where she was, what she was doing, hoping one day she would have answers. And now she will have answers but they will only bring more grief. Her baby died just a few months old. What happened to me was awful but at least I have my happy ending. I found you. That poor woman, her partner, her whole family have nothing.'

'I know.' I put my arm around her, waiting for the shuddering of her thin frame to cease. It was tragedy upon tragedy.

'It makes me realise how lucky I am.' The choke in Selina's voice was still there but, as she pulled away, I saw the beginnings of a tremulous smile. 'My search could've had a very different outcome. Now, at least, *we* have a future.'

'We do.' For the first time, I believed it. I felt a tide of love for the woman beside me, the woman who gave birth to me, lost me, but who had doggedly refused to believe she'd never see her daughter again. I held out my arms. Suddenly, I wanted to hold this woman tightly, never let her go. 'Mum,' I whispered.

'Oh ... baby.'

Then we were both crying and laughing simultaneously, a bubbling cauldron overflowing with happiness and relief. No matter what happened now, we'd found each other. Our lives may take a new direction, not necessarily together but always close, the journey eased by the inseparable bond of love and support we shared.

Later on, when we sat eating paella and drinking glasses of Rioja, I received a call from Harry.

'I've remembered,' he declared triumphantly.

'Remembered what?'

'You know, the dream you had ... when we were kids ... that thing I was holding and wouldn't let you see ... I've remembered what it was.'

I held my breath. 'What?'

'It was a dragonfly – really pretty. I think it was a hair grip ... something like that. I thought I'd given it to you. It was just before you were taken.'

I smiled. My dragonfly. My secret. No wonder Mariella had wanted to get rid of it.

'You did,' I replied.

***

As the sun set over the Mediterranean Sea, a breath-taking swirl of red and gold, Selina and I talked about Josh.

'What are you going to do?' she asked neutrally.

I let my hand rest comfortably against my ear, twisting the lobe gently between my fingers. I was no longer self-conscious about the gesture; it was simply who I was. 'I haven't decided. It's been three months, after all. He's probably moved on.' I shrugged carelessly, hiding my face behind my wine glass.

'Really?' She frowned. 'Well, if he has, it clearly wasn't meant to be. I don't know exactly what happened between the two of you but I *do* know there were some initial suspicions concerning his involvement in ...' she hesitated, '... recent events.'

'Yes. DS Thorncroft thought he probably switched the DNA test results.'

'What did *he* say?'

I squirmed, discomfited by the question. 'I haven't actually asked him face to face. He denied it in texts he sent but I chose not to believe him ... Then I visited my d ... Geoff Blake and I found out he may have been telling the truth after all ... unless Geoff was lying, of course.'

'Oh Anna!' Selina sighed. 'I can understand why you're finding it difficult to trust any man but, in the end, that's a very lonely path to take. Wasn't it Tennyson who said, Better to have loved and lost ...?'

'... than never to have loved at all. Yes, I know. I guess I made a mistake about Josh. I'm not sure he'll want to forgive me.'

She gave me a pitying look. 'Where's the feisty, little girl who was my daughter? Ask him! What have you got to lose?'

'I'll think about it,' I said. 'When I'm back home ...'

CHAPTER 41

Mariella
HM Prison Peterborough

Mariella sat opposite her lawyer in a secure, airless room. She loathed being incarcerated and was relying on the man opposite to get her out as soon as possible. It was a sobering thought. She tried to keep hidden the irritation she felt as she listened to his whiny voice drone on and on. Jonathan Harvey-Watts was supposedly one of the top defence lawyers in the country but she struggled to believe it. He was so dull. She'd wanted someone with charisma who would show the jury she was a victim of circumstance, manipulated by her husband, and he wasn't remotely that person. But time was running out and he was the third lawyer she'd appointed. She'd fired the first when he twice called her Maria; the second, a grey-faced woman in her fifties, reminded her of weak tea – unpalatable and lacking taste. How could she allow someone like that to represent her? Harvey-Watts was the best of a bad bunch and she could only hope he deserved his reputation.

He looked across at her with a tight smile, steel-rimmed glasses perched on the end of his nose. Following his advice, she'd pleaded guilty to the charge of abduction. She hardly needed a lawyer for that. It was a no-brainer. To the charge of attempted murder, she'd pleaded not guilty. Her statement was very clear. She knew nothing of Geoff's intentions. Yes, she knew he'd hired Ewan Jacobs to investigate Selina Matthews but that was as far as it went. She'd been completely horrified to learn that a man called Kevin Docherty had been hired to kill the woman, or so the police claimed. No, she had no knowledge of that man and had never met him. She'd made sure there was no evidence to the contrary. The court would believe her. The charge of abduction was a trickier one to counter. Harvey-Watts had explained she would serve a custodial sentence but this would be mitigated by evidence he would present to show that, on both occasions when a crime was committed, she was not in her right mind. That's what he was droning on about now. He'd assembled a list of experts prepared to testify on her behalf. She tried to look impressed.

He'd also dropped a bit of a bombshell. Geoff had filed papers for their divorce. 'Clearly he's distancing himself from you,' Harvey-Watts explained, as if she needed *him* to tell her facts about her marriage. 'He's also pleaded not guilty to the charge of attempted murder so I suspect he's going to try to pin the blame on you.'

She gave him a look of distain. 'I can handle whatever my soon to be ex-husband dishes out,' she said smoothly. 'As I've told you before, the evidence will all point to him.'

Did she feel guilty about throwing Geoff under the bus? No. One of them had to take the blame and it wasn't going to be her. Was she upset about the end of her marriage? No, of course not. The very idea filled her with scorn. She'd loved Geoff once, it was true, but that had faded rapidly when Anna had preferred him to her. That child had broken her heart. All she'd wanted was a child to love, someone who adored her. From the moment she'd taken Anna from that seedy Spanish hotel terrace, the child had viewed her with fear and distrust. Despite her best efforts and intensive hypnotherapy, the love she craved was never forthcoming. Instead, the child always gravitated towards Geoff, showering him with affection rather than her. As time went on, the longing disappeared, replaced with irritation and anger. She'd risked everything for a child who remained wary of her and she'd no alternative other than to put up with it. The closeness between Geoff and Anna grew and she festered in her isolation, an unwanted third wheel on their cosy tandem.

You reap what you sow.

Her own father's mantra haunted her dreams. He was a cold, harsh man, stiff and unyielding as concrete. She remembered standing before him, hand outstretched, as he toyed with his cane, a vicious, whippy twitch of hazel about two feet long. He would say those words, rolling his tongue over the 'reap,' giving it special emphasis. Only then would she feel the stinging heat of the cane across her palm, ten strokes, one for each of the ten commandments. She hadn't thought of her father in years but, locked away from the world, enduring her punishment, his voice rang in her ears.

'Do you repent your sins?' he would ask his silently sobbing child afterwards.

'Yes, father.'

One time, she'd said 'no' to spite him. It earned her another ten strokes, repeated until she gave the correct answer. She'd hated her father and despised her mother, a weak woman who stood aside when he inflicted his torture, a passive accomplice to his cruelty. Growing up, alone in her draughty bedroom, bare of any adornments, she'd vowed she would never be like her mother. When *she* had children, she would shower them with love, protect them with a lioness' fierceness, give everything for them. And she had.

You reap what you sow.

'No, Father,' she said to herself. 'Not if I can help it.'

CHAPTER 42

Geoff
HM Prison Wayland

Geoff lay back on his hard, narrow bed with an air of self-satisfaction. Project Anna, as he termed it, had got off to a good start. He was not about to lose his daughter, not when he needed her most. Whatever it took, he would do it or say it; he would use every ounce of determination, charm and guile to restore their relationship. He had no intention, upon release from prison, of giving up all he once had. The fact he was here in the first place was all Mariella's fault. He'd felt no compunction throwing her to the wolves. He had no choice. Survival of the fittest, that's what it boiled down to.

Idly, his thoughts drifted back to those early days. He'd met Mariella through a friend of a friend when he was up in Edinburgh. She was cool and reserved, the type of girl he saw as a challenge, and it wasn't long before they were an item. His lust had grown and he'd asked her to marry him. At the time, he'd thought he was in love with her. She was a stunner to look at; he supposed she still was. But the razor-sharp edges she'd cultivated over the years had shaved away all his desire for her. The terrible secret they shared had ruled out separation and they'd endured a life of mutual conspiracy, shackled together by their daughter and the knowledge of what they'd done. Now the secret was out, it was a relief to rid himself of her. He'd read once that snakes shed their skins to allow for further growth and to remove parasites attached to their old skin. That's what he was doing.

The next step in Project Anna was to encourage further visits. That may prove tricky but he had no doubt he would wear down her resistance. He hoped she would attend the trial, now scheduled for the middle of November. Already, he had a plan for that. From under his mattress, he extracted a sheet of paper – the draft of his next letter.

My darling Anna,

It was so lovely to see you when you visited the prison. I cannot bear to think of you coming to such a place but I'm a selfish man and I wanted so much to see you, to explain things in person.

You are, and will always be, the light of my life. That's why I'd like you to consider my next words very carefully. I don't want you to attend my trial. The thought of you having to go through that, to relive all the distress I've caused you, would tear me apart. Please, my darling, stay away. Remember your old dad as the man who loved you, who dried your tears when you were upset, not as the pitiful man in the dock accused of such horrors ...

He knew his daughter. If you wanted the adult Anna to do something, then tell her to do the opposite. Licking his dry lips, he reread the final phrase. Was it a good idea to describe his crimes as such horrors? Would it alienate her further? Possibly, but he needed to show remorse, contrition for his actions. Underplaying them would make her think he was incapable of change.

And change was what he planned. From now on, in front of his daughter, he would be penitent, blame only himself for his change in fortune. He was happy he'd already done enough to shift most of the responsibility squarely onto Mariella's skinny shoulders. Now, to Anna, he would defend her and, in doing so, reiterate the unpleasant characteristics she'd displayed. She wanted to kill Selina Matthews – yes, he'd admit that after the trial – and he couldn't forget or forgive that. Hence, he'd realised the only possible course of action he could take was, sadly, to file for divorce.

He couldn't achieve what he hoped without allies. When he left prison, he would do his utmost to woo Selina Matthews. She was an attractive woman; it wouldn't be too onerous. It would begin with him prostrating himself before her, begging her forgiveness for the wrong his wife had done her. Yes, alright, he'd have to accept blame too but he'd point out the bond they shared – their love for Anna. He was a good-looking man with an armoury of blandishments at his disposal. Eventually, he would win her over. With Selina as his wife, Anna would inevitably revert to thinking of him as her father. He knew nothing of her real father – he didn't want to know – but he had no doubt it would be easy enough to eradicate the threat he posed. No other man would be a father to the daughter who was rightfully his.

He had one final ace in the hole. It had been very gratifying to see the relief Anna tried to conceal when she asked about Josh Fielding's involvement in his crimes. It was number one on his list of priorities: ensure marriage between Anna and Josh. They would make a perfect couple, not least because Josh Fielding still owed him. Such a partnership would go a long way in securing his own future status. He was confident that Josh would have his back.

The first step was to charm the jury at his trial and receive the minimum sentence possible. Charlotte Greatwood had a wealth of evidence at her disposal primed and ready to point the finger of guilt fairly and squarely at Mariella. He'd made sure of that. Hopefully, he'd done enough. Time would tell ...

CHAPTER 43

Anna

The day after I returned home from Alla Mora, I squashed my reservations and sent Josh a text.

Hi Josh. Hope you're well. Was wondering if we can talk? Anna.

Sick with nerves, I waited for a response. I didn't have to wait long.

Am out now. Back in an hour. Come around then. J

Oh God! The thought sent butterflies fluttering in my stomach. I studied the text, searching for non-existent clues about how he felt. Impersonal, slightly formal, the tone exactly matched the one I'd sent him. Up until this moment, I'd been denying my feelings, thinking I was over him. I wasn't. I only hoped he wasn't over me.

Exactly one hour and five minutes later, I took a deep breath and rang the doorbell. To distract myself from my nerves, I turned to survey the border at the front of the house. It was overgrown. Whilst the lawn was freshly mown, recent rain had encouraged rampant growth of both weeds and flowers. Thistles, docks and dandelions vied with straggly chrysanthemums and woody buddleia.

'It could use a bit of work.' His voice behind me followed my gaze and I spun around. He looked tired and he'd lost weight. His jeans hung low on his hips and his white T-shirt no longer clung to his chest as it once had. Still, he took my breath away. I studied his face, avidly drinking in all its contours and nuances. His expression was guarded but there was hurt in his eyes. I'd wounded him; I wasn't sure how to make it better.

'Hi.' My voice came out as a bit of a croak and I cleared my throat. 'Would you mind if I came in?'

Wordlessly, he stood back and allowed me to pass. I started to head for the kitchen but he called me back. 'Not in there – in here.' He gestured towards the sitting room and my heart sank. The vibes weren't looking good. I stood politely in the centre of the room, waiting for him.

'Please, sit down,' he said stiffly.

'It's been a while since ...'

'Three months,' he interrupted, his voice cold.

'Yes ... I'm sorry.'

'Three months without a word and now you want to talk. Well, go on, what is it you want to say?'

'I was confused.' I looked up at him, my eyes beseeching his understanding. 'It was a difficult time.'

He snorted. 'I get that Anna. What I don't understand is why you shut me out? I would've been there for you ... helped you get through it.' He raked his fingers through his hair, his brown eyes flecked with anguish.

'When you were arrested, I thought you ... I didn't know what to think.'

'Thanks for the vote of confidence! You thought I was involved in all that? Attempted murder? Christ!'

'No.' I shook my head vehemently. 'I thought you might have switched the DNA results. DS Thorncroft thought you had.'

He just looked at me, disappointment etched in every line on his face. Shame flooded through me. He was right. I hadn't given him the benefit of doubt; I hadn't trusted him enough; the fault was mine.

'I'm sorry,' I said once more. My heart was shattering all over again. It was hopeless. I'd lost him.

'I was released without charge, Anna. I thought we had something really special together. Why were you not prepared to believe me? I told you enough times I was innocent. Why couldn't you trust me?' He was angry now, glaring at me.

I met his gaze steadily as I framed my reply. It was a crunch question, a deal breaker. It deserved an honest response.

'You talk about trust,' I said evenly. 'Yes, I should've trusted you. You didn't deserve my suspicions ... but it had become very difficult for me to trust *anyone*. I'd just discovered that everyone close to me, *everyone*, including you ...' I looked at him pointedly, 'had been deceiving me, going behind my back, reporting details of my life to my ... to Geoff. Then I found out that the people I called my parents, the people closest of all to me, had been lying for all those years. No wonder I had some trust issues!'

He lowered his eyes and nodded slowly. 'I get that. You'd been through one hell of an ordeal. I knew that. That's why I gave you time and space. When you refused to see me, ignored my calls and didn't answer my texts, I got the message you thought I was somehow involved. But I'd thought ... I'd hoped you'd realise that I was always, first and foremost, on your side.' He shrugged. 'Anyway, enough of that ... why are you here? Why now?'

His eyes challenged mine and I braced myself for what I knew I had to say. 'I visited Geoff in prison. He told me everything ... and some ... but maybe that can wait for another time.' I shifted closer to him, took his calloused left hand in my right and stared into his face. 'I love you, Josh. All the time, while I was trying to get to grips with everything, I was still in love with you. You kept sending me messages and it broke my heart not to reply but I didn't dare. You see, I didn't trust myself. I knew I couldn't trust my judgment where you were concerned. I had to be sure.' I squeezed his hand hopefully. 'And now I am. I just hope I'm not too late.'

My words hung in the air and the world stood still as I waited for his response. He stared back, his eyes searching my face, his gaze impossible to read. I held my breath ...

'Come here,' he sighed, breaking the silence and pulling me into his arms. 'You're so beautiful. Even more beautiful than I remember ... although that's probably because, in my dreams, you still have a whopping, great, black eye!' He smiled. 'I love you too. When you didn't respond to my texts, when your silence went on for months rather than days, I tried to get over you, forget you, but I couldn't. You're the one, the only one.'

His lips found mine and I lost myself in the closeness of him. He kissed me with all the desperation of the past months and I matched his urgency. As I slid my hands under his T-shirt, seeking the firmness of his bare skin, he released me abruptly and stood up.

'I almost forgot,' he said, grinning at my now dishevelled state. 'I have something to show you. Come on.'

He took my hand and led me towards the kitchen. I could hear something skittering across the floor.

'Is it a dog?' I asked breathlessly.

'No,' he smiled, pushing the door open. 'It's a giant hamster.'

'Hilarious.' A large, hairy body brushed past me to get to Josh, its tail wagging frantically. 'Oh, he's gorgeous.'

'She,' Josh corrected, crouching down on his haunches to fondle the dog. 'She's a rescue dog.'

'Oh!' I exclaimed again. 'We both said we wanted a rescue dog. How long have you had her?' I held out my hand to the dog but she ignored me, frantically licking Josh and spinning excitedly in circles around him.

'About a month. I was lonely.' He looked up at me. 'And she reminded me of you.'

'Gee, thanks. I guess I do look like that on a bad hair day!'

'That's true but it wasn't *that* so much. You see, she's blind in one eye.'

'What?' I wrinkled my nose in puzzlement and his smile widened. 'It makes her clumsy. She keeps bumping into things just like you.'

I laughed and crouched down beside him. Tentatively, the dog edged closer and gave my hand a cautious sniff.

'She's very nervous, poor thing. She was found abandoned, roaming the streets of Norwich and then taken to the RSPCA. She'd been at the rehoming centre for over six months. Nobody wanted her. It's taken her a while to learn to trust me.' His look spoke volumes and I nodded in response, letting the words remain unspoken. Another thing we had in common. The dog moved closer and allowed me to stroke her back. It felt soft and warm.

'Good girl,' I crooned gently. 'You're beautiful. What's your name?'

'Ah well, that's the other reason she reminded me of you.'

'What? She's called Anna?' I asked.

'No.' Josh covered my hand with his. 'Her name is Maisie.'

*****

ACKNOWLEDGEMENTS

I am enormously grateful for all the wonderful people who have encouraged me during the writing of Who To Trust – friends, family and the writing communities on Twitter and Facebook. In particular, I'd like to thank Sandra Simm, Sue Flinton, Sara Proctor and Kerry Bath for their feedback and my husband, Mark, for his invaluable insights.

My brother-in-law, on call firefighter, Mark Proctor, answered all my fire-related questions and read the fire scenes with a critical eye. Mark, you are the inspiration for the unnamed rescuer in the story.

My son, Rob, took on the task of book cover designer. Thank you, Rob, for doing such an amazing job.

My daughter, Alex, was heavily involved in the editing process and her proofreading skills are second to none. Al, you're a star.

Finally, I'd like to thank you for choosing to read my book. I hope you enjoyed it. If so, I'd love to hear from you on Twitter, Facebook or Instagram and you will earn my heartfelt thanks if you post a review.

www.ingramcontent.com/pod-product-compliance
Lightning Source LLC
Chambersburg PA
CBHW022141050726
47590CB00002B/524